BENT, BUT NOT BROKEN

FIRST EDITION
First printing, 1986

Copyright © 1986 by Sandlapper Publishing, Inc., 127 Russell Street SW, P.O. Box 1932, Orangeburg, South Carolina, 29116-1932.
MANUFACTURED IN THE UNITED STATES OF AMERICA

Book Design by Allison L. Stein
Cover Art by James H. Sanders

Library of Congress Cataloging-in-Publication Data

Gillis, Gerald L., 1947-
    Bent, but not broken.

    1. Vietnamese Conflict, 1961-1975—Fiction.
I. Title.
PS3557.I3896B4   1985   813'.54   85-19657
ISBN 0-87844-065-8 (pbk.)

BENT, BUT NOT BROKEN

a novel by

Gerald L. Gillis

SANDLAPPER
PUBLISHING, INC.

This book is dedicated not to the reasons, whatever they were; nor to the outcome, whatever it was; nor to the events which are yet to be shaped, whatever they will be; but, simply, to the efforts of those who, in the heat and the mud and the blood, went and did their very best.

AUTHOR'S NOTE

This book is entirely fictional. The military units as depicted herein are actual components of the U.S. Marine Corps, though these fictional accounts should in no way be construed as a measure of, or a reflection upon, the performance of those units during the Vietnam conflict. Unit locations and movements do not necessarily correspond to the actual historical record with regard to time and place. And any resemblance in name or deed of any of the characters to any person, living or deceased, is wholly unintentional.

The era of Vietnam produced such successive waves of shock, in such profound degrees of depth, that much of the residue in the aftermath has best been described in terms common to psychologists and psychiatrists. The effects of the long war upon the senses of the participants have hardly been inconsequential. Many have recovered adequately and blended into the mainstream of society; others have been less fortunate; none, however, have forgotten. The memories and the scars still exist after a full decade.

Overlooked throughout much of the stringent criticism which followed in the wake of the war was the competence, professionalism, and sense of duty exhibited by the vast majority of American troops. As in other wars, in other times, the American serviceman acquitted himself admirably in the face of hostility and adversity. There were the exceptions, of course, which tended to overshadow much of the rest. But the fact remains that the Americans who took to the bush, to the air, and to the sea, who served and endured, who fought and sometimes died, did so with a measure of commitment and courage comparable to those of any era in our country's history—and more so, in many ways. In very many ways.

The question of the American involvement in Vietnam, in

i

its nobility or ignobility, as one's opinion dictates, is well outside the scope of this novel. That involvement is neither glorified nor vilified in the words that follow. History shall be the ultimate judge of the war's effects upon the course of world events and the shaping of the American character. May history show that the hurt eventually healed, that the dark cloud of the turbulent era finally dissipated, and that those who returned, upright or prone, were remembered by their country-men with dignity and compassion.

Gerald L. Gillis

CONTENTS

PART ONE:
The Preparation

1

Darkness had already begun to settle upon northeast Virginia, partially obscuring Marine Corps Base, Quantico, from the eyes of the members of the newly formed Echo Company, Third Platoon. The sixty-two young men were dressed in their civilian clothes and stood in ragged formation in front of the mess hall where they enjoyed a moment's respite before eating their first meal as Marine Officer Candidates. They were waiting nervously for their initial encounter with that near-mythical figure who would act as the equivalent of a boot-camp drill instructor. The candidates stood rigidly, some pallid with fear, others in a state of disbelief that previous actions of their own volition had resulted in what now appeared certain to become an extraordinary, if not altogether intolerable, undertaking.

They had come from all parts of America, these fledgling candidates, from the farms of the Midwest, from the shores of the Pacific, from the mountains of Appalachia. Nearly all were college graduates. Some were the offspring of the privileged; others were of more moderate means. Their backgrounds and educations were as varied as their geographical origins. They had answered the call of the country, the call to arms. It was a strange call, an inchoate echoing even upon the ears of those whose own fathers had dealt the Axis the defeat of all defeats, the *sic temper tyrannis*. But answer they had. They had come to be Marines, to carry the torch of freedom as their fathers had done when their call had come. It was a strangely different call to a strangely different set of circumstances, and the rally to the perceived threat was anything but smoothly reconciled and heartfully justified. They had come anyway, to Virginia, to the banks of the old Potomac. They would do their part.

Candidate Michael David Billingsley, twenty-three years old, felt apprehensive, slightly disoriented, and manifestly homesick. Images of the past several hours filled his mind—the pleasant flight from Atlanta to Washington, D.C.; the taxi ride to Quantico with other candidates; the small main gate; the old wooden train depot; the brick buildings and Quonset huts; the endless administrative forms; the black ink; the herding as if they were cattle; and the ceaseless, obtrusive, obnoxious shouting, laced with profanity and loaded with a sense of terrible urgency.

Mike Billingsley brushed wind-blown, brownish hair from his eyes while he contemplated his new lot. Strange, he thought. So serene now, with only the sound of the wind off the nearby river. So peaceful in the glorious greening of spring and the transformation of renewed blossoming, in form and spirit, in all that which lives. But he knew this place, Quantico, was going to be different. It was harsh, he had already discovered. It was impersonal. Underneath the illusion of warmth and tranquillity lurked a machine in whose gears and pulleys and rotors he would be unceremoniously ground into a new substance, with a new meaning and a new purpose. He would be re-done and re-packaged as a military professional, a member of another machine, a killing machine. The new product of the grinding bothered him little. It was the grinding itself that disturbed him. He had seen just enough to know that it would not be pleasant, that it would not be without difficulty as he moved along his ten weeks on the conveyor. The thought of it all was unsettling; the coarse aggression his senses had suffered was far beyond anything he had ever experienced.

Billingsley wished that he could excuse himself from the gathering and depart without recrimination. No hard feelings, nothing said, and particularly nothing owed. Just leave the way he came. He began to realize, however, that leaving was irrevocably out of the question. On this day, Monday, March 25, 1968, Candidate Billingsley was beginning a journey of unalterable and unforgettable consequences. He drew a deep breath, exhaled with a sigh, and waited with the rest of the group.

"You people are a sad lot. You're too slow, you're too stupid, you're pitiful. I don't know why any of you would join my Marine Corps. If you think you've made a mistake in showing up here, I'd say you're probably right. The Program's not going to wait on any of you, so if you can't keep up, and many of you won't, then we'll start finding out in the morning. Before any of you pin on those gold bars, I'm going to have to be satisfied that you could lead *me* in combat. You'll have to prove it here, people. Every single day. This is a serious business, and I'm a deadly serious man."

Staff Sergeant O'Brien completed his walk down the length of the barracks and turned to face the candidates. Tall and slim, immaculately groomed in his green uniform, he stood erect, neither shifting nor fidgeting. As he delivered his lecture on their first evening in the barracks, he seemed larger than life.

"This is the United States Marine Corps, ladies, not some candy-assed fraternity picnic. This is the finest fighting organization ever known to man. War is our business and, ladies, business is good. By the time I return in the morning to turn on these lights, your feet had better be on the deck."

O'Brien dimmed the lights and added, "Sleep tight, ladies."

After O'Brien and his assistant, Staff Sergeant Sykes, had departed, Billingsley lay in his bunk in the darkened building and sorted out his thoughts. He held to the feeble hope that he would awaken in the morning to discover that Quantico, O'Brien, and Sykes had all been a dream. The coughing, sniffling, and restless sounds in the barracks led Billingsley to believe that he was not alone in hoping for the Nightmare Solution.

A large, stocky black instructor with a menacing expression on his round face was inspecting candidates outside the Quartermaster building. The men stood in formation, their seabags beside them, in their baggy new uniforms, on the morning of their first full day at Quantico.

"With your right hand, reach down, grasp, and hold up your RIGHT boot," shouted the instructor as he watched closely.

The candidates complied under his frowning gaze.

"With your left hand ... "

Billingsley glanced down at the remaining boot from his second issue and discovered, to his horror, that his second pair consisted of two right boots.

" . . . reach down, grasp, and hold up your LEFT boot."

The instructor quickly noticed Billingsley's left hand remaining stiffly by his side. The instructor moved directly in front of Billingsley.

"Where's your left boot, dumbass?" asked the instructor.

"The candidate received two right boots in his second pair, Sergeant Instructor," replied Billingsley, embarrassed.

"Would the candidate prefer two right boots?"

"No, Sergeant Instructor."

"Did you go to college, genius?"

"Yes, Sergeant Instructor."

"Did you learn anything practical, worm, like which boot goes on what foot?"

"I hope so, Sergeant Instructor," Billingsley mumbled, flustered.

"She hopes so," said the instructor sarcastically, moving closer. "I'm gonna pull your ear off and shove it up your butt so you can hear me when I start kicking your ass if you're not back here in thirty seconds with your Goddamned boots squared away. Go, dammit. Move, MOVE."

Billingsley had suffered his first encounter with a staff member. He felt humiliated and inadequate from the dressing down. He was glad that O'Brien had been busy elsewhere and had not seen the reprimand.

Billingsley stood at attention just inside a doorway, listening to the buzzing of shears and noticing the mounds of hair already accumulating on the floor of the shop.

"Get in that last chair, candidate. MOVE, MOVE, MOVE," Sykes ordered.

Billingsley ran to the end of the shop and was seated. He was sheathed and sheared in moments. With an upward stroke of the shears on Billingsley's temple, the barber removed a small mole from the head of the ramrod-straight candidate. The occurrence did not elude O'Brien, who noticed the thin streak of blood oozing from the side of Billingsley's head.

"Find that mole, candidate," ordered O'Brien. "Then get outside and tell the others that if they have a mole under their hair, they'd better have their fucking finger pointing to it when their ass hits the chair."

Billingsley issued the warnings to those waiting their turn. The small wound still bled, and Billingsley saw several candidates glancing curiously at him. As he turned to make his way through the barber shop to have the wound treated, he overhead a remark from near the front of the line.

"Jesus, what the hell are they using in there, bayonets?"

First Lieutenant Kenneth C. Coleman was a former enlisted man who had risen in the ranks to become a sergeant major, or E-9, before accepting a commission as an officer. His eighteen years of military service had given him the hard-bitten look of a combat veteran, which he was. Lieutenant Coleman had only recently returned from Vietnam where, as a platoon leader, he had been decorated for valor in battle. At thirty-six, he looked worn and much older to the candidates.

"At ease, candidates. Take a seat on the deck," Coleman said gruffly.

"Listen carefully to me. I am Lieutenant Coleman, and I'm in charge of this platoon. It is my direct responsibility to evaluate you, with the help of Sergeant O'Brien and Sergeant Sykes, as potential Marine officers. I happen to consider the job of a Marine officer to be one of the toughest jobs anywhere, and not just anybody is cut out for this kind of work. The three of us have all seen combat, so we have a good idea what it takes to lead Marines in action. I'm gonna tell you now that the Marine Corps will receive no marginal officers from this platoon. If you make it, you will have earned it. And I really don't care how many of you I have to send packing to find the ones the Corps needs."

Coleman paused for several seconds and observed the young faces in front of him.

"You've made a decision to seek a commission in the Marine Corps. But the only way, and I repeat, only way, you'll be commissioned is to do one hell of a job while you're in this Program. Some of you will be dead and buried before a year is over, and almost all of you can count on seeing action. It would behoove all of you to pay a great deal of attention to what you will be told in the days ahead. It would also behoove you to put forth your maximum effort, for anything less than your best will make it clear to me that you don't belong. And I'll be rid of you in one helluva hurry.

"You came here to see if you can measure up, if you can cut it. Believe me when I tell you that you'll have earned it, if you make it. You'll need to put everything you've got into it. Everything. I won't wait on any of you to make up your minds to keep up with the pace. I've never known any of you before, and I don't care who you are or what your grand designs on life are. I don't give two shits about your backgrounds or your opinions of the world. I'm gonna assume that all of you came into the Marine Corps because you wanted to learn how to whip the other guy's ass on the battlefield. And all I want to know about you is whether or not you pack the gear to be able to do just that—to whip the other guy's ass in the jungles, or on the beaches, or wherever it is that you're apt to find him. It's mean, people, this combat thing. And it takes mean people . . . smart people . . . the best people. I won't fail the Corps. I'll pick the ones who can get it done, who can lead, who can go anywhere at any time and be ready to kick ass when the shooting starts. I mean it, people. *I won't fail the Corps.* Only . . . the best. And only . . . when I'm satisfied."

"The name's Mike Billingsley," Billingsley offered his hand to his bunkmate late that first day as they settled into the barracks.

"Dan Redwine, Mike. Glad to meet you. Where you from?"

"Georgia, just outside Atlanta. What about you?"

"Southern Illinois, from a farm."

Billingsley liked Redwine's friendly, thin face and his easy manner. Redwine's movements were slow and deliberate as he marked his name tags. He smiled easily, though it was only a half-smile.

"Isn't this place going to be a barrel of laughs," observed Redwine as he placed his stenciling equipment in his foot locker.

"Yeah, looks like it," Billingsley said laconically.

"If every day's like this one . . . God almighty," sighed Redwine. "I don't know why I left Illinois for this. Maybe I should have let the damned draft get me," he sighed again. "Why did you join the Marines, Mike?" Redwine asked with a trace of sarcasm.

"Oh, I guess it seemed like the thing to do at the time," Billingsley said, remembering his exhilaration when he announced to his friends and roommates at college, to their astonishment, his decision to become a Marine.

"Bet you wish you knew then what you know now, huh?"

Billingsley glanced over to see that half-smile on Redwine's face again.

The candidates were allowed ten minutes to write letters before the lights were dimmed. Sergeant Sykes ordered them to include in their letters the facts that they were being fed three meals each day, that they would receive mail at regular intervals, and that they would receive ample rest and exercise. Sykes also warned the candidates to tell their friends and families not to send packages of food and candy through the mails.

"Tell them that you want for nothing," barked Sykes with a mischievous grin on his face.

Billingsley completed a brief letter to his parents and advised them of his well-being. As he sat by his bed, he wished that he could climb inside the envelope and mail himself to his home. He was greatly disillusioned. He felt intimidated by his complete lack of control over his destiny and the events that seemed about to engulf him. It was too big, too fast. When he thought ahead to ten whole weeks at the pace of the first day, ten horrible weeks, he wanted to cry. He was tempted to beg his parents to extricate him from this interminable hell. It was heavy stuff, he knew. Far heavier than he had expected. But not heavy enough to break him, he grimly resolved. Not yet. No way. He neither cried nor wrote of his concern to his parents. Instead, he sealed the letter and slept.

The second full day began with a series of formal classes covering such topics as Marine Corps policies and procedures, military law, and the specifics of the procedure for voicing a complaint, termed "requesting mast." Billingsley and his class-mates made notes of the crisp, snappy lectures delivered by the officers of the OCS training staff. He was impressed with the quality and confidence of the instructors, and envious of their apparent status and freedom.

In the early afternoon, the candidates of Echo-Three under-went a physical testing and strength inventory. The test not only measured the general fitness of each candidate, but also served as an index against which future progress would be measured. Billingsley performed well on the test which included pushups, pullups, situps, standing broad jump, and a run of one mile. While it was obvious that several of the candidates had come to Quantico in marginal condition, Billingsley was generally pleased with his results.

The late afternoon brought the candidates their first session of close-order drill. Billingsley noticed the near-lyrical way that O'Brien called cadence. It was a slandering, methodical, melodic series of utterances which somehow fit together in a logical, effluent pattern understood by at least a majority of the marching candidates. Still, a few candidates had immense difficulty in marching which at first delighted O'Brien and Sykes, but soon exasperated them.

"WHERE THE FUCK ARE YOU GOING, IDIOT?"

"YOU'RE MARCHING, SHITHEAD. STEP IT OFF. LEFT, RIGHT, LEFT."

"THAT'S IT, ASSHOLE. JUST GET LOST IN BROAD DAYLIGHT."

"ARE THERE ANY MORE AT HOME LIKE YOU?"

"ONE MORE MOVE LIKE THAT, SCUMBAG, I'M ON YOU LIKE STINK ON SHIT."

"YOUR OTHER LEFT, SWEETPEA; YOUR MILITARY LEFT."

"HEAD BACK, CANDIDATE, AND CLOSE YOUR UGLY MOUTH."

"DIG YOUR HEELS IN; HEELS, HEELS, HEELS, HEELS."

"SWING THOSE ARMS, LADIES, LIKE YOU'RE STRUTTIN' YOUR SUNDAY BEST."

"CAN YOU HEAR, CANDIDATE? CAN YOU SEE? CAN YOU DO ANYTHING AT ALL?"

"PITIFUL, CANDIDATE. SIMPLY FUCKING PITIFUL."

Billingsley thought O'Brien was delivering the instructions quickly so as to confuse the candidates and afford the NCOs an opportunity to display their considerable abilities in shaming and intimidating their hapless victims. Sykes, especially, seemed incapable of uttering anything apart from vicious recriminations. Sykes made himself easy to hate, while O'Brien took on the role of the tough but reasonable teacher.

Billingsley also noticed that although each candidate received a measure of harassment, the early objects of a greater than average share of verbal abuse from O'Brien and Sykes were those candidates who stood out. The skinny, the heavy, the short, and the tall candidates were repeatedly chided with references to their physical statures. Their treatment of the few chubby candidates was virtually insufferable. O'Brien and Sykes seized every opportunity to belabor the virtues of leannesss and meanness.

A short, thin candidate made several errors on a marching movement. The candidate had been corrected earlier for other mistakes, and when he appeared ready to step in the wrong direction during a turn, Sykes was there waiting.

"Why don't you tell me what the problem is, squirt. I'm getting sick and tired of your skinny ass. I don't think I like you, maggot," Sykes said from a distance of three inches.

"The candidate has never marched before, Sergeant Instructor," replied the man weakly.

"Has the candidate ever blown another man's head off?"

"No, Sergeant Instructor."

"Listen, dipshit. You're going to be doing that pretty soon, and I think you'd better start getting with the program and stop fucking up. Do you *like* to fuck up, candidate?"

"No, Sergeant Instructor."

"I think you do, candidate. I think you enjoy fucking up. I think you *are* fucked up, candidate. Aren't you, maggot?"

"No, Sergeant Instructor."

"CANDIDATE, ARE YOU CALLING ME A LIAR?"

"No, Sergeant Instructor."

"I think you *are* fucked up, candidate."

"The candidate *is* fucked up, Sergeant Instructor."

"Totally fucked up."

"Totally fucked up, Sergeant Instructor."

"You gonna punch me, worm? Huh? Does the fair little maiden want to strike out at me?"

"No, Sergeant Instructor."

"Huh? Do you, worm? Wanna take a shot?" shouted Sykes, angling his chin obliquely in mock submissiveness. "Go ahead, sweetpea. Knock me on my ass."

"No, Sergeant Instructor."

"I DON'T LIKE REJECTION, CANDIDATE. ARE YOU REJECTING ME?"

"No, Sergeant Instructor. I just don't want to hit you," replied the candidate, on the verge of panic.

"Well, then. What *do* you want to do, candidate? Do you want to blow me? Is that it? You wanna perform an unnatural act on me? Is that it? ANSWER ME, SCUMBAG."

Billingsley and the others stood rigidly at attention while Sykes toyed with his victim. The other candidates would have reacted with joy had the small man flung a right cross on the point of the sergeant's chin and separated him from his consciousness.

"Why not, candidate? Is it because you're in love with me? Or is it because you're angry at me? Which is it, sweetpea?"

C'mon, Sykes, Billingsley thought to himself. The guy's on the verge of tears. Back off, dammit. Enough's enough. Get away and leave him alone.

The two stood directly in front of Billingsley.

"If you don't want to do anything to me, candidate, then maybe I ought to stick my hand down *your* throat. What about *that*, hog?"

The candidate flinched. Billingsley noticed a trembling in the man's legs.

"I said *what about that, hog?*"

Billingsley could feel his pulse in his neck and temples. He risked only quick glances at Sykes while otherwise keeping his eyes focused straight ahead.

"Maybe I should reach down your throat and pull out your heart, sweetpea. You wanna see your own heart?"

The candidate jerked slightly, as if he had momentarily lost his balance. Billingsley looked ahead and held his breath so as not to move. The platoon was frozen in formation.

"You gonna faint, sweetheart?"

"No, Sergeant Instructor," was the man's meek reply.

"You look pale, candidate. You havin' a stroke?"

"No, Sergeant Instructor."

"A seizure?"

"No, Sergeant Instructor."

"ARE YOU ABOUT TO FALL DOWN AND DIE, SCUMBAG?"

Billingsley felt dizzy from holding his breath. He exhaled

slowly when Sykes stepped away from the man. Though he despised Sykes, Billingsley, like most of the others, wanted no part of him.

Sykes moved toward his victim. "HUH, SCUMBAG? ARE YOU?" he screamed.

"No, Sergeant Instructor."

"You're a chickenshit, candidate. You're the lowest form of scum on this earth. The gooks will laugh their fuckin' heads off when they see you come skippin' through the jungle. They'll roll over and fuckin' die laughing. You're funny, maggot. Really funny. Laugh, sweetpea."

"Ha, ha, ha, Sergeant Instructor."

"I said LAUGH, cocksucker."

"Ha, ha, ha."

"LOUDER, GODDAMMIT."

"HA, HA, HA."

"KEEP IT UP."

"HA, HA, HA, HA, HA . . ."

Billingsley watched as the candidate began sobbing while Sykes pushed ever closer, sensing the breaking point. O'Brien said nothing from the front of the column.

"Oh, now she wants to cry. Well, by all means, candidate, stop laughing and give me a boo-hoo."

The candidate's shoulders heaved as he stood at attention and cried in disgrace.

"I said boo-hoo, sweetpea. DO IT."

"Boo-hoo, boo-hoo, boo-hoo."

"LOUDER, ASSWIPE."

"BOO-HOO, BOO-HOO, BOO-HOO."

"AGAIN, LADY."

"BOO-HOO, BOO-HOO, BOO-HOO."

The candidate wheezed and coughed. A line of mucous dangled unattended from his nose, and tears streamed from his reddened eyes. He remained at attention.

"Shut up, candidate."

The man continued weeping.

"I SAID SHUT THE FUCK UP, GODDAMMIT."

A full minute elapsed before the candidate regained control of himself. The platoon's collective hatred of Sykes boiled, though not the slightest move nor expression bore witness to the fury which raged within each of them. Nobody else wanted a session with Sykes, however much they would have loved to have seen him run over and crushed by the Amtrak train which was passing on the far side of the field.

"Get down in the pushup position, candidate. Let me hear you count 'em off. LOUDER, CANDIDATE, LOUDER."

O'Brien and Sykes doled out their punishment in many forms, the most common of which was the tongue lashing. Next, and close behind, was the pushup. Pushups were done in the barracks, on the athletic field, in the staff offices, on the drill field, and any other location where the need arose to correct offenders. The entire platoon would, in many cases, be sentenced to pushups for the errors of one individual. Several hundred pushups were routine in the course of a day. Billingsley's shoulders were tight from the unaccustomed activity.

The remainder of the first week passed in a blur for Billingsley. He rarely knew the day of the week or the hour of the day. Every moment of every day was a struggle. The numerical strength of the platoon had been reduced from sixty-two to fifty-one members by the middle of the first week. Of the eleven candidates dropped, seven were judged to be medically unfit for military service and released from the Marine Corps. The remaining four were sent to a separate area of the base to await another class whose start would commence two weeks later. In the interim, the "recyled" candidates would receive an intense program of physical conditioning to bring them up to the minimum standards.

Classes, conditioning, drill, chow, cleaning the barracks, rifle maintenance, laundry, fire-watch, pushups, boot polish, Brasso, and inspections all served to dominate the waking moments of every candidate. And for some, their sleeping moments. Billingsley began to feel as if he had never known another way of life. He began to learn to deal with incessant fatigue. He began to develop a taste for the food and manage his craving for cigarettes. He began to understand and utilize the particular Marine Corps phrases, such as "bulkhead" and "scuttlebutt" and "by your leave." He referred to his weapon as a "piece." And he even began thinking of himself as a Marine. If it wasn't getting any easier, Billingsley thought, then it must be that I'm getting better.

The candidates were not allowed to leave the base over the

first weekend of the Program. Instead, they were assigned a series of chores which, from Saturday afternoon until Monday morning, were less closely supervised and more leisurely in pace. It was a welcomed relief from the chaotic and frenzied days of the training week, and it gave the candidates a chance to begin to get to know one another. It was an opportunity, as well, for the seven candidates who had been chosen from the enlisted ranks to answer questions and offer advice to the others on the ways of the military. The seven candidates were popular members of the group by virtue of their having experienced the regiment and rigors of boot camp at either Parris Island or San Diego, the two enlisted recruit depots.

Candidate Stephen O. Nelson bunked directly across the aisle from Billingsley and Redwine. A veteran of Parris Island, Nelson had been selected for OCS on the basis of his aptitude tests and his two years of college. Nelson's intelligence and seriousness had so impressed the officers with whom he had served that his application for OCS had been accepted easily. He was even more impressive to the candidates of Echo-Three as he moved about the barracks, tall, sturdy, composed, and confident. Though neither overbearing nor presumptuous, Nelson seemed to know all the right answers and make all the right moves.

Billingsley and Redwine were cleaning their M-14 rifles, using their foot lockers as work platforms. Across the aisle, Nelson also cleaned his weapon.

"Is this as tough as Parris Island, Steve?" Redwine asked.

"Nothing's as tough as P.I.," Nelson chuckled.

"What's the big difference?" queried Billingsley.

"Oh, P.I.'s more physical, I'd say. It seems that the big stress here will be more mental. Seems that way so far," Nelson answered as he applied a thin coat of oil to his weapon.

"Think we'll all make it through?" asked Redwine.

"Hell no," Nelson said quickly. "Probably half. Not much more than that, based on what I've heard."

"What *have* you heard?" pressed Billingsley.

"Only that it's not unusual for an OCS class to be cut in half by the time it finishes. They'll cut some at the five-week boards and some at the nine-week boards, and maybe one or two in-between. The rest will become 'officers and gentlemen' and be off to see the sights of Southeast Asia."

Billingsley considered Nelson to be a credible source and was mildly disturbed at this. A visible tightness in Redwine's jaw betrayed a similar concern, as both pondered whether they would survive the cuts.

"Did you have orders to Vietnam after P.I., Steve?" asked Billingsley.

"Sure. I'd be there now if I wasn't here. Almost everybody in my recruit platoon ended up in Nam," Nelson answered tersely.

"What have you heard about Nam?" Redwine asked.

"That it can screw up your health record in a hurry," Nelson chuckled, then turned serious. "I haven't heard a lot of good things. It seems to be a fairly typical place for Marines to have to fight a war, as far as the heat and jungle goes. It's made to order, Redwine."

"How's that?" asked Billingsley, stopping his cleaning and staring at Nelson.

"How's what?"

"How's it made to order?"

"Because it's nasty, full of gooks, and a good place to get your shit blown away."

"That's good to know," Redwine chimed, unfazed.

"Any of your classmates from P.I. been killed yet?" asked Billingsley.

"Five, that I know of. Coupla more been hit and evacuated. I hear from a buddy every now and then who fills me in on some of 'em."

"Pretty bad, huh?"

"Yeah, plenty. You worried about it, Billingsley?"

"Should I be?" Billingsley answered cockily.

"Probably not," shrugged Nelson. "No need worrying about it when there ain't shit you can do about it."

"I'll go if they send me."

"Me, too," added Redwine.

"Won't be no 'if' in the deal," Nelson said.

The second week began on Monday with the fury of the preceding week. The pace was even stepped up another increment, to the amazement and chagrin of the candidates. The academic classes began emphasizing the workings and nature of Marine Corps weapons, both individual and crew-served.

Billingsley was impressed with the weapons, the tools with which death could be so efficiently and impersonally dealt. He also began to hear repeated use of the term "gook," which represented Viet Cong or North Vietnamese soldiers, and who were the intended targets of those tools of death. The Program began to deal in the specifics of the trade—searching for, finding, and destroying the enemy.

Echo Company made its first lengthy hike. The men hoisted their rifles and packs and felt the burden of the infantryman under the weight. They marched from the Annex, moved uphill past the Air Station, and stopped at the edge of the forest which surrounded the course their hike would follow. The hike would start with the infamous and demanding Hill Trail, a series of steep and tortuous slopes whose summit had seemed an eternity away to the many thousands of preceding candidates who had fought their way to the top.

Billingsley stood in a column of files which paused at the base of the Hill Trail while the instructors shouted their expectations to the candidates.

"Don't let these hills psyche you," a candidate beside Billingsley said. "Take 'em one at a time, and always keep on the move."

"Move out, people," shouted O'Brien, looking natural in his combat regalia.

Billingsley strained as he began moving ahead, keeping the pack of the man to his front within touching distance. The heat and the weight of the pack caused him to perspire heavily as the company began its climb up the hills. The instructors shouted at the candidates to keep the columns moving, ever quicker, ever upward.

"Get up the hill."

As the pace quickened, several candidates were unable to maintain their close intervals in the column.

"I SAID GET UP THE FUCKING HILL, CANDIDATE."

"GET ON YOUR FEET, YOU GUTLESS MOTHERFUCKER. ON YOUR FEET."

"MOVE, FATASS. GET TO THE TOP OF THE HILL. MOVE, MOVE."

"UP THE HILL, MAGGOTS. GET UP THE HILL."

As he struggled to keep moving, Billingsley saw several of

his classmates slump to the ground in exhausted heaps. Soon, it looked as though machine-gun fire from the crest of the hill had driven into the column, dropping casualties along the slopes. Billingsley pushed on, not sure how much longer his legs and lungs would hold out.

"GET UP THE HILL."

The climb was excruciating, straining the legs and backs and wills of even the best conditioned of the candidates. The instructors screamed their insults at those who fell out and quit. Billingsley kept pushing, pushing, nearly blinded by the sweat and wary of his straining, uncooperative muscles. The instructors' screaming intensified with the severity of the slopes. Men fell all around him, gasping, clutching, groping. He kept moving, pushing, straining, one step at a time. More screaming from the instructors. My God, he thought. Not much left in my legs. I can't breathe. Can't see the top, either. Couldn't be far, though. Jesus, I'm dying! I don't know if I can make it. C'mon, dammit. End soon, please. Keep . . . keep . . . keep moving . . . a few . . . more . . . shit . . . c'mon, man . . . end . . . just a . . . little . . . more . . . to go.

"GET UP THE HILL."

I'll make it, he vowed. Or I'll die in a pile. I'll make it! Won't quit. Hurry, dammit. I'm losing it. Not much more to go. Not much more. Couldn't be.

"GET UP THE HILL."

Near the top, the columns squeezed in accordian fashion, jamming the main body which had already reached the summit of the final crest. Billingsley staggered to the top, slowing the final few yards to allow the others an opportunity to spread out. He was winded and dizzy, but he felt exhilarated at being upright and at the top. Below, he could see candidates in a desperate struggle to keep their unwilling bodies moving up the rise while instructors screamed their insults. A few candidates had stopped altogether, oblivious to the shouting around them, and lay coughing and vomiting, gasping for air.

Several instructors stayed back with the stragglers as the remainder of the company continued on.

The rest of the six-mile hike was rapid and challenging, though not nearly as difficult as the Hill Trail. Billingsley's feet ached and his hands and arms were numb from the shoulder straps of his marching pack. His uniform was soaked with sweat and his mouth was dry and gummy by the time the company finally emerged from the forest. He had made it, though. He was on his feet and feeling pleased with himself.

O'Brien called cadence as he marched his platoon back to the barracks. The tired but proud candidates repeated his chants in unison. Echo-Three could be heard throughout the barracks and mess hall complex as it strutted to O'Brien's commands.

"Lift your head and hold it high, Echo-Three is passing by."

"If I die on the Russian front, bury me with a Russian cunt."

"If I die in the Russian rear, bury me with a Russian queer."

"One, two, three, four, I love the Marine Corps."

O'Brien flickered a brief look of satisfaction with his platoon. Billingsley reasoned that the relatively few stragglers from the platoon had pleased the competitive instructor. The platoon was dirty and grimy, but it marched in sharp formation as the dull, distinctive thud of boot heels impacted simultaneously on the asphalt surface.

The remainder of the second week and the third were routine only in that the dawn-to-dusk activity continued. The Program became more varied and provided the staff with early indications as to those whose physical and leadership capacities were suspect. Hikes, runs, and obstacle course sessions provided ample evidence of physical stamina. The leadership evaluation was slightly more subjective, though obvious in several cases were candidates with seemingly little or no ability to lead. And there were those whose desire to lead had dwindled, perhaps somewhere along the slopes of the Hill Trail.

In the fourth week rumors flew as to the names of those who would be dropped from the Program. The candidates had already developed ideas and opinions concerning those who they thought would be marginal, as well as those in their number who were clearly exceptional. It was the large group in the middle who nervously awaited the beginning of the process of elimination.

Billingsley felt reasonably confident that his performance was satisfactory. He had scored well on the academic tests, and he had received no more than an average amount of reprimands from the staff. Still, he worried over the possibility of having made an unfavorable impression on any of the people who made the judgements. Billingsley equated the prospects of failure at OCS to disgrace, a loss of honor. By now he wanted a commission into the officer ranks of the Marine Corps more than anything he had wanted in his life. He was unsure, though, whether he wanted the commission for the opportunities it afforded or, because without it, he would consider himself a failure. He only knew that he wanted it very badly.

"What are you thinking about, Danny?" asked Billingsley as he sorted his laundry near the end of another long day.

Redwine sat on his foot locker looking doleful. "I'm thinking about a cigarette," he answered.

"That all? You look pretty grim to me."

"Well, I'm also thinking about how nice it would be to get laid, get drunk, and get the hell out of here."

"In that order?" asked Steve Nelson who sat shining his boots across the aisle.

"Not necessarily," Redwine said. "Just out the damned gate first. Everything else would follow soon enough. Man, I'd give one of my feet away to have the other one flat so I could get out of here on a medical. Boy, did I mess up by not getting my knee screwed up in football."

"You gotta love it, Danny," kidded Billingsley.

"Yeah, right. I love it so much already that I could just shit. I'd love it all the more if I had a cigarette."

Billingsley and Redwine were immensely relieved to find that the four-week boards had not included their names among the ones who had been dropped from the Program. Altogether, eighteen candidates had either been recycled or sent to Parris Island for recruit training. Along with the eight who had been released during the first week of training, the platoon had been reduced from an initial strength of sixty-two to a current tally of thirty-six. And there would be more, they all knew.

Lieutenant Coleman gathered the platoon at the front of the barracks and again emphasized the seriousness of the work ahead.

"You're through one phase of the screening, but there's still a long way to go before you can become Marine officers. I've told you before that I don't care how many have to be pushed aside to get at the ones I want, I'll do it. If you have any doubts about that, people, just look around. There's still a lot left to be proven. Don't let up and waste the efforts you've already put into this Program. Keep at it."

Coleman studied the faces of the remaining candidates with the calm, detached, but stern expression that few other leaders in professions apart from the military can duplicate. His steely gaze chilled many of those whose eyes met his, including Billingsley.

"Remember what I've told you. You know what we're after, and you know what you must provide. You are dismissed."

Two events during the fifth week of training convinced Billingsley of the grim realities of his undertaking. The first involved Candidate Franklin Reeves who, like Billingsley, was a Southerner. Unlike Billingsley, however, Reeves was small and unathletic. He had stood out, and so he had endured more than a normal amount of abuse from the staff. It was Reeves who had been reduced to tears in a previous encounter with Sykes on the drill field.

At the completion of another daily drill session in which Reeves had been rebuked harshly for his errors, O'Brien had dismissed the platoon to the barracks. While the other candidates put away their weapons, Reeves went directly to his bottom bunk in the center of the barracks area and fell spread-eagled on his mattress. He began to tremble uncontrollably as he lay silently on his stomach. A crowd gathered in front of Reeves' bunk. O'Brien appeared.

"Secure your gear, people. Get back to your own areas," O'Brien said calmly.

O'Brien leaned over the trembling Reeves. "Can you hear me, candidate?" he asked as he attempted to see Reeves' eyes. Reeves did not answer, nor in any other way acknowledge O'Brien's presence.

"Listen to me, candidate. I want you to stay where you are," said O'Brien, as if Reeves might suddenly rise and tremble his way to the mess hall for noon chow. "Medical help's on the way."

In minutes, an ambulance with a team of corpsmen arrived at the barracks. Reeves was quickly placed on a stretcher and removed from the building. O'Brien stayed close to the shivering Reeves until he was placed in the back of the ambulance.

The diagnosis through the platoon grapevine, though

unconfirmed, was that Reeves had suffered a nervous breakdown.

Billingsley wondered what would become of Reeves, as well as Reeves' wife and small child. On the few occasions when Billingsley had spoke to Reeves, the talk had generally centered on their common Southern backgrounds. Reeves, an architect, had impressed Billingsley as being a quiet, introspective loner. Now he had come apart at the seams and been carted away to an unknown fate. It disturbed Billingsley deeply.

The second event involved a chance encounter while Billingsley took his turn at washing trays and dishes as part of a stint of mess duty after evening chow. The man in charge of the mess crew was a sweaty, stocky, dark-skinned individual who answered to the name of Meat, though Corporal Vince Demetros was his more traditional label.

"Take a break, candidate," Demetros said as he noticed Billingsley working near the steamy dishwasher, perspiring heavily.

"Thank you," Billingsley replied cautiously.

"Wanna smoke?" asked Demetros as he held a pack of Camels near Billingsley.

"I do, but I guess I'd better not."

"Hell, take one. Nobody can see you back here, if that's what you're worried about. And I sure as hell don't give a shit," said Demetros, still extending the pack.

Billingsley accepted a cigarette and lit it from the end of the one held by Demetros. He inhaled deeply and immediately became dizzy. It was the first courteous gesture extended to him by a member of the regular Marine Corps establishment. He felt the need to be reserved, nonetheless.

"So how's OCS? Getting along okay in all that bullshit?" asked Demetros as he wiped his face with a paper towel.

"It's okay, I guess."

"Well, enjoy it here while you can, man. I don't just mean here at Quantico, but civilization, man, 'cause where you'll end up ain't no place to write home about."

"Where is that?"

"Fuckin' Nam."

"Have you been to Vietnam, corporal?"

"Yeah, I been over there. Got this motherfucker for a souvenir," proclaimed Demetros, opening his utility shirt to expose an eight-inch scar that ran from his stomach to his side.

"Damn. What happened?" The red scar was still clearly outlined by the stitching marks.

"Got my ass mortared. Part of a convoy that got hit. I was getting out of the damned truck when I got zapped."

"Looks pretty bad."

"It was weird, man. Strangest trip I've ever taken, that's for damn sure. Spent three months in a lousy hospital."

"Anybody else get hit?"

"Christ, yes. The gooks even got the medevac chopper my buddy was on."

"Kill him?"

"Killed 'em all. My buddy was already hit in the head, so I don't know if he woulda made it any damn way. It was some fucked up sight, man. Dudes screamin', dudes cryin', dead dudes. And me lookin' at my own Goddamned guts comin' out. I thought I was one dead little snuffy. Ready for the body bag and the whole nine yards."

Demetros sighed heavily at the thought of his past, though he was enjoying the role of combat veteran. He had a captive audience and, besides, talking about war beat cleaning the mess hall.

"Hey Fogarty," Demetros shouted to one of his crew members who was half-heartedly mopping a section of nearby floor. "Be sure to swab the deck in the officer's mess. One of the clumsy motherfuckers spilled his fuckin' coffee all over the Goddamned world, and it'll be my ass if it's sticky in the morning."

Billingsley grinned softly and relaxed with Demetros.

"You wanna soda, candidate?"

"I'd love one."

Demetros shouted at another worker who dutifully produced two cans of Coke and brought them to Demetros. Demetros waved off Billingsley's thanks.

"Don't worry about it, candidate. Like I said, you better enjoy yourself while you can."

The chilled, burning carbonation of the soda felt sensational to Billingsley's mouth and throat. He felt talkative and at ease, away from the barracks and O'Brien and Sykes and the whole stiff, demanding routine.

"Ain't got but three more months to pull in this green

mother, and then I'm out," Demetros said.

"What are you gonna do when you're out?"

"My uncle runs a grocery up in Chicago, so I'll probably get on with him. My old lady wants to go back, anyway. Her and me are both from up there. Ever been to Chicago, candidate?"

"No, I haven't. I hear it gets a little cold, though."

"Gets more than a little cold, I shit you not. It's as cold as Nam is hot. Those are *extremes*, man."

Demetros lit another cigarette, noticed Billingsley's glance at it, and offered the pack to the candidate. "Here, keep 'em all," he said.

"Just one more will do. I'd better not go back with a half-pack," Billingsley said, taking one last smoke and lighting it.

"Suit yourself, man."

A cigarette and a Coke, a simple pleasure which only weeks before would have been as normal as morning, was an extraordinary delight to Billingsley. He savored each puff and each sip as if he were paying handsomely for them.

"Glad you went to Nam?" Billingsley asked innocently.

Demetros grimaced and exclaimed, "Are you *shittin' me*, man?"

"No, why?"

"Worst fuckin' thing that ever happened to me, for damn sure. Gives me the DTs just thinkin' about it sometimes. I swear to Christ I'd rather go to the fuckin' brig than to go back to the Nam. My old lady'd leave my ass in a minute if she knew she had to go through me comin' home and actin' crazy again. No more of that bullshit for this kid, though. I'm too short for the friggin' bastards to send me back. Naw, man. I ain't glad I went for shit."

"You'll be out by the time I get over there."

Demetros smiled. "That's fine with me. You're not gonna be a grunt, are you?" he asked.

"Yeah, I think so."

"Jesus, man. You're fuckin' askin' for a dose of it. Those grunts I was around at Chu Lai were the craziest motherfuckers on the face of this earth. Used to heat their C-rats with C-4. Crazy, I mean. And didn't give a shit, either. Must be all the shit they had to put up with, or something. You oughta get in something besides the damned grunts, man. You'll be humpin' until you're blue in the friggin' face, I shit you not."

Demetros wasn't envious of infantrymen, Billingsley gathered.

"No jokin', man. You'd better give that some thought," Demetros emphasized.

"I will. I appreciate the advice, and the soda and cigarettes."

"Try to stay out of Nam altogether if you can, man. That'd be the easiest way to skate by. Just get yourself in a position to where you can fuck off over here, Stateside. That'd be the way to do it."

The conversation with Demetros remained with Billingsley as he returned to the barracks.

Echo-Three plunged into its sixth week of training. Its members were becoming physically fit and hardened. They were also becoming familiar with the array of weaponry in the Marine Corps arsenal, though their closest familiarity rested with small arms, and particularly the M-14 rifle. The newer, lighter M-16 rifle had been introduced into Marine units in Vietnam, while training organizations retained the reliable and proven M-14. The candidates knew their weapons well, both in function and in purpose.

Billingsley was progressing satisfactorily, if not actually excelling. His performance was near perfect on the academic tests, and his leadership qualities were apparent to the staff as well as his peers. Although Billingsley was generally soft spoken, his endurance and his ability to think on his feet had impressed Lieutenant Coleman and Sergeant O'Brien. Both agreed that Billingsley was one of several candidates with outstanding potential.

The seventh and eighth weeks of training included classroom sessions in tactics, with trips to the field for practical applications. Patrolling, attacking, and defending positions were rehearsed. The fitness routine was continued with hikes and runs. Most of the candidates reached the peak conditioning of their lives. Classroom lectures covered the basics of squad tactics. There was little slack in the pace.

Billingsley's bunkmate, Dan Redwine, also progressed in a satisfactory manner. While skillful, Redwine often irritated

O'Brien and Sykes with his flippancy. Inwardly, though, Redwine was serious and purposeful. He worried that he would irritate O'Brien to the point that his name would be included in the final list of candidates to be dropped at the very end of the Program.

Billingsley and Redwine buoyed one another when depressed and shared enough humorous anecdotes about their common plight to maintain their perspective. Their friendship was solid, developed not only through their training but also by the weekend trips taken together to Washington, D.C., and the northern Virginia area. They shared many thoughts, many concerns, and more than a few beers. They wondered where their respective journeys would take them once their training had been completed. Vietnam seemed a certainty, though their youthful feelings of immortality caused them little concern over the inherent dangers of combat. They viewed battle as something exciting, something challenging, something wholly honorable. And they saw not the least incongruity in the idea of Americans slaying Communists in the name of freedom and justice. They talked, and discussed, and hoped, though they knew nothing of the realities of war.

Billingsley and Redwine returned to Quantico after a weekend of merriment and relaxation in Washington, D.C. They still felt the effects of the previous night as they changed into their uniforms and folded away their civilian clothes. Their disgruntlement over an encounter with a pair of attractive government secretaries also lingered.

"You owe me twenty bucks, Danny my boy," Billingsley said as he laced his boots.

"For what?" Redwine protested.

"For your part of the tab for drinks and dinner."

"God, Mike. I paid for a bunch of rounds. No kidding, I really did."

"Yeah, but while you were outside the restaurant begging them to stay, I got the damned check for the dinner and the drinks we had afterwards."

"Left us high and hard, didn't they?"

"Sure did. I thought we were doing okay until you made that comment to yours that you'd like to meet her anti-war brother in Canada so you could blow his shit away. Damn,

Danny, they were out of their seats and gone as soon as you said that."

"Pretty smooth, ain't I?"

"You were the one who told them to order anything they wanted from the menu when we had dinner. Did you see the prices of the shit those two ordered?"

"Ah, don't sweat it, Mike. You know what they say about people who can't take a joke."

"Yeah, I do. And I was planning on doing that until you did your number on 'em."

The beginning of the ninth week brought no relief to the candidates as the academic and field pace continued unabated. They all noticed the extra scrutiny with which Lieutenant Coleman observed their activities. Coleman, they all suspected, was making his final decisions on who would, and would not, take part in the commissioning ceremony soon to take place.

During a routine physical training session, the candidates performed a series of exercises known affectionately as the "daily dozen." Then they reported to the pull-up bar where they performed their repetitions and called out the number to the nearby Coleman.

"Sir, eight pullups," reported Candidate Gary Archer, an ex-enlisted Marine.

"Negative, Archer. You only did *five*," snapped Coleman.

Archer stood motionless in front of Coleman. The others around them went about their routine, though everyone listened intently. Archer's face paled as he awaited the confrontation with Coleman.

"Do you stand by that number, candidate?" pressed Coleman.

"Sir, the candidate did eight pullups."

Coleman moved close to Archer, positioning himself only inches from the ramrod-straight candidate. Archer's expression became pained, as if he would have preferred to snap his fingers and disappear into the clouds.

"Archer," Coleman said softly, "I don't tolerate liars. I don't tolerate lying privates and I don't tolerate lying sergeants, and I damn sure don't tolerate lying officers. And you *are* a liar. Aren't you, candidate?"

Archer said nothing.

"AREN'T YOU, CANDIDATE?"

Sir . . . sir, the candidate didn't—"

"THAT'S RIGHT, ARCHER. THE CANDIDATE DID-N'T. THE CANDIDATE DIDN'T WORK, THE CANDIDATE DIDN'T TRY, THE CANDIDATE DIDN'T TELL THE GODDAMNED TRUTH. AND YOU KNOW WHAT ELSE, ARCHER?"

Archer's eyes blinker, his only movement.

"I SAID, DO . . . YOU . . . KNOW . . . WHAT . . . ELSE . . . ARCHER?"

"No, sir."

"THE CANDIDATE WON'T," shouted Coleman as he backed away from Archer. "I'm taking you to the end of the line, hotshot, and then I'm going to shitcan you. You can count on that. Now get away from me, Archer. You make me sick."

Archer joined in the line of candidates who made ready to start the obstacle course. The lesson was not lost on the remainder of the group. The Program was unfinished and the final list was incomplete.

The May sun and high humidity drained the hardened candidates during the final field exercises. An occasional rain was a welcomed relief to the already soaked men. Heat, mosquitos, fatigue, C-rations, loose bowels, and dirty clothes were, they were learning, tolerable if viewed as the standard condition. They found that misery and discomfort were indiscriminate, that by merely being in the field one could find enough of each in ample portions.

Yet Billingsley, like many of the others, found the forest and the outdoors to his liking. He was uncomfortable with the spartan living conditions in the field, but he enjoyed the naturalness of the forest. He had grown up spending a lot of time in the piney Georgia woods that surrounded his home. As a child, he had imagined himself as a Confederate scout, stealthily moving around the lines of the Union invaders while using his familiarity with the terrain to avoid detection. Many of his trips to the field as a candidate reminded him of his pleasant childhood fantasies. After all, he was back out in the woods, playing war again.

The end of the ninth week brought the beginning of the

final week of training. It was a week which had seemed an eternity away during those first few days after reporting. Final uniform fittings were made by Post Exchange tailors. Arrangements were made for those few friends and relatives who planned to make the trip to Quantico for the Friday ceremony. A discernible relaxation of the tight discipline enabled the candidates to enjoy an evening smoke. A scheduled twelve-mile hike was shortened to half that length as a reward, of sorts, for the level of effort put forth by the candidates throughout the Program. In inter-company competition in such events as close-order drill, the rope climb, and tug-of-war, Echo-Three made a clean sweep. Sergeant O'Brien was ecstatic.

A suite of motel rooms was reserved in nearby Dumfries for a platoon party on Wednesday. Thursday brought the graduation parade. Billingsley's parents and younger brother arrived in time for the parade, and even managed a short visit immediately afterward. Billingsley could tell that his father, who had served as an infantryman in the European Theater during World War II, appreciated his accomplishments.

The last serious business was completed on Thursday evening when Lieutenant Coleman advised three members of the platoon that they were being dropped. As promised, Candidate Archer was among the three. Thirty-six of the sixty-two candidates originally in Echo Company were scheduled to receive their commissions as officers of Marines.

Finally, it was over.

"Second Lieutenant Michael David Billingsley," called the speaker as the commissions were awarded in a formal ceremony in the Auditorium. He had finished near the top of his class, barely missing out on the distinction of being the Honor Graduate. He received his first salute from Sergeant O'Brien after his mother had pinned the gold bars onto his uniform, sealing the attainment of the goal for which he had worked so hard. When the brief gathering outside the Auditorium with the families and friends had concluded, Billingsley and the others drove the few miles to the Basic School complex to check in and receive their room assignments in the BOQ. Then it was off to join his parents at their motel room.

Billingsley's parents were overjoyed at the achievements of their eldest son. Their sacrifices had been rewarded innumerably, especially by Mike's graduation from college—a first on either side of the family. He was young and bright and handsome; he was everything they had ever hoped and dreamed he would become. He shared his parents' values—love of family, the work ethic, the Bible, and individual dignity. And now, with their son on his own and in the service of his country, Billingsley's mother and father gave each other the looks of admiration—the gleaming eyes and warm smiles—which indicated not only a pride in their son, but an appreciation for what they had produced as parents, as husband and wife.

The thought of her son going off to war deeply disturbed Dorothy Billingsley. The thought of Mike and his younger brother, Kevin, age sixteen, both serving in Vietnam caused her moments of physical revulsion. She held those feelings within, hoping that the war would somehow reach a conclusion before involving her sons. The news reports gave her little reason for comfort, however.

Raymond Billingsley had grown up in modest surroundings on the outskirts of Atlanta. He had vowed during the early years of marriage that his children would enjoy a higher standard of living, and the opportunities it brings, than he himself had known in his youth. His years as a warehouse manager had enabled him to fulfill his ambition to improve the lot of his children. He was proud of Mike, proud beyond description. And he, too, hoped the war in Vietnam would end quickly. But he also felt that young men of the caliber of Mike might come away with the victory which had thus far seemed so elusive.

Kevin Billingsley idolized his older brother. At the same time, Kevin suffered slightly from the intimidating prospects of meeting the high standards of achievement which his brother had set. An average student, Kevin had not found success in academics, athletics, or popularity to the degree which Mike had experienced with relative ease. Instead, he struggled to find an identity to which he could cling, and in which he could be regarded with admiration. Kevin hardly knew where Vietnam was, and certainly wanted no part of any activity which involved the act of killing. Of that much, he was certain.

"Are you going to Vietnam, Mike?" Kevin asked as he stood with his brother on the balcony outside the two rooms reserved for the Billingsleys.

"Not for a while, yet. I've got five months of Basic School before I go anywhere."

"Do you want to go?"

"Hell, Kevin, I don't know right now."

"Then why did you join the Marines?"

"Because."

"Because why? Because you wanted to go to Vietnam?"

"That's it, Kevin. Why not?"

"Why *not*? Because you might get *killed*, Mike. That's why not."

"Don't talk so loud. Mom and Dad are asleep, like most of the others in this motel."

"Think you'll stay in?" Kevin asked after a while.

"I don't think so. I'll probably just do my time and get out. It'll be nice to talk about in ten years."

"Yeah, if you're *around* in ten years."

"Christ, Kevin. I can't tell you how good it is to talk to you after all these weeks." Billingsley stared at Kevin. "You've really picked me up, pal."

"I'm sorry, Mike. I just hate to see you get involved with that stupid war. It's a joke, man. Really, it's a complete bummer."

"Tell you what, Kev. You can have all my old baseball cards if I get blown away. And my car, you can have that, too. And my—"

"All right, Mike. I said I was sorry. Let's don't get into that. Okay?"

"Okay," Billingsley said as he smiled and slapped his brother on the shoulder. "Let's get into the room and hit the rack. You're worse than Sykes."

"Who is Sykes?"

"A former acquaintance who also used to ask difficult questions."

Billingsley returned to the base on Sunday afternoon after the melancholy farewell at Washington's National Airport.

2

On Monday, June 3, 1968, Company N convened in a large classroom at the Basic School complex referred to as, simply, TBS. Some 220 new officers made up the Officer Basic Course. The function of TBS was similar to that of a finishing school; the rudiments of their training would be examined in greater detail, both theoretically and practically. The course would last five months, with major emphasis on the duties of a rifle platoon leader. Included with the recent OCS graduates in November Company were NROTC and Naval Academy graduates, as well as those from summer commissioning programs known as Platoon Leaders Class.

The orientation at TBS was organized and crisp, providing the officers with a course outline, platoon assignments, and a summary of what they would be expected to accomplish. While the atmosphere was by no means leisurely, the officers were made to feel much more at ease than was the case at OCS. Gone were the references to the men such as "worm" and "maggott," though the new officers were still wary of those of higher rank.

After the orientation, the officers settled into their new environment. Their dormitory-style rooms at the BOQ consisted of small but reasonably private two-man quarters with a bath in between. Married officers were allowed to live off the base.

Billingsley had been assigned to the First Platoon, along with his new roommate, a sandy-haired Californian named Bill Blanton. An OCS graduate, Blanton had been a member of a platoon other than the one in which Billingsley had finished. Although Dan Redwine was located in another area of the BOQ and had been assigned to a different platoon, Billingsley still saw a lot of him.

Blanton and Billingsley joined Redwine after dinner in the small but jovial lounge in the main building. The beer was cold and the conversation plentiful. They managed to find a table vacated by a group intent upon a night on the town.

"Man, this sure beats the hell out of OCS," Redwine said as they took their seats.

"Yeah. This is pretty classy," mused Billingsley as he admired the clean and orderly arrangement of the lounge.

"I still can't believe I'm not a candidate anymore," Blanton said. "The sight of one of those instructors would send a cold chill through me."

"How was the visit with your family, Mike?" asked Redwine.

"It was good. I think my little brother is becoming an anti-war type, though. He seemed a little distant."

"Do you think he's using drugs?" asked Blanton.

"Nah, I don't think so. He's only sixteen. How was your visit, Dan?"

"Fine. Mom's doing well and the farm seems to be surviving, in spite of my sister and that dipshit she's married to. I can't complain as long as everything finds a way of working. Did your family come over from California, Bill?"

"No, my parents are divorced. When we get a long weekend during the Fourth of July, I'm going to have my girlfriend fly to D.C. and meet me."

"Is she from California, too?" asked Billingsley.

"Yeah, L.A. She's a senior at UCLA. Sure wish she was here now."

"God, it's been so long since I've held a breast, I'd probably have a coronary and keel over in a pile," lamented Redwine.

"Bullshit, Danny. I've seen you work. And the only thing about you that keeled over was your damned wallet when it came time to pay the bar bill," chided Billingsley.

"Not so, brother. Just to show you, the next round is on me," said Redwine.

Three more beers were brought to the table as the reminiscing continued. They were as relaxed as they had ever been in their short careers. It was a fine thing, indeed, to be an officer instead of a tense, struggling candidate. As they downed the last of their beer and prepared to leave, Redwine leaned toward Billingsley.

"I'm a little short, Mike. Can you handle the tab?"

"November Company, ATTEN-HUT," shouted the student officer designated for the week as the CO. At his command, the officers rose to their feet in the large, amphitheater-style classroom as the instructor for the session entered and stepped up to the podium.

"Be seated, gentlemen," said the instructor, a highly decorated infantry officer named Captain Richard Travis.

"Welcome to Individual Weapons. The purpose of this period of instruction is to review the individual weapons assortment found in a Marine rifle company." Captain Travis delivered his lecture in a professional, thorough manner. An overhead projector was used to illustrate each of the weapons discussed. The body of a well-endowed female was flashed momentarily on the screen to gain and maintain the attention of the students.

"The M-16A1 rifle, gentlemen, is a 5.56mm, magazine-fed, gas-operated, air-cooled, shoulder-fire weapon. It is designed for either semiautomatic or fully automatic fire through the use of a selector lever. The weapon is equipped with a flash suppressor. As an aside, gentlemen, let me mention that being on the receiving end of this piece could tend to ruin what could otherwise be a very nice day," joked Travis.

The officers laughed approvingly, enjoying the detached humor so frequently employed in Basic School lectures. The instructor ended his fifty-minute session with a summary before excusing the class for a short break. Thus was the schedule: classes, noon chow, physical training, and more classes. Practice in the field came only after the subject matter had been adequately covered in the classroom.

Each officer was informed that an evaluation would be made of his performance in three distinct areas while at Basic School. The Academics assessment would be based on the average from tests given for each of the subject areas. Military Skills identified performance associated with physical conditioning and endurance, such as the physical fitness test, the obstacle course, and the like. Leadership was the category in which the officer would be judged on his performance in handling his duties. Each officer was also told that his class standing would, in large measure, determine the Military Occupational Specialty, which each would receive later. The higher the class standing, the greater the likelihood of obtaining the MOS of one's choice.

Billingsley had decided during OCS that infantry would be his first choice of specialties. He enjoyed the outdoors, wished to be close to the action, and felt that the "grunt" was the true essence of the Marine Corps. He knew that he would have little or no difficulty in being assigned to the infantry since the Corps needed replacements in its ground units at a far greater rate than those of the other disciplines. After all, he concluded, somebody's got to fight. And he was rapidly learning how.

As the routine of the classroom continued, field demonstrations showed the destructive capabilities of such weapons as the M-60 machine gun, the flamethrower, and the recoilless rifle. Napalm delivered in a demonstration by attack aircraft created an impressive spectacle of fire and smoke to the front of the seated officers.

"I'll bet you gentlemen can't wait to get in-country and use some of that stuff on the VC," an enlisted instructor said to Billingsley and several others. "Nothing but crispy critters and the smell of flesh. I just love the Goddamned sight of it."

Billingsley stared at the instructor for a moment. He wondered how the sight of charred bodies—enemy bodies, notwithstanding—could ever be viewed with pleasure. Ambivalence, perhaps. Maybe even detachment. But certainly not glee.

"Do you really enjoy that sight?" he asked when the instructor turned his way.

"They're gooks," the instructor replied tersely. "And they're dangerous. They look a helluva lot better dead than alive and, Lieutenant Billingsley, there ain't no mistakin' 'em being dead when they're crispy."

Billingsley remained silent as several classmates laughed loudly.

Classes ended on Wednesday afternoon before the long Fourth of July weekend, leaving the students four free days. Dan Redwine left for Illinois, and Bill Blanton drove to Washington for the planned rendezvous with his California sweetheart. Billingsley decided to remain at Quantico and use the time to relax and visit the nation's capital. He spent the Fourth with several married officers and their wives, picnicking at the pool of an apartment complex in nearby Woodbridge. He and his married friends swam, grilled steaks, drank beer, and laughed at stories about OCS, Sergeant O'Brien, and the events that only a few weeks ago had seemed far from funny.

On the following morning he got up early, now an almost natural function, and made the forty-minute drive to the Arlington National Cemetery. After viewing the Iwo Jima Memorial, he visited the Tomb of the Unknown Soldier and the gravesites of the Kennedys, John and Robert. He was still shocked and disappointed over the recent murder of Senator Kennedy, and he left the cemetery in low spirits. After a trip to the Jefferson Memorial, the Lincoln Memorial, and the Washington Monument, he decided to have a late lunch.

He drove to Georgetown, parked his car, and went into the first restaurant he saw, a fashionably adorned, overpriced hamburger outlet. He slid into a booth and began reading the menu, enjoying the air-conditioned comfort. In the next booth, a strikingly attractive girl, with long, brown hair pushed behind her ears and sunglasses resting atop her head, was intently reading a paperback. She was alone, sipping her soft drink through a straw, and seemed oblivious to anyone or anything else in the restaurant. She faced Billingsley, but did not look up from her book until her lunch was delivered. Her facial features were soft but nicely defined, her appearance clean and trim. She had a touch of class, of elegance, Billingsley thought. Her dark sleeveless blouse, exposing her tanned arms and shoulders, was tantalizing unbuttoned beneath the neck and permitted a glimpse of her white bra when she leaned forward to sample her hamburger. A thin gold chain, supporting a tiny cross, dangled from her neck and disappeared into the dark hair resting upon and behind her shoulders. A small gold ring was on the little finger of her right hand. Her only other jewelry was the sleek gold watch which slid up and down her trim wrist with each movement of her hand.

She looked up only once, and that for a short glance and approving nod to the waitress, signaling that her lunch was satisfactory. She noticed Billingsley staring but ignored him completely. She returned to her book.

Billingsley ate quickly. He realized that he had limited time in which to create an opening and deliver a clever line. She looked up only once more before finishing her hamburger, taking a quick gaze around the restaurant. She appeared to him to be approximately his age, and certainly no older. Probably a teacher, he thought. Or maybe a tourist. Or maybe even a student. She definitely wasn't the hippie type, he decided.

Just as Billingsley took the last bite from his sandwich, the girl looked up and peered directly into his eyes. He stopped chewing and the food bulged in his mouth, nearly gagging him.

"Why do you continue to stare at me?" she asked in a soft tone that moderated the bluntness of the question.

He lurched forward, grinning sheepishly, and pointed to his full mouth as his excuse for his inability to offer an immediate response. He chewed hard and swallowed with a gulp, again nearly gagging.

"I ... uh ... I suppose ... uh ... I have been staring, haven't I?"

"I suppose you have."

"Well, I could have stared at my sandwich, but it kept getting smaller. Sorry about that," he said with a grin. "Am I forgiven?"

He noticed a trace of a smile as she left the question unanswered and closed her book after bending the edge of the page. She reached for her purse and began sliding across the bench seat toward the aisle.

"Not in a million years," she said as she started to leave.

"Wait a minute," he called, gulping his water and standing. "That's an awful long time. Couldn't you be a little more reasonable? Say, ten thousand years?"

"Semper fi," she said, walking toward the cashier near the entrance to the restaurant, with Billingsley close behind.

"How did you know that? Do I know you from somewhere?"

The girl ignored him until she had paid the cashier with a crisp twenty, stuffed the change into her red billfold, and dropped it into the overstuffed leather purse which dangled by its strap along her side.

"You're *not* a Marine?" she asked, looking squarely at him before lowering her sunglasses into place.

"Well, yeah, I am. But how did you know? I don't have any

tattoos, or anything," he said with a grin.

"You don't have any hair, either."

She turned and walked toward the door.

He noticed her slimness, well accented by her white slacks and dark blouse. Her clothes fit snugly but tastefully, and she was nicely proportioned, petite. He followed her outside the restaurant after he had paid his own check. She had already started down the sidewalk. He had to trot to catch up with her. The Georgetown sidewalk was mostly clear of other pedestrians.

"Don't leave yet," he called as he caught up.

She turned and stopped to face him, lowering her sunglasses on her nose and looking over the rim. "What do you want?" she asked with some annoyance.

"Well, for starters, tell me how you knew I was a Marine."

"Look," she said as she raised her glasses, "I've got to be going. I don't have the time nor the inclination to stand out on the street and talk to you."

"Yeah, right," he said, following at her side and persisting in his attempts at conversation. "You can talk to me. I'm not an axe-murderer, or anything like that. Honest, I'm really very normal. Can you hear me over there? Hello?"

They walked the block and a half to her parked car with Billingsley continuing his monologue. She searched for her keys in the disorganized leather bag. He was encouraged by her faint smile.

He hesitated for a moment, fearful that his moment of opportunity was escaping. He groped for a gimmick, for anything that would continue the flow. Anything. Something. And fast.

"Wait a minute, just hold it right there," he commanded. "Are you aware of what could have happened to your car while you were away?"

She looked at him curiously and paused before stepping toward the car door. She remained silent.

"Huh? Are you aware of what could have happened?" he pressed.

"Why don't you tell me," she demanded sarcastically, her hand on her hip.

"Okay, I will. By God, I will," he said as his mind searched in desperation for a rejoinder.

"Well?"

"I have every reason to believe that your car has been the object of a search. Illicit, perhaps. And for causes unknown to me. But I must tell you that everything points to the fact that your car has been searched."

"What kind of search? For what?"

He stepped from the curb and glanced inside the late-model, red MG. He then shook his head in mock disgust. He turned and looked at her.

"Yep, just as I thought," he said. "You can't get into that car now. It may be rigged to blow. I'm afraid you'll just have to stay for a while."

"Are you out of your mind? I've got to be leaving. Please excuse me," she said as she stepped away from him.

"Okay. Now I know. I know how you knew I was in the Marines. It's clear to me now."

She paused again, with her keys in her hand.

"You used to go with a Marine, didn't you? Or maybe you still do. Which is it?"

She looked at him, interested in spite of herself, and made no further attempt to unlock the door. "Okay," she said. "You guessed it. I used to date a guy who was in the Marine Corps. Lucky guess, wasn't it?"

"It's all I had left. Nothing else worked with you. Tell me the jerk's name and I'll tell you if I know him."

"His name was Hugh Jernigan," she said, looking at the ground, "and he was killed in Vietnam six months ago yesterday."

He drew a deep breath and exhaled slowly. His face tingled from the sudden rush of blood to his cheeks. The girl glanced up and, noticing his embarrassment, looked away.

"God almighty," he said. "I am sorry. I wish now I hadn't said anything at all. Will you accept my apology for such a foolish remark?"

"I accept your apology."

"I am sorry, really. I feel like taking off one of my shoes and hiding underneath it."

She smiled again, a forgiving, reconciling smile.

"You'd still be visible," she said.

"And I'd probably make a fool out of myself *again* if you ever walked by the shoe."

She laughed out loud and greatly eased his discomfort.

"Will you tell me your name?" he ventured.

"Andrea," she said after a moment of hesitation. "Are you stationed at Quantico?"

"Yeah. I really am sorry about the wisecrack, Andrea. I feel rotten about having tried to be cute like that."

"It's okay," she said with a smile.

"My name's Mike. Mike Billingsley."

"Hello, Mike Billingsley."

"And I was just kidding about your car."

"Were you kidding about not being an axe-murderer?"

"Yeah," he grinned. "I mean *no*! No, I wasn't kidding about that."

They stood talking politely for a bit longer. She giggled at his admitted embarrassment when he explained his desperate and unsuccessful attempt to think of the perfect line. She liked the way he recounted his bungling of the conversation. He was open and honest with her, though she still remained reserved and formal. She smiled wonderfully, he thought. Perfectly aligned teeth. Soft eyes. And the hair, the dark, lovely, long-flowing hair, parted in the middle and draping over her shoulders. He could sense a flicker of receptivity as they talked. Slight, but definitely there. He was emboldened.

"Will you do me a favor, Andrea?"

"Probably not, but ask anyway."

"Will you get out of the street before you get run over?"

"How else will I get into my car?"

"You don't have to get into your car. If you'll look just across the street, right over there, you'll see a lounge that looks like a perfect place for me to buy you a drink and make up for my stupid remark. If you don't want to, of course there'll be absolutely no pressure."

"Thanks, but I've got to be going."

"Wait a minute, now. If the bartender went to all the trouble to stock all that booze, then shouldn't we, as Americans, feel some obligation to support our system of free enterprise?" he asked as he cocked his head to the side and grinned. "Just one? Please, Andrea?"

Andrea couldn't help laughing at the sight of his pleading. She folder her arms across her front. "I thought you said there would be no pressure."

"I can't help myself." Billingsley stepped alongside her and extended his hand for her to follow. "C'mon, let's hurry before your car blows up."

She looked at his extended hand for a moment, her face reflecting neither acceptance nor outrage at the gesture. Her pale-blue eyes, softly textured and clear as a cloudless sky, gazed at the boyish expression on the face of this cocky new acquaintance. A moment longer and it was there again—The Smile.

"I can't believe I'm doing this," she said, shaking her head as she reached for his outstretched hand.

There were few other customers in the dimly lit lounge. Their corner table was illuminated by a single candle-lit lantern. He ordered the drinks—gin for Andrea and beer for himself. He looked into her shadowed, lovely face and delighted in his extraordinary good fortune.

"I appreciate this," he said.

"Just think of being here with me as one small way for me to serve my country," she laughed.

"Oh, you're a patriot. I didn't think there were too many of those left anymore."

"A patriot, yes. In favor of that crazy war, absolutely *not*!"

The drinks were brought to the table. He took a light sip of his beer before saying, "I don't blame you for feeling that way."

"It's such a *waste*. It's almost criminal."

"All wars seem to have a lot of wasting," he said, smiling faintly at the ludicrous thought of the Marine Corps infinitive "to waste," and its invariable reference to the act of inflicting mortal harm on an individual of Asiatic and Marxist persuasion.

"But especially this one. It's so silly."

He avoided any further reference to Vietnam and succeeded in shifting the topic of the conversation. He discovered that Andrea Strickland was a law student in her second year, home for her summer vacation. She spoke of how her father and grandfather had both studied and practiced law. Her father, she related, was a member of a prestigious Washington firm for whom she worked occasionally in the summer months as a legal assistant. Though her physical attractiveness was obvious enough, the longer they talked, the more apparent her intellect and wit became. She was sharp and opinionated, and seemingly of independent mind. Billingsley felt comfortable with her. And she seemed to feel at ease in his company.

The subject of her deceased friend never surfaced again, so he was unable to learn the degree of her previous involvement with the other Marine. He didn't mind not knowing; he could then hope that her prior misfortune wouldn't close him out because of his military status. Her company was delightful, her charm considerable. She could tease him with a coy turn of her head, yet show sincere interest in what he had to say. She listened well, nodding her understanding, raising her eyebrows in surprise, interjecting a mild disagreement. She was well informed and versatile as she spoke her piece in her soft, pleasant voice.

After an hour and a half, she had taken him by storm.

"I've enjoyed it, Mike," she said. "I've got to be leaving for home now."

"Can I see you again?"

She reached for her purse, offering no response.

"Hello? Still with me over there?" he called as he leaned toward her. "Did you hear me?"

She took one last sip of her drink before remarking softly, "I heard you."

There was a moment of silence as she fidgeted with a paper napkin. He could see that her eyes were focused upon the napkin. Her thoughts, he sensed, were far away.

"Thanks for having a drink with me," Billingsley said, finally. "And I still want to see you again. Okay?"

She looked directly at him for several seconds while remaining in her seat. She appeared to be unsure of the appropriate response to offer. She looked uncertain, skeptical.

"And now, Miss Strickland, I shall ask *you* why do you continue to stare at *me*?" he asked, grinning.

"I've enjoyed it, Mike," she said without a change in her expression.

"I'll walk you to your car."

They left the lounge and squinted in the late-afternoon brightness of the outdoors. He escorted her by the arm across the street to her car. He stood at her side while she gathered her keys from her purse and unlocked the door. Before she climbed into the seat, he touched her gently on the elbow.

"I meant what I said, Andrea. I want to see you again."

"Do you live at the Basic School?"

"Yes, at the BOQ. Why?"

"Then I'll contact you," she said as she entered her car with Billingsley still standing in the street.

"Why don't you let me call you?"

"No. Let's do it my way. Okay?"

"Okay, counselor. Drive carefully."

She started the engine of her car as he stepped away onto the sidewalk. He was unsure of whether he would ever see her again. He watched the car pull away and disappear into Georgetown's traffic.

He walked to his own car with the thought of her firmly fixed in his mind. As he began the drive to Quantico, he attempted to downplay the chance meeting and the hope of seeing her again. He concluded that the chances were indeed small, and it would be best for him to keep his mind on the work ahead. She can stick to her torts and replevins, he thought. And she probably goes with a pipe-smoker who always wears a necktie to supper, anyway. Besides, he concluded, one bad experience with a Marine was probably enough for her. The guy went and got himself killed, for God's sake. He drove along, silently struggling to erase her image and voice from his active memory. He couldn't shake her from his thoughts. He slammed his fist into the empty seat next to him.

"I should have gotten her telephone number. Now she's gone. I should have gotten her GODDAMNED TELEPHONE NUMBER," he shouted.

The return to the routine of the Basic School brought Billingsley a certain stability. There he could immerse himself in his work during his duty hours and retire to the bar in his off-duty time. Thoughts of Andrea came less frequently in the steady pace of the activity, which included qualifications at the rifle range, countless classroom sessions, and field exercises under simulated combat conditions.

Billingsley enjoyed commanding squads of other students as he led them in simulated attacks. He learned how difficult it is to stay in control in the midst of the noise and movement of even a mock battle. He wondered how anyone ever determines what is really going on during real war. When he posed the question to the instructors, their answers confirmed the difficulty in ascertaining the true situation in any given moment of a battle. It got easier with experience, he was told. And he noticed that Marine Corps tactics were designed to lead men in one direction only, and that direction was forward. A stroke of genius, he thought. If combat was as confusing as it appeared from the field exercises, why then not simplify it by eliminating 'movement to the rear' as a possible course of action? Brilliant! Read the book, follow the guidelines, and move forward toward the enemy. If he's there, find him and kill him. If he's not there, and he can't be found, then the hell with him. He can't win if he won't fight. Simple enough.

The hot, sultry days of July finally ended. Platoon tactics began dominating the classes as August brought its own heat and humidity. The officers of November Company had neared the mid-point of their training. They were also nearing the MOS assignment which they had previously requested. Some would receive additional training before reporting to a regular Marine unit, as in the case of artillery and armor officers, after completing Basic School. Billingsley was among the leaders in class standing, so he worried very little about getting his request for assignment into an infantry MOS.

Bill Blanton sat with Billingsley in the lounge at the Basic School after they finished studying for a tactics quiz. They had gone over the material thoroughly and decided to reward themselves with a round of beers. The lounge was sparsely populated with the student officers, though the laughter was loud and the bartender was busy. They sat at a table and enjoyed the cool of the lounge and the beer. Sure beat tactics, they both agreed. They quickly relaxed and emptied their minds of the acronyms and maneuver schemes of academic warfare.

"Lieutenant Billingsley, sir?" called the enlisted bartender. "You've got a phone call. You can take it over here, sir."

Billingsley arose, glanced at Blanton inquisitively, and walked around the bar to the telephone. "Lieutenant Billingsley speaking."

"Hello, Mike. This is Andrea Strickland. Do you remember me from Georgetown?" came the soft voice on the other end of the line.

"Andrea?"

"Yes, Mike. How have you been?"

"I've been fine."

"I don't think you remember me. We met last month in—"

"For God's sake, Andrea, of course I remember you. I just thought I'd seen the last of you, that's all. You've surprised me, to say the least."

"Mike, I called to see if maybe we could meet at the same place again."

"I can be there in an hour."

"No, no," she laughed. "I mean this weekend."

"That sounds great to me, Andrea."

"How does Friday night sound? Will that work out okay with Basic School, and all?"

"Friday night's perfect. Can we have dinner together?"

"Sure. Will you keep my car from being searched?"

"Absolutely. What time?"

"Eight o'clock okay?"

"I'll be there, counselor. Same place."

"Good, Mike. See you then."

He hung the telephone up and, smiling broadly, returned to the table. He felt euphoric over the delightful and unexpected turn of events. He had virtually erased her from his thoughts, though the memory was as clear as ever.

"Can you believe that, Bill? Up and calls me, right out of the blue. Can you believe that?"

"I can believe it, man. How many times you gonna ask me?"

"I can't believe it, Bill. I can't *even* believe it."

The remainder of the week dragged by for Billingsley. The dull, tedious, uninspiring lectures on the Uniform Code of Military Justice, the basis of military law, bored him. His interest in law was low, but his interest in a certain person who studied law of a different sort was exceedingly high.

When the classes finally ended on Friday, Billingsley showered hurriedly and changed into his civilian clothes, including jacket and tie. He then left for Georgetown in time enough to assure an early arrival in their scheduled meeting place. As it turned out, he was an hour early. He took a seat at a small table near the entrance and braced himself with a beer. A mix of patrons, predominantly middle-aged, gathered noisily in the lounge to begin the end-of-the-week celebration.

Andrea arrived punctually, dressed conservatively in a white cotton dress, but with a look of elegance in the fit of her clothes and the darkness of long, soft hair. Billingsley stood as she approached the table.

"Good evening, Miss Strickland. You look as lovely as I remembered," he said, smiling.

"Thank you, Lieutenant Billingsley. Why so formal?"

"I didn't think I'd ever be in this place and in your company again when I last left Georgetown."

"I didn't think so either. Will you order me a glass of white wine?" she said as she was seated with Billingsley's assistance.

As before, they talked politely about the events of their respective days. After the drinks were served the conversation seemed to warm.

"Why did you call me, Andrea? I can't sit here and not ask you that," he said.

"I just decided that I'd like to talk to you again. You don't mind, do you?"

"Of course not. I'm delighted with your decision."

They chatted idly. Eventually, the conversation slowed and he suggested that they depart and walk the short distance to the restaurant she recommended.

The fashionable restaurant was crowded with young professionals. Billingsley felt slightly awkward; his close-cropped hair was noticeably different from the longer lengths of the other men. The service of the restaurant was excellent, though, and he soon felt at ease with his surroundings and his date. Andrea laughed at his stories about life in the military. Their common selection of prime rib was excellently prepared.

"Good choice of restaurants, Andrea. I haven't eaten this much or this well in quite a while," Billingsley said between sips of steaming coffee.

"Thanks. I've always liked it. Do you eat out often?"

"Pretty often, yeah. We have C-rations in the field."

"Are they good?" she laughed.

"If you're hungry enough."

"What choices do you have?"

"Eat or starve, I guess."

"No, I mean what types of meals," she giggled.

"Oh, there's several. Turkey loaf, ham and limas, beans and franks. They're not too bad."

She ignored her coffee and sat with her chin propped upon her clasped hands. Billingsley correctly sensed that she was comfortable in his company, because of the way she smiled and her relaxed expression.

He reached for his cigarettes and offered her one. She politely declined.

"They aren't good for you, you know," she said as he lit up.

"I know. I'm gonna quit soon."

"When?"

"Haven't set the date yet. I don't think it'll be tonight, though. What would you like to do now?"

"I'll have to be leaving, Mike."

"There's a place near here that has some live music. Want to give it a try?"

"I don't think so," she responded. "If you like, you can follow me to my home in Reston, and we can have a drink there."

"I'd like that. It won't be an inconvenience, will it?"

"Not at all. Are you ready?"

They drove to suburban Reston, Virginia. Billingsley followed her car closely to avoid becoming separated and losing another opportunity to be with her. You old dog, he thought to himself, smiling. Nice job of working your way in. And the part about making sure it wouldn't be an inconvenience, that was a good lick. Damn, don't lose sight of her.

The drive seemed interminably long. At last, they reached the long, winding driveway to Andrea's home. The size of the two-story brick residence confirmed his guess that the Stricklands were prosperous well beyond the standards to which he was accustomed. Jesus, he thought. Got to act right around millionaires.

Andrea led him through a wide foyer and into an adjacent family room. He noticed the thick carpeting, the dark walnut paneling, and the oil paintings. A well-stocked bar was located along the near wall, across from the bay windows overlooking the front lawn. A large bookshelf, filled with dozens of hardbound volumes, stood at the far end of the large room facing the entrance. Big enough to sleep a platoon, he concluded.

"Make yourself comfortable, Mike. My parents are away for the weekend, so take your coat off if you like and make yourself a drink. I'll be back in a moment," she said, leaving him.

He mixed drinks for both of them while admiring the room and the adequacy of the bar. Andrea soon returned with a tray of snacks and placed it on a table in front of the couch on which Billingsley sat. She sat down in a lounge chair across from him and sipped her gin and tonic.

"Nice place," he commented.

"Thank you. I've lived in Charlottesville for most of the last five years, but it's always nice to come home." Andrea relaxed in the chair.

"When will you leave for school again?"

"The middle of next month. I'm beginning to look forward to it already. I hope this year isn't as bad as last year, though. The first year of law school isn't a lot of fun."

"That's what I hear. Will it get easier?"

"I hope," she replied vehemently.

Their talk ranged from the study of law to the surge in student unrest, with international politics and space exploration wedged in between. Andrea was bright, and she was impressed as well with Billingsley's intellectual versatility over such a variety of subjects. They talked on, solving little, disagreeing mildly on occasion, but exploring the ideas and opinions of one another. It became late.

"I suppose I'd better be making my way back to Q-town," he sighed, feeling the effects of a long day.

He rose from his seat on the sofa and slipped into his jacket, leaving his shirt collar unbuttoned and his tie loose.

"I'm glad we could be together, Mike. I feel very comfortable with you. I hope you didn't mind my calling you," she said, also standing.

"Of course not. You know that."

He met her glance and held it for several seconds before she looked away.

"You're still very vulnerable, aren't you?" he said.

"Why do you say that?" she responded, looking downward.

"How deeply were you involved with—"

"Hugh?"

"Yes, Hugh."

"Deeply enough. We were quite close for a time."

"I'm surprised you'd have anything to do with me."

"So am I, really. I thought long and hard about seeing you

again. You're such an easy person to like, Mike, and I enjoy your company a great deal. I just don't understand what it is about war and killing and suffering that compels you and many others to want to be a part of it. It's so illogical, and wasteful, and confusing. Does what I say make any sense at all to you?"

"I think I understand better what you're feeling than what you're saying, Andrea. And I have no overwhelming desire to take part in a war. I just want to do what I think is right."

"Nothing makes much sense to me anymore. I oppose the war with all my heart, yet I don't feel strongly enough about it to take to the streets with the protestors."

"I wouldn't think you'd call *me* if you spent a lot of time protesting," he said with a short chuckle.

"Does the idea of killing another human being bother you, Mike?"

"In war?"

"Yes, in war."

"The idea doesn't. The *act* might. I don't consider war a criminal activity, Andrea. I don't relish having to kill another man, but I'm not sickened by it, either. That much is obvious by my job status. Do you consider me to be cold-blooded?"

"No, I don't think you are cold-blooded. I think you are actually very sensitive," Andrea said with a slight grin.

"And very sleepy."

It was clear that Andrea had exposed feelings to him which she had repressed for quite some time. She was also visibly tired. He walked toward the foyer.

"I've enjoyed it, counselor. I appreciate your having me in your home, too. I'll be in touch soon," Billingsley said.

"How? By phone? You don't have my number."

"If it's the same number on the telephone next to the bar, then I have it. Reconnaissance, Andrea."

She grinned and followed him into the foyer. He turned to her as he stood near the door and took both her hands gently.

"You're pretty cocky, Lieutenant Billingsley. But you already know that, don't you?"

"Just a poor little ole country boy, ma'am, trying to impress a very pretty lady."

"Oh, please. Not another 'poor Southern boy' gimmick. Better stick to the line about the search."

They smiled warmly at each other as he continued to hold her hands. He leaned forward and kissed her lightly on the cheek. The smell of her perfume and the softness of her face intoxicated him. She raised her head slightly and he found her moist lips while he began to embrace her firmly. He could feel the pounding of her heart, as well as his own, as she returned the kiss and embrace with equal passion.

"God, I may detonate at any moment," he whispered softly into her ear as he held her tightly.

He continued to hold her against him. He rocked gently from side to side and could feel her long hair in his face. She was soft and delicate and beautiful and all the things that caused him to want to remain in the embrace forever, oblivious to the outside world and its goings on. He closed his eyes and enjoyed the feel of her body next to his.

"I'm joining my parents in New England tomorrow, Mike. I won't be back for another week. I'll let you know when I'm back," she said quietly while still in his embrace.

"The minute," he said.

He kissed her again, slowly, and cradled her head with his hand.

"Good night, counselor."

"Good night, Mike. Thank you for a lovely evening."

"Gentlemen," spoke the instructor, "test your gas masks before you get inside. Have your sleeves rolled down and button up your collars. If your mask does not function properly once inside, then immediately leave the trailer. Each of you will be required to unmask and report to me your name, rank, and service number. You will then be free to leave the trailer. Two men will be stationed at the door to assist you down the steps."

Billingsley stood outside the trailer where he and the officers from November Company were set to encounter their first direct contact with riot control gas, termed CS. The officers were divided into groups and waited to enter in a single file.

"This shouldn't be too bad," remarked Bill Blanton as he adjusted the strap on his mask.

"Some of the guys who went through this at Parris Island said it helps to start running when you get outside. Helps blow the shit off you, they said," Billingsley offered.

"Ah, this ain't gonna be any biggie. There probably won't

be enough gas in there to matter," countered Blanton.

"Why the hell would it be used to break up riots if it wasn't some pretty potent stuff, Bill?"

"No sweat, man. It'll be a piece of cake."

"Group One, form up outside the door. Single file against the bulkhead and facing me when you're inside," ordered the instructor, Major Munson.

The first group of fifteen officers, which included Billingsley and Blanton, fitted their masks over their faces. They tested the masks by placing the palms of their hands over the mask's filtering device to ensure an air-tight fit when they attempted to inhale. They walked up the steps of the trailer and stood alongside the inner walls. When the entire group had entered the trailer, the instructor closed the door. He then began filling the inside with the white smoke of the CS by burning a candle-shaped object. The officers immediately felt the skin on their throats and the backs of their hands begin to tingle.

When the haze had grown sufficiently thick, the instructor, speaking through his mask in a muffled tone, ordered the first officer in the group to unmask and offer the required recital. The others watched the procession of gasping, struggling students until it came time for their exposure to the gas. The afflicted students groped forward toward the doorway when finished, coughing violently to rid their lungs of the disabling chemical.

Billingsley breathed deeply as he readied himself for his moment before the instructor. As he stepped forward and removed his mask, his eyes burned as if lye had been thrown in his face. The shock of his stinging eyes caused him to inhale a sizable gulp of the cloudy CS. He recited his lines with great difficulty, and then moved quickly to the door. His eyes, nose, and mouth watered profusely as a coughing spasm overtook him at the bottom of the steps. He managed eventually to steady himself, but continued to feel slightly nauseated.

The door to the trailer opened again and Blanton fought to retain his balance. Blanton ambled out as if in a drunken stupor, weaving unsteadily with his body bent forward at the waist and his arms dangling limply at his sides. Blanton interrupted his coughing seizure long enough to vomit all over the tops of his boots. The sight of the sick and embarrassed Blanton diverted Billingsley from his own discomforts.

"Pretty bad shit, huh roomie," mumbled Billingsley as he walked to Blanton's side.

"I thought I'd fucking die," was all Blanton could manage as he knelt with one knee on the ground.

"Piece of cake, Bill," chided Billingsley.

Blanton raised his head and looked weakly at his recovered roommate. His nose still dripped and his eyes were red and watery from the irritation of the gas. A Blanton tirade was made mostly unintelligible by a coughing and sneezing seizure, though Billingsley did catch the suggestion to "Blow it out your ass, hotdog."

The introduction to the effects of CS upon the officers was followed by lectures on the employment of gas in combat situations. The widespread use of underground tunnels by the Viet Cong offered obvious opportunities for its employment. The experience in the trailer had convinced the young officers of the effectiveness of the gas.

The hard work continued for November Company. Tactics instruction advanced from the platoon to the company level. Field exercises continued unabated in the August heat. The officers maintained their physical conditioning with regular and frequent periods of strenuous exercise. They were also becoming increasingly confident in their abilities as leaders. Map reading, radio procedures, scouting, patrolling, and ambushing were becoming second nature to them. The months of intensive training had begun to yield competent, motivated junior officers who impatiently awaited their chance to enter the "real world" of the Marine Corps. All the pieces had begun to fit together in a coherent pattern, spoken of in terms of grid coordinates, lines of departure, final protective fires, call signs, five-paragraph orders, and estimates of the situation.

Billingsley often wondered about commanding regular troops in the Corps. He wondered about their expectations and opinions of junior officers and how they would respond to his leadership. He wondered about the level of training of the troops, the level of motivation and competency he would find in them when he joined a unit. He wondered about the older NCOs upon whom he would have to rely so heavily. The TBS instructors, all of whom had experienced combat, were always complimentary when assessing the quality of the troops.

There were exceptions, the instructors noted, but on the whole the quality of the troops was generally agreed to be, in a word, superb. Properly led, the senior officers said, the individual Marine was unsurpassed in spirit and fighting ability.

It was as if the slogan Billingsley saw sewn onto the backs of the jackets worn by many Marines in their off-duty hours summed it all up.

"Yea, though I walk through the valley of the shadow of death, I will fear no evil ... 'cause I'm the meanest motherfucker in the valley."

Belleau Wood, Guadalcanal, Tarawa, Saipan, Iwo Jima, Okinawa, Inchon, the Chosin Reservoir. Now there was already talk of Khe Sanh and Hue City. The green machine. Mother green, the killing machine. Renowned the world over. The Marines hymn. Once a Marine, always a Marine. First to fight. The Marines have landed, and the situation is well in hand. Uncommon valor. Eagle, globe, and anchor. Tell it to a Marine.

"'CAUSE I'M THE MEANEST MOTHERFUCKER IN THE VALLEY."

It was hardly unexpected that the young officers were influenced by the tradition and mystique of the Corps. More than the tailored uniforms and the glitter of the gold bars, it was a *feeling*. Subtle, yet profound. Understood, yet inexplicable. Invisible, yet woven into the fabric of each of them. Perhaps it was a result of some subconscious need, or of the need to identify with the organization. Whatever the reason, it was there. It was bigger than the men who carried it, bigger than anything previously experienced. And it probably would be bigger than anything they would ever experience again.

Billingsley continued to see Andrea after she returned from her vacation. They were together on weekends, and often they would dine and take in a movie during the middle of the week. Their relationship grew into a genuine affection for one another. Each looked forward to the company of the other with anticipation and excitement. They found that the time spent together passed all too quickly, especially as the time neared for Andrea to return to school. Her presence was invigorating to Billingsley, and the thought of her leaving was equally depressing.

Billingsley arranged for the two of them to spend the final

weekend of her summer vacation together on the beaches of the Virginia coast. He had rented a cottage from the friends of a fellow TBS officer who was familiar with the area. Andrea's initial reluctance had posed a serious obstacle. She had finally consented when she had been able to manufacture an adequate cover story for her parents' benefit.

Finally! Billingsley rejoiced.

Andrea met him at Quantico, where she left her car, and accompanied him on the Saturday morning drive to the shores of the Atlantic Ocean. They reached Virginia Beach by late morning and located the multi-unit complex. He registered them as Mr. and Mrs. and unloaded their belongings into the small but clean concrete-block structure, one of a dozen such buildings within sight and sound of the ocean. The interior of the cottage was modest and frugal.

"Thoughtful of you to select a cottage with twin beds, Mike," cracked Andrea as she glanced at the furnishings.

"Just my way of providing adequate shelter to ladies in distress," he answered.

"Am I in distress?"

"You may be before the new day dawneth, ma'am. The distance between those racks is hardly a difficult distance for a man in my condition. Wanna find a place for lunch?"

They left the cottage and found a nearby restaurant where they ate fresh seafood, with oysters as appetizers, and drank mugs of icy beer. Afterward, they came to an amusement park and stopped to idle away several hours on the rides and miniature golf course. Billingsley's insistence upon approaching each of the rides with a demonstration of daredevilry left each of them dizzy from the motion and the laughter.

They purchased wine and cheese for Andrea and beer and chips for Billingsley and returned to the cottage to put the drinks in the refrigerator. Then they strolled the short distance to the beach. The cool evening breeze and the sounds of the sea soothed and relaxed them. They rolled up the legs of their slacks and waded, and watched their footprints disappear into the sand. The foamy water rolled over their feet. They walked slowly and quietly, close together, with their hands clasped and swinging between them. Andrea's hair blew in her face as the wind slapped at the light jacket she wore.

Andrea had noticed that Billingsley had become noticeably

less talkative since they left the amusement park. He glanced at her while they walked along the beach, catching her eye and smiling faintly, but for the most part he remained silent. Andrea's attempts at conversation were met only with nods and shrugs. His eyes watched the surf and the sand, his expression distant, his mood diffident.

"You okay, Mike?"

"Yeah."

"Are you sure?"

"Will you come home often when school starts?"

"Not that often. You can come to Charlottesville, can't you?"

"I suppose I can. That is, if you want me to."

"If I want you to? Do you think I'd come here with you if I didn't want to be with you?"

He walked along at her side, offering no response.

"Well, do you, Mike?" she pressed.

Still, he remained silent.

"Will you, or will you not, visit me at school? Or will I just become another nice memory for you after this weekend? Which will it be?"

"I got my MOS and duty assignment this week," he said casually.

"You didn't answer me, Mike."

"Andrea, for Christ's sake, you know I'll visit you every chance I get. But I'm going to be going away, too, in early December."

"Oh God, Mike," she said as she stopped and turned toward him. "Where?"

"The Third Marine Division," he answered, noticing the tightness in her unpainted lips.

"And where is the Third Marine Division?"

"It's in Vietnam."

"Oh, no," she said as her voice began to break. "Oh dear God, no."

They fell into silence as he reached for her hand. They began walking again, neither looking at the other, their heads bowed into the wind.

"Let's sit here for a while," Andrea said as she sat on the soft sand with her legs crossed. She felt his arm slide around her waist. They stared out into the wide sea, with Andrea's head resting on his shoulder.

"You volunteered for Vietnam, didn't you?"

"Yeah, but I would have been sent over there eventually, anyway."

"Look at me, Mike," she said, raising her head.

He turned and gazed directly into her eyes.

"Why did you volunteer?"

"I'm not sure I can explain it, Andrea. Don't pressure me."

"I'm not pressuring you. I just want you to be honest with me. And I want to know why you volunteered."

"I volunteered because I'm an infantry officer in the U.S. Marine Corps, and because Vietnam is where the war's at. I want my turn at it, Andrea, because I went to school on a deferment while the others went to Vietnam. It's my way of settling up."

"You don't owe your life for having gone to school, Mike. You've got so much to offer. My goodness, you're intelligent, sensitive, witty, and so much more. Why take such a foolish chance?"

"What does that make me, then?" he snapped. "An intelligent, sensitive, witty fool?"

"No, no. I didn't mean it that way at all. What I meant to say was that—"

"I'm very much in love with you, Andrea," he interrupted.

She blinked and swallowed.

"That's right," he continued. "I had to come right out and say it before I exploded. I'd thought about how I might tell you, with all the right words, all the right gestures, all the right everything. But then I just threw it all out and decided to blurt it out. It's the way I feel, and I thought you might like to know."

Andrea's blue eyes moistened. She bit her lower lip gently as she weighed the meaning of his words.

"Are you hearing me, Andrea? Loud and clear?"

"I'm hearing you, Mike. Loud and clear."

He leaned forward and kissed her softly on the lips, then whispered, "Now get off my ass about Nam, counselor."

She leaned her head forward and rested it on his chest. He draped her with his arms and noticed her wiping at the tears streaming from her eyes.

"You've sure managed to complicate my life, Billingsley."

"Crazy, the way it works. Isn't it?"

"Of all the people in this world I could become involved with, I fall off the deep end for a reckless charmer who's about to go marching off to war."

"Are you mad at me or mad at yourself?" he laughed as he gently removed the dark hair blowing in her tear-stained face.

"I'm not mad at you, Mike. Just in love with you."

"I'm glad," he said as he leaned forward and kissed her.

They locked themselves in a solid embrace, blocking out everything but the sand and the sea and, of course, each other. He could feel her breasts pressing against him and her hair blowing in his face. They kissed again, this time more fervently, with Andrea's hand reaching for the back of his neck. Her kisses were sweet and moist and passionate, all as good as Billingsley had fantasized during countless boring lectures and dozens of long nights in the BOQ. Andrea, sweet, loving, dazzling Andrea. At long last. She was his, suddenly. Almost like a dream. Her scent and her image filled his head. "I love you," he whispered and heard the same words softly returned, the same words which echoed and reverberated through his brain like a hundred cathedral bells in an eternal, ethereal resounding. Sweet, sweet Andrea. Never let it end.

The sun had already begun to fade behind them. Not so their passion.

"Want to change and go to dinner?" asked Billingsley. "Or do you want to go as we are?"

"Why don't we dine-in?" she said, lifting her head and smiling naughtily.

"All we have are chips and cheese."

"Who cares?"

They loved one another, and made love to one another, feeling as if they were one, the same. Finally exhausted, they slept. Warmly, peacefully, closely, they slept.

Billingsley awakened first, aware of Andrea's presence by her arm draped across his chest. He nudged her and pulled her close, enveloping her in his hold. Her dark hair fell across her shoulders and onto his arm. He gently caressed the back of her shoulder with his fingers.

"Are you awake, Miss Strickland?"

"Barely," she replied softly. "I want to stay here forever, just like in a fairytale."

"We'll have to be shoving off soon. Do you realize how long we've occupied this bed?"

"Are you complaining?"

"No, just hungry," he announced. "I want you dressed and outside in formation in twelve minutes. Move it."

"Don't start that Marine Corps business with me, hotshot. I want to stay here for a while."

"That's a negative. We're gonna saddle up and leave."

He slid onto his side and faced her. She grinned sleepily and closed her eyes. He ran his hand over her silky smooth skin, from the middle of her back, over her soft rounded hip, to the side of her thigh. She smiled again as she opened her eyes and rested her hand on his shoulder.

"Well, maybe a little while longer," he whispered as he drew her close to him, absorbing her in his grasp.

They ate breakfast afterward at a restaurant just outside Virginia Beach. Eggs, bacon, toast, and, at his prodding, grits. Soon they were on the highway headed toward Quantico, laughing, joking, and promising their continued love to each other. They sang along as the radio blared the sounds of an endless stream of rock oldies.

They reached Quantico in the early afternoon and drove to Andrea's car in the parking lot at the Basic School. She suggested that he join her for dinner at her home on the night before her return to school.

"What time should I be there?" he asked.

"As soon as you can get there. Come early if you can. We'll plan on having dinner at eight. Okay?"

"I wish you weren't leaving next week, counselor."

"I don't feel so good about it myself. I'm going to miss you terribly, Mike," she said as she put her arms around him while they stood near her parked car.

"I'm not real sure how to say this," Billingsley said, groping for words, "but I just want you to know that you mean a great deal to me. And I don't think I'm able to tell you how much, either."

Andrea squeezed him tightly, her head against his chest. He felt bothered by her imminent departure to her home and, later, to school. Why can't things be the way you want them, he thought.

She pushed away and looked at him.

"You make me feel so special, Mike. Not so much by what you say, but the way you look at me, and hold me. It doesn't have to be in your words. It's in your eyes, in the way you turn your head and smile at me. You're so disarming. I've always been so competitive all my life, with being an honor student, and a class officer, and law school. And you come along one day in Georgetown and sweep me away. You may have gotten more than you bargained for when you followed me out of that restaurant."

"Wrong. You may be the one who gets more than you bargained for. Who knows, I may show up in Charlottesville and abduct you."

They embraced again.

"I suppose you'd better be leaving if your family is expecting you for dinner," Billingsley said reluctantly.

"Every time we do this, it gets a little harder," Andrea said. "Will you promise me that you'll come as soon as you can on Tuesday?"

"I'll be there, counselor. I love you."

"And I love you, too."

November Company scheduled exercises in the field on Monday and Tuesday. The reactions of the student officers were tested while each had an opportunity to command a squad of other students. As a patrol of the officers advanced in search of "aggressors," a TBS instructor would, at some point, ambush the patrol with the aid of several enlisted Marines who played the part of the hostile force. Blank ammunition gave a degree of realism to the affair.

Billingsley had served as a squad member while others had been appointed as leaders of the squad. He had carefully observed their reactions and noted the immediate critiques from the instructors who accompanied each patrol. For all practical purposes, the element of surprise was eliminated since the squad knew that ambush was inevitable somewhere along the way. The essence of the exercise, then, became one of controlling the group once the shooting had started.

"Okay, Lieutenant Billingsley," called the instructor after a review of a previous patrol. "I'd like for you to move your squad along this road to our front and follow it for a distance of three hundred meters. You will come to a recognizable trail running perpendicular to the road, on your left. Move your squad onto the trail and join up with your platoon about one hundred meters into the treeline."

"Aye-aye, sir."

"Any questions?"

"No, sir."

"I'm ready when you are," noted the instructor as he picked up his clipboard.

Billingsley issued the appropriate orders to those who had been appointed as fire-team leaders. He saw that the men maintained the five-meter intervals as the squad set out onto the road. They moved along the shoulder of the unpaved road, with Billingsley slightly forward of the squad's center. The instructor walked behind Billingsley and wrote an occasional note on his clipboard.

The distance to the trail's intersection was covered without incident. The squad made the ninety-degree turn and walked toward the treeline. Billingsley turned to several members in the group and spoke quietly, "Move through here slowly and don't bunch up. Listen for my commands. If we get hit, you break your team to the left, Britt, and you take yours to the right, Ackworth."

The patrol moved perhaps seventy-five meters along the trail. The entire length of the column was within the treeline. The popping of blank ammunition erupted to their front, prompting Billingsley to drop quickly to one knee to assess what was unfolding. Since no radios were used in the exercise, Billingsley began shouting commands for the others to move up in the prescribed fashion. When he had managed to form a line of his squad, facing the opposing force, Billingsley heard the ambush group commence firing from directions on both his flanks. His squad was caught in a volume of noise that came from three directions.

What the fuck? Billingsley thought in his surprise. Gotta keep moving, stay on line, don't panic. Where'd all these people come from? It ain't supposed to be like this.

"KEEP MOVING. STAY ON LINE," he shouted at his advancing men.

As soon as the blank firing had ceased, Billingsley discovered that the opposing force numbered over twenty men, compared to the three or four who had been employed on other, more typical ambushes. He also noticed the grinning of the two instructors—the one who had walked with Billingsley and the one who had accompanied the aggressor force.

"Lieutenant Billingsley," called the instructor who had accompanied his squad, "you've just become a victim of a horseshoe ambush."

"There were no survivors," offered the instructor with the ambush party.

Billingsley realized that, late in the day, the two had conspired to enliven the field event. The enlisted Marines within the aggressor force all smiled broadly while the squad members, the victims of the fun, looked at one another with expressions of relief over the fact that the "fun" had been conducted with blank ammo.

"Your reaction was good, Lieutenant Billingsley. You did a good job in controlling the squad," summarized the primary instructor.

"But I just lost all my men, sir," Billingsley countered.

"Yeah, but you were at a slight disadvantage. I thought your orders to keep moving were good. You can't stand still when you're that exposed, so it's best to do something. And moving forward is generally better. Unless," added the instructor with a laugh, "you get caught in a box like the one you just died in."

The instructor with the aggressor force walked over to Billingsley and displayed a sketched diagram of the ambush plan.

"They're a lot of fun to set-in, Lieutenant Billingsley, but they're a bitch to walk into when everybody's using real lead. Keep your eyes open. Okay?"

"I will, sir."

"And if you ever move Marines into a terrain configuration similar to this one, remember the lesson you learned at Basic School about horseshoe-shaped ambushes."

"Will do, sir."

"The penalty for miscalculation should be obvious," explained the officer. "And remember that ninety-nine percent of the time, the first symptom that you've walked into an ambush like this will be sudden death."

"Yes, sir. My own death."

"That's right. Your own death."

"Good evening, Mike. Please come inside," spoke the attractive, middle-aged woman who answered the doorbell. "It's good to see you again."

"It's also good to see you again, Mrs. Strickland. I hope I'm not too early," Billingsley said as he stepped into the foyer.

"No, not at all. Andrea will be down in a moment. Why don't you join Charles for a drink before dinner."

She led him into the family room where the tall, distinguished father of Andrea awaited. The elder Strickland removed his eyeglasses and folded his newspaper before rising from his chair to greet Billingsley with a handshake.

"How are you, Mike?" he asked firmly.

"I'm fine, sir. And you?"

"Fine, just fine. Would you join me in a drink?"

"Thank you, sir. Beer will be fine."

Mrs. Strickland excused herself and returned to the kitchen.

"Take a seat, Mike," commanded Strickland after he had produced the drinks. "I've heard so much about you from Andrea that I regret our having so few chances to chat."

"I regret that too, Mr. Strickland. Andrea always speaks so highly of Mrs. Strickland and you."

"Margaret and I are both very proud of Andrea. She's quite a young lady."

"I would agree with that, sir."

"A bit independent at times, but I suppose that's to be expected. Am I correct in understanding that you've received orders to Vietnam?"

"That is correct, sir. I report in early December."

"What abominable timing," said Strickland with a grimace. "I do hope everything works out for you, at any rate. The war's becoming more and more of a political albatross the longer it continues. Wouldn't you agree?"

Billingsley felt the measure of Strickland's calculating gaze. His eyes were penetrating as he cocked his head slightly and awaited Billingsley's response. Dude's a lawyer all right, Billingsley thought. He seems to listen carefully and think ahead at the same time.

"I suppose so, Mr. Strickland. I tend to look at the war more in military terms than political terms, though. And from the looks of things in the papers and on television, I think I'd rather fight it in-country than try to manage it in Washington."

Strickland paused for a moment before asking, "Do you look forward to going?"

"Not as much as I did before I met your daughter, sir."

Strickland smiled slightly and sipped from his drink.

Andrea walked into the room. She wore a navy blue dress, trimmed in white. As usual, the mere sight of her stirred Billingsley, who, with her father, rose from his seat.

"Hi, Michael. Has Daddy been bending your ear?" she asked with a wink in her father's direction.

"Not at all. You look lovely, Andrea."

"Thank you."

"Could I fix you a drink, dear?" asked Mr. Strickland.

"No thanks. I've come to tell you both that dinner will be served in five minutes. Mike, I hope you like chicken cacciatore."

"Sounds delicious," said Billingsley, unfamiliar with the dish but unconcerned about anything created from poultry.

"Good. I'll leave you two to finish your drinks. Five minutes, Daddy."

"We'll be there," said Strickland who, after Andrea had departed, motioned for Billingsley to take his seat.

They remained silent for another moment, with Billingsley grinning uncomfortably at the elder Strickland whose looks gave Billingsley the feeling that the family room was suddenly a courtroom. He's sizing me up, Billingsley thought. He's got something on his mind and he's getting ready to get to it.

"You're evidently quite important to Andrea, Mike," said Strickland. "She can't seem to concentrate on much of anything unless the subject somehow involves you."

"She's important to me also, sir."

"I assume you'll visit her at school."

"I plan to, sir. At least within the limits of our schedules."

"You know, of course, that her work at law school involves quite a great deal of preparation."

"I do, sir."

"And that she'll require a great deal of time for that preparation."

"I understand that, sir."

"Unobstructed time, I suppose you could say."

Billingsley stared ahead into Strickland's face. "Mr. Strickland, I understand your concern over the possibilities of my becoming a nuisance to Andrea. And I understand your concern over the importance of her work in law school. I also want you to understand that her success means a great deal to me, also."

"I'm glad to hear that, Mike."

"I'm very fond of your daughter, sir, and I want to see her as often as possible. But I'll be in a combat zone in less than sixty days, and between now and the time I get to Vietnam there's plenty in the way of preparation for me, also. I think you would tend to agree that the prudent thing for me would be to prepare myself as best I possibly can."

Strickland looked at him with admiration.

"Andrea's work is important," Billingsley continued, "but so is mine. It wouldn't pay for me to go where I'm going and not be prepared. The stakes for me will involve a good bit more than posted grades on the classroom door."

"Yes," agreed Strickland with a smile, "I would tend to agree. Let's join the others for dinner, shall we?"

Strickland directed Billingsley into the spacious dining room. The food was already on the large table, and the seating arrangements placed Billingsley alongside Andrea and across from her parents. The meal was excellent and the conversation was light and comfortable. Billingsley spoke of his native Georgia, his interest in history, and his love of the outdoors. He carefully deflected questions from Andrea's parents concerning his future plans, though his degree in finance would likely serve him well. Mr. Strickland's occasional ribald humor, which inevitably drew rebukes from his wife and daughter, made Billingsley feel at ease in the company of the family.

The time seemed to pass quickly. An after-dinner drink in the family room eventually led to Andrea's parents excusing themselves and retiring to another part of the house. Andrea and Billingsley used the time alone to make plans for their future visits. They masked their emotions and repressed the uneasiness which gripped them as the time for their parting neared. It had happened so suddenly, this relationship, and the prospect of separation loomed heavily within each.

The time finally came. They embraced, said their good-byes and embraced again. The barrier of Andrea's composure began to crumble as she held onto the quiet, somber Billingsley. He kissed and held her, then started to leave only to have Andrea call him back for one last embrace. It was as difficult as each had feared beforehand it would be. Perhaps even more so.

Billingsley drove back to Quantico with her picture in his head and a sinking feeling in his stomach. His world was changing, and the pace of the events and the thoughts of the prospects confused and disoriented him. Tough to sort out, he thought on the drive to the base. Damn tough. Tougher than it was when all that mattered was showing up for class and deciding which party to attend on the weekend. Those were the days, he realized. Those *were* the days.

The month of September concluded and the officers of November Company began their final month as Basic School students. The majority of officers were scheduled for duty in Vietnam, some immediately, others after specialty training. Several had decided during TBS to embark upon aviator training and had been ordered to flight school at Pensacola, Florida. A few others had been assigned to duty stations within the continental United States and Hawaii. It was clear from the heightened attention in the classroom, however, that most of the group would soon be headed to war.

The final stages of instruction at TBS were deliberately narrowed to those applications which were particular to Vietnam. The students examined a replica of a Vietnamese village, exacting in detail and complete with secret hiding places. They were instructed on the techniques for the search of the village. They were exposed to the noise of an AK-47 rifle, with its distinctive cracking sound in contrast to the thumping sound of an American M-16 rifle. They became familiar with the enemy's creative and lethal use of booby traps, and the wide range in their sophistication. And they learned to distinguish areas where booby traps might typically be found. There appeared to be precious few places where the VC might not choose to leave a surprise.

"You know what, Mike?" lamented Bill Blanton, who was also under orders to Southeast Asia. "Nam ain't nothin' but one big tripwire. You can step on booby traps, fall in booby traps, have them fall on you, and who knows what else. I don't know whether I want to go, now. Maybe we ought to catch the midnight bus to Montreal."

Billingsley made no response as he sat in the bleachers and focused his attention on a demonstration on the identification of booby traps.

"Watch those Vietnamese students," Blanton whispered, looking over at several South Vietnamese Marine junior officers assigned to November Company as exchange students, of sorts.

"What about them?" asked Billingsley.

"Did you see the way they grinned and looked at one another when the Major held up the booby traps? I'll bet you that half the bastards are V fuckin' C."

"I doubt that, Bill."

"Bullshit. The odds are high that at least one of 'em is. And it wouldn't surprise me if all of 'em were."

"Why don't you just go ahead and shoot one of 'em, if you feel that way. You can tell the colonel that you were just doing what he had taught you to do. He might give you a Congressional, or something."

"All I'd get is a long tour at Portsmouth," said the irate Blanton. "Those little dipshits. They're VC, man. I'd bet my ass on it."

"Keep an eye on 'em, bunkie," Billingsley said with a grin.

The question of the loyalties of the South Vietnamese students had long been disturbing to Blanton, and for no apparent reason. But especially so, it seemed to Billingsley, in the past few weeks. Mostly, though, it was the idea of going off to war that troubled Blanton. As with many others, the bravado of training had eventually turned into the sobering reality that soon the rehearsals would cease, soon the stakes would be raised, and soon the curtain would open. And then the performance would count.

The effect upon Blanton was typical, in many ways, of men who wait the final few days before going to war. Some were openly edgy while others turned inward, introspectively searching, examining, questioning. Still, there was time left to prepare. Time left to enjoy. And time left to be comforted by the youthful assurances of full and long lives. Each preferred to believe that somehow he would see it through, no matter the degree and quantity of unknowns associated with Vietnam. Each also knew, though, that Vietnam was replete with unknowns.

The long months of training were almost over. It was nearly time for the bigger things toward which they had all been pointing. It was nearly time for the real instead of the simulated; the distant instead of the nearby. For most, it would soon be Vietnam. The time was nearer than any of the young officers dared think.

Field operations, classroom sessions, weekends in Charlottesville, and quiet moments of reflection characterized Billingsley's final days at Basic School. He finished among the top ten graduates in the final standings. It all ended with a formal ceremony in which they were awarded their diplomas and sent on their respective ways.

"Good luck and good hunting," they had been told.

Billingsley lunched with several classmates after the ceremony. Resplendent in their dress blues, Billingsley, Blanton, Redwine, and others drank a final farewell beer with their lunch at a local Quantico establishment. They ate and drank and joked as brothers, as Marines. Cocksure, proud, and filled with anticipation. They had arrived. The world would soon be theirs. They had paid their dues.

"Good luck and good hunting," they told one another.

After a quick call to Andrea to confirm their plans for the days of his leave, Billingsley drove away from Quantico. The emotional good-byes to Blanton and Redwine had been sealed with the words, "Good luck, babe. Stay in touch. And good hunting." The packing, the loading, and now, the driving. One last glance at the statue at the entrance to the base. Then came the interstate highway. He was going home to Georgia.

It was nearer than any of the young officers dared think.

3

The Billingsleys were reunited on Georgia soil again, their first such reunion in their suburban Atlanta home since Mike's departure the previous March. It was a happy occasion for all members of the family. Thoughts of war and further separation were avoided as much as possible so as not to detract from their togetherness. Billingsley was treated as a returning hero, enjoying the finest of his mother's cooking and regaling his father and brother with descriptions of his training experiences. Kevin, especially, was eager to hear of the details and difficulties associated with life in the Marines.

"Was it as tough as it's made out to be?"

"Did they beat you up? Did they gang up on you?"

"Did anyone try to commit suicide?"

"What were the drill sergeants like? Had they all been to Vietnam?"

"Did you learn karate?"

"Will you be in the fighting when you get over there?"

Billingsley responded to the questions with honest, sincere answers, neither glorifying nor dramatizing. His training has been strenuous, he related, as was the fashion of the Marine Corps. And, he added, it had been thorough and professional. The quality of the officers had been high. The instructors had been knowledgeable and experienced. There had been no instances of physical abuse directed at himself nor anyone else, he explained, though he understood that occasional hazings occurred at the enlisted training facilities. Contrary to regulations, he insisted.

His letters to his parents had told them about his burgeoning relationship with Andrea, and they questioned him about her. His parents, Billingsley noted, seemed favorably impressed with his description of Andrea, though he preferred that they make their own judgements of her. And so he explained his and Andrea's plans for her to fly to Atlanta and join the Billingsleys for the Thanksgiving holidays. The visit would be the couple's last chance to be together before he left for the West Coast and the Western Pacific. His mother and father enthusiastically endorsed the plan.

The days following his arrival were slow and easy, a dramatic change of pace from the previous months of intensive, dawn-to-dusk activity. Sleeping late was an unaccustomed luxury. He maintained his conditioning by running two miles each night. He visited several friends from his school days who had been exempted for various reasons from active military service. He stayed in contact with Dan Redwine in Illinois and Bill Blanton in California, mostly through letters. And he kept in touch with Andrea, writing and receiving daily letters and accumulating a sizable telephone bill.

Billingsley watched many hours of television during his leisurely days, especially news coverage of the battle scenes from Vietnam. He also saw ample coverage of those who opposed the war. College students and other protestors carried banners and placards and chanted slogans, many of which explicitly sympathized with the Viet Cong's National Liberation Front. Commentaries speculated about a peaceful solution and a gradual withdrawal of American troops from Vietnam, though the casualties continued to mount. A new president had been elected, and settlement of the Vietnam issue had been the central theme of the campaign. One way or another a settlement was needed, and with honor, Billingsley thought. The collective patience of the nation was wearing thin.

Billingsley watched the newscasts attentively. Naturally, he was curious about developments in the conduct of the war. But he was also interested in the statements and activities of the protestors who, more and more, were becoming central to the news coverage. Billingsley viewed some of the protestors with a grudging respect, especially those whose efforts seemed to be directed at something other than the personal evasion of military service. Others he held in contempt as cowards and deadbeats and, in the extremest of cases, traitors. He could understand why some were upset about the inconvenience of military service. He could also understand the abhorrence some felt toward war, in a general sense. What he couldn't understand was why these people wouldn't go ahead and serve, anyway. That's the way it was supposed to work, after all. And it had worked that way since before Cornwallis' thrashing.

The war, Billingsley discovered, had claimed the lives of several members of his high school class. Three of his classmates had died, and five others had been injured. None of the classmates who had been killed in action had been his close friends, but their deaths touched him nonetheless. He kept remembering scenes from their school days together. He was curious—perhaps morbidly so, he thought—to discover the circumstances of each of their deaths. When he learned that one of the dead friends had been shot in the throat, Billingsley dismissed any further thought or mention of the entire matter. Just another burden, he reasoned.

Mike had lived in the house in suburban Atlanta, with its three bedrooms and one bath, all his life. The large backyard had so often been the scene of frolicking neighborhood games when he and Kevin were children. When Mike had departed for college, his larger room had been claimed by Kevin upon their mutual agreement. The room arrangements held during Billingsley's leave stay in the house.

Billingsley lounged in the cramped bedroom, gazing at a black-and-white television which was featuring a program on Nazi Germany. It was late when Kevin opened the door and stumbled slightly as he walked toward a wooden chair in the corner of the room.

"What's on, Mike?" Kevin asked, his eyelids drooping and his general expression conveying little in the way of alertness.

"A documentary."

"Any good?"

"Yeah, real good. Where have you been?"

"At a friend's house. Hear anything from your girl?"

"Sure."

"What's her name again?"

"Andrea. What the hell's the matter with you, Kevin? Are you drunk?" asked Billingsley as he stared at his brother.

"I'm not drunk."

Kevin stood as if to leave.

"Sit down," requested Billingsley. "You don't have to leave. C'mon, stay and talk a while."

Kevin seated himself again on the wooden chair and avoided eye contact with his brother. He glanced around the room. "Want the bigger room?" he asked. "I'll move back in here, if you want."

"Of course not. I'm fine right here. Thanks, though."

Kevin watched the television program for a moment, giggling at the sight of goose-stepping German soldiers passing the reviewing stand before a somber Adolf Hitler.

"Kevin, look over here at me," Billingsley said as he sat up in bed.

Kevin looked in his brother's direction briefly, defensively, then turned away.

"What have you been drinking?" Billingsley asked.

"Nothing."

"That's bullshit, Kevin. You're all screwed up. What is it you've had?"

Kevin looked down toward the floor, his shoulder-length hair falling forward, and smiled faintly. "A little herb, Mike. Now get off my case," he announced.

"Marijuana?"

"Yeah, grass. It's no worse than that beer you drink and those cigarettes you smoke. Know what I mean?"

"Where'd you get it?"

"Around," Kevin answered, lowering his voice and looking toward the closed door of the bedroom. "It ain't hard to come by. You want some?"

"Hardly. Do you use anything else?"

"No need to," Kevin said with a giggle.

"How long have you been smoking that stuff?"

"Ah," said Kevin with a shrug, "maybe six months, or so. Not regularly, though. Just when the mood strikes me."

"Does Dad know?"

"You kiddin'? He'd throw me out in the street."

"You're breaking the law, Kevin. You realize that, don't you?"

"So what? It's a bad law. I'd do it more often if I had more bread."

"I'm surprised at you, Kevin," Billingsley said reprimandingly.

"Are you for real, Mike? Where have you been, man? This ain't the Dark Ages, you know."

"You could mess yourself up, you know."

Kevin rose from his chair and saluted his brother with an exaggerated wave. He smiled and added, "Here's a guy who's goin' off to Vietnam, and he's tellin' *me* I might mess *myself* up. C'mon, Mike. Who are you shittin'?"

"Are you leaving?"

"Yep. Sleep well, 'cause I know I will," Kevin said with a sheepish grin.

Kevin left the bedroom, leaving Billingsley alone to worry about the changes taking place in his home. And of the changes taking place in homes all over the country. Changing values, changing habits, changing expectations. Drugs and war and rebellion and chaos. Political assassinations and sit-ins and flower children and communal living. Each piece of the puzzle infinitely different in shape and form, making it hard to fit them into a meaningful pattern. No solutions, no conclusions. Just a puzzle with a lot of incongruity and contrast.

Billingsley fell asleep only to awaken later to the glare of the blank television.

"Telephone, Mike," called Mrs. Billingsley as she prepared breakfast in the kitchen.

Billingsley got out of bed and ambled to the hall telephone. "Hello," he called sleepily.

"Did I wake you?" came the voice of Andrea.

"Yeah, but I'll forgive you. How are you?"

"I'm fine. Almost studied out, but fine. I was just thinking of you and decided to call. You really haven't been too good about calling me."

"I really haven't had much time, counselor."

"Oh? Somebody else monopolizing your time now?"

"Look, I sleep late, eat a late breakfast, watch a few game shows, eat lunch, watch a few soap operas, eat supper, run, and on and on. See what I mean?"

"Poor baby. Listen, my father told me recently that there's already talk in Washington of a troop withdrawal. Have you heard anything?"

"Not really. I mean, my orders haven't been rescinded, or anything."

"Well, he says there's a good chance that it could begin to

happen soon. Gradually at first, then more later. Isn't that fantastic?"

"Andrea, the war's still hot. They're still workin' out on one another over there."

"*Nothing* moves you, Billingsley."

"You do, baby. I miss you."

"I miss you, too. Mike, are you sure it's okay with your family about my coming to Atlanta?"

"It's fine, as long as you bring your own towels."

"Oh, stop it. You're hopeless, you know.'

"I know I'll be a lot better off when you get here."

"Me, too."

Billingsley helped his mother decide the details of food selection and sleeping arrangements for the Thanksgiving holidays. Nearby relatives were expected on Thanksgiving day, a tradition which had held for as long as Billingsley could recollect. Nearly thirty relatives, along with the guest from Virginia, would fill the house for the festive gathering.

The day before Andrea's arrival, Billingsley and his father strolled in the backyard in the cool twilight. They both were under the spell of so many fond memories of the house, of the yard, of the bygone days of the warmly remembered past. They walked along, their hands in the pockets of the light jackets they each wore, reminiscing, laughing, sharing. There had been good days, many, for this family. They each felt the warmth which comes with the shared remembrance of pleasant times. But there was still the ominous spectre of Vietnam, and the possibility of the unspeakable.

"How do you feel?" asked Billingsley's father as they walked across the brown grass and fallen pine needles.

"About what, Dad?"

"About going off to Vietnam."

"A little nervous, I suppose. The waiting bothers me, now that it's almost here."

"Got any idea about what you'll be doing when you get over there?"

"No, not for sure. I hope to get a platoon, but I could end up with a staff job."

"Which would you prefer?"

"I want a platoon."

Billingsley noticed his father's slight wince.

"There's something I need to tell you, Dad."

"Okay."

"I made out a will before I left Quantico. I've got some insurance benefits, too. It's all spelled out, and if you need it, it's in the desk drawer in my room."

"We won't need it," his father said slowly. "You'll be back in a year and everything'll be just fine."

Raymond Billingsley didn't fancy the idea of his son going off to war, particularly as the time neared. His own experiences with war as a combat soldier in Europe had inculcated a distaste known only to those who had sampled and endured it. He wanted so badly to plead with his son to remain alert, to be ever mindful of the danger, but he said nothing. He had confidence in his son's judgment, and in his sense of responsibility and thoroughness. He just hoped and prayed that everything would somehow work out.

"I suppose you're excited about seeing your girl again, aren't you?" his father asked in an attempt to lighten the mood.

"Yeah, sure am. I'm even kinda nervous about that, too."

"Well, just try to relax and enjoy yourselves. Your mother and I will leave you two alone as much as possible."

Billingsley turned to his father and placed his hand upon the shoulder of the shorter, greying man. "You've both been very good to me, Dad. And I'll always be grateful, for as long as I live."

Billingsley's father, wordless, smiled faintly and then embraced his son tightly. They turned afterwards and walked toward the house, assured that their bond as father and son was strong, and that their bond as friends was equally as strong.

Somehow, someway, they both thought.

The Atlanta airport was crowded on the morning of Thanksgiving. Billingsley arrived early, fighting his way through the throng of travelers to reach the concourse where he would meet Andrea's flight. He glanced at his watch and then looked outside. Twenty minutes, he thought. Twenty more minutes. He walked to a coffee shop near the concourse, took a seat, and ordered a cup of coffee. He lit a cigarette and waited.

A stranger seated at the counter alongside Billingsley offered a section of newspaper. It was declined. When the same man made several attempts at friendly conversation, Billingsley responded only with polite shrugs and nods. He was nervous about seeing Andrea again. And excited. And impatient. He was nearly out of cigarettes. His fingernails were bitten to the quick. He kept glancing at his watch.

The time passed slowly. The coffee was gone when the cigarette was extinguished. Finally, the arrival announcement came. He walked into the concourse and saw the sleek airliner outside, facing the window and snuggled against the jetway. Hot damn, he thought. It finally did get here.

Andrea soon walked through the passageway behind a stream of other passengers. She was lovely in her orange sweater and tan slacks. Her leather purse was slung over her shoulder and she carried a paperback novel in her hand. As she quickly scanned the faces in the waiting crowd, she noticed Billingsley moving toward her. Her face broke into a wide smile as she hurried to reach him.

"It's about time," said Billingsley as he embraced her firmly before guiding her aside, away from the flow of arrivals.

"Real smooth, Mike," Andrea admonished. "No 'I'm glad to see you, Andrea,' or 'I've sure missed you, Andrea,' or 'I've been counting the moments until you arrived.' "

"I'm glad to see you, Andrea. I've sure missed you. I've been counting the moments until you arrived."

After a long embrace, they walked slowly, arm in arm, to the escalator which led to the baggage claim area.

"I hope you know the grief I've had to endure about not being home for Thanksgiving," Andrea said while they awaited her luggage. "And, about running off to Georgia to spend the holidays with some fascist who's ready to go off to war."

"Don't hand me that, counselor. You've been stuck on me ever since I picked you up that day in Georgetown."

Andrea raised her eyebrows, then reached up and pulled at Billingsley's neck. "You smug bastard," she whispered into his ear before kissing his cheek.

"And you, my dear," he whispered in return, "have the cutest nose and the prettiest ass of any *rich* girl I've ever known."

She backed away a step, placing her hands upon her hips, and forced an expression of sternness. "Okay, so tell me how I compare with the *poor* girls you've known," she demanded.

"Let's see now," said Billingsley as he lowered his head and rubbed his chin. "I'd say that you dress better and the poor girls eat a helluva lot more when you take them to a restaurant."

Andrea threw back her head and laughed out loud. Billingsley pulled her toward him and held tightly to her.

"I'm glad you're finally here, counselor. The sun's finally shining," he said as he held her.

Andrea's luggage finally arrived on the conveyor. The two heavy suitcases, makeup kit, and garment bag drew a look of disbelief from Billingsley. "Christ, Andrea. This is more than I'll take with me to Vietnam," he muttered as he sought the assistance of an attendant.

They drove from the airport toward downtown Atlanta. Billingsley exited the interstate ten minutes later and drove along famous Peachtree Street, pointing out items of interest. Traffic in the city was moderate and they soon completed an abbreviated tour of the central district. They turned to the northeast, toward the Billingsley home.

The introductions went smoothly. Andrea's warmth and charm were apparent immediately—not to mention her obvious physical attractiveness. With some effort, she gracefully concealed her own apprehensiveness over meeting the family. She laughed easily, kidding, complimenting, and thanking, and all at the right moments, Billingsley thought. She was received well, and she took an instant liking to the family members.

They ate the traditional turkey and dressing, with the accompanying additions brought by the relatives. It was well into the evening before the relatives began to leave for their own homes. The embraces which preceded the relatives' departure were especially touching when Billingsley met them at the door to say his farewells. Andrea stood nearby, smiling politely and watching as the aunts, uncles, and cousins embraced Billingsley and inevitably added something to the effect of, "God bless you, son. Hurry home." Through it all, Andrea smiled, remaining poised and dignified. Inside, however, she was shaken by the realization that the time approached when she, too, would reach for that last embrace.

By nightfall, the last of the relatives had departed.

Andrea and Billingsley drove downtown among the many thousands of others who had come to witness the traditional lighting of the giant Christmas tree atop Rich's department store. The occasion was festive, complete with amplified caroling from groups within the glass-enclosed bridge which spanned the crowded street below. A roar of approval went up as the tree was spectacularly illuminated. Andrea wrapped her arms about Billingsley's waist and held back the tears that welled in her eyes.

The couple spent Friday in Billingsley's college town, Athens. Several of his friends lived in the area and provided plenty of beer and tales for their unexpected guests. They drove later to a remote area, on the banks of the Oconee River, and enjoyed the solitude of the rural setting. Sleepiness pulled at them as they rode the seventy miles back to Atlanta at the end of the day.

Each awakened on Saturday eager to begin their last full day together. Billingsley jumped up from the den couch on which he had slept and shouted at Andrea, in the smaller bedroom, to get up, too. Mrs. Billingsley had a large breakfast ready by the time they ventured into the kitchen.

Billingsley had arranged to use an apartment which was shared by two of his former classmates from college. Billingsley had quickly accepted their offer of the apartment, which would be empty while they were away for the holidays. It was a convenient solution to an awkward problem. The idea of a motel room was uncomfortable to Billingsley, and he was sure that Andrea would feel the same way.

They arrived at the apartment after lunching in a Mexican restaurant. Andrea had held out for Chinese food until Billingsley protested, "Hell, I'd be suspicious of everything and everybody in an Oriental joint." They brought refreshments with them, though they planned to have dinner at a Southern-style restaurant Billingsley liked. The inside of the apartment was uncharacteristically neat and orderly, to Billingsley's surprise. His recent visit had shown that housekeeping was a low priority to the inhabitants. Not an empty beer can nor a full ashtray was in sight. Even the kitchen sink was void of mugs and dishes.

"How did you manage this?" Andrea asked as she surveyed the surroundings.

"Case of beer and a frozen pizza," he answered.

Andrea sipped a glass of wine while Billingsley nursed a can of beer. "Pretty nice," Andrea said. "I'll bet this place has seen some wild times with two bachelors living here."

"Unless those guys have changed a lot since I went to school with them, I'm sure this place has seen its share of parties."

"What do they do?"

"One's in sales and the other's an auditor. The other things they do I shan't mention," Billingsley said with a wink and a smile.

"Why not?"

"It's lewd and lascivious," he said as he leaned toward her and kissed her.

He put his arms around her and embraced her, their drinks forgotten on the coffee table. He kissed her again, feeling her tongue flicker inside his mouth. Their longing for one another took over. The kisses continued, long and passionate. He unbuttoned her blouse and ran his hand over her smooth back and side. He held her firm breast, still inside her bra, and stroked the nipple with his fingers.

"Not here, Mike. Not on the couch," Andrea whispered when he reached for the zipper of her slacks.

He kissed her again and then led her to a bedroom in the back of the apartment. There they stayed, immersed in the warmth and comfort of each other. The passion and love flowed freely, from one to the other, as they pressed closer, closer, building to volatile, volcanic climaxes, then building once again.

It had been well worth the wait, they agreed afterward.

"What am I going to do without you for a whole year?" she asked while smoothing the damp mat of hair on Billingsley's chest.

"We really haven't talked much about it," Billingsley said.

"The thought of a whole year without you depresses me terribly."

"Does the same to me, too."

"Maybe the war will end and you can come home early. Daddy says the talk's still pretty heavy in D.C. about the troop withdrawal thing."

Billingsley hoped for such a development, though he realized that the likelihood of his coming home early would probably involve death or serious injury. "Maybe so," he said laconically.

"We'll just hope for the best, anyway."

He sat up in the bed and lit a cigarette. Andrea remained propped upon a pillow with her hair spreading over her shoulders.

"Listen, Andrea. We haven't talked much about what *you're* going to do while I'm away."

Andrea wrinkled her brow as she looked at him. "What do you mean?" she asked.

"I mean, I think it would be a good idea for you to date other people. It would be okay with me, if you wanted to."

Andrea sat up quickly, covering her bare chest with the sheet of the bed. "*What?*" she asked sharply.

"That's right. I think it would be the fair thing to do."

"Why, Mike? Are you planning on seeing other women?"

"Who the hell am I going to strike up a love affair with, Andrea? Suzy Wong? I just don't want to be unreasonable with you. I want you to feel free to live your own life, and see the people you want to see. A year's a long time, counselor."

"So what are you telling me, Mike? To go back to normal while you leave the country? To act as if nothing's ever happened? To forget about you, and us, go on for the next year with a happy smile and not a care in the world or a second thought about Mike Billingsley and the way things were before—"

"Andrea . . . "

"And maybe get a letter from you once in a while and think to myself how nice you were and how much fun we had and then—"

"Andrea . . . "

"And maybe drop you a line if I can find the time between my busy social life and my second year of law school but otherwise just keep on truckin' like everything is just peachy—"

"Andrea, wait a minute."

"What is it, Mike? What the hell are you telling me?" she said heatedly.

"Jesus," he said, shaking his head. "Calm down and listen to me for a minute. Okay?"

Andrea sighed deeply and reclined on the bed. She took another deep breath and exhaled slowly before answering, "Go ahead."

"I didn't mean to get you all stirred up," he began as he crushed his cigarette into an ashtray. "All I wanted to do was to let you know that I don't mind if you want to date someone else while I'm gone. I can't promise you anything. I can't even promise you that I'll be back, for God's sake. Much less promise you marriage and security and all those regular things. I don't want to sound melodramatic, Andrea, like in the movies where the dude tells the girl to 'let's just live for today,' and all that shit, but I don't know *what's* gonna happen. I've never been through anything like this before, where the two extremes are living or . . . "

He reached for another cigarette. Andrea remained silent. He dragged deeply once, then again.

"I don't want to lose you, counselor. I didn't know I could love another person the way I love you. I'm just trying to be fair with you, Andrea. And I don't know exactly how, but I'm trying as best I can."

He turned and looked at her. Her face was expressionless and her manner was calm.

"I understand you, Mike. I know what you're trying to say."

"Good."

"Honestly, though, doesn't the thought of my being with other men bother you just a little bit?"

"Yeah, more than just a little bit."

A long, tense silence ensued. Billingsley sat on the bed, looking away from her. He was afraid his well-intentioned comments would ultimately serve as the epitaph for this relationship which he so cherished.

"Can I tell you something?" Andrea asked in a hushed tone.

"Sure."

"Look at me, then."

Billingsley turned to her. Still, there was no discernible expression to reveal her feelings.

"I'll be waiting for you when you get back, Michael."

He leaned forward and kissed her tenderly on the lips. She then pushed him away, smiling, and looked into his eyes.

"You can be such a jerk sometimes, Billingsley. A lovable jerk, but a jerk just the same."

"Are you aware of the penalty for disrespect to an officer, madam?"

"Ten minutes in an exercise of exotic lovemaking for each

offense, I hope," she answered with a mischievous grin.

"There it is. Now how many offenses would you prefer to be charged with?"

"Jerk, jerk, jerk."

"You'll never last that long."

"Try me."

"I have, in case you hadn't noticed. My friggin' elbows are raw."

"All talk, huh?"

He leaned toward her, removed the sheet which covered her chest, and pulled her on top of him. They kissed, renewing the fire, rekindling the heat. Billingsley reached around her, across her silky smooth back, and pinched her on the buttocks.

"Ouch!' she complained in the middle of a kiss. "That's not exotic, dammit. That's bestial."

"That's what your naked body does to me."

Andrea's hand slid along Billingsley's leg as they kissed again. She returned the pinch.

"Ouch, Andrea!" he yelled, pulling himself from her fingers. "You'll cut me with those fingernails and I'll end up bleeding to death with all that pressure down there."

Andrea giggled and kissed him again. "Truce," she said through a slight parting of their mouths.

"Meet me in Hawaii, baby," Billingsley whispered.

"Not until I've had supper."

"No, I'm serious," he said, rolling Andrea onto her side.

"What?"

"Yeah. When I come up for R&R, why don't we meet in Hawaii and spend two weeks there."

"Are you serious?" Andrea asked as she propped herself with her elbow.

"Of course, I'm serious. I'll be able to take an R&R next summer and you could be there waiting for me. That way, we won't have to wait a whole year to see each other. What do you say?"

Andrea's eyes sparkled as she thought of it, and her smile indicated her approval.

"I could arrange that," she concluded. "The summer would be perfect. June in Hawaii."

"June in Hawaii with me."

"June in Hawaii with you. Yeah, I could arrange that."

"Let's plan on it, then."

"God, Mike. That's a fantastic idea! I can't wait. I'll have to shop for clothes and get another swimsuit, the one I've got is horrible, and make the—"

"Andrea, it's not until *June.*"

"So?"

"Let's just live for today."

Andrea grabbed him and began wrestling playfully. "Aloha, Hawaii. Aloha, aloha, aloha. It'll be great, Mike. I've always wanted to see it. It'll be so romantic and beautiful, with that blue water and . . . "

Darkness had fallen over Atlanta as Andrea and Billingsley returned to his house. "I hope you two had an enjoyable day," Mrs. Billingsley greeted them.

"I had a very enjoyable day, Mom. How about you, Andrea?" he teased, seeing Andrea's suddenly embarrassed expression.

"I had a very nice day," she said quietly.

Billingsley led Andrea into the den. When he straightened up after turning on the television, Andrea kicked him squarely on the shin.

"Dammit, Andrea. I think you broke my friggin' leg." He raised his trousers to examine the damage.

"Oh, I'm sorry, Mike. I didn't mean to hurt you. Here, let me have a look," she said and proceeded to kick him in his other shin. "That'll teach you to embarrass me, you inconsiderate brute."

Billingsley grabbed her and held on as they both fell onto the couch. He began tickling her, and she squirmed and giggled as she tried to get away.

"Stop, you'll have everybody in here," she said between the giggles. "Stop, Mike. Stop it."

He finally did stop. He held her close while she caught her breath. She really is small, he thought. And so delicate. And so beautiful. He loosened his grasp and gently embraced her.

Their moods changed, together, as if both had been charged by the same surge. The time was nearing.

"We're running out of time, baby. It keeps moving and I can't seem to slow it down," he whispered.

"Hold me, Mike. Please, just hold me."

"I'll be back, Andrea. I *am* coming back."

"I know you will. And I'll be waiting. I love you."

"I *am* coming back."

The time did move quickly. The loudspeaker inside the Atlanta airport terminal announced, "Delta Flight 901, non-stop service to Washington, D.C., is now boarding at Gate G. All departing passengers are requested to have their boarding passes available for the flight attendant at the door ... "

They stood and looked at each other. Andrea's lip quivered as she fought the tears. She smiled faintly, knowing that to do otherwise would only prompt the tearful surrender.

"Oh God, Michael. It's finally here."

"We've got Hawaii to look forward to. We'll plan the details when I get over there."

Billingsley pulled Andrea close to him. She buried her face in the red sweater he wore underneath his windbreaker.

"I don't think I like this kind of thing," Billingsley whispered, with a nervous chuckle.

Most of the other passengers were already on the plane. They stood apart, holding hands, trying desperately hard.

"Call me every night before you leave. Okay?" she said, trying to ignore the tears flowing freely.

"I will."

"And don't make me be the one who does all the writing."

"I won't. I'll write often."

"And promise me that you'll please be careful."

"I promise."

"Please hurry home again, Mike."

"I will, Andrea. I love you."

She held onto him once more, whispering her love. Her face was damp and her eyes reddened. She pulled away and stared for a moment. She turned and walked away, wiping her eyes. When she reached the end of the corridor, she turned once more to see the strained smile upon Billingsley's face. He stood with his hands in his pockets and his head cocked slightly.

They waved before she stepped out of his sight.

Billingsley knelt at the altar of the church, alone and undisturbed in the early morning. Outside, his father waited in the car. The good-byes with his mother and brother had been accomplished with emotion, yet with dignity. His bags were packed and his flight was due in two hours. He closed his eyes and clasped his hands together.

"Dear Lord, I come humbly to you in this moment of need. I will probably have many such moments in the days ahead. Be with me, Lord, and with my family. And please, Lord, remain close to Andrea. Help me to do what is best, and what is right. Please help me to see this thing through. I am afraid, Lord, and I ask you to help me with that, too. Please stay close to Andrea. Please, God. Amen."

He rose slowly. He studied the empty sanctuary as if trying to affix the image in his memory, available for recall if he needed a comforting thought. He turned and left the church.

His father drove him to the airport. The skies were dreary and misty, and there was a cold chill in the air.

"Take care, Mike. Our thoughts and our prayers go with you, son."

"Thanks, Dad."

The final boarding call was announced. He embraced his father quickly, then followed with a handshake. He turned and made his way to the corridor, erect and proud in his green uniform. The gold bars glittered on his shoulders. He stopped when he was nearly out of sight and glanced back at his father.

He gave his father a short salute and a smile, and was gone.

PART TWO:
To the Sound of the Firing

4

The helicopter's engines whined a stream of noise into Billingsley's ears as it headed northeast. Billingsley sat next to the bulkhead of the long CH-46, with a dozen other Marines and several pallets of C-rations, smoke grenades, and star clusters. The chopper's helmeted crew chief closely watched the ground passing slowly beneath him from his position in the front of the aircraft. The passengers, all new replacements, occasionally glanced out the portholes on either side. They also watched the actions and expressions of the crew chief. Beneath them lay Indian Country.

Billingsley turned around and looked to the east, toward the Coastal Plain, where he could see rice fields, marshlands, and winding, glimmering rivers. When he looked out the opposite windows, he could make out the shadowy form of the Highlands. Below him, he could see intermittent bomb craters, orange-colored depressions. The green lushness of the terrain gave it the appearance of a tropical wonderland, disturbed only by village clearings and occasional military encampments.

The destination of the flight was Dong Ha, in Quang Tri Province, and near the DMZ. There Billingsley was scheduled to join the Third Marine Regiment. He sat back, wondering what type of unit he would join, what his CO would be like, what his troops would make of him, and what life in a combat zone would bring. He guessed that all of the replacements with him aboard the chopper were having similar thoughts as the flight neared its end. So far, so good, Billingsley thought, while his mind raced through his Far East journey highlights thus far: the twenty-hour journey from California's Travis Air Force Base to Okinawa, with refueling stops in Anchorage, Alaska, and Yokota, Japan; three days on Okinawa—stowing personal belongings, firing weapons, receiving immunizations, relaxing with a beer; the bumpy C-130 flight of four hours from Okinawa to Vietnam; the processing in Da Nang; the hop to Phu Bai to catch the hop to Dong Ha. No particular memory stood out above the others. It was only a collection of insignificant impressions.

The helicopter created a whirlwind of red dust as it touched down in the landing zone. Billingsley collected his gear and walked down the ramp in the rear of the craft, noticing a jeep and driver parked nearby.

"Headquarters, Third Marines. Where is it?" he shouted to the driver who sat leaning forward with an unlit cigarette dangling from his lips.

"Throw your gear in the back, sir, and I'll take you there," he shouted in return.

The driver shouted to a Marine standing nearby that he would return shortly. Other Marines were unloading the chopper of its cargo while its engines still ran.

As quickly as Billingsley could be processed and assigned to First Battalion, Third Marines, he found himself headed west on Route Nine in the middle vehicle of a truck convoy. An uneventful and unimpeded journey of 8,000 meters found a SeaBee company clearing an area of thick scrub growth, among gently rolling hills, in preparation for a fire support base and landing zone.

"You'll find Bravo Company over there, sir." The driver of the six-by pointed toward a group of tents whose sides were lined with sandbags.

Billingsley carried his pack and weapon by their straps as he approached a solitary figure standing near the first of several tents. "Can you tell me where I might find the CO of Company B?" he asked, noticing no rank insignia on the helmetless man.

"You're looking at him," spoke the man, his hands on his hips and staring straight at Billingsley.

Billingsley dropped his pack and weapon and saluted. "I'm sorry, sir. My name's Lieutenant Billingsley."

"Welcome aboard," smiled the CO. "Captain Clarke here. Glad to have you in Bravo Company."

"Come with me inside," ordered Clarke as they shook hands.

They walked into the tent, where the air was hot and heavy,

unventilated. Maps of the area, laminated and taped to plywood squares, were propped against empty ammunition boxes. The cot and folded poncho liner indicated that the tent served as Clarke's quarters.

"We've been expecting you. Would you care for a soda?" asked Captain Clarke.

"Thank you, sir. I certainly would."

The soft drink was warm, the can slightly rusted across the rim, and the flavor was metallic. Billingsley drank it anyway.

"You can start by taking off those gold bars, lieutenant. And there's no need to salute out here. You're going to command a platoon. Your men will know that you command the platoon. And I will know that you command the platoon. But there's no need to let Charles know that you command the platoon. Enough said?"

"I understand, sir."

"We'll take you over to First Sergeant Day in a bit. He'll get you squared away with your orders, and what have you."

"Fine, sir."

Captain Reginald Clarke sat on his cot and motioned for his new officer to drop his gear and take a seat on a stack of wooden ammunition boxes fashioned into a work bench. Clarke moved slowly, looking older than his thirty-two years. He was razor thin, almost emaciated, and his dusty utility trousers appeared to be at least two sizes too big. He took a rag and wiped the sweat from his face and neck between long gulps of the soft drink. He grumbled something about the "damned lousy dust" before tossing the rag on his helmet and gear, which lay near his feet. He drew a deep breath, belched slightly, and turned his gaze to his new lieutenant.

"First, I want to tell you that you're getting Second Platoon. Most of 'em are out on patrol, at the moment. They'll be in here before dark, though. Staff Sergeant Tyler has been acting as the platoon leader for the past three weeks. First and Third platoons are led by officers, so we're in pretty decent shape now. Second Platoon has a good blend of troops, good experience and good squad leaders. There are a few birds, and you'll recognize them soon enough. Tyler's good, though he's better as a platoon sergeant. Anyway, I want you to keep their asses in gear and give 'em some fire."

"I'll do my best, sir."

"Where are you from, Billingsley?"

"Georgia, sir. Just outside Atlanta."

"That's a good town. I like Atlanta."

"Where are you from, sir?"

"Midwest. I grew up in St. Louis."

"Been in-country long?"

"Eight months. This is my second tour."

"Has there been much action in this area?"

"Very little. Our mission is to provide security. We patrol, stay in communication with battalion, and stand watch around the perimeter. I have no XO at present, my FO is a corporal, and my platoons are not at full strength. I'll be counting on you to pick up the pace in Second Platoon."

Clarke finished his soda and tossed the can into the corner of the tent. Billingsley drank the remainder of his, and threw the can into the corner only after Clarke motioned for him to do so.

"What's your background, Billingsley?"

"I majored in business, sir."

"Play any sports?"

"Played 'em all in high school, sir. Nothing at the college level but intramurals."

"Married?"

"No, sir."

"The other two officers in Bravo Company are doing a good job, and I think you'll like 'em. I would recommend to you that you keep your eyes and ears open, and take advantage of the experience you'll find in the men here. Get to know your people quickly because you'll get to know your enemy soon enough. Feel free to ask me any questions, at any time. We don't have any secrets here in Bravo Company. Just Marines doing their jobs."

"Yes, sir."

Clarke stood, prompting Billingsley to do the same.

"Let's get you checked into the unit. Top Day will arrange with the gunny to get you over to meet your platoon," Clarke said as he led Billingsley out of the tent.

First Sergeant Day came to his feet from behind his field desk when Clarke and Billingsley entered the tent which served as the headquarters facility.

"Look what I found." Clarke gestured toward Billingsley. "A brand, spanking new one. First Sergeant Day, I'd like you to meet Lieutenant Billingsley. We've already had a chance to chat briefly, so why don't you introduce him to the gunny and arrange for him to get over and meet his new platoon?"

"Will do, skipper," said the tall, grizzled sergeant.

Clarke left Day to give his account of Bravo Company: its personnel, its character, and some of its previous actions. Billingsley filled out some forms and then met Gunnery Sergeant Kennerly, a subdued and portly veteran of fifteen years of Marine Corps service. Kennerly eventually led Billingsley to an area at the edge of the clearing. This area was the sector of Second Platoon, whose members lounged in pairs in or near their holes, sweaty and dirty. They approached a Marine sitting alone on a sandbag, cleaning his rifle.

"Sergeant Tyler, meet Lieutenant Billingsley," said Kennerly. "He'll be your new platoon leader."

"Glad to meet you, sir," spoke Tyler, a former drill instructor with ten years of military service.

Tyler was a large man, tall and muscular. He spoke to Billingsley courteously, but with a measure of caution. Tyler, Billingsley decided, was one who was instinctively uncertain of junior officers, and perhaps all officers.

Billingsley dropped his gear and took a seat near Tyler on the sandbags that ringed the open hole. Tyler reassembled the pieces of his M-16 rifle while discussing the affairs and personnel of Second Platoon. Billingsley reviewed with Tyler his own understanding of the duties each would perform as the platoon's two senior members. He watched Tyler's expression for signs of agreement or disagreement, pleasure or displeasure, acceptance or rejection. But Tyler said little, and his face showed no expression. Occasionally he glanced up at his new leader or nodded his head as he said a perfunctory, "Yessir." Billingsley was left feeling uncertain as his conversation with Tyler began to ebb.

"Sergeant Tyler, what became of the last platoon leader?" asked Billingsley.

"You're looking at him, sir."

"I meant the last officer."

"Stayed down when he should've stayed up, and stayed up

when he should've stayed down. I'll let you guess which one got him a round in the brain-housing group."

"Didn't listen, huh?"

"No, sir. Never did."

Tyler later took Billingsley on a walking tour of the sector. The entire compound was formed in a circle, surrounded by triple concertina wire and measuring 350 meters in diameter. Outside the wire, a cleared area of approximately 70 meters was designated as the kill zone. The Second Platoon sector faced to the south, opposite Route Nine, with First Platoon on its left and Third Platoon on its right.

Billingsley watched the men of the platoon fill sandbags that would surround the outsides of their two-man fighting holes. Some had stopped to eat C-ration meals, complaining loudly for Billingsley's benefit about the chronic lack of hot food. They glanced at Billingsley as he passed with Tyler, surmising that their new platoon leader was making his rounds. The word of Billingsley's arrival had traveled quickly, as is usual in an infantry outfit.

Tyler summoned the squad leaders after he and Billingsley had eaten their evening meal while sitting on sandbags at Tyler's hole. The squad leaders, two corporals and a lance corporal, gave brief accounts of their squads: numerical strength, experience in combat, and assigned sectors of fire. Billingsley asked several perfunctory questions, but on the whole said little. He expressed his pleasure at having command of the platoon, and told each of the squad leaders that Sergeant Tyler's value to the platoon would remain considerable. Tyler concluded the meeting by dismissing the squad leaders.

Tyler and Billingsley discussed the plans for the following day, which would include a morning patrol of squad size. The previous two days in the position, Tyler explained, had been routine. The only contact had come when a patrol from Third Platoon had happened upon five Viet Cong soldiers in the adjacent forest. A brief fire fight had ensued before the VC had been either chased away or killed, with no human cost to the Marines.

Captain Clarke met with Billingsley and Tyler after nightfall in his dimly lit CP to issue general instructions for the morning patrol. Clarke showed Billingsley the areas in which pre-planned artillery targets had been plotted, in the event of need.

Clarke pointed out that an artillery battery would begin to occupy their current position by early afternoon on the following day. Furthermore, Clarke said, he believed that a battalion-sized operation was in the offing, with Bravo Company earmarked for an active role. The arriving battery would support the operation, he surmised. Details had not yet been announced, however.

Lieutenants Tom Compton and Steve Page, platoon leaders of First and Third platoons, respectively, came in and were introduced to Billingsley. They greeted him enthusiastically, for they were also relative newcomers to Vietnam. Compton had been in his capacity for three months, while Page had joined the company only six weeks previously. Once the handshakes and welcomes were completed, Billingsley left with Tyler to return to the platoon area.

Sleep that night came in uneven snatches for Billingsley. He leaned against the walls of his freshly dug hole, with its top covered by a poncho and its outside surrounded at the top with sandbags. It had finally happened, he thought. In Vietnam, with a platoon of Marines, ready for duty as a combat officer. He hoped that his platoon would accept him, that Tyler and the squad leaders would support him and cooperate with him. He hoped that his remarks had been well received. At last, after all the anticipation, all the waiting to be in a combat zone, he was now in a combat zone, waiting.

The buzzing of insects was the sound he mostly associated with that first night in the field. He fell asleep only shortly before daybreak.

"Sir? You awake, sir?" called PFC Mark Martindale, Billingsley's radioman. "Lieutenant, sir, it's first light."

Billingsley awakened to see a boyish-looking Marine squatting and peering into the hootch. He held a box of C-rations and smiled self-consciously at Billingsley as if afraid to intrude upon a sleeping officer.

"What's up?" asked Billingsley, immediately feeling the stiffness in his back and shoulders.

"The patrol leaves in an hour, sir. Sergeant Tyler wants to know if you'd like to take it out. You know, sir, to kinda get to know what's goin' on."

"Yes, I would."

"Here, I brought you some chow . . . beans and franks. Not bad if you load 'em up with sugar. There's a heat tab on top."

"Thanks, Marine. What's your name?" asked Billingsley as he poured water from his canteen into his hand and then splashed his face.

"PFC Martindale, sir. I'll be your radioman."

"Good morning, PFC Martindale. Where you from?"

"Encinitas, California, sir," responded the nineteen-year-old communicator.

Martindale's jet-black hair was just long enough on the top to curl slightly, Billingsley saw as the radioman crouched helmetless in the entrance to the hootch. He was slender, of medium build, with smooth skin on his face that probably didn't need shaving too often.

"I appreciate the chow," offered Billingsley.

Tyler walked up to the hole and leaned for a look inside. "Good morning, sir," he said, already shaved and fed.

"Good morning, Sergeant Tyler. Have you briefed the patrol?"

"Yessir. I've gone over it with Corporal Ambrosetti. You want to go?"

"Sure do. I'll be out shortly." Billingsley wondered what effects the breakfast of beans and franks would have on his digestive system. Probably get the damn runs, he thought. "Ah, what the hell," he muttered as he reached for the C-rations box.

"Sir?" called Tyler who was walking away with Martindale.

"Nothing," Billingsley replied.

Corporal Lyn Ambrosetti, a twenty-year-old Chicagoan, had his squad assembled near the perimeter wire and ready to depart. Billingsley and Martindale stood off to the side and made a final check of their radio equipment. Ambrosetti and Billingsley studied a map for a moment to confirm their course for the patrol. They took the squad out in single-file through the opening in the wire.

The weather was warm and dry, and not especially uncomfortable. Billingsley noticed that most of the men carried at least four canteens of water, and many had five. He hoped that his two canteens would be adequate. The patrol moved through the cleared, bulldozed area and approached a line of trees to the south. Ambrosetti was positioned near the front while Billingsley walked in the middle of the column. They moved into the treeline, thick with brush and undergrowth, with each man keeping about twenty feet behind the man in front of him.

The objective of the patrol was to head south into the forested area for 2,000 meters, coming to a dirt trail which was suspected to be a VC conduit. They were to check the trail for signs of enemy activity and, if finding nothing, to continue further south for another thousand meters until coming upon a shallow stream. They were to examine the stream area and return to the compound.

The squad moved slowly and carefully, anticipating that the area was likely to have been booby trapped by the elusive VC. The column halted after about an hour. Billingsley looked ahead, seeing only the backs of the next few men in front of him. The thick undergrowth made it difficult to see for more than a few feet.

"Lieutenant up," came the whispered request down the line moments later.

Billingsley joined Ambrosetti at the head of the column. A short, black, well-built Marine stood with Ambrosetti to the front of the others. PFC James Rosser was considered an ideal point man—perceptive, calm, and fearless.

"Here's our trail," Ambrosetti said quietly.

"Anything moving?" Billingsley asked.

"Nothing, sir. Not a thing," spoke Rosser.

"I think we ought to send two men across, move 'em in thirty meters, have 'em split and come back to cover us," Ambrosetti suggested.

"Okay. Get 'em across in a hurry," ordered Billingsley.

Ambrosetti called two men forward and issued the orders, all in a hushed voice. The two men scrambled across the wide path, low and on the run. They moved slowly once they were on the opposite side, remaining alert and cautious. When they reappeared a short time later, they signaled for Ambrosetti to move the column across the trail. Rosser went ahead, resuming his point position. Ambrosetti and Billingsley fell into their places as the column hurried over the openness of the trail. They pushed on ahead, each man perspiring from the rising temperature and scratched by the thick brush. Though their packs were only moderately heavy, the heat and rolling terrain caused their mouths to feel dry and gummy. The air seemed to hang heavily around them, with little circulation to cool them in their damp uniforms.

After another thousand meters, they reached the stream objective. Finding no movement other than the murky water along its bed of rocks, they followed the stream east for 100 meters, staying just inside the treeline.

Billingsley ordered a short rest break as he and Ambrosetti checked the map. Ambrosetti's dark features had caused the men in his squad to refer to him as "Dago," an affectionate characterization that he seemed not to mind. His men trusted Ambrosetti and respected his competency and fairness.

Their break completed, the squad began its return trip to the perimeter. Rosser, who moved lightly and quietly, like a cat, continued on the point at his own request. The pace was moderate in the still, tranquil forest. Rifles were carried at the ready, with each man glancing quickly from side to side for signs of movement or disturbance. Fingers remained on the triggers.

In addition to his .45 caliber pistol, Billingsley carried an M-16 rifle so he would look like the other Marines. He had removed its nylon sling to eliminate the inevitable noise of the sling's metal clips, something he had noticed the men doing before they left the compound. He wanted very much to look as though he knew what he was doing. He had long since emptied his two canteens, and he berated himself for not bringing more water.

The patrol soon intersected the trail once again, crossing in the same way as before. To avoid retracing their exact steps over most of the return trip, Billingsley ordered Ambrosetti to turn the patrol due west when they were about 500 meters from the perimeter. The offset compensated for the travel along the stream and, upon turning north again after a hundred meters, would take them near their original entering point in the treeline.

Only shortly before Ambrosetti was set to turn Rosser to the west, three sharp, rapid thumping sounds echoed through the forest. The sounds had come from a clearing to the left-front of the alerted and anxious squad. Billingsley moved to the head of the frozen column, crouching as he went. Martindale moved up behind him, a few feet back. When he reached Ambrosetti at the front, three muffled explosions were heard in the distance to the north. "Mortars," Ambrosetti said softly as he strained to get a glimpse of the clearing ahead. "Not sure how many. Maybe just one."

Martindale's radio suddenly crackled. *"Bravo Two, this is Bravo, over,"* called the voice over the radio.

"This is Bravo Two, over," answered Martindale.

"Advise your position, over," came the request.

Martindale shoved the handset to Billingsley. "This is Bravo Two. Position is five hundred meters south of your position, over," Billingsley answered calmly.

"Roger, be advised the shelling is coming from your general direction."

Billingsley was still holding the handset to his ear when Rosser and several other Marines suddenly opened fire at three figures moving quickly to the left of, and parallel to the column. The fleeing enemy soldiers returned the fire, still on the run. Billingsley noticed whooshing sounds as bullets flew over his head.

"This is Bravo Two. We have contact with an undetermined number of enemy. Will advise, over," he radioed.

The entire squad answered with a burst of heavy gunfire as the Marines fired in the direction of the barely visible enemy. Several more shots were returned from the enemy before the fusillade of bullets from the squad silenced the three. Ambrosetti then shouted to his men to approach the enemy soldiers on a line, all the while continuing to fire. They warily crossed the thirty meters of undergrowth, ceasing their fire only when three bleeding, unmoving men were in view. A 60mm mortar and two AK-47 rifles lay on the ground nearby. The three enemy soldiers wore sandals and khaki uniforms. Martindale announced via the radio that the firing had ceased.

Ambrosetti maneuvered the squad into a defensive posture, shouting commands and ordering everyone to remain alert. None of the Marines had been hit by the enemy rifle fire. It had begun and ended quickly.

Billingsley walked over to the dead soldiers. "These are NVA regulars, lieutenant," Ambrosetti said, as he turned one of the corpses with his boot. "I'd bet my ass on it."

Billingsley was stunned at the damage done to the bodies by the multiple gunshot wounds. Two of the bodies had been hit repeatedly in the head and chest. A baseball-size chunk of skull had been shot away from one, exposing the mangled brain in strings of red and grey. Blood oozed from his ears and nose. The other body was soaked in blood from massive upper chest and facial wounds. The third soldier showed feeble signs of life as he lay on his side in the fetal position with his knees drawn toward his chest. The man's eyes blinked quickly.

"This one's still alive," Billingsley said, noticing a slight jerk of the man's hand and hearing a low, gurgling sound.

"He's bought it, sir. Dude's shot clean through," commented Ambrosetti. Intestines protruded from the man's stomach and groin wounds, as well as from the gaping exit wounds in the back.

Martindale approached.

"Skipper's on the hook, sir."

"This is Bravo Two, over," spoke Billingsley, feeling a weakness in his knees and a trembling in his hands as he turned away from the bodies.

"Understand you've solved our problem, over," came the voice of Clarke through the handset.

"That's affirmative. Three enemy KIAs and weapons."

"Any friendly casualties?"

"Negative, no friendlies hit. What about these KIAs?"

"Drag 'em to the edge of the perimeter."

"Roger."

"Thanks much, out," concluded Clarke.

Billingsley suddenly realized that his report to Clarke had been inaccurate, since one of the enemy soldiers had seemingly survived. He wondered for a moment whether he should report his error to Clarke. Unsure what to do to correct his erroneous report, he stood with the radio in his hand.

"He's dead now, lieutenant," said Ambrosetti, grinning and standing over the body. "Motherfucker didn't want to make a liar out of you, so he bought it like a champ."

"Give him my regards," Billingsley replied, not bothering with a confirming glance at the dead soldier. He wondered briefly how Ambrosetti could be so flippant in the midst of such a gruesome scene. And after such a short but violent encounter. He still felt the weakness in his knees. He quickly moved away from the corpses when he detected the odor of feces. "Saddle up. Bring 'em on in with us."

The Marines claimed the bodies and the weapons and set

out over the final few hundred meters to the compound. Before they broke out of the treeline, Billingsley ordered Martindale to announce their arrival over the radio while Ambrosetti popped a red smoke grenade to mark their location to the perimeter defenders. They then crossed the open area and entered the encampment.

Tyler greeted Billingsley after the patrol had woven its way through the opening in the wire. "Welcome back," Tyler said. A slight grin creased his face.

"Thanks. Where did the mortar rounds hit?"

"In the kill zone. None of 'em made it inside."

Ambrosetti walked up with a cigarette dangling from his mouth and a green towel draped over his head.

"Came right to us," said Ambrosetti, looking at Tyler. "Can you believe that? They made it easy on us, the stupid cocksuckers."

"Looks like they may be NVA regulars, according to Corporal Ambrosetti," Billingsley said.

"Better get that word to the captain. He wants to see you, anyway," Tyler said. "The artillery gets here in an hour. Ambrosetti, have 'em clean their weapons and eat chow."

"Good job, Ambrosetti," Billingsley said.

"Thanks, sir," answered Ambrosetti as he left for the area occupied by his squad.

Billingsley removed his gear and went to the CP, where he found Clarke talking to Tom Compton. They were bent over studying a map as Compton made ready to lead a patrol to the east of the camp. "Come in, Mike," said Clarke as both he and Compton greeted Billingsley with a smile. "It didn't take you long to get into the swing of things, did it?"

"Sorry we didn't get there a little earlier," said Billingsley with a sheepish grin.

Clarke and Compton completed their discussion. Compton slapped Billingsley on the shoulder as he left. Clarke folded his map and placed it inside its small carrying case, then rested his hands on his hips and turned to Billingsley.

"Well, what do you think of life in a combat zone so far?" Clarke asked.

"I'm glad I got to go out, sir. It gave me a good feel for things."

"That's good. There's nothing quite like the smell of powder and the sound of shots fired in anger to give you a picture of what combat is. You've got to bust some caps before you find that out."

"Sir, my squad leader seems to think that the three bodies are those of NVA regulars," advised Billingsley.

"That's not surprising. We've known about an NVA battalion in or around this area for quite some time now. We know they're out there, just not sure where. Wherever they are, though, they're probably three short on the head count now," Clarke said, winking at Billingsley.

"They had no documents," Billingsley added.

"Not surprising, either. At least, not in a small group of that size."

Billingsley took a seat on an empty ammo box as Clarke sat down on his cot. "As soon as the rounds impacted, Sergeant Tyler was on the horn telling me that you should be near to where the mortars were being fired from. He told me to hold off on returning fire," Clarke said, smiling at the thought of Tyler's uncharacteristic excitement.

"I'm glad he did, sir," concluded Billingsley. "And I'm glad you did, too."

"Hell, I knew about where you should be," Clarke sagely added.

Billingsley liked Clarke immediately. He sensed Clarke's knowledge and professionalism, though his contact with his CO had been limited to less than thirty minutes of conversation so far. He felt comfortable with Clarke and thought that Clarke was genuinely concerned over his Marines as people rather than merely as tools with which to enhance his own career.

Clarke told Billingsley about the change in plans for Bravo Company. The company had been ordered to remain in its current position, Clarke explained, and provide security for the artillery battery. They would also serve as the reserve force for an operation scheduled to begin the following day. Unless the sweeping operation conducted by companies A and C of the First Battalion escalated beyond expectations, Clarke surmised that Bravo would continue in its present fashion.

"My guess would be a coupla more days," Clarke concluded.

"That gives me a little more time to get to know my platoon," Billingsley said.

"Speaking of your platoon," said Clarke as he unfolded his

map, "I'd like to set up an ambush along the trail to the south of here. I've found a good location, to the southwest, with some high ground on the north side of the trail. It's about three hundred meters west of where you crossed it today."

Billingsley looked over the CO's shoulder at the proposed location on the topographic map.

"We can support it with the artillery that'll be in here soon," Clarke said. "No need for anything bigger than a squad. We'll also have the mortars if you need 'em in a hurry."

"I'll take it out." Billingsley continued studying the map.

"That's up to you. But be out by dusk and set-in by dark. Take a claymore with you."

Billingsley returned to his platoon area. The guns began arriving as the Seabees began departing. The 105mm howitzers of the artillerymen dangled on nylon slings beneath the choppers. The guns were gingerly set into the newly created positions before the slings were released by the helicopter crews. Ammunition came in the same way. The compound was enveloped in a dusty, reddish haze from the rotors of the hovering choppers, while the cannoneers went about their business of aligning the howitzers so that the tubes pointed toward the northwest. They put out aiming stakes and uncrated ammunition and were soon ready to take on a fire mission, if needed. The personnel were quartered only after the battery was prepared for action.

The other infantrymen watched the activities of the battery. Rock music could be heard at various intervals along the perimeter from dozens of transistor radios blurting the familiar sounds to the lounging troops. Activity continued throughout the afternoon. Patrols left and returned. The artillerymen worked on adapting to their new environment, and adapted their new environment to suit themselves. Jeeps and trucks traversed the area, ferrying supplies. The weather remained warm and dry; dust stirred with every least bit of provocation from foot or vehicular traffic.

Billingsley used the late afternoon to write short letters to his family and Andrea. He could hardly avoid feeling homesick when he thought of the months that separated him from his return home. He wrote the news from his little part of Vietnam, and requested a steady stream of letters in return. He already appreciated the significance of mail to men in the field.

Lance Corporal Dennis Sanchez, twenty-one by only a few days, had been a squad leader for only five weeks. His predecessor had been evacuated with serious wounds suffered when a booby trap had exploded nearby during a patrol. Sanchez came from a large family, three brothers and two sisters, the son of a Mexican-American oilfield roughneck from the flatlands of east Texas. A year of football at junior college had proven less demanding than anticipated, prompting Sanchez to seek the excitement and challenge of the Marine Corps. Though not physically large, Sanchez had excellent strength and stamina. Those qualities had earned him the distinction of being the top graduate of his recruit training platoon, a feat that impressed Sergeant Tyler, the former drill instructor. Tyler was of the opinion that, given experience, Sanchez would become an outstanding leader.

"We're ready to shove off, sir," Sanchez told Billingsley, who was finishing his meal of ham and limas.

"Got the flares and claymore?"

"Yessir."

"I'll be there in five minutes." Billingsley chased the last mouthful of C-rations with warm water from his canteen.

Martindale checked his radio and made sure that he packed a spare battery, and he and Billingsley fell into their usual place in the departing column. The patrol walked through the opening in the wire as the evening sun disappeared in a orange glow to the west. Sanchez had placed PFC Grady on the point as the patrol headed southwest. Billingsley noticed that the pace was slightly quicker than that of the morning patrol; Sanchez wanted to reach the ambush location before darkness overtook them.

The squad reached its destination eventually, but not before the dark of the night had indeed surrounded them. Billingsley moved quietly to the front of the column after it suddenly came to a halt in the quiet night. He found Sanchez and Grady near the trail, straining to detect any signs of movement along its length.

"Everything's quiet, sir," whispered Sanchez.

"Where's the rise? There's no high ground on this side," queried Billingsley, gauging from his walk past the column's length that the terrain remained low and fairly even.

"We must have missed it," Sanchez concluded, embarrassed.

Billingsley recollected from his Basic School experiences the tendencies toward drifting off the course of an azimuth. He calculated quickly that for 5 meters of drift every 100 meters of travel, the patrol should be within 100 meters of its objective. "Okay, Sanchez. We've drifted, and probably to the right. Send a couple of men along the trail to the east for no more than a hundred meters, and we'll see if they can find our spot," ordered Billingsley.

"Shaw, you and Ivey get up here," Sanchez called in a muffled tone.

"Have 'em stay off the trail, Sanchez. We'll wait here until they get back," added Billingsley.

Sanchez sent the two men on their way, ordering them to move as quickly and quietly as possible. Meanwhile, Billingsley strained to see the terrain around him from his position just off the trail. He certainly wanted to avoid moving the squad up and down the trail in search of their assigned location. And he didn't feel comfortable with the knowledge that the squad was backed up behind him. The darkness caused his usual confidence to waver slightly. He had to resist the temptation to cover himself with his poncho, light a match, and refer to his map.

The minutes passed slowly as they waited for the return of the scouts. Billingsley knew that he wasn't lost, since they were on the trail, but he also knew that fire support would be made more difficult and certainly more hazardous to his patrol if he didn't know their exact location. Finally, there was a rustling noise to the left and a loud whisper.

"Sanchez."

"Yeah, Shaw. Over here. Did you find the rise?"

"Right. Sixty or seventy meters down the trail. Ivey's still there."

"Let's go," said Billingsley, feeling tremendously relieved that their location had been fixed. "Get the claymore out ASAP when we start to set-in, Sanchez."

"Okay." Sanchez nudged Grady toward Shaw to get the column under way again. They moved off to the side of the trail and began the short walk to their ambush position. Billingsley noticed the slight uphill pull as they climbed the small ridge which would serve as their waiting and, perhaps, their fighting location for the duration of the mission. The troops took their places along the ridge, quietly dropping to the ground and aiming their weapons toward the trail beneath them. Sanchez personally emplaced the single claymore along the far shoulder of the path, facing up the trail. Billingsley planned to signal the start of the ambush by detonating the mine once an unsuspecting enemy was within the kill zone.

With everyone and everything in place, the squad began the interminable wait. The darkness and silence combined to create an eeriness and uneasiness among the Marines. Only the insects—at least one of every insect number and type in the universe, Billingsley thought—moved about the ridge.

Billingsley's mind wandered as he lay on the hard ground, listening and watching. He saw the Christmas scenes in Georgia, with the decorations adorning the homes and shopping centers in bright reds and greens. So familiar in his memory, yet so far in distance. And he thought often of Andrea. Especially Andrea. Her softness and her spirit . . . a million miles away . . . a hundred years from seeing her. Wonder what she's doing, right this minute? Hope she's okay. Hope she stays okay. Hope I stay okay. Damned bugs. Damned hard ground. Damned Republic of Vietnam.

He heard a noise. Oh Jesus, he thought. Here we go. Then he heard a giggle and realized that a nearby Marine had expelled gas onto the ridge.

"Shut the fuck up," he heard Sanchez whisper at the offenders.

The World's Finest, he thought, amused. They never taught us in Basic School about farting on an ambush mission. Matter of fact, they never covered farting under any tactical conditions. Somebody must've covered it with Sanchez, though. He knew exactly how to handle it. Speaking of farting. *Damn* these bugs!

He wondered also about the size of the force which might appear suddenly in his ambush location. Up to a squad would be fine, he decided. Finish 'em off and slide on away. But what about a platoon? Or a whole company? What if a whole battalion of hardened NVA regulars came hoofing through? God almighty, he thought. Better let 'em on through and hope nobody fires a burst. Or farts.

The minutes slowly turned into hours as heavy fatigue gripped Billingsley and the others. He was extremely uncomfortable. Martindale continued his periodic signals to the CP to confirm the patrol's security by keying the handset three successive times. Billingsley guessed that some of his troops were losing the battle with fatigue. He would occasionally hear the sound of a steel helmet rim as it made contact with the barrel of a rifle. Heads were nodding, unavoidably. Nothing moved, no footsteps, no words spoken, no coughs, no sneezes, no signs of the enemy. They waited. Still, there was nothing. More waiting. Only the silence. Only the dreadfully slow passage of time.

The enemy didn't come.

Daybreak finally arrived, a reward to the tired Marines. Billingsley felt numbed as he gazed around the area of the ambush site, able to see his surroundings clearly for the first time. His legs were stiff and his joints ached as he stood up.

"Tell the CP that we've had negative contact and that we're on our way back in," Billingsley told his puffy-eyed radioman. "Back the way we came, Sanchez. Don't forget the claymore."

"All right, people," called Sanchez, bringing the squad to life. "On your feet. Same order of march. Grady on the point. Shaw, you get the claymore. Let's go, let's get rolling."

The men began making their way through the brush, some grumbling when they stumbled coming off the ridge.

"We gonna get to crash when we get back in, Sanchez?" asked a young private as he passed the squad leader.

"Who knows, man," replied Sanchez. "Just keep moving."

"This ain't for shit, man. This ain't for jackshit."

When they were within several hundred meters of the compound, a pair of loud booms shook the ground. Billingsley recoiled from the surprise and the loudness. He trotted up the column to find Sanchez, who was walking along, unfazed.

"You hear that, Sanchez? Where the hell is that coming from?" asked Billingsley, concerned.

"It's okay, sir. It's the 05s in the position," Sanchez replied casually.

Another volley from the guns followed as Billingsley remembered the operation of which Clarke had spoken. He was embarrassed that his fatigue and edginess had so clouded his memory.

"Right," he replied as he turned and went back to his spot in the column.

The howitzers continued to fire at their targets to the northwest as the patrol entered the compound. Attack aircraft, F-4s and A-6s, rumbled overhead trailing a thin stream of black smoke from their exhausts. An occasional shout of *"get some"* could be heard over the noise of the guns and the jets as Marines on the ground looked toward the sky.

"Looks like we've got us a little war goin'," Billingsley remarked to Tyler once the patrol was fully inside the wire.

"They're probably prepping the LZs. Alpha and Charlie companies ought to be on the ground soon," said Tyler, glancing at his watch. "Any luck, Mister Billingsley?"

"No, just a lot of mosquitos."

"Why don't you get some rest. Skipper said just to hang loose until they see what develops."

"I will after I drop by the CP. Was it quiet here last night?"

"No problems, sir."

"See that Sanchez and his people get some chow and rest," Billingsley ordered as he rubbed his stubby growth of beard. "Any hot water to shave with?"

"Sure, lieutenant," Tyler said with a chuckle. "Just pour some from your canteen."

Billingsley looked at Tyler for a moment before grinning and shrugging.

After a brief report to Clarke, Billingsley retired to his hole and stowed his gear. A light rain had started to fall, and the sound of the raindrops on the outstretched poncho which covered the hole lulled him into a deep and refreshing sleep. Even the sound of the howitzers did little to interrupt his several hours of rest.

Corporal Rick Stacey, two months short of his twentieth birthday, returned to the compound in the early afternoon from a short patrol to the southeast. Stacey was the only son of a widowed wheat farmer from northern Kansas, his mother having died not long after Stacey had begun elementary school. His father had raised his son to become independent and resourceful, in many ways the product of the farmer's incessant struggle for the harvest. Stacey had volunteered for service in the Marine Corps within hours of receiving his high school diploma. He intended to use his GI benefits to help pay his tuition for an agricultural degree. Tall and blond, Stacey would have looked just as natural walking through the campus quadrangle, dressed in his letter sweater, as he did in his jungle utilities and boots.

Stacey approached Ambrosetti's hole and found Ambrosetti cleaning his weapon, sitting on the sandbags. Music played from the small radio at Ambrosetti's side.

"How'd it go, Stace?" called Ambrosetti.

"Not too bad, if you don't mind a little rain."

"It don't rain on the Marine Corps," Ambrosetti joked in the clear, warm weather. "Every day's a holiday and every meal's a feast. Throw me those patches over here, will ya?"

"What's the scoop on the new brown bar?" inquired Stacey, tossing the rifle patches in Ambrosetti's direction.

"Hard to tell. Seems to have his shit together, though. He might be just another screaming asshole, for all I really know."

"Sanchez told me this morning that the dude's pretty good in the bush. And he doesn't seem to mind going out."

Ambrosetti elevated the barrel of his weapon and scrutinized the condition of the bore. "Yeah, he might be okay," Ambrosetti said with a shrug. "I think Tyler's glad the dude's here. Tyler doesn't seem to be on the rag anymore, like he was when he was the platoon leader."

"I noticed that, too. Maybe Tyler doesn't want to be in charge of a bunch of snuffies. Might be feeling his years."

"The thing about Tyler is he's good when the shit hits the fan. Don't nothin' else make a rat's ass out here but that, man," Ambrosetti added.

"Well, I hope it works out."

"What the hell, it all counts on thirty."

"Where's he from, Dago?"

"I think he's a grit. Talks a little like one, anyway. Why don't you ask him, Stace. He's coming up behind you," said Ambrosetti as he nodded in the direction from which Billingsley approached.

"Afternoon, sir," called Ambrosetti. "Get any crash time?"

"Sure did. I feel a lot better. How did your patrol go, Corporal Stacey?" asked Billingsley as he rested his foot upon a sandbag.

"Routine, sir."

"Any contact?"

"No, sir."

"They gotta be out there somewhere. The guns woke me twice."

"You'll get used to that, sir," said Ambrosetti. "It's when it's comin' instead of goin' that it gets a little hard to sleep."

"Or maybe sleep forever," Billingsley cracked as he turned to leave.

Gunny Kennerly ambled toward Ambrosetti's hole after Billingsley had departed. Kennerly's flak vest and helmet cover were new and clean, unlike the frayed, worn equipment used by most of the troops.

"Seen Sergeant Tyler?" Kennerly called.

"Over there, gunny," Stacey answered, pointing.

"Get a shirt on, Marine. And a steel pot," Kennerly barked to the half-naked Ambrosetti.

Ambrosetti pulled his shirt toward him and began dressing himself. He watched as Kennerly turned and walked away, then removed his shirt and tossed it on the sandbags. "Stick it up your ass," he muttered quietly.

Billingsley and Steve Page were discussing the forthcoming patrols and security matters with Clarke when word came over the radio in the CP that Bravo Company should prepare immediately for participation in the operation to the northwest. Tom Compton was summoned to the CP as Clarke looked over his notes taken during the conversation with battalion. Clarke reviewed with his platoon leaders the few details with which he had been provided.

"Looks like maybe Charles has decided to stand and make a fight of it," Clarke mentioned in reference to the enemy's resistance to the sweeps of companies A and C. "We're to be ready to move out by chopper in an hour."

None of Bravo Company's patrols remained in the field, so it was able to respond quickly and smoothly. The platoons were ready in short order, though Clarke ordered them to remain in their respective locations. Billingsley and his counterparts were later summoned to the CP for another meeting. As they assembled in their full combat gear, Clarke set out the order of movement.

"Third Platoon will be out first," Clarke ordered. "Second will follow, then First. The CP will go out with Second. Understood?"

The officers nodded their heads in the affirmative.

"Make sure your embark teams are organized. Once we're on the ground, we'll set up in our usual manner," continued Clarke.

"You may need to explain the part about the set-up, sir. I'm not sure I know what the usual manner is," Billingsley said.

"With due north at twelve o'clock, your platoon will set from the four to eight o'clock position. A circular perimeter. You with me?"

"I understand, sir."

"Any other questions?"

First Sergeant Day, dressed in combat attire, stuck his head into Clarke's tent. "Skipper, they want you on the admin net," advised Day.

Billingsley turned to Tom Compton as Clarke and Day left the tent for the radios in the adjacent tent. "Think the LZ will be hot, Tom?" Billingsley inquired.

"Possibly. Always assume it's going to be hot and get 'em on the move when you get on the ground," answered Compton.

"A and C companies have stirred up a hornet's nest, huh?" asked Steve Page.

"Sounds a little like it," said Compton, grinning.

"As you were on the arrival of the birds," Clarke said as he returned to the tent. "Just rest easy in your areas until I give you the word. It'll be at least another hour."

The artillery battery began firing anew as Billingsley left Clarke's tent and walked to his hootch. Two guns fired until the distant observer located the bursts on or near the target; then all six of the guns would follow with their volley. Billingsley watched briefly, and he was able to follow the projectiles for a short distance as they sped through the overcast skies toward their targets.

Billingsley used the delay to review with Tyler the procedures for movement of the platoon by helicopter. Tyler, ever attentive to details, had organized the teams and briefed the squad leaders. The value of Tyler's knowledge and experience became immediately apparent to Billingsley. Tyler's presence would permit him to continue to get his bearings without omitting an important detail or procedure which could adversely affect the platoon. Tyler was a professional in every sense of the word.

"Maybe we'll go up by truck convoy," Billingsley suggested after an hour's wait.

"Matter of fact," said Tyler, "we might even hoof it up there."

"If Alpha and Charlie are in trouble, don't you think we'd already be on the move?"

"Probably. I kinda doubt they've let it get out of hand up there. You never know for sure until you get there and see for yourself, though. You'll hear all kinds of shit when you're away from it," said Tyler as he cleaned the mud from the soles of his jungle boots.

The artillery continued, with mission upon mission. Still, no choppers. Word eventually came from Clarke that Bravo Company would not leave its present position until the following morning. Adequate security was ordered, though no patrols were scheduled.

"I'll get the watches set, sir," spoke Tyler as he left to gather the squad leaders.

The night passed without incident.

Bravo Company was in the air by 0700 on the following morning. The company was ferried to an LZ within the perimeter established on the previous day by companies A and C. They disembarked quickly and were directed to positions along the eastern flank of the battalion enclave. Clarke joined the Battalion Commander, Lieutenant Colonel Walter Fletcher, and Fletcher's staff, at a Buddhist shrine near the center of the position. The shrine served as the CP. Clarke was quickly brought up to date on the progress of the operation and assigned his unit's mission for the succeeding portions of the plan.

The First Battalion position was 2,000 meters southeast of Con Thien, a prominent rise above the surrounding rice paddies, which had been the scene of sporadic fighting for the past several months. The DMZ stretched to the north for some 5,000 meters. Open rice paddies faced Bravo Company to the east, beyond which a thick hedgerow was clearly visible. The weather remained clear, though slightly overcast and cloudy.

The troops of Bravo Company went immediately to work on improving the existing fighting positions in their sector. They dug deeper, piling the fresh soil around the outside of the holes before tamping with entrenching tools. The platoon leaders walked about their respective areas, inspecting the positions and assigning fields of fire. Squad leaders distributed some of the additional ammunition which had been delivered into the position on the previous evening.

Bravo Company had been in position for nearly an hour, enough time to have settled in, when a single mortar round exploded with a loud *carumpf* to the north of the perimeter. Before the black smoke had cleared, another round reached the perimeter's forward edge. A third shell exploded soon thereafter in the middle of the compound. A mixed barrage of artillery and mortars followed. The deafening explosions scattered dirt and debris in all directions. The jagged and lethal fragments from the bursts reached the size of flashlight batteries.

The shelling ceased after ten minutes.

Shouts of "corpsman" came from several parts of the dusty perimeter. Only those assisting the injured ventured into the open from the relative safety of the deep fighting holes which circled the position. The calls for medical assistance were coming mostly from First Platoon. As he crouched in a hole, with Martindale at his side, Billingsley watched as several wounded Marines were carried through the dust to await medical evacuation. He could see the blood of some of the wounded as they were carried either on litters or by other Marines. Tyler reported that Second Platoon had escaped the shelling without suffering a casualty.

After a wait of forty minutes, and with no repeated harassment from the NVA gunners across the DMZ, friendly artillery began firing into and beyond the hedgerow country to the east. Marine F-4 Phantom jets made a half-dozen low-level runs at the same area once the artillery had lifted. The explosions from the artillery and air attacks shook the ground and left clouds of dark smoke hovering over the near horizon.

Clarke called his platoon leaders together and briefed them in the cramped confines of an open trench. The plan called for companies A and B to move east across the rice paddies, on a line, with Company C following in trace. The search and destroy operation, Clarke explained somberly, was ready to shift into the "destroy mode."

A fifteen-minute barrage from the battalion's organic mortars saturated the hedgerow while the maneuver elements took their places. The 360 Marines began moving across the open ground, two companies abreast and one following. Friendly artillery continued to concentrate its fire on the trails and road junctions to the rear of the hedgerow, and well forward of the advancing Marines. Billingsley, with First Platoon to his left, moved through the paddies from his position in the middle of his own platoon. His group formed the extreme right flank of the entire advance, so he glanced often at the openness to his right. Behind him, and centered between First and Second Platoons, came Third Platoon, where Clarke also traveled.

They had crossed most of the open terrain and had come to within 150 meters of the hedgerow when Company A, to Billingsley's far left, suddenly came under sporadic small-arms fire to its immediate front. They returned the fire while attempting at the same time to advance forward to the better ground. Billingsley shouted at his platoon to keep moving and stay on line with the others. Then the entire hedgerow seemed to erupt in a simultaneous volley of small-arms and automatic-weapons fire. Both the lead companies advanced under a hail of bullets. Several Marines slumped to the ground. Billingsley passed the fallen forms of two of his men during the assault. The shouting and firing became chaotic as he pushed his men forward into the teeth of the enemy. He felt weak in the knees, though the adrenalin surged throughout his body, pushed by the rapid pounding of his heart.

"Keep moving," Billingsley shouted as loud as he could manage. "Stay on line . . . keep moving, keep it up . . . don't stop . . . keep moving, dammit."

He reached the hedgerow with his platoon in time to see Marine helicopter gunships searching for targets on the far side. The bodies of perhaps thirty NVA soldiers lay mangled in the nearby area, mostly victims of the pre-assault fires. The stop in the hedgerow lasted only long enough to receive Clarke's call to continue in the assault toward the treeline which lay across 100 meters of open terrain on the hedgerow's far side. The two companies continued the chase, below and behind the gunships which were raking the treeline with its mini-guns.

Billingsley was breathing heavily by the time his platoon had swept into the trees. The Marines were immediately pinned down by the fire from NVA who remained to protect the withdrawal. Concussions from grenades and rocket launchers reverberated through the shallow forest to Billingsley's left. The fighting was close, close enough that the defending NVA soldiers could be seen periodically when they hurled a grenade or moved to another position. The fighting was also close enough that the effectiveness of the gunships was diminished. They circled overhead nonetheless, available for use as Fletcher and his commanders saw fit.

"Bravo Two, this is Bravo. Advise of your situation, over," called Clarke from his location behind Billingsley.

"This is Bravo Two. We are pinned down along the point, fifty meters into the treeline. Heavy resistance, over," replied Billingsley as he and Martindale lay prone on the ground with bullets flying over their heads.

"Roger, hold on to your right flank. Kick 'em outboard and notify me if they try to move on you."

"Roger," replied Billingsley, looking quickly to his right to ascertain some type of order in the confusion to his front and sides.

Attack aircraft were soon heard. The jets made low passes along the perpendicular axis of the advance. When their bombs were released over the treeline, the ground shook violently from the explosions. The bursts were well away from the forward positions of the Marines, though the noise and concussion from the blasts were almost deafening.

"Son of a bitch!" shouted Martindale, flat on the ground.

The Marines were soon able to push forward again, advancing perhaps 200 meters into the treeline before being halted by Fletcher. They met only light resistance during the final thrust, and that mostly by snipers. Bodies littered the ground, mostly NVA, Billingsley was glad to see. Some of the corpses had been hideously dismembered from the aerial bombardment.

"Bravo Two, this is Bravo. Turn your right flank and set-in," came Clarke's order.

Billingsley halted his platoon and then directed the emplacement of two squads on the right flank. The Marines took positions within or behind anything which would afford them cover—shell craters, fallen trees, stumps, and, occasionally, the bodies of NVA soldiers.

The flank was secured.

Billingsley found Tyler checking on the condition of the platoon's squads. The firing had ceased and the air was filled with the acrid smell of cordite. Billingsley saw a corpsman attending to a group of Marines to the rear of the platoon's sector.

"We've got six WIAs, two of 'em bad," said Tyler. "And one KIA."

"Get 'em further to the rear. Skipper says the medevacs are on the way," ordered Billingsley, surprised that his casualties weren't twice as high after the violence of the brief fight.

The injured were taken to the open area to the rear of the treeline, and the evacuation helicopters began arriving. The gunships remained on station, circling menacingly over the position. The medevacs wasted no time in taking on their torn and damaged human cargo and lifting into the air. Ten minutes later they were gone.

Company A had discovered arms and food caches in the enemy positions it had taken over during the attack. Stocks of rice, small-arms ammunition, grenades, rockets, and medical supplies were confiscated by the Marines. The main enemy position comprised a network of supporting trenches, complete with a command bunker and small aid station. Colonel Fletcher surmised that the fortifications had been recently constructed by an NVA rifle company, coinciding with a general upswing in the enemy's activity in the area. Fletcher later ordered the spoils removed by helicopter, with the exception of 200 Chicom hand grenades, which were blown in place by the Marines.

The battalion moved north during the afternoon, traveling 2,000 meters by foot before establishing a new perimeter. The three rifle companies were dug into their new positions two hours before nightfall. Night patrols and ambushes were scheduled for the areas to the north, east, and south. Bravo Company secured the western flank of the compound.

Clarke gathered his platoon leaders and advised them that the operation had, at least so far, been considered a success. Ninety-two NVA bodies had been claimed from the day's action, bringing the running total from the operation's beginning to 223. The friendly casualties for the day, Clarke pointed out, numbered 12 Marines killed and 30 wounded. All but two of the wounded had been evacuated to medical facilities. Billingsley contemplated the casualty count, perplexed and bewildered. He was sitting in a trench with Clarke and the others, leaning against its sides and smoking a cigarette with his hands cupped. Clarke noticed Billingsley's expression. "Something bothering you, Lieutenant Billingsley?"

"Nothing, sir. I was just thinking of all that ordnance spent in bagging a measly ninety-two gooks. It just seems like it would've been more," replied Billingsley.

"I'm quite sure they carried away a number of their dead. There were blood trails when we broke contact," Clarke added.

"I don't know, sir. It just seemed when all the firing was going on that we were killing them by the hundreds."

"Welcome to Vietnam," quipped Tom Compton, drawing a laugh from the others.

The briefing concluded and Billingsley walked to the hole Martindale had prepared for the two of them. Martindale sat outside the hole, smoking a cigarette and nursing the blisters on his hands. His muddy entrenching tool and his helmet were beside him, and his radio was propped against the parapet.

"Did you dig this yourself?" Billingsley asked as he admired the hole.

"Damn near, sir," beamed Martindale, showing the space between his two front teeth. "Rosser dug awhile. Even got us a grenade sump."

"First prize, Martindale. This hole takes first prize."

"What *is* first prize, sir?"

Billingsley pondered for a moment, stroking his chin. "An all-expense paid vacation," he answered.

"To where, sir?"

"Three guesses, Martindale."

"Vietnam?"

"There it is. You guessed it right off."

"What's second prize, sir?"

"Ain't no second prizes. Everybody here takes first prize."

Billingsley stood next to the hole and surveyed the adjacent terrain in the subdued light of dusk. The countryside was mostly open. Good observation and fields of fire, he thought. An abandoned airstrip, small and overgrown, lay 200 meters to the east. Con Thien was clearly visible to the northwest. To the west, the vegetation thickened considerably into tropical rain forest and rugged hills. Nightfall was less than an hour away, and the air was still and comfortably warm.

Billingsley heard a muffled concussion to the north, then another. Then several in rapid succession. "INCOMING," someone screamed from a nearby hole. He and Martindale jumped into their hole and crouched at the bottom. They were both thankful for the depth of it as they waited for the shells to hit. Seconds later the first of the rounds exploded on the fringes of the encampment.

"Bastards," muttered Martindale as the bursts moved closer to the positions along the perimeter. Martindale suddenly realized that his radio and helmet remained outside the hole. He raised himself and extended his arms, trying to reach his gear without leaving the hole.

"My radio's out there," he said.

Billingsley grabbed him by the collar of his flak jacket and jerked him down. He pushed Martindale to the bottom of the hole and then crouched on top of him, shielding him. An artillery round exploded within several meters of the hole and temporarily deafened him. Dirt and debris were still falling into the hole when three more shells exploded nearby. Billingsley's ears rang with a high-pitched echo after each of the rounds. It was as if the bursts sucked all the oxygen from the hole, making breathing difficult from the flash and hearing impossible from the concussion. Billingsley clenched his teeth, dreading that the next shell would drop into the hole and blow them into oblivion.

Perhaps two dozen rounds fell into the position before the shelling ceased. Billingsley waited a full minute after the last explosion before breathing deeply again. The air was choked with dust and the smell of cordite. He was still on top of Martindale.

"You hit, sir?" Martindale called from beneath the weight of his platoon leader.

"What?"

"I said are you hit?"

"I don't think so."

"It's quit, sir."

"What?"

"The shelling. It's lifted."

Billingsley straightened and discovered that his body parts

were intact. He looked outside the hole and saw corpsmen running among several positions, offering assistance to the wounded. He climbed out and gazed around. He then turned to Martindale.

"Keep your damned gear on you or in the hole," Billingsley snapped impatiently.

"I will, sir," responded Martindale. "Thanks much, Lieutenant Billingsley."

Two Marines had been slightly injured, neither requiring evacuation. The deepness of the holes had reduced the number of casualties, a lesson not lost on the troops.

Dust hung over the position.

Colonel Fletcher had hoped to entice the NVA into a full-scale conflict in which he could fix and destroy an enemy force of significant size and strength. A reserve force, elements of the Ninth Marines, had been designated as available to him in the event of such an engagement. But the operation had encountered only pockets of resistance. And though the pockets were numerous, the size of the NVA forces which had been drawn into battle had yet to exceed that of a reinforced rifle company in any singular action. So the battalion pushed farther to the north, past Phu Oc and Hao Son. The results were predictable; the NVA employed delaying tactics while keeping on the run. Mortars, snipers, artillery, occasional booby traps and skirmishes. And in no particular order of delivery. The Marines followed, in a sequence of movement, casualties, halting, evacuating, movement, encampment, and harassment.

The routine continued for three days before the tired men of the battalion were withdrawn from the region. Nearly 300 NVA soldiers had perished in the sweeping operation. The cost to the Marines was 58 casualties, of whom 19 had died.

Showers and hot food awaited the troops of First Battalion when they arrived at Camp Evans in Thua Thien Province. A beer ration was especially welcomed. Once the accumulated grime and filth had been washed from their bodies in the portable showers at the camp, and once a full, hot meal of roast beef had been served, the morale of the troops rose decidedly. Mail was like the sweet topping on the pudding.

Compton, Page, and Billingsley shared a tent during the break. It was a large tent, draped over a frame of wood and reinforced at the top by corrugated tin. The three officers had it to themselves, spreading out on their cots and feeling clean for the first time in quite a while. Billingsley lounged on his cot and savored the last few sips of his beer. Compton read a letter from his wife in Baltimore as he sat upright on his cot. Steve Page lay reading an old issue of *Playboy*, borrowed from an officer in Alpha Company in an adjacent tent. Clarke had stopped by the tent earlier to express his appreciation for the manner in which the officers had performed during the operation.

"Well, Mike. What's your impression of Bravo Company so far?" asked Compton after he had folded his letter away.

"It's a good impression. I like the company, and I like my platoon," Billingsley answered.

"You've got a good man in Tyler. He's a cool head."

"Yeah, I'm lucky to have him."

"He was busted on the drill field a few years back. Did you know that?"

"No, I didn't. Why was he busted?"

"Unauthorized PT, or some such shit. He was busted two ranks. That's why he's not a gunny now. God knows, he's better than that worthless Kennerly, and by a factor of at least ten," Compton explained.

"He told me about his tour as a drill instructor, but he didn't mention the part about being busted."

"He came in after a few drinks one night and took his recruits out on a late night run of three miles."

"I'll bet he was hell-on-wheels as a drill instructor," Page interjected.

"I'll bet he was, too," agreed Billingsley. "What do you guys think of Captain Clarke?"

There was no immediate response to Billingsley's question, though Compton squinted as he thought over his response.

"He's a lifer, no doubt about that. But we could have done a whole helluva lot worse," Compton finally said.

"Sure could have," agreed Page. "He's treated me and my platoon fairly. I don't think Clarke much gives a shit about body counts. He just gets the job done in the best possible way."

"Yeah, and the least costly," added Compton. "I know he wasn't real keen on this sweeping operation. It's a bunch of bullshit, really. Especially against regulars."

"How do you mean, Tom?" questioned Billingsley.

"Clarke and I talked about it. We shouldn't be moving a whole Goddamned battalion around without a specific objective to attack. He didn't come right out and say it, but I know Clarke felt that way. You can get away with that kind of crap against those VC shitasses, but not against NVA. They couldn't miss us, wherever we went. Unless they wanted to," Compton offered.

"We got three hundred of the cocksuckers," Page argued.

"We couldn't help but get some of 'em, Steve. Look at what we threw at them. We didn't hurt him *that* damned bad, I'll *guarantee* you," countered Compton.

Compton sat up on his cot and looked at Billingsley. He sipped his beer, keeping his eyes fixed on the newcomer. "What do you think of Captain Clarke, Mike?"

"Seems to me like he knows what he's doing. He's made me feel comfortable in the short time I've been aboard. I'd have to say that I'm impressed with him."

"One thing you need to remember about Clarke," said Compton. "He's got a helluva good head on his shoulders. He is one smart dude. And don't ever try to bullshit him. As long as you're straight with him, you'll have no problems."

"Tom's right," offered Page. "Clarke ranks up there with the best of 'em as far as IQs go. With a head like he's got, I often wonder why he decided to stay in the Marine Corps. He could do anything he wanted to."

"I think he's *doing* what he wants to do. His family life was all botched up. He told me that he was raised by an aunt, and that he worked his way through college by running a lawn care business. I mean he *ran* it, and never once cut a blade of grass. He'd make enough in the spring and summer to pay for school and his car," admired Compton.

They talked on, of Clarke and others in Bravo Company. Billingsley was keenly interested in all of it—the information and the chance to get to know Page and Compton. They spoke freely, an indication to Billingsley that he had been accepted into the fold. Besides, they had been under fire together, the stuff that bonds infantrymen.

Tom Compton was the senior platoon leader in the group of three. Clarke considered him to be an excellent officer, tactically sound and wise to the ways of the enemy. Big and muscular, Compton stood six feet two and weighed slightly over 200 pounds. He was tough and steadfast, though fair and impartial with the troops under his command. His intense and serious approach to his work made him appear aloof and arrogant at times. His degree in civil engineering had trained him to think quantitatively, in terms of problems and their solutions. Dark hair and a dark moustache made him look rugged; he could have been a macho figure in a cigarette commercial. Compton was quite seriously considering a military career since he had found the Marine Corps to his liking. His wife preferred otherwise, however.

Steve Page, on the other hand, had no interest whatsoever in serving the Marine Corps beyond the three years for which he had obligated himself. He would rather have started his life's calling as a public schoolteacher in his native Wisconsin, ice fishing in his spare time, than lead combat troops. He was short and heavyset, open and spontaneous—in contrast to Compton's methodical and deliberate style. Page was an American History major, yet he was intrigued by the Far East culture to which he had been exposed. He studied Vietnamese language and customs to satisfy his own curiosity. A bachelor, Page also found the women of the Far East to his liking.

Page opened the centerfold from the magazine and held it aloft. "Have a look, gents. Just a quick look for you, Thomas. You're a married man," he said.

"Very nice," Billingsley observed.

"Listen, Steve," countered Compton. "If they want to show it, then I'm gonna damn sure look at it. You two bachelors will find that out later."

"When is Chris due?" asked Page.

"March," Compton replied.

"Congratulations, Tom. I didn't know your wife was expecting," offered Billingsley.

"Yeah, it'll be our first. Wish to hell I could be there with both of 'em when it happens. That would be a mind-blowing change, huh? Going from killing to birth ... what a trip," Compton mused.

"You could handle it, couldn't you?" asked Page.

"In a minute, man. In a minute."

At least I'm not married, and with a pregnant wife, Billingsley thought.

Replacements caught up with Bravo Company during the brief stay at Camp Evans. Billingsley had an opportunity to speak with each of his new men before Tyler assigned them to the various squads. Though he hardly knew the names of all his men, Billingsley had spoken with every man in the platoon at least once. Their names and faces and hometowns and duties were beginning to come together. The replacements brought the strength of his platoon to a total of forty-four effectives.

"Forty-two effectives and two shitbirds," Tyler had countered, expressing immediate displeasure at the sight of two slightly obese newcomers. "That's all we need—a coupla whales. Those two should have been given typewriters instead of M-16s. They ain't nothin' but office pogues."

"Think they came from Parris Island?" kidded Billingsley.

"No way, sir. They're fuckin' Hollywood Marines. They start to straggle, I'll have my boot affixed to their assholes."

Billingsley thought of the absurdity of such a predicament laughed heartily. Tyler remained stern and expressionless, though he privately enjoyed his platoon leader's reaction to his graphic description.

The break concluded and Bravo Company packed its gear and headed back out to the bush. Their objective was to search the area to the south and southwest of Con Thien for the enemy. Companies A and C were scheduled to operate in the same general vicinity, with each available to support the other.

A village of perhaps eighty inhabitants, suspected by intelligence to be sympathetic to, if not actually under the influence of, the enemy, stood on the outskirts of the rain forest to the southwest of Con Thien. Bravo had been assigned to search the village before continuing on into the canopied jungle to the west. A Vietnamese scout, who also acted as an interpreter, traveled with the Marines.

The company moved in a column formation along the trail that led to the village's south entrance. They passed open rice fields and encountered several villagers, mostly elderly, who neither looked at nor in any other fashion acknowledged the presence of the Americans. Billingsley's platoon led the column as it neared the village. They were within 200 meters of the entrance when a terrific boom at the front of the column jerked the platoon, and thus the entire company, to a halt. An orange and black cloud of dust and debris rose ominously from the head of the column as the explosion echoed throughout the area. Billingsley, startled, flinched at the sound of the blast. He moved ahead to near the front of his platoon and saw Ambrosetti setting up a small defensive perimeter.

"We need a corpsman up here," Tyler called as he knelt near one of the felled Marines.

"Corpsman up," shouted Billingsley. "What the hell was it, Sergeant Tyler? Booby trap?"

"Yep. Had to be command detonated. Stacey's got a group in the bush to our left lookin' for 'em."

"Did you see anybody?" Ambrosetti called from the side of the trail.

"I didn't see nothin' but the flash," replied Tyler.

"I got the wires," shouted Stacey. "Whoever did it looks like they beat feet to the ville."

"Motherfuckers," Ambrosetti said in disgust. "We oughta go in there and string somebody up by their Goddamned dong."

The corpsman administered first aid to the Marine whose leg had been severed just below the knee by the explosion. His left foot, still in its shredded jungle boot, stood upright ten feet away from him. Another man had been peppered along the upper thigh and groin by the hot fragments. A third man—Billingsley recognized him as one of the overweight newcomers—was sprawled in the center of the trail. The man had been struck by a large fragment, just above the eye, and had been killed instantly. The body was slumped forward, face down with arms underneath.

The Marine with the severed leg began to moan loudly.

Billingsley contacted Clarke and requested a medevac. Clarke said the helicopter had already been summoned and Billingsley was to confine his search for the enemy soldiers to the immediate vicinity of the trail.

"I'm sliding Bravo Three across your right flank to seal off the northeast. Spread your people out and remain in position until I notify you, over," Clarke advised over the radio.

Billingsley shouted the order to Tyler to spread the platoon off the trail. He also passed through his column and alerted the men to the movement of Third Platoon in the trees and brush to the right. He then went to the two wounded men, who had been removed to a slight clearing off the trail. The lesser injured of the two rested on his side, bandaged heavily on the thigh and lower abdomen.

"Hang on a little longer, tiger," Billingsley spoke as he knelt before the groggy Marine.

"Right, sir."

"We'll have you out soon."

"Thanks much, sir," replied the young Marine as he rubbed his forehead.

The other wounded man had calmed down after several minutes of thrashing and wailing. The corpsman was with him.

"We'll have you on a chopper in just a few more minutes," Billingsley said comfortingly.

"My leg's gone, sir," the man cried softly, in disbelief. "My leg's been blown off. It's gone, sir."

"You're gonna be okay. It won't be much longer."

"My leg's gone, sir. Doc, do something . . . it hurts bad . . . please . . . oh dear God, please . . . don't . . . I don't want . . ."

The thumping sound of the helicopter's rotors was heard from the rear of the platoon, away from the village. Billingsley could see the dense red smoke which had been used to mark the landing site.

"Get 'em up. The chopper's in the area," called Billingsley.

The dead Marine was placed in a poncho and carried off by two other men. The wounded were taken to the LZ as the chopper made its nose-high landing in the grassy open area. The helicopter left unmolested.

Stacey approached Billingsley on the blood-spattered trail. "There weren't any trip wires, sir. I walked by there myself just before it went off. We followed the det cord into the bush, but they were already gone. They're in the damn ville. They gotta be," he concluded.

Clarke ordered Second Platoon, along with Third Platoon, to proceed ahead and begin the search. They entered the village cautiously, walking slowly with their weapons at the ready. Billingsley and Tyler organized searches for half the straw huts and left the remainder for Steve Page's group. The Vietnamese interpreter entered with Billingsley and spoke briefly to the village chief in high-pitched, hurried phrases.

The atmosphere in the village was tense. The children stayed to themselves, not following the Americans as they usually did. The adult villagers avoided eye contact with the Marines. Many of the women continued to cook their noon meals over pot stoves, seeming to ignore the searches which went on about them.

"The Kit Carson scout's got a young dude in the far hootch over there," Tyler pointed. "Everything else looks okay."

"Call the skipper and tell him that everything checks out with Bravo Two, except the questioning of one suspect," Billingsley called to Martindale.

Billingsley walked to the straw hut where the scout interrogated the young Vietnamese man. Inside, he found the scout holding a revolver and occasionally pointing it at the expressionless suspect. A young woman, apparently the man's wife, held an infant which, along with its mother, sobbed incessantly. The scout slapped the suspect's face with his open hand. He then continued his rapid questioning of the squatting man, paying no attention to Billingsley. Billingsley watched the routine for several minutes—questions from the scout, no answer from the young man, slaps from the scout, still no response from the man, the pointing of the pistol by the scout, and the continuous crying and wailing from the wife and child.

"Is this our man?" asked Billingsley, stepping to the side of the scout.

"May-be VC," replied the scout without looking away from the suspect.

"Is he the one? Is he the man who set off the booby trap?"

"May-be VC. Ask more ques-tion."

The scout cocked the hammer of his revolver and placed the barrel against the suspect's head. Billingsley thought the scout was bluffing until he saw his index finger begin to take up the slack on the pistol's trigger. The tension produced by the terrified expression of the suspect and the crying and pleading of the woman was almost palpable. The young man squatted, motionless, with the pistol at his skull. He perspired heavily.

"Outside, cowboy," Billingsley said to the scout with a motion toward the opening.

The scout stared at Billingsley for several seconds before uncocking his weapon and storming out of the hut. Billingsley followed him.

"Keep an eye on the dude in the hootch," Billingsley called to Sanchez.

The scout, Tri, found Clarke near the south entrance to the village and told him about the suspect, adding that the chances of the suspect's being VC were high. But, Tri noted, it was unlikely that the man had participated in the booby trap detonation. The quick escape of the enemy from the scene caused Tri to believe that the nearby jungle likely protected the enemy soldiers. Tri, in his broken English, also registered a complaint of what he deemed to be unwarranted interference from Billingsley during the interrogation process.

Clarke found Billingsley listening to the reports of his squad leaders.

"What's the scoop?" Clarke asked as he and Billingsley stepped away from the group.

"Nothing but one suspect, sir. No weapons or explosives."

"What the hell happened with Tri?"

"I had to throw him out of the hootch. I really thought he'd shoot the dude. And I wasn't real sure that he wouldn't blow *me* away," Billingsley said, removing his helmet and wiping at the sweat on his face and neck.

"I don't think we've got the one we want."

"I don't know, sir. I don't understand gook, and Tri didn't tell me jackshit."

"I had First Platoon follow the det wire to see if they could find any tunnels, but Tom reported there were none."

"Where the hell did they go? Stacey and Ambrosetti and their people didn't see a thing."

"They're in the jungle. I didn't think they'd try to hide in the damned ville, not with a Marine rifle company on the outskirts."

"What about this dude?" Billingsley asked with a point toward the hut.

"Leave him. I don't want to take the time to evacuate his ass. The guy's probably VC, like Tri says, but he's got plenty of company in *this* village."

"Sanchez," Billingsley shouted. "Bring your man out and let the guy go."

Bravo Company went on from the village into the heavily canopied jungle, where movement was slow and cumbersome. The stench from the rotting foliage and the lack of air circulation caused the Marines almost as much discomfort as the loads they carried on their backs. They moved in a column, alternating platoons on the point. Radio contact was erratic both within the company and with battalion headquarters in the rear. The rolling terrain did little to enhance the ease of movement.

Billingsley's thoughts kept flashing to the scene of the booby trap as he trudged along through the vines and bushes. The picture of the still body of his dead Marine was frozen in his memory. The second of his men to meet death in the field, with the poncho covering all but the protruding jungle boots. What odds, he thought. The fat guy's first outing, and he dies. Two hours ago he was alive, and now he's probably in a morgue. One piece of metal out of ten thousand, and he gets hit in the head. Could have just as easily missed him, or hit him in the shoulder or foot. But it hits him flush in the skull. Ripped open his brain. Jesus, what lousy luck. Wonder what'll be done to notify his family of the news. They probably don't even know yet. Nah, not yet. Wonder how many more? he thought. How many more of my troops will I see like that? Wonder if they'll ever see *me* like that. The boots stickin' out from under the poncho. God, what a sight. What a dismal fucking sight.

Six hours of searching in the stifling jungle produced no contact with the enemy. Bravo Company set up its perimeter outside the jungle, 2,000 meters to the east. The area was flanked by rice paddies and open in every direction. Fields of fire were excellent. Clarke assigned his platoon leaders their portions of a coordinated fire plan. Listening posts were emplaced outside the perimeter to provide early warning. No patrols were ordered so as to keep the forces together. Pre-planned artillery targets ringed the area, along with claymore mines. Clarke considered the regions to the north and north-west to represent the most likely avenues of approach for an enemy force.

As darkness fell, Billingsley inspected his positions and then returned to the hole he shared with Martindale. All was quiet within and outside the perimeter, and reports from the listening posts gave no indication of enemy movement. The watches were set, and Billingsley nodded off to sleep in the coolness of the fresh hole. The trek through the jungle had exhausted him, and he was able to rest even though slime and filth covered his skin like a thin coating of oil.

He was jolted from his sleep three hours later when a mixed barrage of rockets and mortars burst in the perimeter. The explosions came slowly at first, building over the next fifteen minutes until the flashes and bangs came so fast Billingsley feared the entire North Vietnamese Army had targeted Bravo Company for a massive demonstration of firepower.

"The LP, sir," shouted Martindale over the noise. "There's a problem."

Billingsley accepted the radio's handset from Martindale.

"Holy SHIT!" came the frantic radio transmission from the listening post. *"They're all OVER the place! They're headed in your direction. I say again, they're headed in your direction."*

"Get back in here," Billingsley radioed, only to hear a wild burst of gunfire from the LP's direction.

Automatic-weapons fire announced the arrival of the enemy force as they crossed the open terrain to Billingsley's front, on the dead run. The mortars and rockets lifted when the first elements of the NVA neared the forward Marine positions. Some of the NVA were able to hurl grenades and satchel charges before they were caught in the exploding claymores. The gunfire increased. Muzzle flashes flickered in the night like a New Year's Eve fireworks demonstration. Red tracers snaked over the ground in both directions. The noise was incredible—the gunfire, the explosions, and the shouting—far beyond anything Billingsley had yet heard.

"This is Bravo Two. Request the arty, over," Billingsley radioed to Clarke.

"Roger," was Clarke's terse reply.

The NVA slammed into the outer perimeter from the north and northwest, as Clarke had anticipated, right into the face of Billingsley's platoon. The assaulting enemy closed the distance to thirty meters from the position, and individual rushes came within easy hand grenade range. Several enemy actually penetrated the perimeter before being felled by gunfire from the Marines.

Billingsley's LP could not be contacted. He had difficulty determining what was going on only a few feet away, much less at the LP. Mortars, augmented by artillery fire from a nearby Marine battery, pounded at the enemy to his front.

Machine gunners, firing their M-60s until the barrels glowed in the dark, raked the area of the enemy advance. The NVA were close enough so that Billingsley could hear shouted commands as their commanders tried to keep control of their advancing forces. He could also see them sprint toward the perimeter with an occasional halt to fire a quick burst at the Marines.

"Jesus God," Martindale kept exclaiming. His tongue felt as if it were sticking to the roof of his mouth when he spoke. He breathed in short, quick heaves. His hand trembled uncontrollably each time he raised the radio's handset to transmit or receive a message.

Clarke tightened the noose by moving the artillery fire closer to the fringe of the perimeter, and closer to the pressing NVA. He also ordered illumination rounds fired into the skies over the attackers. The first of the illumination shells exposed a silhouetted area to the front of the position where dozens of enemy soldiers could be seen. Sizable numbers of enemy dead were accumulating on the ground. The fighting raged for over an hour before Clarke determined from his platoon leaders that the integrity of the perimeter was intact. The enemy showed no signs of weakening, however, as the level and intensity of the gunfire continued at a fever pitch. Clarke and his young FO kept the artillery moving ever closer, bursting in orange clusters less than 100 meters to the front of the most exposed of the company's positions.

Billingsley was never sure which side had the advantage. He was only sure that his sector had not been overrun.

"What is your situation?" radioed Clarke.

"We're still getting hit hard," Billingsley replied.

"No shit. Are you still holding?"

"Affirmative."

"Roger. Keep an eye on your ammo."

Reports from his squads indicated to Billingsley that his men were beginning to run low on ammunition. Their firing had thus become more selective. Many of the Marines had their combat knives unsheathed and within easy reaching distance. Billingsley knew that, in the worst of cases, bandoliers of ammo could be rushed into his sector by Marines from First and Third platoons. He waited, instead. He was using

Ambrosetti's squad as the platoon index since they were the most exposed. And they still had ammo.

The NVA continued to press the assault. Their troops rushed the nearby positions, sometimes inflicting casualties with a burst of gunfire or the toss of a hand grenade. As the NVA moved in even closer, hand-to-hand struggles broke out at some of the forward holes.

"Bring it in closer," Ambrosetti radioed in reference to the artillery. *"Some of 'em are startin' to get by."*

"Drop it in another fifty meters," Billingsley called to Clarke.

"You sure?" was Clarke's reply.

"Negative, but do it anyway. They're about to climb in here with us."

"Roger, get the word to your people up ahead and tell 'em to let us know to back off if it gets too close."

Billingsley radioed and shouted the warnings to his troops before the rounds were shifted closer. Soon, explosions were cracking as if giant hardwoods were being snapped, sucking the air and spreading debris over the Marines. The enemy soldiers who were caught in the open by the shelling were struck repeatedly by the deadly fragmentation. The closest of the explosions were a scant twenty meters from the positions of some Marines. Second Platoon members crowded the bottoms of their fighting holes.

"Keep it coming, just like it is," called Tyler from his forward location.

The shelling continued for another ten minutes before Clarke radioed Billingsley that the rounds were being shifted further away from the perimeter.

The gunfire resumed.

An NVA soldier who had penetrated the perimeter had been wounded by the artillery shelling. He lay near the hole of Billingsley and Martindale, and overheard the platoon leader in a radio conversation. He could see Billingsley rise to make quick scans of the battle area.

"How does it look?" Billingsley called to Stacey via the radio.

"Still close," was Stacey's reply.

"Closer than it was?"

"Just as close, roger."

The NVA soldier took hold of his AK-47 and staggered

toward Billingsley's hole with his severely injured arm dangling at his side.

"Goddamn, *lookout!*" screamed Martindale, fumbling for another magazine for his M-16.

Billingsley turned in time to see the wounded NVA soldier standing ten feet away, attempting to support his weapon on his hip. Instinctively, Billingsley raised the .45 pistol which he held and fired a single shot, striking the man in the upper chest. At almost the same instant, rifle fire from other nearby Marines ripped through the man's torso and blew pieces of flesh and clothing away from his body. The enemy soldier fell over hard, limp and unmoving.

"Motherfuckin' gook," shouted Martindale shrilly as he fired several more rounds into the still body.

The explosions and the gunfire flashed from all sections of the embattled area. Billingsley glanced over the top of his hole, the radio's receiver in one hand and his .45 in the other. He could still hear shouting, some of it clearly from his Marines, the rest an unintelligible garble lost amid the booms and cracks and pops of the pitched battle. His squads reported that the sector was still intact. He felt fear, though he was not obsessed by it. He felt confusion, though he was reassured by the presence of his troops and the calm voice of Clarke over the radio. Mostly, he felt powerless, a feeling of being helplessly pulled into a swirling, violent cataclysm whose duration and eventual outcome seemed totally removed from his own control. He held on, doing his small part and bracing himself to ride it out. It was nothing like he had imagined. Nothing at all.

The artillery and the gunfire chased the last of the NVA force from the battlefield. After the remaining ammunition had been distributed, the only movement came from the corpsmen who crawled about attending to the wounded. Within an hour and a half, the first light of day appeared in the east and exposed a frightful picture of the price in lives that had been paid by the enemy. Bodies of NVA soldiers were literally piled atop one another in places. Billingsley, who emerged from his hole at dawn to inspect his platoon, was stunned at the carnage.

"God, look at the gooks," he marveled, with pride and surprise. He moved through his platoon sector, directing medical attention to his wounded and assessing the extent of the damage. Sanchez organized a search party for Shaw and Forbes, his two squad members who had been assigned to the listening post. Ten minutes later Sanchez and his patrol returned with the bullet-riddled bodies of the two men.

They had been shot repeatedly in the head.

The choppers evacuated the wounded and dead while the morning mist still clung heavily to the ground. Billingsley's platoon had lost five men dead and nine wounded, one-third of his entire force. Of the nine who had been wounded, two were so critical their chances for survival were minimal. One died before reaching the hospital, the other only shortly thereafter.

Ambrosetti leaned forward in his hole, alone, with his head resting on his arms. His face was dirty and pale and his eyes were closed.

"You okay, Ambro?" called Tyler when he and Billingsley passed nearby after the departure of the choppers.

"I'm all right."

"You hit?"

"I ain't hit. Just leave me fuckin' alone for a few minutes."

Ambrosetti's grenadier, an Italian-American named Ciccarelli, had been shot in the throat and mouth during the fighting. Ciccarelli had choked on his own blood while fighting at the side of his best friend, Ambrosetti.

One hundred enemy bodies were reported to battalion headquarters as part of Clarke's radio report of the action. "There's more than a hundred, sir," Compton argued after Clarke finished the report.

"Well go *count* the sons of bitches, Tom," replied Clarke.

Compton looked at the corpses of the enemy soldiers spread around and inside the position. He turned back to Clarke with a slight grin. "Looks like about a hundred to me, skipper," he said.

Lieutenant Colonel Fletcher visited the Bravo Company position for a firsthand look at the destruction which had been dealt to one of the enemy's better outfits known to be operating in the region. He seemed impressed as he toured the area with Clarke, stopping occasionally to speak with an enlisted Marine. He congratulated Billingsley as the leader of the platoon that had repulsed the major thrusts of the attack. Fletcher and his party left by helicopter after spending thirty minutes in the position.

For two more days Bravo Company stayed in the field. Contact was limited to occasional sniper fire, and no major actions were recorded. Finally, the choppers came for the tired company. They were going back to Camp Evans for a rest.

It was Christmas Eve. There was mail, and plenty of it. Life at Camp Evans was slow and easy. The food was hot and ample. Beer was available. All the comforts of home, or at least enough comforts to please the troops—veterans and newcomers alike.

Billingsley had two letters from Andrea and one from his parents. The letters from Andrea had been scented with perfume and contained several snapshots of her taken at her Virginia home. One of the photographs showed her standing in front of her family's Christmas tree, wearing a white sweatshirt with the words "U.S. Marines" emblazoned across the top of the eagle, globe, and anchor symbol. Billingsley placed the picture in the liner of his helmet after staring at it for several moments. All seemed well at home. Andrea complained of her upcoming course workload and blamed Billingsley for her average performance of the previous fall term. Too many important distractions, she suggested.

> Oh well, I suppose I can do better. Daddy might pack me off to India with the Peace Corps if I don't. He's not altogether sure of my motivation, sometimes. Thinks maybe I'm just a lovestruck hippie. By the way, my parents send their best. They really think quite highly of you. And I can understand why. After all, they take after me in that regard. Please, please be careful, Mike. I miss you every moment of every day, and I wait impatiently for your return. Have a merry, wonderful Christmas, my darling, and know that I'll be thinking of you constantly. Please write to me.
>
> I Love You,
> Andrea

Billingsley stared at her handwriting and imagined the day he would see her again. He tried to picture her look when she would answer the doorbell to find him standing on the porch. The surprise, the smile, the embrace, the kiss, the whole sweet, romantic, loving scene. Soothing thoughts, they were. Soothing enough that he fell off to sleep in the quiet of the tent.

Two hours later Steve Page entered the tent and shook Billingsley awake.

"Let's go," Page said.

"Where?"

"Captain want us ASAP."

"Are we mounting out? What the hell's coming down, Steve?"

"You'll see. C'mon, dammit. Get a move on," said Page as he walked to the entrance of the tent and waited.

Billingsley grabbed for his utility cap and went with Page to Clarke's tent. Compton was already there, seated on the ground and propped against a foot locker. A small plastic Christmas tree, sent from home, stood on an ammo box next to Clarke's cot. A plastic holly wreath was attached to the side of the tent with boot laces. From the transistor radio near Compton came the sounds of Elvis' *Blue Christmas.*

"Come on in," called Clarke with a motion toward the two.

"Thank you, sir," Billingsley said as he took a seat on the ground next to Compton.

Four empty C-ration cans, filled with chunks of ice, rested on the empty cot alongside Clarke. Beneath the cot was an unopened bottle of blended Canadian whiskey. A canteen of water and three cans of Coke flanked the bottle of whiskey.

Compton winked at Billingsley and pointed toward the bottle.

"Inasmuch as it's Christmas Eve," said Clarke as he sat down on his cot, "I think the officers of Bravo Company ought to enjoy a little yuletide spirit."

Clarke filled each cup to the rim with whiskey. "Tom even managed to scrounge us some ice," he said while pouring.

"There's some Coke and water if you want it, guys. I like mine straight," Compton grinned.

Billingsley accepted a drink from Clarke and, watching the others, refused the offer of a mixer. The water and Cokes went undisturbed.

Compton offered up cigarettes and Page opened a can of mixed nuts for the impromptu party. The whiskey warmed a path through their throats and into their stomachs with each sip. They drank slowly, except Compton.

"First-rate hootch," admired Page.

"We're not going out tonight, are we, skipper?" asked Compton.

"Not supposed to," replied Clarke.

"Then I'll have another."

"Read all your mail, Mike?" Clarke asked.

"Twice," Billingsley answered quickly, drawing a laugh from the others.

Billingsley poured himself another drink, as well as a refill for Clarke and Page. They discussed several items of business while they relaxed, with each of the lieutenants assuring Clarke that the replacements had all been blended into the unit and assigned into squads. They talked leisurely for the better part of an hour. The effects of the alcohol helped to counter the strain and fear that still lingered from the field.

"Everybody freshen their drinks," Clarke ordered. "We're gonna have some toasts."

Clarke stood after each of the tin cups had been refilled. "A toast," he said as the others rose.

Billingsley felt delightfully wobbly when he stood.

"I propose a toast to the Corps. Gentlemen, may Marines exist for as long as the country," said Clarke.

"To the Corps," repeated the others in unison, raising their drinks and then sipping.

"I have a toast to propose," said Compton.

"This ought to be a good one," joked Page with a giggle.

"I toast the grunts," said Compton. "The little green men who jump in the holes and kill the motherfuckers."

"To the grunts."

"Okay, Steve. Let's hear yours," ordered Clarke.

Page rubbed his chin for a moment, grinning. "I propose a toast to the USA. May she win all her wars and produce millions of round-eyed beauties."

"To the USA."

"To war," added Compton.

"To the production of round-eyed beauties," Billingsley said.

They stood and awaited the offering from Billingsley.

"Well?" Page said.

"Hang on a sec, Mike. Let me get another hit," Compton said as he reached for the bottle. "This is the best shit I've ever had the honor and the privilege to taste, skipper."

"A toast to Canada," Billingsley finally said, raising his cup, "for the foresight to make this excellent booze for us."

"To Canada."

"To this excellent booze," Compton added.

"To foresight," said Page. "That's something we don't seem to have much of since we're spending Christmas near the DMZ."

"To Christmas," said Billingsley.

"To the DM fucking Z," laughed Compton.

They all laughed, especially Clarke. The CO finally raised his hand and summoned his tipsy officers to silence. Clarke looked at the ground for a moment, then took a deep breath.

"I want to make a few comments, gentlemen, before we all end up mostly shitfaced."

The lieutenants stood quietly and gave Clarke their full attention.

"We're all a long way from home during this special night. A long way from our loved ones, the people who mean so much to each of us. It's not easy, particularly at this time of the year. It never is. And I don't suppose it ever will be.

"We've got a heavy load to carry. A lot of young men in our care. A lot of futures. A lot of life. Our people depend on us to make good decisions, to provide them with the type of leadership they all deserve. Anything less, and we cheat a lot more than just ourselves. We cheat the best troops in the world. We cheat those futures, those lives. We cheat the men of Bravo Company, First Battalion, Third Marines."

Billingsley thought he saw moisture in Captain Clarke's eyes.

"I look at this group as a team . . . a damned good team. We need each other to make the whole thing work out. And if it works out, then by the very nature of working out, we give our Marines the kind of leadership they deserve. I just want each of you to know that I'm very proud to have you as part of my team. We've been under fire together . . . a lot of miles together . . . a lot of good times and, for damn sure, enough of the bad times. I know that you'll continue to do your very best, at all times, to keep this the best rifle company in the Corps.

"We do a job that doesn't pay all that well, that takes us a long way from home, that subjects us to a fair amount of risk ... but we do it well ... because we care ... because we're Marines ... because we're a team. I'm happy to have each of you in my unit, and in my tent tonight, on Christmas Eve.

"Gentlemen, Merry Christmas," said Clarke, raising his drink.

"Merry Christmas, sir."

Billingsley wondered if Clarke could see the moistness of his own eyes.

5

The new year, 1969, brought few changes to the lives of the men of Company B, First Battalion, Third Marines. The holiday season had passed with little fanfare or festivity. Bob Hope had come and gone in Vietnam. Richard Nixon had come and Lyndon Johnson had gone in Washington. Formal truce negotiations had begun in Paris in late January, offering a glimmer of hope. There was talk of Vietnamization, of the shifting of the preponderance of the military burden to the South Vietnamese. But it all had little effect on the lives and actions of the Americans in the field. They still fought and they still died. They still came and they still went. The talks, the commitments, the dollars, the protests, and the change from the Democrats to the Republicans meant little to the men in the field. There was still a shooting war.

Billingsley had become increasingly proficient as a combat leader. He had earned the respect of his troops for his competency and his fairness in his dealings with them. He had come to know his people quickly, their tendencies and their strengths. He had a good group, he knew, the best group in the company. He was impressed with his men's aggressiveness and resiliency. He had seen them fight with the ferocity of wild animals and later complain like spoiled children about the numerous discomforts of Vietnam. They always responded, though, and he enjoyed his command of them.

Billingsley also came to know his enemy. He was impressed as well with the cunning and courage of his foe. He had faced the NVA often enough to know that they were a disciplined and determined adversary, a far cry from the rag-tag Viet Cong. The NVA wasted nothing, for they carried their ammunition and supplies much too far to expend them needlessly

137

or foolishly. They could be beaten, Billingsley had discovered, but to take them lightly could be extremely injudicious.

As January drew to a close, Billingsley had completed nearly sixty days of his tour in Vietnam. Out of necessity, he had become hardened to the harshness of the war, with its cruelty and its suffering, its agony and randomness. Clarke had taught him that command in combat was a tough, no-nonsense endeavor. There were no vestiges of the glory so often illustrated in sagas of war. It was mean and dirty, where young men screamed for their mothers as they lay hopelessly mangled far away from home. There was no melodrama, no "higher principles" echoing across the silent battleground, no sensationalism. There was only fatigue and fear, images of horrible violence, and comfort and stability in the presence of one's buddies.

Bravo Company had continued its routine of patrolling the areas surrounding Con Thien. Contact had been limited and sporadic. Quang Tri Province was considered as secure as any area of the country, and more so than most. Quang Tri was not, however, without its share of enemy soldiers. Much infiltration of North Vietnamese soldiers into the south continued. A fight could generally be found in Quang Tri without an exhaustive search, particularly if the NVA so chose.

A Marine reconnaissance unit operating well within the jungle canopy to the southwest of Con Thien had observed enemy movement along a well-concealed jungle trail. They were taking troops and supplies to several strongpoints in the area. Bravo Company was ordered into the jungle to attempt to interdict the enemy's chain of supply. The company set up a base of operations on a ridge that had been partially cleared during previous aerial bombardments. The ridge extended for approximately 200 meters and provided sufficient observation in all directions. Clarke sent his platoons into the thick jungle to try to locate an enemy base camp.

Billingsley was ordered to set his platoon along the trail in question for a night ambush. Artillery targets had been plotted by Clarke to cover the platoon's movement to and from the point on the trail some 800 meters to the west of Bravo Company's position on the ridge. Billingsley waited until darkness to move his platoon off the ridge and toward the trail.

Getting to the ambush site was slow and cumbersome in the dark, thick jungle. The clinging vines and the undergrowth made it difficult to move silently, for the men kept tripping.

They struggled forward, moving cautiously and deliberately. Nearly three hours later the column halted and word was sent through the line for Billingsley to come to the front.

"This must be it," Stacey whispered as he and Billingsley strained at the head of the column to see the small opening along the jungle floor. "It ain't for shit, though. But it's gotta be the one we want."

"Well, it's running north to south. And the distance from the ridge seems about right," Billingsley surmised.

"What do you think, sir?"

"We haven't passed any other trails. I thought it'd be wider than this, though."

"I woulda thought so, too. Wanna push on ahead and come back to it if we don't find nothin' else?"

"Not especially. Do you?"

"Not especially, sir," Stacey whispered cautiously.

"Dammit, this has got to be it. It's just overgrown to beat all hell. This is our spot, Stacey."

"Wanna set 'em in?"

Billingsley strained in the darkness of the jungle for any visual signs to confirm his judgement. He saw little apart from the shadowy figure of Stacey. Billingsley knew all the signs pointed to his location as being the correct one, though there was always doubt at night when positive identification was hampered. And he didn't want to push the platoon further into the foreboding jungle.

"Yeah," he whispered quietly.

Tyler assisted in spreading the platoon along the trail. Billingsley placed a team with a radio on the far northern flank to provide early warning in the event the enemy moved toward them from the most-likely direction. He told the radioman on the flank to key the radio's handset three times to indicate the enemy's appearance, then a quick succession of times if the size of the enemy force appeared to be larger than that of a squad. Billingsley would then gauge the appropriate time to initiate the ambush with a burst of automatic fire from his own weapon.

The wait began. The trap was set. The darkness was nearly total. Each man had experienced the same sort of scene before: the same fatigue, the same nervousness, the same bother from the insects. The Marines waited for their prey on slightly higher ground about fifteen feet from the trail. The foliage was thick around them, though patches of the trail could be seen.

Billingsley's senses were sharpened, as was typical on an ambush mission. He waited near the trail, prone, with one hand underneath the flattened plastic stock of his M-16 and the other near the trigger housing. He listened in the eerie quiet for any indication of movement along the trail. Nothing yet. Only the sound of his own breathing. Could they get through here undetected? Could they actually slip through? Could they come up behind us?

The wait continued.

Martindale was stretched out alongside, with the radio. Billingsley glanced at the luminous dials of his watch. 2325. They had been in place for over two hours. His muscles had already begun to ache. Damn, he thought. Should've taken a crap earlier. Another glance at his watch. 2332.

Nothing moved on the trail.

Another night without sleep, another long tomorrow, he concluded. Andrea walked slowly along the beach as his imagination began its inevitable takeover. She was alone, and so naturally beautiful. Her hair blew in the wind. There, on her face, as clear as the sun, was The Smile. She was perfect. Another glance. 2350. He returned to Andrea. He could almost hear her voice, smell her perfume, taste her kiss. He owned nothing that he wouldn't have given in triplicate to be with her again. That very moment. Another glance. It was midnight.

Nothing moved on the trail.

Hope everyone's awake, he thought. Sleep could come so easily. Heavy eyes and nodding head. He struggled with his fatigue. They aren't coming, he concluded. They'd rather us lay out here like dumbasses, nervous and sleepless, than to walk through here and give us a chance to kick their skinny butts. Always like this, always the same. Wait, wait, wait, and then nothing.

Suddenly, Martindale leaned over and touched Billingsley three times on the arm. The signal from up the trail had been sent. Someone was moving on the trail.

How many? The question screamed in Billingsley's head.

No further signals were sent.

The first detectable noise from the trail was that of a weapon sling as it slapped against the wooden stock of a rifle. Then the faint slap of a sandal as an unseen foot stepped into a slight depression in the trail. *They're here!* Billingsley adjusted his gaze above the trail and darted his eyes quickly from side to side. He thought he saw movement, though he wasn't certain. Now? he thought. Should I jump 'em now? His heart pounded with such a fury that he feared the enemy soldiers would hear it.

Billingsley fired the first burst at the trail, followed by an immediate fusillade from his Marines. Flashes from the trail indicated that the stunned enemy soldiers were attempting to defend themselves. The quiet of the night air was shattered by deafening gunfire. Billingsley sprayed the trail with a full magazine and then waited. He watched for signs of further movement and resistance while his men continued to rake the area with fire.

It was over in less than two minutes.

"This is Bravo Two. Does it look like we got 'em all?" Billingsley called to the team on the flank.

"Negative. Coupla stragglers booked up the trail. Should we go after 'em?"

"Negative. Stay put and cover us while we search the trail."

"Roger, we've got the front door."

Billingsley rose from his position and shouted to Ambrosetti to seal off the other flank. Tyler was already on the trail, with two others. They groped around in the dark, eventually searching the bodies and collecting the weapons. Billingsley inserted a fresh magazine in his rifle and moved toward the trail, toward Tyler. Martindale, attempting to follow Billingsley, stepped into a slight depression and fell. He landed heavily on his side, causing his helmet to go flying from his head. He muttered a disgusted "well, shit," and then felt Billingsley's helping hand underneath his arm. He never stopped to search for his helmet.

"Looks good," said Tyler. "One of 'em has papers."

"How many you got?" Billingsley asked.

"Five."

"Anybody hit?" Billingsley called to the squad leaders.

"The doc's got a flesh wound," replied Stacey as he bandaged the creased skin above the eye of the corpsman. "It ain't bad."

"Anybody else?"

"Negative," came the replies from Sanchez and Ambrosetti.

"Martindale, tell Bravo we've got five bodies. One friendly WIA, not serious. Tell 'em we're on our way back in," ordered Billingsley.

Billingsley knelt beside Tyler, who was busy slinging a load of enemy rifles across his back.

"Let's get the hell out of Dodge," advised Billingsley.

"No shit. We can't hide now."

"Sanchez, you're on the point. Get 'em on their horses."

"Right."

"Ambro?"

"Yo, over here."

"You've got the back door."

"Roger that."

"Stacey?"

"Over here."

"Can the doc make it?"

"He's on his feet."

"Skipper wants to know if you want the arty, sir?" relayed Martindale.

"Tell him I'll want the trail blasted when we're clear. I'll let him know. And Martindale, call the team on the north flank and tell 'em to join up with the rest."

As soon as the two men had joined their squad, Billingsley ordered Sanchez to begin moving toward the company position. The hacking through the jungle continued as the invigorated Marines remained on the alert. When the platoon was approximately 200 meters from the trail, Billingsley radioed Clarke to shift the artillery to the north of the ambush point, 400 meters up the trail.

"Let it rip whenever you're able," Billingsley called.

"Roger, it'll be on the target soon," Clarke replied.

The projectiles were shrieking overhead within five minutes. The trail was pounded for another five minutes as the platoon continued on toward the Bravo position.

The return to the ridge was slow and uneventful. Once back, the weary men of the platoon were able to gather a few hours of sleep before dawn.

Clarke and Billingsley examined the captured documents when morning came. One of the maps detailed the area surrounding Con Thien. A map of Cam Lo was also included, with notations written in the margins. Both maps were accurate and current. Clarke sent the documents to the rear via the re-supply helicopter which came later in the morning.

The company went back to its patrolling. Within two days, a Bravo Company patrol had discovered an enemy fortification deep within the jungle to the west of the position. A bunker complex, housing an estimated platoon of NVA soldiers, was located on the slopes of a spiny ridge which was covered by a thick, sheltering canopy. Steve Page's platoon had discovered the camp during a routine patrol. The ensuing clash had brought Page's group under withering small-arms and automatic-weapons fire, pinning them down and inflicting heavy casualties. Since then, Page had aborted a third attempt at dislodging the enemy from their stronghold after having been repulsed on two previous occasions.

By the time Clarke arrived on the scene with his command group and his remaining two platoons, a pair of Marine F-4 Phantoms were already on station. Clarke immediately directed his Forward Air Controller to concentrate on bombing runs upon the crest and reverse slope of the ridge. The FAC, himself a Marine aviator, coordinated the runs. Soon the ground shook and the air rumbled with the explosions. The pilots then fired rockets into the opening in the canopy created by the bombs. The ground troops readied for an assault.

Third Platoon had been somewhat depleted with casualties, among them Steve Page. Page had been hit twice, once during each of the attempts to reach the crest. He was near death by the time Clarke had arrived on the scene to oversee the battle. A medevac chopper was met by a hail of enemy bullets when it attempted to land in a small clearing to the rear of the position. The enemy gunners fired on the craft so heavily that it crashed in flames in the clearing. Only one of its crew escaped the inferno.

Steve Page, shot in the arm and lower abdomen, died from his wounds while a corpsman worked feverishly over him in an effort to control his profuse bleeding.

The cost, Clarke realized, would be even heavier.

Billingsley's platoon was assigned to attack the enemy from its southwest flank while First and Third platoons created a base of fire to the NVA's front. The flanking movement required an uphill thrust, the thought of which chilled Billingsley, who was already tense. He issued the orders to his squad leaders in as calm a voice as he could muster, though he knew his concern must be visible. The platoon was in a tough spot, he knew. It almost seemed like suicide.

"Any questions?" he asked after issuing the orders to his wide-eyed squad leaders and the cool, professional Tyler.

There were none.

"Okay, get in position and wait for the word to jump off."

Second Platoon maneuvered to the base of the ridge. The base of fire from the other platoons slammed into the NVA front as Clarke ordered Billingsley to commence the attack up the slopes. Two of Billingsley's squads moved alongside one another before the NVA detected the attempt at envelopment and directed their fire upon the Marines. Billingsley saw two of his men at the front of the platoon fall. The two bodies were continuously riddled as they lay exposed only thirty meters from the first of the NVA bunkers. The confusion and noise of battle was extraordinary, and Billingsley felt that the attack was bogging down from the very start. He wanted napalm on the ridge, but his troops were too close to the enemy to risk it. His men moved singly and in pairs, sometimes able to advance perhaps ten feet before diving for cover or being hit.

The small advances continued for the next thirty minutes. Still, the platoon was short of the objective.

"What is your position, Bravo Two?" radioed Clarke.

"Twenty meters from the right flank. We can hardly move."

"Roger. I've got gunships on the way and I want you to hold on to what you've got. Can you mark your pos?"

"Affirmative. I have smoke."

Billingsley strained to hear the chopper over the noise of the gunfire. He heard only the fury of the firing and an occasional grenade explosion. He ordered the squads to halt as he awaited word from Clarke.

"Okay Bravo Two. Gimme the smoke." Clarke sounded calm and controlled.

"Roger, wait one," replied Billingsley.

Billingsley and Martindale dashed to a position just behind his lead elements. They dove for cover in a fresh bomb crater while bullets from nearby NVA defenders whooshed overhead. Billingsley leaned on his side and hurled the smoke grenade as far as he could at the enemy. He then heard the chopper's rotors in the background.

"This is Bravo Two. My smoke is on the ground. Keep the fire at least twenty meters to the northeast of the smoke, on the uphill side. Any closer and it'll be in here on us," advised Billingsley.

"Roger, understand. I can see white smoke. That yours?" asked Clarke.

"That's affirm."

Soon the single gunship was firing its rockets into the fortified bunker complex. The chopper flew along the axis of the ridge and made its passes quickly to avoid the return fire. When its rockets were expended, the gunship opened up with its mini-guns.

"Bravo Two, I will advise when the fire has lifted. Then I want you to jump 'em while I bring the rest over the top from the front. Set up and pinch the flank, and we'll assault through," Clarke ordered.

"Roger. See you at the top."

Billingsley passed the order to his squads for the final phase of the attack. The gunship still made its darting passes. Martindale paled, and he suddenly turned on his side and retched. Bile dripped from his chin.

"Get hold of yourself, Martindale." Billingsley shook his young radioman by the shoulder. "We'll be okay. C'mon, dammit! Stay close to me when we move out."

"Oh, Jesus," Martindale said as he wiped his chin.

The chopper made another pass, its mini-guns popping, and then quickly peeled away from the ridge. The NVA gunfire continued, but not so heavily.

"Okay, Bravo Two. Do your thing," Clarke radioed.

Billingsley responded with a "roger" and jumped up. "LET'S MOVE. UP AND MOVING. C'MON, DAMMIT, LET'S GET IT ON. MOVE UP, MOVE."

Billingsley and Martindale rushed forward with the others. Tyler shouted orders also, trying to keep the advance intact, despite the fire from the NVA. The platoon swept ahead. They were able to reach the extreme right flank of the enemy and fired at point-blank range at the few NVA soldiers still alive. Bodies of the enemy dead littered the trenches, with some in piles of three and four. Billingsley saw his grenadiers firing their M-79s at pockets of NVA who were attempting to escape down the far side of the ridge.

"We could use the air again to cut off the escape. Get the CO on the horn," Billingsley shouted to Martindale.

First and Third platoons rushed over the crest of the ridge and destroyed most of the remaining enemy while Second Platoon held onto the flank. Marines covered the top of the ridge, still exchanging gunfire with the NVA.

"I can't raise the CO," advised Martindale.

"Keep trying."

Only light resistance continued once the sweeping Marines penetrated the NVA bunker sites. Billingsley maneuvered his platoon on a line and remained on the flank until the firing had ceased. The smell of powder hung in the air like a fog.

It was over, finally.

Billingsley started counting casualties taken by his platoon. He saw Tyler who, with a corpsman and several others, knelt over a fallen Marine behind the existing positions. Other wounded were being assisted up the hill.

"It's Stacey," Tyler said.

Billingsley looked down at his squad leader as the corpsman continued to administer first aid.

"How bad?"

"He ain't movin'," Tyler said grimly.

The corpsman tried to find a pulse in Stacey's wrist and neck. The young squad leader's utility shirt was drenched in blood from a gunshot wound squarely in the center of the chest. His flak jacket, open and unzipped, had protected Stacey's upper torso from the sides and back only.

"Nope, he's bought it," the corpsman finally mumbled.

Billingsley stared at Stacey's youthful face. The eyes were partially opened, the lips slightly parted. And the blood. God, the blood, he thought. Several of Stacey's squad members covered their leader with a poncho when the corpsman left to attend to the other wounded.

"Son of a bitch," Billingsley said, disgusted. "How many others do we have?"

"At least three more KIAs. Nine WIAs, and some of 'em ain't gonna make it unless we get 'em the hell out," Tyler advised.

"Bravo One's on the horn, sir," Martindale called as he ran up.

"This is Bravo Two," Billingsley said.

*"Bravo One. The Six is WIA, and the CP is now with me.
Get your casualties ready for evac and report to me in zero-five."*
It was Compton's steady voice.

"Roger. Anything else?"

"Set your people four to eight."

"Four to eight, roger."

Billingsley turned to Tyler, who was smoking a cigarette and gazing over the adjacent terrain.

"Set 'em in, four to eight. And get the casualties ready to go out," Billingsley said.

"Aye-aye, sir."

Billingsley made sure the casualties were ready and the platoon sector was established before he went to find Tom Compton in a trench in the middle of the position. Compton alternately held two radios to his ear as he coordinated the medevac and reported on the action to higher headquarters. Resting against a tree stump was Captain Clarke. Clarke's left trouser leg had been cut away, exposing a bloody mass of thick bandages covering his knee. He sat upright, pale and weak, and was attended by a corpsman.

"You okay, sir?" Billingsley knelt by Clarke.

"I'm all right," Clarke answered, holding his cigarette with a trembling hand.

"His kneecap's busted all to shit," the corpsman whispered. "Rifle round, dead on it."

"Mike?" Clarke called.

"Yessir."

"When Tom gets off the radio, tell him to make sure the badly wounded get out first."

"No problem, skipper. He knows to do that."

"I'll go out last, with Page and the rest of the dead."

"Page, sir?"

"Yeah, Steve's KIA."

The news stunned Billingsley, as if cold water had been thrown in his face. Page. Page with the smiling, jovial face. Now Page, like Stacey, was only a memory.

"Choppers," several Marines shouted as the thumping rotors were heard in the distance.

Billingsley glanced at Clarke, who looked drugged. "Take care, sir."

"Good luck, Mike."

The medevacs came in one at a time, taking on the casualties and nosing forward as they flew off the ridge. Billingsley watched as nearly one-third of the company was removed. His remaining men had a distant look on their dirt-stained faces, a look that did little to betray the feelings and emotions hidden behind their glazed eyes. They seemed so old to be so young. He wondered if he looked that way, too. Sherman was right about war, he thought.

Billingsley sat in a crater to the front of his position and peered into the jungle, looking and listening for any signs of the enemy. All was quiet on the ridge and the areas around it in the waning light, but an uneasiness was in the air. Tom Compton startled Billingsley when the new CO unexpectedly jumped into the crater with a thud. "I've been looking all over the friggin' hill for you, ace."

"I've been right here for a while."

"We're pulling out."

"When?"

"Soon, as quickly as it's good and damned dark."

"Where to?"

"To an extraction point about a klick east of the jungle. We'll be picked up at first light."

"Then what?"

"Back to Evans, I think."

"Will they let you keep command of the company?"

"Don't know. Probably not, if they have any spare captains floating around."

"Okay, skipper. Lead the way, and I'll follow," Billingsley grinned and shrugged.

"That's what I want to talk to you about."

"What's that?"

"I want your platoon on the point for the night movement."

"Thanks a shitload, Tom."

"No, listen to me. You're the only officer left in command of a platoon. Sergeant Kupton has mine now, and Sergeant Baird has Third. I want you and Tyler up there ahead, getting us out of this damned jungle. If you can do that, I'll manage the rest."

"You can count on me, Tom. I ain't got any bitches about leaving here."

"I know I can. But I don't know about Baird. And that Gunny Kennerly is a total fucking waste of a Marine."

"Tom, what happened to Steve?"

"Gut-shot, mainly. I didn't see him until he was already dead. They did a number on our command structure, didn't they?"

"Sure did. It was lunacy, Tom. Complete Goddamned lunacy. The whole thing."

"Once you're in it up to your ass, there ain't no turning back."

"It was still lunacy."

"Right. Get up to my CP and we'll go over the route. Make sure your people are fed."

Billingsley watched Compton trot off toward the crest of the ridge. He sat for a moment longer, contemplating the ability of war to alter events so quickly. Clarke, the father figure, the patient professional, was gone. The likable Page was gone forever. And Corporal Stacey would be going back to Kansas prematurely, in a pine box, ending a promising career in agriculture before it had a chance to begin. He felt dazed by it all, and numbed, sitting there alone. Finally, he got up and left.

The order of march out of the jungle was detailed by Compton as he convened and briefed the platoon leaders at the CP. Billingsley's platoon was assigned to the point position. Compton intended to move the company to the fringe of the jungle, still inside and underneath the canopy, where the men would rest for a few hours before moving to the rendezvous point in the early morning hours.

Billingsley installed the squad of Sanchez at the front of the column as Bravo moved off the ridge and into the dense darkness of the jungle. The leaders had emphasized the obvious importance of noise discipline, but the difficulty of movement produced the inevitable chopping, stumbling, and profanity, especially along the point.

"*Fuck* this shit, man!" Billingsley heard the familiar sound of a man's feet entangled in vines and then a fall.

"Damn bush, man. Damn *sorry ass* bush."

"Cut the bullshit and keep it moving," Billingsley whispered, silencing the man.

Billingsley rotated the point men and point squads evenly to distribute the misery and maintain a higher level of alertness at the front. Because of the darkness, there was frequent stopping and starting in the column as the point men struggled to keep the company on course. They took numerous compass readings, sometimes only after thirty or forty meters in the dense and dark jungle. Many of the men in the column actually reached out and touched the pack or entrenching tool of the man to his front. The fear of separation was always present. Word came from the rear of the column on four occasions that contact had been broken. Each time, there was a delay until the separated Marines were found.

Three hours later the denseness began to thin. The company was nearing the open country beyond the jungle. When the clearing beyond was confirmed, Compton halted the company just inside the cover of the jungle. A perimeter was established, with Billingsley's platoon facing to the east, toward the open ground. The temperatures dipped, and the men in their damp uniforms were chilled.

Billingsley's feet ached as he lay under his poncho on the jungle floor. He was exhausted from the strain of leading the movement, even though the distance had not been excessive. Cuts and scratches from the foliage smarted on his hands and arms. Adding to the discomfort was a steady rain which had begun to fall shortly before the company had settled into its position. Though the rain was bothersome, it did lessen the persecution by insects.

A few hours of rest, however uncomfortable, did have a positive effect upon the tired troops. The company got up before daybreak and covered the final distance to their pickup point, arriving only minutes before the sun rose. The helicopters came on schedule and the extraction was executed smoothly.

Once again the greenness of the countryside flowed beneath Bravo Company as the formation of helicopters returned the men to Camp Evans and to hot chow, showers, and dry clothes. Many of the men had skin infections, and several had respiratory ailments which, in the severest of cases, resembled pneumonia. Replacements were greeted and augmented into the ranks of the depleted company. And the word circulating throughout the camp indicated that Operation Dewey Canyon, involving the Ninth Marines, was proceeding successfully in the Da Krong Valley area.

Compton met with Colonel Fletcher and was advised that a new platoon leader was scheduled to join Bravo Company. Command of the company was to remain with Compton until further notice.

Compton and Billingsley shared a CP tent and enjoyed the well-earned break. Billingsley had taken time from his rifle maintenance to read a letter from Andrea. She wrote of her conclusion that the Paris talks would precipitate an end to the fighting and would permit an early departure of the troops from Vietnam. She was certain of it.

"My girlfriend says the war will be over by summer," Billingsley grinned as he sat on his cot holding the letter.

"How did she arrive at that?" Compton was cleaning his pistol.

"Listen to this: 'So don't worry, Mike. Nixon will have you out in a jiff. Then you can come home and tell everyone that you personally saw the war to its conclusion. Just please be careful in the meantime. Please, please, please.'"

"Sounds a little like a Beatles tune, doesn't it? Please, please, please," Compton said as he laughed along with Billingsley.

"Yeah. I hope she's right."

"Honest to God, Mike, I have trouble remembering what it's like back in the world," Compton sighed.

"Big cars, big cities, big girls with big asses."

"It seems like I've been over here humping through the boonies all my life. I'm getting Asiatic, I think."

"Your eyes *have* taken on a noticeable slant, Tom. Ever get a craving for rice and fish?"

"I crave several things, but not any Goddamned rice and fish."

"Would one of your cravings involve a certain young lady who goes by the name of Chris and resides in Baltimore?"

"Bet your ass, cowboy!"

"How is Chris?"

"She's having some morning sickness, still. But she's a feisty little shit. She'll be okay."

First Sergeant Day opened the flap of the tent and stuck his head inside, looking for Compton. "Knock, knock," he called.

"Come on in, top," said Compton.

"You've got a new officer, sir. Just reported aboard. Want me to bring him in?" asked Day.

"Sure," replied Compton, "Bring him on in."

Day was followed into the tent by a man in a clean uniform. Day introduced Second Lieutenant Art Ivester, a tall, spectacled newcomer to Vietnam. Ivester was greeted enthusiastically by the two while Day left to procure another cot.

"Bring your gear in, Art, and put it in the corner over there," Billingsley said, offering a hand.

"Where you from, Art?" Compton asked when his new officer's gear was brought inside the tent.

"Indianapolis, sir."

"You don't have to 'sir' me. And you won't need those gold bars for a good while. Did First Sergeant Day get you checked in, and all that bullshit?"

"He sure did. I also met Gunny Kennerly, too."

"Good. I'll take you down to Third Platoon's area in a bit and let you meet Sergeant Baird and the others. You'll be taking over that platoon, effective now."

"That's great. I understand the former platoon leader was killed yesterday. Is that correct?"

"That is correct. And I inherited the job as CO yesterday, too. Does that give you the impression that yesterday was a complete fucking bummer?"

"It certainly does."

"Well, you're right."

"Are you married, Art?" Billingsley asked.

"Sure am."

"Any kids?"

"Not yet," Ivester smiled. "I've only been married a little over six months."

"When did you last eat?" asked Compton.

"Early this morning, in Da Nang."

"Here's a box of Cs." Compton tossed the box to Ivester. "Something and potatoes, I think. It ought to hold you until morning."

"Will we be going out soon?" Ivester asked.

"Tomorrow, to the southwest of here. We'll be out for a good while, I do believe," Compton predicted with a wink toward Billingsley.

Ivester ate heartily while continuing the small talk with Compton and Billingsley. Neither Compton nor Billingsley made any reference to Steve Page, but both silently felt the loss. It just wasn't the same without Page in the tent, though Ivester appeared as if he might easily fit. He was unpretentious and deferential toward his two more-experienced fellow officers. He appeared serious, unlike the flippant Page, but he seemed to enjoy the ribald humor. He talked softly and smiled a faint, uneasy smile that reflected his basic shyness. He spoke unhurriedly and listened intently while the others told him of Bravo Company, of life in Vietnam.

Compton later escorted Ivester to the Third Platoon area to meet Sergeant Baird and the squad leaders. Compton left Ivester to get to know his key personnel. Ivester's relaxed and easy way of dealing with people served him well.

The three officers finally settled into their cots around midnight. Billingsley and Compton shortly discovered that their newest addition snored with the unbounded fury of a choking rhinoceros. It started only minutes after Ivester leaned back upon his cot and showed no signs of easing after a full hour.

"Well, *shit!*" Billingsley sighed, unable to sleep.

"The bastard's going to suck the tent down around us," Compton observed, awake as well.

They listened to Ivester's open-mouthed rumblings until Compton could take it no longer.

"Hey, Art. You awake?"

The snoring continued unabated.

"ART, WAKE UP."

"Yeah, what is it?" Ivester said, stirring and licking his dry lips.

"Did you hear it?"

"No. What was it?"

"How about you, Mike? Did you happen to hear it?"

"Damned right, I heard it."

"*What?* What the hell *was* it?" questioned the aroused Ivester.

"I hope to God it's not what I thought it was," said Compton.

"So do I, man. So do I," added Billingsley in an ominous tone.

"Goddamn, what's the deal?"

"Probably nothing, Art. Better keep quiet for a little while, though. If it's what I think it is, we'll know soon," Compton said as he rolled onto his side.

"Yeah, just try to relax and stay calm, Art. Hopefully, it'll just pass," Billingsley said.

Once Compton and Billingsley stopped silently laughing, they fell asleep. Meanwhile, Ivester felt for his weapon, pulling it close while he waited and wondered. The remainder of the night passed peacefully. And silently.

Bravo Company departed early the following morning and traveled by truck convoy to the paddy and dike country northwest of Camp Evans, and north of Route Nine. Then they moved on foot through the mostly open terrain to the west, while companies A and C operated to the north and east. All of the first day of the operation Bravo Company searched for an enemy whose presence in the area was known by intelligence experts to be of at least battalion strength. Bravo Company had a quiet day, making no contact with enemy units.

They continued to the west on the second day, through several villages and across Route 561. Then it was back into the paddies, the thick, sucking mud pulling at the feet and clinging to the boots of the Marines. The barefoot villagers worked in the warm sun, transferring rice from seedbeds and ignoring the heavily equipped intruders who sloshed through the countryside. Third Platoon discovered a small enemy force while sweeping on the far left flank of the company, and there was a brisk fire fight for ten minutes. The surviving enemy soldiers disappeared into a thicket of trees, leaving behind two of their dead, one of them a woman. Art Ivester had heard and seen combat for the first time. The Marines suffered no injuries.

Compton was ordered to swing the company to the south-west on the third day, toward the Cam Lo River. They reached the river by late morning and followed its snaking course for approximately 3,000 meters. The explosion of a booby trap beside a river trail killed one of Ivester's men and severed the right hand of another. A third man was hit by fragments along the hip and leg. Coincidentally, two snipers from the opposite side of the river opened fire with small arms on the Marines. The Marines' heavy gunfire discouraged the snipers from pressing the matter, and they withdrew before inflicting any further damage. Ivester was nearly sickened when he saw blood dripping from the foliage near the booby trap, along with pieces of flesh and uniform in the middle of the trail. A medevac chopper was hurried into and out of the area within fifteen minutes of the explosion.

On the morning of the fourth day, Compton moved Bravo to the north to serve as a blocking force while companies A and C pushed into a concealed enemy position in an island of trees. The company set out on a forced march, quickly closing the 3,000 meters to their assigned location. They arrived nearly exhausted, though they were able to set themselves into a position west of and behind the enemy's emplacement. Colonel Fletcher circled overhead in his helicopter, directing Alpha and Charlie companies as they prepared to assault from the east. The plan was simple but classic—attack the enemy frontally and push him into the 300 meters of open space to his rear where he can be finished off by the blocking force.

Bravo waited as the attack began. The NVA unit resisted in its usual determined fashion, though they soon realized the numerical strength of the Marines was decidedly unfavorable. When pressure from Alpha and Charlie began to crumble the enemy's defenses, a dozen NVA soldiers sprinted desperately across the open ground to their rear. When they were within 100 meters of the waiting Bravo Company, a wild burst of gunfire from the Marines kicked up the dirt around the falling NVA. Billingsley watched the slaughter as the exposed enemy soldiers were riddled with bullets. One NVA soldier, wounded in the upper body, fell over on his back after being hit. He attempted to regain his feet and turn away from the blocking force. Mud flew off the man's shirt as several rounds hit and passed through his body. Only a few of the wounded NVA who were caught in the open were able to fire their weapons at the Bravo Company position before being subdued by the sheer volume of fire.

Resistance from those NVA who had chosen to stand and fight in the treeline continued savagely for nearly two hours before the maneuvering Marines eventually destroyed them with small arms and hand grenades. Fletcher stayed in his airborne control position until the fighting had subsided, later landing in the open area in front of Bravo. Fletcher watched as over forty enemy bodies were stacked near the treeline. The medevacs came to collect the twelve Marine dead and twenty wounded.

Compton met with Fletcher and the other commanders in a CP established within the treeline where the bulk of the fighting had taken place. Fletcher spoke of the plans to enter Cua Valley, to the south, to search for VC who were presumed to be using part of the area for a rehabilitation and rest center, the exact locations unknown. The operation was to begin on the following morning.

The briefing concluded in an hour and Compton walked across the open area to Bravo's position. The low sun had begun to fade behind puffy clouds. When the platoon leaders had been briefed on the latest plans, Compton motioned for Billingsley to join him on the ground for a meal of cold C-rations and warm canteen water.

"This is unusual, ace," Compton said between sips of the thick, sugary juice from his can of peaches.

"What's unusual?"

"*This!* Being *here!*"

"Why is being here unusual, Tom? This is Vietnam, isn't it?"

"It's unusual because we've denied the enemy a piece of ground, and we're *staying.*"

"Okay with me. Beats the hell out of the friggin' jungle," Billingsley shrugged.

"Fuckin' A it does. This duty is joe-toe. I even saw Fletcher tell his radioman to take his camera and get some pictures of the dead gooks," Compton said with a mischievous grin.

"How many dead gooks were there?"

"About forty, I heard. Probably report eighty, though."

"Sometimes I think I'm the only one in-country without a damned Instamatic," Billingsley complained. "You got one in your pack?"

"Hell yeah. I want to be able to capture those unforgettable moments."

"Now I know why I don't carry one. I'd like to forget everything about this place."

"I took a bunch of pictures a while back. You know, scenery and all that shit. I had one picture of a dead gook that a recon buddy had snapped and given to me. You know, showed the gook all shot to shit—guts and blood everywhere—and all in living color, too. Well, damned if I didn't screw up and accidentally send the friggin' picture off with all the others, to Chris. Boy, was she pissed. She wrote and chewed my ass royally. Took me two pages to explain the fuckin' thing to her."

"Nice goin'," Billingsley chided, laughing at Compton's embarrassment.

"Yeah, right. Listen, that reminds me. Fletcher's hot on everybody's case about mutilating dead gooks. Somebody in the area must've been collecting ears and fingers. Get the word to your people that the shit'll hit the fan if any 'souvenirs' are taken."

"I've heard some of 'em joke about it, but I haven't seen any of it. I'll get the word out."

"Good. I'll tell Art and Kupton."

"How is Art doing for his first time out?"

"He was scared shitless down on the river. Pale as a fuckin' ghost, I mean. But he didn't freeze. I'll bet he's gonna do okay."

Billingsley placed his empty cans in the cardboard box and started to leave.

"One more thing, Mike."

"What?"

"You know a guy named Bill Blanton, don't you?"

"Yeah. He was my roommate at Basic School. Why?"

"He's a platoon leader over in Alpha Company. Joined 'em in the field a few days ago. He told me to tell you hello when I was over there with the CO. Said he'd heard you were with Bravo."

"I'll be damned. I though he was on some bird colonel's staff at Third Marine Division Headquarters."

"Not anymore. He's a grunt now. Even had his hand all bandaged up."

. "Knowing Bill, he probably cut it on a beer can at Dong Ha," Billingsley said with a laugh.

It was nearly dark when Billingsley returned to the sector of Second Platoon. He was excited about the prospect of a reunion with Bill Blanton. His reminiscing about their good times together was interrupted when Tyler called out from a nearby hole.

"We got us a problem over here, sir. I think you'd better have a look."

"What's up?" Billingsley asked. Tyler looked stern.

"It's Cain, here. He's got a pain in his side and he can't hardly straighten up."

"What's the matter with him, doc?" Billingsley asked the corpsman.

"I'm pretty sure he's got appendicitis. All the symptoms are there."

"What symptoms are those?"

"Fever, nausea, the shits, and acute pain in his right side. I got it myself four years ago, and it sure as hell looks familiar."

"What about it, Cain?" Billingsley asked.

"I'm hurtin', sir. I thought it was just a stitch from all the humpin', but it ain't got no better."

"Okay, Fralich. Do we need to get him out tonight?" Billingsley asked the corpsman.

"I'd say so. It can be a bitch if it bursts."

Billingsley stepped away from the hole with Tyler. "I guess we'd better get him out," he concluded.

"I agree," said Tyler. "Fralich's a good doc, and I trust his judgement. Cain's not any good to us if he's that sick, anyway."

"What about a replacement for him?" Cain had taken over as squad leader when Stacey was killed.

"Maroney's the next senior man. I'll put him in charge."

A medevac chopper collected the sick Marine. It was guided into the open area near the position by Marines with flashlights. The extraction was not hindered by enemy fire.

Within ten minutes, however, artillery was fired by the NVA into and around the Bravo Company position. The shelling lasted scarcely more than fifteen minutes, but one of the rounds scored a direct hit on two of Billingsley's men. One died instantly. The other was left to experience a hideously agonizing death—his lower torso was blown off at the waist. Fralich pumped morphine into what remained of the body, easing the pain in the final few moments of the man's life.

Alpha Company was flown at dawn into the Cua Valley, where they secured an LZ northwest of a Montagnard village. A Buddhist shrine was nearby. Camp Carroll, whose batteries were set to support the operation, lay to the far northwest. The valley was in an area of rolling, spiny, thickly forested hills. The VC had been using the region as a haven and conducting political and military actions there.

Bravo and Charlie companies followed Alpha into the valley.

The landings were uncontested, much to the relief of the troops. Aerial observers, buzzing overhead in the fast OV-10 Broncos, searched the hills and valleys for signs of an enemy presence. Colonel Fletcher and his command group had traveled with Bravo on the way to the LZ.

Fletcher moved the battalion to the north, well away from the populated regions, once the landings had been completed. Popular and Regional Forces, in conjunction with U.S. advisors, assumed the responsibility for the inhabited areas. Since the local forces rarely did more than defend their own compounds, Fletcher had a free rein over the hills and in the valley area north of the settlements. Route 566, connecting Cam Lo and Cua Valley, was deliberately avoided when the battalion began moving along the valley floor. The road was typically mined and often ambushed, so Fletcher chose a slower route along the foot of the hills.

Bravo was assigned to patrol a group of hills to the east of Route 566, with Charlie Company to its north and Alpha Company to the west, across the valley. Once Compton reached his initial objective, a long ridge between two slightly elevated knobs, he sent his platoons to patrol the adjacent area. Billingsley took Second Platoon off the ridge to patrol a series of hills further to the east. All was routine until intermittent small-arms fire was heard to the north. A platoon from Company C had been ambushed by an estimated two squads of VC, resulting in a brisk exchange of gunfire. Billingsley monitored the radio frequency and discovered that another platoon was speeding to the scene of the fight to offer its assistance.

"Charlie Company's in some shit," Billingsley noted to Tyler as Second Platoon took a short break on the crest of a hill.

"Again?"

"Yeah. Got themselves a pretty good little scrap going."

They could see bluish-grey smoke rising from the wooded draw where the fighting continued. Billingsley checked his map; the fighting was about 1,000 meters away.

"They need any help?" inquired Tyler.

"Nah. They said they thought it was only a couple of squads. But another platoon was nearby, so they ought to be able to handle it. Gimme a cigarette."

"Nice way to earn a living, huh?" Tyler handed over his

pack of Marlboros and lay on the ground to watch the distant battle.

"It'd be better if we had a coupla cool ones," laughed Billingsley.

"And a bag of beer nuts, too."

"Yeah, I forgot. Might need a program so we could tell the players."

"Hope our side wins," Tyler grinned. "I don't want to have to leave. Yessir, Mister Billingsley, I could sit up here and watch the war effort of the United States of America for the rest of my tour."

"I'm surprised at you, Sergeant Tyler," kidded Billingsley. "An old pro like yourself, content to sit one out. Why, I woulda thought that you'd want to sprint over there and jump right in the middle of the ass kicking."

Tyler rolled onto his side and glanced mischievously at his platoon leader. "Do you realize, sir, that we're collecting the same combat pay as those fuckers down there shootin' at those gooks?"

Billingsley and Tyler both laughed until they noticed a lone, single-engine plane sputtering as it was hit by heavy ground fire from the VC in the distant draw. Its reduced airspeed indicated that the pilot was losing the struggle to remain airborne.

"He's looking for a place to put it down," Tyler observed.

The plane banked sharply over a nearby hill, its engine still coughing, and crashed on another, wider crest, all in plain sight of the two men. The aircraft disappeared into the trees, with no sign of fire.

"This is Bravo Two. We've got a downed bird about half a klick to the northeast," Billingsley radioed.

"Roger, I saw it," Compton answered. *"Can you get to it?"*

"Affirmative."

"Roger, stay in touch."

"Shoulda known," Tyler said as he mounted his pack and donned his helmet.

The platoon hurried down the hill. They traveled along a narrow valley, crossed another hill, and eventually reached the high ground where the plane rested. Billingsley spread his troops out for the climb to the crest. The VC could have just as easily seen the crash, he knew, so he resisted his inclination to barge recklessly to the top. They moved up slowly, wary of ambush and cognizant of the continued fighting from Company C's position. Billingsley was positioned in the center of the advance.

Ambrosetti's squad was the first to reach the crest. The top of the hill was partially clear of trees, and Ambrosetti quickly spotted the plane. The plane's right wing had been sheared in the crash. The cockpit windshield was shattered and there was damage to the fuselage. By the time Billingsley arrived, Ambrosetti had maneuvered a fire team along the crest to a point thirty meters from the aircraft. They knelt, studying the scene for signs of life—either from the aviators or the VC. A single pistol shot rang out from a thicket of trees and brush to the fire team's front, away from the plane. Another shot was fired, and Ambrosetti radioed to Billingsley to hold the fire of the remainder of the platoon.

"Hey, can you hear me in there?" Ambrosetti called from his prone position near the hill's slope.

There was no reply.

"I SAID CAN YOU HEAR ME IN THERE?"

"I can hear you," came the muffled call.

"WELL HOLD YOUR GODDAMNED FIRE, THEN. WE'RE AMERICAN."

"I need a corpsman over here."

Ambrosetti shouted for the corpsman while he and the remainder of his team rushed toward the thicket. Fralich left his position near Billingsley and trotted off in trace. Billingsley kept the rest of the platoon in place until Ambrosetti emerged moments later and signaled the remainder of his squad forward. He reported that a medevac was urgently needed. Billingsley moved into the thicket and Tyler began setting the platoon into a cordon around the hilltop.

A darkened hole in the pilot's cheek, below and to the right of his left eye, oozed a steady stream of blood. The pilot was stretched out on his back, unconscious, with his head propped on the observer's mapcase. The pilot also bled freely from the nose. The observer, who had dragged the pilot away from the crash, bled profusely from scalp and facial lacerations. His right eye was swollen nearly closed from the impact with the windshield.

"This is Bravo Two. I've got two WIAs up here. We need a priority medevac," Billingsley called.

"Got enough room up there to get it in?" Compton radioed.

"That's a roger."

"Is the LZ hot?"

"Negative."

"I'll get it on the way."

Billingsley walked over to the AO, who was propped against a tree. The man strained to get a clear look at Billingsley from underneath the bandages which covered his face and head. The corpsman, Fralich, still attended to the critically injured pilot.

"How you feelin', hoss?" Billingsley asked the AO, who was a Marine lieutenant.

"I'll be better when I'm off this hill. Sorry about the reception I gave you," the AO said with a weak grin.

"No sweat. You'll be out soon."

"Is the pilot, Captain Collins, still alive?"

"Yeah."

"Jesus, how he managed to get that plane down with a wound like that, I'll never know. The only thing he said after he was hit was 'hang on,' " said the AO.

Billingsley glanced at Fralich, who continued to monitor the breathing and pulse of the unmoving pilot.

Small-arms fire erupted on the opposite side of the hill as a squad of VC ventured up the slopes. Maroney's squad took the first of the VC under immediate fire, killing two.

"Martindale, call the CO and tell him we've got contact. Tell him we'll keep him advised," ordered Billingsley.

"Yessir."

"You people keep your heads down in here."

Crouching, Billingsley made his way to Maroney's side as the shooting continued. Maroney's men were exchanging gunfire with the enemy, keeping low, in the prone position.

"Not that many, sir. Want to slide off and flank 'em?" Maroney asked, excited.

"No. I want you to stay right where you are. Keep the heat on."

Billingsley ran to where Tyler was kneeling and firing at the VC. "Get the bloopers over here and let's work out on the bastards," Billingsley said.

"Right." Tyler slid backwards and ran off.

"Chopper," Martindale shouted from the trees.

Billingsley popped a white smoke grenade and threw it off to his side, near the middle of the platoon's position. He then sprinted to where Martindale knelt with the radio.

"Sir, they want to know how hot the LZ is."

"This is Bravo Two, over," called Billingsley, taking the handset from Martindale.

"Roger, Bravo Two. This is Golden Rod. What's your LZ like down there?" inquired the chopper pilot.

"Warm, but not sizzling. Try to approach from the west and you should be okay. Do you see my smoke?"

"Roger, white smoke. Understand you have two WIAs?"

"Affirmative, both counts. One of 'em is in a world of hurt. He needs to go quickly."

"Roger, we'll take the western approach."

The chopper made a wide swing around the hill, avoiding the area to the east where the sporadic firing continued. The pilot maneuvered his craft into the landing area with the assistance of one of Billingsley's men, who directed it to a level spot. As soon as the chopper was on the ground, Fralich and another man carried the wounded pilot out of the trees, Fralich supporting the pilot under the arms while the other man carried his legs. The AO was able to board the chopper under his own power. The chopper rose and banked sharply to the west, escaping unharmed.

Once Tyler had directed the fire from the grenadiers onto the VC, the outnumbered enemy broke contact and scurried down the hill. Maroney and his squad gave a brief chase and found the bodies of three VC on the side of the hill.

"Will that guy make it, Fralich?" Billingsley asked the corpsman, who had returned to the trees to retrieve his medical gear.

"I doubt it. He was gurgling."

"Gurgling?"

"The 'death rattle,' as your people call it. He may not even make it to the aid station."

Billingsley stood for a moment, as if lost in thought, before turning to Tyler. "Let's get 'em off the hill. We've got two more to sweep. We'll blow the airplane in place. Ambro's got the C-4."

"Aye-aye, sir. Okay people, saddle up. Sanchez?"

"I'll take the point," Sanchez shouted, knowing what Tyler wanted.

"You take the point," Tyler confirmed.

Billingsley studied his map as the airplane was set afire with a C-4 charge. The platoon then tramped down the hill, into a draw, up another hill, down it, and up one more. Compton ordered them to return when Billingsley reported that the sweep had been concluded. They got back to the company position with two hours of daylight left, ample time for preparing fighting holes along their portion of the ridge.

More of the same patrolling and searching routine continued for the next four days. Patrols during the day and ambushes at night were the order of business. Though the results were less than dramatic, the three companies killed more than 120 VC and bagged two prisoners. Across the valley, one of Alpha Company's squads bumped into a friendly Regional Force patrol during the night. The exchange of gunfire left one Marine and three PF members wounded before the accident was detected. The American adviser to the PF platoon was also slightly injured in the mishap.

With the operation concluded, the battalion marched seven kilometers to Route Nine where they were moved by truck convoy to the east, toward Dong Ha. Together with an ARVN battalion, they took up positions alongside Route One in the flat coastal area. The region was covered with scrub growth, now brown from repeated defoliations. Apart from small farm parcels, the terrain was generally crisscrossed by long hedgerows. The vast logistics complex of Dong Ha was to the south, across the Cua Viet River. Further to the north was Gio Linh, near the DMZ. To the west lay the flat piedmont which made up the bulk of what was known as Leatherneck Square. Five miles to the east lay the South China Sea.

Bravo Company moved into a fortified position west of Route One. The hot, dry weather sapped their energy as they entered the wire-encircled compound which was large enough for two rifle companies. Billingsley and Ivester shared a musty bunker, supported by timbers and covered on top by runway matting and sandbags, while Compton set up in a slightly larger bunker which also served as the CP. No patrols were scheduled for the remainder of the afternoon, so the tired Marines could relax as they settled into their new positions.

Alpha Company also moved into the compound and occupied the northern portion. Billingsley saw to his platoon, establishing sectors of fire and locations for listening posts, and then returned to his bunker. He and Ivester laid out their gear and filled their air mattresses, hoping to get a few hours of rest before hot food was brought in for the evening meal. The hot chow was a reward from Colonel Fletcher, who, according to Compton, had been pleased with the week's work. Fletcher maintained his command center to the north, in position with Company C and the ARVN units.

"Lieutenant Billingsley, you in here?" someone shouted from the entrance to the bunker.

"Yeah, come on in," Billingsley answered, not moving from his air mattress.

"How are you, you sorry prick?" Bill Blanton stepped into the bunker with a wide grin on his face.

"I'll be damned. The surfer boy, himself. How the hell are you, bunkie?" Billingsley said, jumping up.

It was their first meeting since leaving Quantico. Billingsley immediately set upon Blanton about his minor hand wound after introducing Blanton to Ivester.

"Caught a fragment from a grenade," Blanton explained, adjusting the fresh dressing on his hand.

"Did you throw the grenade yourself, Bill?" Billingsley asked.

"Of course not, idiot. Some slope did. The damned thing's been infected for so long that it oozes all kinds of nasty crap."

Blanton took off his helmet and sat on it with his back braced against the dirt wall of the bunker.

"Well, how were things at headquarters while you were there?" Billingsley asked.

"Oh, it wasn't bad duty. I was tight with a major from G-1 who helped me get into the field. Otherwise, I might still be up there color-coding maps in the G-3 shop."

"So you come out to the bush and get a Heart in your first fight, huh?"

"Yeah, first time out."

"You always did have a sense of the dramatic about you," Billingsley laughed.

"Yeah, well, I read a few reports on Bravo Company. You guys haven't been too inactive, either. When I found out you were in Bravo, I kept an eye on some of the operations you guys were on. Didn't you people get in some shit over near Con Thien?"

"That's about *all* you can get in up there. There were hordes of 'em, man. Right in the damned position with us, too."

"No shit?"

"Damn sure were. It took everything we had to keep the bastards from overrunning us."

"Do you hear anything from Andrea?"

"Oh, yeah. She's been good about writing. Much better than I've been. She'll get a kick out of hearing that you dropped in on me with your damned hand bandaged up."

"How is she?"

"She's doing well. Bitches about school and all those civilian things that don't seem so important anymore."

"Yeah, it's funny what a couple of months over here can do for your outlook," Blanton shrugged.

"What about your girlfriend?"

"Ah, we split before I came over here," Blanton responded nonchalantly.

"I'm sorry to hear that. What happened? You two were pretty tight, weren't you?"

"She said she didn't want a long-distance romance. She needed her freedom, she said."

"What did you tell her?"

"What *could* I tell her. I told her she could *have* her God-damned freedom."

"You could have begged, Bill."

"Bullshit! I got one farewell piece of ass off her and rode away into the sunset. Tipped my hat and galloped away, just like 'Cowboy Bob' would have," Blanton said, grinning.

Billingsley turned to Ivester, who was laughing at Blanton's account of the crumbled love affair.

"See what I mean about the dramatic sense, Art?" Billingsley cracked.

"While we're on the subject, Mike, have you had any of this Oriental stuff?" Blanton asked.

"Nah, I haven't. Have you?"

"Hell, I had me a regular when I was at Dong Ha. She worked in a bar outside the base. It was some fine tail, I mean."

"She didn't have razor blades or broken glass stuffed up her snapper, did she?" Ivester asked, winking at Billingsley.

"If she did, man, I didn't notice it."

"There's not much out *here* for you to chase, if you don't like water buffalo," Billingsley said.

"Don't bet your ass on it, Mike. I hear there's a friendly ville just west of here," Blanton said.

"I've heard that. We'll be too busy to mess with it, though, as soon as the patrols start cracking."

"What's in your goody package?" Blanton asked, pointing to the partially opened parcel on Billingsley's air mattress.

"Andrea sent me an Instamatic."

"That reminds me," Blanton said with a wry smile. "Do you know the definition of a Marine rifle squad? One lootin', one shootin', and ten takin' pictures."

This got a good laugh, especially from Blanton himself. Billingsley and Ivester were still laughing as Blanton moved to leave.

"I'd better get back to my unit. Nice to meet you, Art. Take care of my bunkie," Blanton said, as he slapped Billingsley on the shoulder.

"Good to meet you too, Bill."

"Take care of yourself, hotshot. I'll return the visit soon," Billingsley promised as he walked outside with Blanton.

Billingsley watched Blanton make his way across the encampment to the Alpha Company position. The heat was oppressive, with little wind to move the dense, heavy air. Sweat kept his skin continuously damp and sticky. Blanton turned and waved when he neared his sector. Just like old times, Billingsley thought.

The hot chow came in on trucks from Dong Ha. Beef, along with potatoes, peas, bread, butter, and cold milk. True to his word, Fletcher and several of his staff came into the position to dine. Compton was invited to join Fletcher as they sat in the shade of stacked C-ration boxes which had been unloaded earlier from the truck convoy.

Soon after the meal, Billingsley and Ivester were called to the CP. They found Kupton already there, together with Day, Gunny Kennerley, and, sitting next to Compton, an unfamiliar figure. The FO and FAC came into the cramped bunker behind Billingsley. The newcomer sat ramrod straight, his eyes measuring each man in the room. He was thin, of medium height, with close-cropped hair and a bony, sharp face. His uniform was clean and his boots were polished. Compton shot a quick glance toward Billingsley before standing to address the group.

"Listen up, gentlemen. I'd like to introduce to you the new CO of Bravo Company. Effective immediately, Captain English, to my right, is in command of this company. Captain English is an experienced infantry officer, and we're fortunate to have an opportunity to work with him. This is his second tour in-country, so he's familiar with the situations we're faced with."

Compton drew a deep breath and exhaled.

"I'd like to express my appreciation to each of you men for giving me the support and cooperation I needed in order to run this company. I deeply appreciate it, and I've told Captain English that this is an outfit of professionals. I know you'll continue to do your best for the new skipper," Compton said, looking slightly uncomfortable.

Billingsley was surprised and disappointed.

"With your permission, sir, I'd like to introduce these officers and staff," Compton requested, receiving a nod of approval from English.

Each man was introduced by name, rank, and billet. English greeted each with a slight smile, carefully listening to Compton's comments. Then Compton yielded the floor to English.

"Thank you for those introductions, Tom," English said as he rose slowly.

"When Colonel Fletcher welcomed me into the First Battalion, he informed me that I was gaining command of an outstanding rifle company. He told me that Bravo Company was a solid performer, with a group of motivated and professional Marines. Colonel Fletcher thinks quite highly of this unit," English spoke in a cool, deliberate manner.

"That tells me that the leadership being provided by those of you here is of a high quality. And you are to be complimented for that. I am extremely pleased to take command of this company. For me personally, I could wish very little more in terms of assignments. This is where it's at, this is where it counts the most. The nature of the war is not quite the same as in '66, when I was here last. It's gone from small-unit actions to larger, more conventional methods, and now has begun to shift back to the small-unit emphasis. We have more men and more gear now, but the major difference I see is that it's not building anymore.

"I'm probably not telling you anything you don't already know. There *are* three things, however, that I want you to remember at all times. I will expect these three things of you each and every day that I remain in command here," said English, pausing as the men reached into their pockets for pen and paper.

"Number one: Follow the book. It works. Always has. The Marine Corps has over one hundred-ninety years of success because Marines followed the book. Tactical geniuses are nothing more than extremely sound fundamentalists.

"Number two: Lead. Your troops are a reflection of you. There's too much at stake here for failure of leadership. Leadership failures should remain with the civilians, because they don't know any better. When we fail, somebody dies.

"Number three: Helmets, flak jackets, kick ass and take names. I don't imagine any of you misunderstand that. We have the best fighting men in the world. If we follow the book and lead them well, then I'll guarantee you we'll kick our share of ass.

"Okay, I won't go any further. I look forward to working and getting acquainted with each of you. Are there any questions?"

There were no questions. English turned to Compton.

"Lieutenant Compton will serve as my Executive Officer. He'll be of tremendous assistance to me, and he'll continue to be an asset to Bravo Company. Thank you, gentlemen. You are dismissed."

Billingsley and Ivester left the bunker and checked on their platoons, passing along the news of the change of command. The troops accepted the news in their typical fashion, showing little surprise or emotion. They had little choice, actually, but to hope that the new guy had his stuff together. Just go with the flow and see how it works out.

For the rest of February they patrolled the flat, scrubby terrain. Casualties from booby traps were numerous, almost commonplace. The NVA and VC chose to harass rather than engage the Marines, except for an occasional skirmish. The weather was uncooperative, as seasonal rains periodically drenched the men and their positions, sometimes lasting for days before clearing. Bravo Company, with its new CO, did its part in securing its portion of Route One and in ensuring that the Cua Viet waterway supplying Dong Ha stayed open. They searched for the enemy persistently and aggressively, staggering the time and place of their patrols to avoid predictability. The penalty for predictability in movement was nearly always booby traps, so English went to great lengths to avoid a set pattern.

Patrols of squad size permitted adequate coverage of the battalion area of responsibility. The enemy in the area were kept off balance by the light, mobile Marine and ARVN units which fanned out along the countryside. Artillery, air, and naval gunfire support added a lethal assist whenever and wherever needed, so long as the weather cooperated. To the southwest, in Operation Dewey Canyon, the Ninth Marines were enjoying considerable success in finding and destroying enemy units in the Da Krong Valley.

As March began, several Marine and ARVN encounters with NVA units at Gio Linh, to the north along Route One, signaled a potential step-up in the infiltration rate along the DMZ. Elements of Company C had seized upon an enemy company along Jones Creek, to the east, and engaged the force while reinforcements were hurried to the scene. Before the fighting had ended, and with the assistance of tanks and recoilless rifles, the Marines and ARVN had pushed the NVA into a pocket where the sixteen-inch guns of the battleship *New Jersey* finished them off with a deadly swiftness.

Billingsley's platoon was active. The squads became familiar with the areas to the east and west of Route One. The friendly village to the west of the position supplied the passing Marines with beer and soda and, time permitting, the services of prostitutes who seemed to time their arrival into the village concurrent with that of the rich Americans. Some of the villagers also sold or traded marijuana to those Marines who wanted it. Business with the villagers was brisk in all categories.

A patrol sent on a mission to the west of the compound had passed through the village on its way to search for signs of the enemy further to the west. No contact with, nor any sightings of the enemy had been made during the four-hour march. The patrol headed back, once again approaching the village. PFC Dobrinski walked the point position, with Lance Corporal Maroney, the squad leader, close behind. Billingsley and Martindale were positioned near the center of the formation. Scattered trees along the sides of the main trail were of no great concern, since visibility was generally good over the flat terrain. The village itself could easily be seen 200 meters up the trail. The afternoon sun parched the Marines' throats and burned their faces and necks. Their uniforms were soaked with perspiration.

When the column was 50 meters from the village, Dobrinski was met by a small Vietnamese boy, perhaps ten years old. The boy wore a faded USMC utility cap which drooped over his ears. His baggy black trousers dragged the ground. He was a familiar fixture to those Marines who had been by or through the village before. He sold bottled drinks at impromptu roadside stands made of discarded wooden pallets and ammo boxes. He had been nicknamed, aptly enough, "Billy the Kid" for his ability to negotiate virtually anything he wanted from the big Americans.

Billingsley saw Dobrinski stop when the boy began his pitch for the soft drinks. Dobrinski looked toward Maroney, who in turn glanced at Billingsley for permission to stop the column and take a break. Billingsley walked to the front of the patrol where Dobrinski and Maroney stood with the boy.

"There's some shade off the trail, sir. Wanna take five?" Maroney asked.

"Cold so-da, boocoo cold so-da. You buy?" questioned the boy, pointing to his bamboo basket nearby.

The boy was pulling at Dobrinski's trouser leg. "Open the basket and bring it over here, Billy," Billingsley said softly.

The boy opened the basket, lifted it by its handle, and ran over, the bottles rattling inside.

"You buy, honcho? Have boocoo so-da?"

Billingsley looked inside the basket and saw the dark bottles, an inviting piece of Americana. A scan of the adjacent trees and scrub growth showed nothing of concern. He decided that the progress of the patrol had been sufficient enough to allow for a short break. "Aw, what the hell. Get 'em off the trail, Maroney. We'll take five," he directed.

"You buy, honcho? You buy?"

"I buy, Billy. I buy."

The boy began thrusting sodas and collecting money from the Marines as they moved off the trail into the shade.

"These aren't cold, Billy. They're hot," Billingsley protested after the first burning swallow.

"No have ice."

The men sat on the ground and removed their helmets, glad to be out of the afternoon sun. They relaxed on either side of the trail, drinking the warm Cokes and exchanging small talk. Another long day, another patrol, another walk in the sun had neared its end.

"I'll bet Billy's already had a piece of ass, the little hustler," cracked Maroney who sat across the trail from Billingsley.

"Hell, I'll bet he's got kids of his own. That's why he's such a businessman. He's got a motherfuckin' family to feed," Dobrinski said, provoking laughter.

"If this fuckin' war lasts long enough, he'll probably grow up and marry one of those Donut Dollies and go live in the States," Lance Corporal Willingham, the grenadier, joked.

"There it is," Martindale agreed. "Little dude ain't no fool. I'd want to leave this shithole, too, if I was a damn gook."

"Tell you what," interjected Maroney. "*I* want to leave it and I *ain't* no gook."

"There it is," Dobrinski agreed.

"Shit yeah." Martindale looked dreamy. "Climb on that Freedom Bird and start banging the stews right in the aisle."

"I'd bang 'em in the pussy. I ain't never fucked no aisle before," Dobrinski said.

"You ain't never fucked nothin' but your Goddamned *hand*, Ski," Martindale countered.

"Your ass. I've had more nookey than you have, shithook."

"Bull fucking shit."

"Naw, man. No shit. I started gettin' laid when I was twelve."

"I don't believe that, Ski. You were probably screwin' animals, or somethin'. What do you call it when a dude screws animals?"

"An animalscrewin' dude," Willingham said.

Billingsley leaned back, smiling at the stream of banter from his troops. He enjoyed listening to their verbal taunts, each trying to outdo the last in absurd vulgarity.

Billy returned from his final sales efforts and walked to where Billingsley was leaning against a stump.

"Honcho, you have Ja-pan cam-ra?"

"No, Billy. What's the matter with Kodak?" Billingsley grinned.

"You souvenir me Kodak? Have more so-da," the boy said, pressing for another deal.

"Can you get me some boom-boom, Billy?" asked Maroney. "I've got a Kodak that I might make a deal on."

Billy's eyes sparkled as his little mind raced through a potential transaction. The laughter resounded along the trail.

"Can do boom-boom. You souvenir me Kodak, can do," he offered.

"What that means, Maroney," explained Dobrinski, "is that if you give him the camera, you're fucked."

The laughter continued while the small boy pursued the deal for the camera. Billingsley, caught up in the spirited jostling, finally glanced at his watch. Before his mind registered the time, he was distracted by what he thought to be the sound of movement behind him. He turned and looked among the scrub growth, but the bushes were thick and high. He couldn't see beyond them. The five-minute break had turned into fifteen minutes. The others were still laughing at Billy and Maroney and belching from the warm drinks. Billingsley extinguished his cigarette on the sole of his boot.

A metallic sound was closely followed by a thud in the center of the trail.

"GRENADE!" Willingham shouted instinctively at the sight of the explosive device.

Billingsley quickly turned his back toward the trail, hoping to absorb most of the blast with his flak jacket and helmet. The grenade had been thrown from his side of the trail and had rolled about ten feet away from him. It exploded. The ground shook and Billingsley felt as if he were suspended in mid-air for a moment. His ears rang loudly from the terrific concussion and his mind was fuzzy for several seconds afterward. His head was unsure of the condition of the rest of him. He realized that his limbs were still attached. He had no searing pain. He moved his arms, then his legs. He shook his head. He was whole. He rose to a crouch and pointed his weapon at the brush.

At the rear of the column, PFC Sharpe had seen two escaping VC soon after the grenade exploded. Sharpe opened fire with his M-16, dropping one of the VC. The other streaked away in a desperate gallop. Sharpe's fire team took up the chase.

Dobrinski sat upright across the trail swatting his bloody face as if attempting to defend himself from a swarm of angry hornets. Maroney was nearby, with blood pouring from his head and neck. At Maroney's feet was the body of the small boy, his lower abdomen ripped open by the blast.

"Get up here, doc," Billingsley shouted. "Get us a medevac coming, Martindale."

Billingsley's legs were wobbly as he ran across the trail to Dobrinski. Dobrinski's face had been peppered from the uneven blast from the Chicom grenade, leaving him partially blinded but conscious. Billingsley failed to notice the wound in Dobrinski's upper arm until the warm, spurting blood from the gash splashed him on the side of his face. The corpsman arrived and began applying a pressure bandage to the arm of the moaning Marine.

"Maroney and the kid bought it, lieutenant," Fralich advised as he brought the bleeding under control.

Billingsley turned away from the blood and the death and tried to spot Sharpe and his team. He shouted to Sharpe and then saw the others searching the brush. He called to Sharpe to order that the search for the remaining VC be limited to within 100 meters of the trail.

"Choppers on the way, Martindale?" Billingsley asked.

"Yessir. Skipper wants to know what's comin' down."

"Well fuckin' tell him!" Billingsley snapped. "Willingham?"

"Yessir."

"Get a fire team up the trail and set up an LZ in the clearing we passed on the way in," Billingsley ordered, throwing a smoke grenade to the young Marine. "And Willingham?"

"Yessir."

"You're the squad leader now. I'll handle things here, and you get us an LZ established."

"Okay, sir," the red-haired corporal said as he and his team moved out at a trot.

"Skipper wants to talk to you, sir. He wants to know what's the deal," Martindale explained defensively.

"Goddammit, tell him I don't fuckin' *know* what the deal is! I'm trying to find out," Billingsley shouted, disgusted.

"We got one of 'em," Sharpe called from thirty meters away. "The other one's got away. Can't find no blood trails, either."

"Drag him over here. Keep a couple of men in there until you hear the birds, then pull 'em back to the clearing up the trail," Billingsley called.

Several villagers, perhaps a half-dozen, had ventured up the trail and spotted the dreadful sight of the dead boy. It wasn't long before the word of the boy's death reached the village and his family. Others appeared, screaming and wailing. Three Vietnamese women, whom Billingsley guessed to be the grandmother, mother, and sister of the boy, ran to the small, limp figure at Maroney's feet. The mother became highly hysterical, alternately looking at the dead boy and then placing her hands to her head, screaming.

"Fralich, can you move Dobrinski?" asked Billingsley over the screaming of the boy's family.

"I can get him to the LZ."

"Then do it. Get somebody to get Maroney the hell out of here, too."

Martindale approached Billingsley warily, the handset of the radio extended. "The CO's getting pissed, sir. He wants to talk to you," he said weakly.

Billingsley took the receiver and noticed blood on his fingers and the back of his right hand.

"You're hit, sir," Martindale said, opening the first-aid kit attached to the back of Billingsley's cartridge belt. "You took something just above the elbow. I'll wrap it for you."

"This is Bravo Two, over."

"Be advised that I have attempted to contact you every minute for the past ten. Give me a report on your situation, over," English called sharply.

"We've taken a frag grenade from unknown number of Victor Charley just west of the ville. One KIA, one WIA, one villager KIA."

"Is the position secure?"

"Affirmative."

"What about the local KIA?"

"A small boy. There's quite a scene here now."

"And he's a definite KIA?"

"Very."

"You bring it in when the dustoff leaves. Leave the village deal to us. You got any Victor Charley KIAs?"

"Roger, one."

"Find out if the chief can make a pos ID."

"Roger."

"Keep me advised."

"Roger, out."

The medevac chopper soon arrived and claimed the injured Dobrinski and the dead Maroney. Billingsley remained on the trail with the tearful family of the boy while Martindale and Sharpe's fire team stood nearby. Once the evacuation from the clearing was completed, the rest of the squad returned. They fanned out around the trail, ready to intercept any further interference from the VC.

"Hey, doc, take a look at this," Martindale shouted as he pointed to the bloody bandage on Billingsley's arm.

"No, I'm all right. Stay where you are, doc," Billingsley insisted, though the wound above his elbow had begun to throb and tighten.

Billingsley looked back at the villagers and noticed an elderly male who had appeared while the helicopter was taking off. The old man stood in the middle of the trail, only a few feet from the boy's corpse and the grieving women.

"Are you the village chief?" Billingsley asked.

The old man nodded tentatively and smiled, showing his bad teeth.

"You the honcho?" Billingsley said, seeking confirmation.

"Ah, yes. Honcho," grinned the old man.

"Sharpe, where'd you drag the dead dude?" Billingsley shouted.

"Over here," Sharpe said, walking toward the body.

"Come with me, honcho. I'll show you the VC who killed the boy," requested Billingsley, pointing in the direction of the dead soldier.

The body of the VC lay sprawled in the bushes.

"He killed the boy. Hurt Marines, too. This man VC. Do you know him?" Billingsley asked.

The old man looked at the body of the dead VC but was unable to recognize him; the face had been completely destroyed, along with much of the skull. The head was a mass of blood and brains from the multiple gunshot wounds. The old man shrugged his shoulders and smiled self-consciously at his inability to identify the man on the ground.

"Jesus Christ, Sharpe! Did you guys get *enough* of the cocksucker?" Billingsley said, showing his irritation.

"I guess we were pissed, sir," offered Sharpe.

"You're not the only ones pissed, Sharpe. I can tell you that for damn sure."

Billingsley escorted the old man back onto the trail, thanking him for his efforts, and making a slight bowing gesture.

"Willingham, get your point on the trail. Let's get the fuck out of here. Martindale, get over here with the damned radio. Hurry up."

Billingsley called English and told him of the problem with the identification. English seemed perturbed.

"Was the chief able to tell that the Victor Charley was NOT from the village?" English asked.

"The village chief can't tell a thing," Billingsley answered. "The Victor Charley's body is in one place but his face is somewhere else. This whole thing's a mess. It's not a pretty sight, at all."

"Roger. Get 'em back in here."

Martindale watched as Billingsley drew a deep breath and exhaled slowly. The strain was plenty evident on the face of his platoon leader. Billingsley's injured arm was hurting; he winced as he held the radio's handset.

"Let's move, Willingham," Billingsley called, ready to separate himself from the village and the villagers.

The column got underway, wasting little time in setting about on its march back to the company position. They stayed on the trail, moving quickly, though conscious of the threat of another VC attempt to harass them. Rifles remained at the ready as the men glanced from side to side, watching for anything the least bit unnatural.

The patrol reached the compound with the afternoon sun still beating down upon them. As Billingsley took off his gear and stored it in his bunker, he was reminded of his wound with each movement of his arm. He went to the CP where he found English discussing the events of the patrol with a member of Fletcher's staff via the radio. Billingsley listened as a plan was drawn up for an extensive search of the presumably friendly village. When the radio conversation was completed, English's eyes were drawn to the dried blood on Billingsley's arm.

"I thought you reported only one WIA," said English.

"I did, sir. I didn't know at the time that I was hit."

"Well, get yourself over to the aid station and have it seen about."

"I will, sir. But let me tell you what went on out there."

"By all means. You told me very little while you were out there," English replied with a trace of sarcasm.

English took a seat on a metal folding chair while Billingsley sat on a foot locker and recounted the events at the village. English listened quietly and intently, occasionally interrupting for clarifying information. It became clear to English that Billingsley felt solely responsible for the results of the attack, because he had permitted the patrol to stop for the break. Billingsley was distraught; it showed on his face and in his words. He wanted badly to have those moments again, before the rest break, before the grenade attack, before the deaths of Maroney and the boy, before the injury to Dobrinski. If only he could have it to do over again, he seemed to say to English. If only he'd known. If only.

"I just feel rotten about it, sir. If only I'd kept . . . "

English looked at his platoon leader's lowered face. English was commander enough to know when a swift kick was needed. He also knew when a word of encouragement was altogether appropriate.

"You can't look back, Mike. If you make a mistake, then you obviously don't repeat the same mistake. But you can't keep looking back on it and stewing about it."

"I suppose so, sir."

"You're not the first Marine officer to let his guard down and get hit. As innocent as things appear sometimes, there's always risk. Especially in this war. You're a good officer—you were yesterday and you are today, regardless of what's gone on. And I expect you to be a good officer tomorrow."

"Yessir."

"Now get over to the aid station and get that arm seen about."

"I will, sir." Billingsley rose to leave. "I really appreciate your hearing me out."

The aid station was near the center of the perimeter and served as a forward emergency facility. Portable generators outside the bunker provided lighting.

Inside the bunker wooden sawhorses were stacked, available to support the stretchers bearing the wounded. The medicinal smell of a hospital added to Billingsley's discomfort. He had always loathed hospitals, and especially that smell.

"What can we do for you?" asked a corpsman posted near the entrance.

"I'm Lieutenant Billingsley from Bravo Company and I've got a frag wound in my arm."

"Okay, sir. Have a seat over here and we'll have a look at it."

A single lamp dangled from its cord over Billingsley's head. The corpsman cleaned and examined the wound, while another man gathered information: his blood type, known allergies, unit, service number, and the like. The area of the wound was injected with a local anesthetic, and Billingsley was taken to a makeshift operating table. It was several minutes before a surgeon appeared.

"How do you feel, lieutenant?" the doctor asked as he felt the flesh around the wound.

"Not bad, sir."

"I'm going to probe around and see if I can find the fragment. It feels as though as it may be rather deep."

Billingsley, who lay on his stomach on the table, watched the doctor take a metal probe from a tray of instruments. Billingsley could feel the probe in his arm, but the pain was only moderate. The fragment was soon found and removed. It was the size of a small kernel of corn.

"You've got a souvenir," the surgeon said. "Get your corpsman to change the dressing twice daily for a week. Try to keep the area of the wound as clean as possible."

"Thanks, doc."

The doctor left, leaving Billingsley with the crew of corpsmen. He was given an injection and his wound was dressed with a sterile bandage.

"You guys busy today?" Billingsley asked.

"Not too bad. Some dudes from Alpha tripped a booby trap. Killed one of 'em, so there was nothing we could do for him except tag him and send him on. A lieutenant got some fragments in his leg, and lost one of his testicles. Other than that, it was pretty quiet. The people from your outfit were sent on to Quang Tri."

"There was only one. The other was KIA."

"Yeah, I know."

Billingsley winced at the thought of hot shrapnel penetrating, of all places, a testicle. It was a horrible thought. He suddenly had another disturbing thought.

"What was the officer's name from Alpha?"

"Don't remember, sir. Hey Kwalick, what was the lieutenant's name that got his nut blown off this morning," the corpsman shouted.

"Uh, Lieutenant Blanton," was the reply from across the bunker.

Billingsley began to feel dizzy and nauseated, as if he might faint. "I'm going to need to lie back for a minute," he said.

"You okay, sir?"

"I'll be fine. Can you give me something for a headache?"

"Sure. Hang on a minute."

"Oh merciful God," Billingsley prayed, almost in a whisper. "I'm going to need a hand down here. I sure could use your help."

The corpsman returned with a Darvon capsule and a cup of water. Billingsley gulped the pill. Five minutes later he was able to stand.

"Where was Lieutenant Blanton taken?" he asked.

"Third Medical Battalion at Quang Tri, sir."

As Billingsley left the aid station, the evening sun was disappearing on the horizon. He checked with Tyler to find that all was well with the platoon before retiring to his bunker. He was alone. Ivester had left with one of his squads for a night ambush on the eastern side of Route One. There was a letter from Andrea on Billingsley's air mattress.

He felt low, as low as he had ever felt in his life. And he felt alone. He was alone with recurring images of the grenade being tossed upon the trail, and of the aftermath of the explosion. He thought of the boy and his family, and of his dead and wounded Marines. He thought of Bill Blanton, and the pain he, too, must be feeling. He sat staring at the letter from Andrea, thinking of her and wishing he could be with her. He wondered if he would ever again see her. Tears streamed down his face, as deep grief, sorrow, and confusion seemed to virtually consume him. His arm throbbed, his head ached, and his depression intensified his physical hurting.

Tom Compton came in. He saw Billingsley sitting on the ground, holding the letter from Andrea. Compton could see the tears in Billingsley's eyes, on Billingsley's face. He walked over and sat down beside his friend. He slapped Billingsley lightly on the thigh and passed a lit cigarette into his trembling hand. Billingsley made no effort to wipe the tears from his face.

"How you feelin', stud?" Compton asked.

"Pretty low, Tom. Pretty damned low."

"Were you hit bad?"

"Not really. Did you hear about the patrol?"

"Yeah. I tried to get English to mobilize a group and go level that fuckin' ville."

"I don't think that would help. Just make more VC."

"Maybe so. Must've been pretty shitty, huh?"

"It was. Still is, for that matter. I can't seem to get it out of my head. Maroney, Dobrinski, the kid, the women screaming. And then I come back and find out that Bill Blanton got hit."

"Yeah, I heard about that, too. Just hasn't been your day, comrade."

"No shit," Billingsley said, wiping his face with his sleeve.

"It'll get better, babe."

"I hope so, Tom. God, it's got to."

"It will. I've got some good news."

"Lord knows, I could use some. What is it?"

"I've heard from Chris. We've got a little girl," Compton said.

"That is good news, Tom. I'm happy for both of you. What's her name?"

"Karen. I can't wait to see a picture of her. Miss Karen Ann Compton."

"Pretty name. I'm sure she'll bring a lot of joy into your lives," said Billingsley, unable to show anything more than token enthusiasm.

"Anything I can do for you, buddy?" Compton asked sympathetically.

"No thanks. I'll be okay."

Compton rose and stood in front of Billingsley, kicking him lightly on the bottom of his boot. "Hang in there. Let me know if I can do anything, will you?" he offered.

"I will. You write and tell Chris that I'm proud of her."

"Try to get some rest, Mike. You look like warmed-over shit."

Billingsley was finally able to laugh softly as Compton turned and left the bunker. He listened to the steady drone from the lantern, still crying until he fell asleep with Andrea's letter on his lap.

Captain English moved Bravo Company through the perimeter wire at precisely 0700 the next morning. The three platoons moved west, toward the village, with Kupton's platoon in the lead. Ivester, looking tired after his night ambush, followed with English's CP. Billingsley brought up the rear. The heat was already building as the company traveled the short distance to the village. Just outside the objective, Billingsley maneuvered his platoon around the area to the north of the settlement, through the farmed fields, to take up positions to the west. English's plan called for Ivester's platoon, with an interpreter, to conduct the search while Billingsley and Kupton sealed the village with a circle of troops around the outside.

"Better let the skipper know the fields are unattended. That ain't the way it's supposed to be," warned Tyler, always observant.

Billingsley contacted English by radio at his CP near the eastern entrance to the village. "This is Bravo Two. Be advised that there's nobody in the fields to the north. You'd better step lightly," he radioed.

"Roger. Lock us in tight and advise when you're in position," English answered calmly.

Second Platoon was moving toward its assigned sector on the fringes when Rosser, Ambrosetti's point man, halted the column. Billingsley hurried over to Rosser and Ambrosetti. He saw nothing out of the ordinary except the drawn faces of Rosser and Ambrosetti.

"What the hell gives," he snapped impatiently.

"There's some bad shit over there in the grass," Ambrosetti pointed.

"What is it?"

"Dead gooks from the village," Rosser spoke.

Some thirty men from the village lay dead with their hands tied behind their backs. All of the bodies showed the signs of fatal blows to the head. The sight was grotesque, with many of the victim's skulls literally split open to expose the grey brain matter.

"God!" Billingsley exclaimed.

"Wide fuckin' open, ain't they?" Ambrosetti observed faintly.

"I've seen a lot of hawgs like that before, but never no damned person," added Rosser. "Even the *old* motherfuckers."

They stood and stared for a moment.

Billingsley collected himself and radioed a report to English. Billingsley was advised to continue with the disposition of his troops around the village. Ivester's platoon, accompanied by English, spent two hours searching and questioning, while Billingsley and his men endured the glare and heat from the outskirts of the village. Finally, English notified Billingsley to set up a perimeter around the open area. The area would again be used as an LZ, this time for Colonel Fletcher.

Soon two Huey's appeared and landed in the clearing. Fletcher and members of his staff got out, while the choppers kept their engines running. Billingsley couldn't hear the conversation, though he watched as Fletcher viewed the slaughtered village men. A young radioman in Fletcher's party turned away from the sight and vomited his breakfast into the tall grass.

"Dude lost his cookies," Ambrosetti chuckled.

"Keep looking outboard," Billingsley snapped.

After Fletcher left, English summoned Billingsley to where he and Compton and Gunny Kennerley stood. Kupton also joined the group. English told them that, according to the villagers, the VC had appeared shortly before dawn; the VC had apprehended as many adult males as could be found; and, finally, the VC had promised death to anyone who followed their departure to the west.

"So the village women don't know about these bodies?" Billingsley asked, thinking of the chaos of the previous day with the dead child.

"That's affirm. They were too frightened to leave, and then we showed up within an hour."

"How big a force?"

"A platoon, as best we can figure."

"What now?"

"We're going to leave one of Art's squads in here for a couple of days until these people can be resettled. You swing around the way you came in and then we'll tell the women where the men are."

"They didn't fire a damned shot, did they?" Billingsley asked.

"Not one," Compton answered quickly.

The villagers were eventually resettled to a larger, neighboring village. They showed little emotion during the course of the resettlement, as they were protected by armed Marines from Bravo Company.

Routine patrolling and security details filled the rest of March, with only minor deviations. The compound was shelled three nights in a row near the end of the month; Alpha Company ambushed the VC mortar squad. The following night, Billingsley's platoon intercepted and destroyed an NVA squad as it set up rockets and mortars to the northwest. The shellings ceased.

Word finally came that the position was being turned over to a battalion of ARVN troops who were moving over from areas to the west. Rumor had it that the Third Marines were headed to Con Thien, after a few days of rest at Dong Ha.

When the day came for the Marines to turn over the position to the ARVN, Billingsley formed his platoon inside the compound, ready to board the trucks for Dong Ha. The ARVN units waited outside the perimeter in their company formations. Billingsley's own men stood slumped and tired, many wearing tattered boots and clothing that had literally rotted away. Several wore bandages, evidence of encounters with booby traps. They seemed anything but the spit and polished image of recruiting-poster Marines. But they straightened up and assumed an air of cockiness when the ARVN units began to enter the compound. Some of the ARVN soldiers grinned and waved at the Marines while passing to the front.

"Hope you enjoy yourself, peckerhead," Ambrosetti cracked at a waving ARVN.

"Too bad we're leaving, ain't it. Now you assholes gonna have to steal from each other," Rosser offered.

"Hello there," Martindale smiled at a passing ARVN soldier. "Nice boots. Send 'em to me if you get your legs blown off."

"Okay people, you can knock off the wisecracks," Billingsley ordered. "I don't want to hear any more of that bullshit."

After the ARVN troops had passed, Billingsley turned to his silent troops. "I'm surprised at the behavior of you people," he said, looking into their faces. "To make the kinds of comments you made to those troops is a disgrace. And I don't suppose any of you know why, do you?"

No one attempted to speak.

"Well, I'll *tell* you why. It's a disgrace because these people are our *allies!*"

The troops remained silent and motionless.

"And besides, what would I do for a platoon if these ARVN troops took offense at your remarks and commenced to attack and kill every one of you in a gang butt-fuck?"

The troops stifled their laughter until Ambrosetti let out a loud guffaw, causing most of the others to laugh until tears came to their eyes. Even the shoulders of the grizzled Tyler shook as he lowered his head and attempted to hide his laughter at Billingsley's surprising and uncharacteristic remark. Billingsley saw a displeased stare from English, who stood ceremoniously nearby, and tried to quiet them.

They finally stopped laughing after Billingsley shouted, "At ease, dammit!" Only an infrequent snicker reached Billingsley as he stood to the front of his platoon and waited for English to start the boarding process. Gunny Kennerley had been moving about the platoons, speaking with the NCOs and looking over the troops. He ambled toward Second Platoon and realized that he would have to pass by Billingsley to get to Tyler. "Morning, lieutenant," he spoke as he approached Billingsley.

"Good morning, gunny. Anything I can help you with?"

"I've got some word to pass on some things that have to be done when we get to Dong Ha. I'm gonna talk with Sergeant Tyler."

Billingsley smelled alcohol on Kennerley's breath. The gunny avoided eye contact with him, looking instead over Billingsley's shoulder.

"Tell me first. I'm in charge."

"I'll tell Sergeant Tyler. That way I'll be sure it gets done," Kennerley said aloofly.

"Tell *me first!*" Billingsley snapped.

Kennerley glared.

"I'm gonna want haircuts for these men before we leave the rear. And I want those moustaches trimmed even with the corners of the mouth and one-eighth of an inch above the lip."

"Is that all, gunny?"

"That's all, lieutenant," Kennerley said, looking back at Billingsley's troops.

"Gunny, step over here a little closer."

"Sir?"

"That's right. Step over here where you can hear me and nobody else can."

Kennerley inched closer, still refusing to look at Billingsley.

"Gunny, you can take your order and shove it one-eighth of an inch up your ass," Billingsley whispered.

Kennerley recoiled as if he had been shown a poisonous snake.

"Lieutenant, that order comes from Captain English. If you remember correctly, he's the CO of this Goddamned company!" Kennerley said, livid.

"I know who the CO is, and I know that order didn't come from him because if it did, I'd know about it. And if I knew about it, there'd be no need for you to come over here and repeat it. Like I said, gunny, I'm the one who's in charge here."

"I'll tell you *one* thing, Captain English ain't gonna be happy with this *at all!*" Kennerley threatened.

"Before you go running off to Captain English, gunny, you'd better get the smell of that booze off your breath."

Kennerley walked away in a huff, gritting his teeth. Tyler asked Billingsley about the short, curious exchange.

"It was nothing, Sergeant Tyler. Just a quick discussion on some organizational matters. By the way, make sure our people get trimmed and groomed when we get to Dong Ha," Billingsley said, looking straight ahead.

"Aye-aye, sir," Tyler said cheerfully, returning to his place in the formation.

6

At the Dong Ha facility, the men of Bravo Company washed away the accumulated dirt and grime of nearly fifty days in the field. The typical working parties were arranged during the day, but they were free at night. Most of them headed for the EM Club, where the beer was cheap and the atmosphere was rowdy.

Billingsley, Compton, Ivester, and several junior officers from Alpha Company moved into a Quonset hut where they drank beer, ate peanuts, cleaned their gear, caught up on their correspondence, and simply enjoyed their leisure. Compton was even able to commandeer a pair of small, rotating pedestal fans. Transistor radios carried rock music throughout the hootch.

Billingsley learned that Bill Blanton had moved to the naval hospital at Yokosuka, Japan. He wrote to Blanton, explaining that the battalion was currently in lusty search of the girl with whom he, Blanton, had carried on a romance prior to joining Alpha. He promised to tell Blanton of the results, concluding his letter with a prediction that Blanton would probably be a better man with one testicle than were most who carried around a full complement. One less to scratch, he added.

Compton invited Billingsley to join him on a foray into Quang Tri City, eight miles to the south. "Even got us a jeep," he beamed.

"How'd you get it?"

"I just asked around. Wasn't hard. Art's got the duty so let's get rolling. We'll be back before too late."

The steady stream of military traffic along Route One was reassuring as Compton drove the jeep to Quang Tri City. They parked near a string of bars, where men in uniform moved

187

from club to club. Loud music from jukeboxes poured into the street from the gaudy bars. They looked inside several, hoping to find one that was relatively uncrowded. Most were brimming with American patrons. One bar was filled with black servicemen, who stared indignantly at the two white officers. They turned and left quickly.

"Don't think they wanted us in there," Compton remarked.

They finally discovered an uncrowded bar near the end of the string of such establishments. They took seats at the counter, though a half-dozen tables were unoccupied.

"Stay with beer," advised Compton. "And drink it out of the bottle. These people don't worry too much with cleanliness and shit like that. Some guy with the clap could have been in here drinking from a glass that they wipe off and give to you."

They were served their bottled beer by an attractive Vietnamese girl. Her long hair, black and silky, fell along her back as she moved gracefully around the small area behind the bar. Her *ao dai*, the gossamer skirt which was split to the waist and worn over trousers, accented the roundness beneath. Several other women moved among the dozen customers, but none were as appealing as the girl behind the bar. Her olive skin was smooth, her eyes narrow and dark, and her smile was radiant.

There was no air conditioning and the inside of the bar had a stale, smoky odor. There were other odors, also.

"You, know, no matter where you go, it all smells like shit," Compton said as he scraped at the label on his bottle of beer.

"I've noticed that," Billingsley agreed with a laugh.

"You smell it in the camps when they burn it, you smell it in town, the swamps smell like it . . . it's everywhere. Fuckin' everywhere. You can't get away from it. R and R in Hong Kong, and it's there. Okinawa, and it's there. Anywhere in Nam, and it's there."

"Yeah. It's getting hard for me to remember anything that exists outside of I Corps. Do you remember what it's like to sleep in clean sheets?" Billingsley asked.

"Nope. Do you remember what it's like to soak in a tub full of hot water?"

"Nope. Do you remember what it's like to sleep until you're ready to get up?"

"Nope. Do you remember what a chili dog tastes like?"

"Nope. Do you remember what it's like to take a shower every day?"

"Nope," Compton replied as he watched the movements of the girl behind the bar. "Do you remember what a piece of. . ."

"Barely," said Billingsley as he, too, became caught up in watching the shapely, sensuous girl.

They drank and watched and talked idly. Billingsley enjoyed Tom Compton and now considered him his most trusted and loyal friend. They talked about things that Billingsley was reluctant to discuss with anyone else, and he always knew that Compton's opinion would be objective and candid. He told Compton about Andrea, of his deep feelings for her. He spoke of Bravo Company, and of the war and its dismal effect upon him. Compton's reasoning was sound and his answers frank and logical. Billingsley put a lot of store in what Tom Compton thought and said.

The two of them had not noticed when Gunny Kennerley and his counterpart from Company A had entered the bar and taken seats at the opposite end of the counter. They were alerted to Kennerley's presence when he complained obstinately over a drink the girl served him.

"This ain't scotch, dammit! Get over here and get this piss and gimme some Goddamned scotch," Kennerley said loudly, drunk.

Gunny Rousseau from Alpha Company pointed at Compton and Billingsley and suggested to Kennerley that they seek another bar.

"No way I'm leavin'," Kennerley insisted, tapping his index finger on the counter. "Ain't no dipshit officers gonna chase *me* away from *any* damned place!"

"Of all the assholes to have to see," Compton sighed, sipping the remnants of his beer.

"No kidding. You ready, Tom?"

"Yeah. Let's make like shepherds and get the flock out."

They paid their tabs and walked toward the door. Billingsley could feel the eight beers he had consumed over the past two hours. They had to pass by Kennerley.

"Good evening, Mister Compton, sir," Kennerley said.

"Good evening, Gunny Kennerley. Hello, Gunny Rousseau."

"Enjoying yourself?" Kennerley slurred.

"Yeah, right. Good to have a little huss every now and then."

"And what about you, *Mister Billingsley?*" Kennerley asked with a sneer.

"What *about* me, gunny?"

"You havin' a good time, too?"

"Yeah, gunny. A real good time."

"That's just fucking dandy."

Kennerley raised his glass and gulped the contents. He requested another by banging the glass on the counter.

"Need a ride back?" Compton asked.

"We're fine, sir. Thanks."

"Okay. See you later," Compton said, nodding at the two NCOs.

"Did Second Platoon get haircuts?" Kennerley asked gruffly when Billingsley was nearly out the door.

Billingsley stood silently for a moment, half in the doorway and half on the sidewalk. The temptation raged within him to respond in some way, and preferably violently. He wanted to knock the drunken sergeant off his barstool. He kept his composure, however, and continued out the doorway.

"Asshole. Goddamn motherfuckin' son of a bitchin' *asshole!*" Billingsley said through clenched teeth as he climbed into the jeep.

Compton managed to drive the jeep back safely to Dong Ha. He abandoned it on a gravel road near their Quonset hut.

"How'd you get the jeep?" Billingsley asked as they ambled toward the hootch.

"Greer," Compton replied. "I just told Greer, that damn crazy hippie-ass clerk, to get me a jeep even if he had to shit one. I think the little crook could have gotten me an amtrack if I'd asked him to. He's the best scrounger there is, Mike. He showed me how to forge those forms to get the fans for the hootch. He's offbeat as hell, but he always produces. He's smart, too. Twice as smart as those other vegetables we've had in admin."

Everyone else in the Quonset hut was asleep as Compton and Billingsley stumbled around in the dark, feeling for their bunks. They were guided by the sound of the whirring fans.

"Don't stick your hand in the friggin' blades," Compton warned.

Billingsley spent the final day of the short break at Dong Ha ensuring that his troops were ready to move to the field again. He enlisted the assistance of the enterprising clerk, Greer, in the procurement of clothing and equipment. Greer was able to locate jungle boots, utility uniforms, camouflage helmet covers, and much more. Billingsley saw that Greer was a man of extraordinary value. The "proper channels" of distribution were slow and cumbersome, whereas a well-disguised lie or bribe by Greer precipitated the movement of materiel.

The two days of rest went a long way toward restoring the spirits of Billingsley's platoon. Several replacements had joined the unit, bringing its numerical strength higher than it had been in some time. Only Rosser was missing when the platoon embarked by helicopter to Con Thien with the rest of Bravo Company. Rosser was enjoying his two weeks of R&R in Japan.

The entire battalion was flown by chopper to Con Thien, where they found plenty of fire support in the compound— sufficient to have convinced the NVA of the futility of a large-scale assault upon the base. Tanks, Ontos, howitzers, mortars, dusters, and heavy machine guns augmented the infantry force. An ARVN battalion operated from the high ground to the southwest, called "Yankee Station." Observation on a clear day was excellent from Con Thien, though the Marines knew that they could likewise be seen by the enemy gunners from across the DMZ.

The Marines spent their first full day improving their fighting locations. Patrols searched the surrounding fields and hedgerows for signs of NVA forces in the area. Enemy activity in recent weeks had been sporadic. No one was sure what the enemy intentions were.

Tom Compton walked into Billingsley's sector to find his friend sitting on sandbags over a bunker studying a map of the region. The warm April sun was drying the dampness from the previous night's rain.

"Ain't too shabby a place, is it?" Compton asked as he sat down beside Billingsley.

"Not too bad for government work, I don't guess," Billingsley replied, not looking up from his map.

Compton picked up a stick and poked at the mud on his boot. "Skipper's got the patrol schedule. You need to get up there and take a look," he said.

"Anything going out tonight?"

"Nah. Looks like the patrols will be fairly small potatoes. Not much bigger than companies, with platoons and squads in close. This area's been quiet for a while. The most gooks anybody's seen in the last five weeks was a platoon of 'em."

"What are they doing, Tom? Just catching their breath?"

"Probably, although Captain English keeps telling me that they're beaten, for all practical purposes. He's got a theory."

"Hope he's right."

"Yeah, me too. His theory makes sense."

"How does it make sense?"

"Because of Tet, last year. English says we ripped them such a new ass that they can't mass in large numbers anymore. He thinks it's just a matter of time, especially the way the body count figures have looked for the last eighteen months," Compton said.

"Tom, those body counts are a ration of crap. You've inflated 'em, I've inflated 'em, and you know damn well they get higher on up the line. The gooks are the only ones who know how many we have *really* killed, and they wouldn't tell us if we asked 'em."

"Everybody's under pressure for results, Mike. I didn't fully understand that until I was CO, then XO."

"Nothing wrong with that. But who the hell are we kidding with all these dead gooks we're claiming?"

"Don't get your panties in a wad over it, hotrod."

"My panties are fine," Billingsley said with a wink. "A good officer keeps his boots polished and his panties unwadded."

"I'm gonna tell English that you think his theory stinks."

"Tell English that I'll kiss his ass if he can keep the gooks from massing. And tell him that I'll kiss his ass and buy him a steak dinner if he can end the war. And I don't mean theoretically. I mean *end* it. But don't tell him that I think his theory stinks, 'cause that would wad his panties really bad," Billingsley grinned.

"Yours, too," Compton laughed.

North Vietnamese artillery from across the DMZ greeted the Marines during the battalion's first night at Con Thien. Two dozen rounds exploded on the promontory in the short but intense bombardment. With the exception of a metal CONEX box and the slight wounding of one man, no damage was sustained. Just a few more craters in the red-clay mud.

The patrols began in earnest on the next morning as Billingsley led his men off the hill to conduct a sweep to the northeast. First Platoon swept due north while Third Platoon, with English and his group, set up a blocking position. English hoped to push any enemy soldiers in the area of the sweep into the blocking force for a quick annihilation. A light rain in the early morning had turned into a downpour by the time the men began sloshing their way along the assigned routes.

Second Platoon moved northeast toward a thick hedgerow, L-shaped and dense. They were to search it and then turn northwest. It was hard to see in the downpour. They were fifty yards from the hedgerow when Sanchez, whose squad was on the point, suddenly slowed the pace. Billingsley could see the tenseness on the faces of his wet troops when they reached the shorter portion of the hedgerow which terminated at a right angle to the longer, more dense section. Nothing could be seen within the thicket, and there were no noises other than the falling rain and the sloshing sounds of the Marines' movement.

Sanchez's point man, a stocky black Marine named Jarvis, had gone about five meters into the brush when he tripped a booby trap. It shattered his leg and hip and killed the man immediately behind him. As it exploded, the NVA who were hidden in the main hedgerow opened up with automatic weapons and RPGs, catching the majority of the platoon in the open. Sanchez pushed his squad past the victims of the booby trap and attempted to return the fire to allow the rest of the platoon to advance to cover. A bursting RPG stopped Sanchez's movement and wounded two more of his men. His grenadier was virtually decapitated. Sanchez grabbed the dead Marine's M-79 and fired repeatedly at the NVA stronghold.

Meanwhile, Billingsley and the remainder of the platoon had dropped to the ground and returned the fire. They were exposed and pinned down. Several Marines had fallen and lay writhing on the ground, bleeding and calling for help. When he reported his situation to English, he was informed that the other two platoons were also engaged with light enemy contact.

"This ain't light," Billingsley shouted over the radio as the bullets passed over his head and the RPGs streaked toward them in loud, searing whooshes before exploding behind the platoon.

"*Hang loose*," advised English.

No shit! Billingsley thought.

The rain intensified, making air support out of the question. Billingsley had to get the men to cover before the NVA drew an accurate enough bead on the exposed Marines to destroy them. Sanchez had secured a portion of the smaller, connecting hedgerow from which he and his squad fired at the enemy, ninety meters away. Billingsley judged the size of the enemy force to be at least that of a platoon, and likely larger.

Rifle slugs were hitting around Billingsley, kicking up clumps of soil and geysers of water. He ordered Willingham, whose squad was the most removed from cover, to remain in the open and provide covering fire while Ambrosetti's squad made a dash for the trees. Sanchez's squad poured rifle and machine-gun fire into the enemy's position as Ambrosetti's group made it to cover. Billingsley ran into the trees with Ambrosetti. He felt an AK-47 round slam against the stock of his rifle. The men dispersed once they were inside the treeline and took up firing positions within the brush. Fralich, the corpsman, began attending to the wounded, the majority of whom were from Sanchez's squad.

Willingham and his men were still in the open, forty meters from cover. Tyler was with the exposed squad and was attending to a seriously wounded man, ignoring the bullets splashing around him as he put a dressing on the man's shoulder. Billingsley ordered Willingham to move his men into the trees in fire team rushes, protected by the fire of the other two squads. A few minutes later, the last of the exposed squads had made it to cover, bringing with them their two wounded. One of the wounded Marines had been struck in the hip and leg by small-arms rounds. He screamed uncontrollably as he was dragged the last few feet into the treeline by Tyler. Fralich rushed over with morphine and bandages.

"*Bravo Two, advise of your situation, over*," radioed English.

"Still have heavy contact. Estimated enemy platoon. Friendly casualties moderate. I'm going to call for artillery fire and adjust it myself," Billingsley reported.

"*Roger. Can you hold until I break contact over here?*"

"Affirmative."

"Load 'em up and advise," English calmly ordered.

The NVA fired another RPG into the Marines' position. It burst high in the trees, but it was close enough to spray fragments onto one of Ambrosetti's men. "Corpsman," someone shouted. Then another RPG blast echoed through the position.

"Corpsman, over here."

Billingsley contacted an artillery battery to the south of Con Thien and provided them with the necessary grid coordinates and direction so that the target could be plotted. He asked them to send the initial rounds away from the NVA, and opposite the position of the Marines, so he could then "walk" the explosions toward the enemy. The NVA were close, so there was an extremely narrow margin for error. Billingsley had never before adjusted artillery fire in combat, and he wasn't all that sure of what he was about to do. He didn't want it too close, at least to begin with.

"Roger, Bravo Two. Standby one," came the reply from the artillery battery.

Billingsley rolled onto his side and shouted for the word to be passed that artillery would fire on the NVA. He was gripped with fear, the fear that only a slight error could kill more of his own troops than that of the enemy.

"Jesus, I hope to hell he knows what he's doing," Ambrosetti remarked to one of his nearby men. "It'll be a bitch if he doesn't."

Another NVA RPG exploded in the trees above the Marines.

"Hang on, Martindale. I hope this works out," Billingsley cracked nervously, noticing his radioman's paleness.

The gunfire continued from both sides. The rain and the clouds cast a dull greyness over the area. Billingsley's heart pounded. Please be there, he thought. Please don't make a mistake and blow us apart, he wished of the artillery battery, far away and unseen by those who needed their help. Please be there.

"Shot, over," came the signal from the battery. The rounds were on the way.

The shells screeched when they neared the target.

The two rounds exploded well to the rear of the NVA position. Billingsley's fears that his target location had been incorrect were greatly allayed.

"Drop one hundred, over," Billingsley called into the radio.

"Roger, drop one hundred."

Tyler ran up. "I'm gonna get us a few more men on the right flank. They may try to put a move on Sanchez if you get that shit too chose to 'em," he explained.

"Yeah, good. Tell Sanchez to let us know the minute he feels like they're tryin' to flank us," Billingsley said.

"Shot, over."

Again, the screeching approach of the rounds.

The next explosions roared just behind the NVA, impacting simultaneously. Tyler was up and running toward the far end of the position.

"Okay babe. Drop five-zero. You're close," requested Billingsley.

"Roger, drop five-zero. You want a fire-for-effect?"

"Negative, not until I see the next ones."

"Roger, drop five-zero."

"Oh God . . . I'm crippled. Please . . . get me out of here . . . I'm shot all to hell." The Marine with the hip and leg wound was still moaning. "Oh, it hurts bad . . . oh . . . oh . . . oh, God."

"Has he had morphine, Fralich?" Billingsley called.

"Yessir."

The gunfire and the rain continued. The NVA made no attempt to leave their positions and flank the Marines. Tracers flew in both directions.

"Shot, over."

C'mon, Billingsley thought. Get it on 'em.

The concussion from the bursting rounds was terrific, shaking the ground underneath the Marines. Billingsley saw black smoke and debris rising from the enemy location. The target had been hit.

"You're right on. Fire for effect," he shouted, exhilarated.

"Roger, fire for effect."

"We're gonna bust their ass, Martindale," Billingsley said to his much-relieved radioman.

Tyler came running back over to Billingsley's side and dropped to one knee. "Good shooting," he offered.

"Thanks. Think we ought to rush 'em?"

"Let's see what gives when we lean on 'em again. You get that stuff on top of 'em and we might not have to do anything," Tyler said.

"*Shot, over.*"

"GET DOWN," Billingsley and Tyler shouted.

Six rounds impacted like close thunder. The closest of the explosions flung soggy debris onto the Marines. The ground rolled and shook as if the world had come to an end. Indeed, for many of the NVA, the end had come. Their firing was considerably reduced, though intermittent muzzle flashes were still visible from the adjacent hedgerow.

"Hit 'em again!" Tyler said. "One more lick like that and we can jump 'em, no sweat."

"Repeat, over," called Billingsley over the radio.

"*Roger, repeat.*"

Billingsley and Tyler formulated a quick plan for an assault upon the enemy position and notified the squad leaders. The plan was simple—as soon as the rounds were completed, an all-out assault by the Marines would sweep through and destroy any remaining NVA. The platoon would have to move fast through the open terrain once the command was given to attack.

Billingsley felt both exhilarated and desperate as he pondered the prospect of attacking an unknown number of enemy soldiers who were likely well dug-in.

"We gotta jump 'em fast, lieutenant," said Tyler. "We gotta be out and on the move before the damned dust clears."

"Right," Billingsley agreed. He saw Martindale go pale again.

"*Shot, over.*"

Again, the treeline opposite the Marines erupted violently from the explosions of the 155mm projectiles. Mud and pieces of trees were flung into the air around the target area.

"LET'S GO," Billingsley screamed.

"GO, GO, GET UP AND MOVE," Tyler shouted.

Billingsley, Tyler, and the squad leaders led the men forward and out into the open. The NVA fired sporadically as the Marines sprinted at them. Sanchez and the few survivors from his emaciated squad reached the enemy bunkers and trenches first. Grenade explosions reverberated. The few NVA still alive held savagely to their positions until they were shot at close range by the storming Marines.

Ten minutes later, it was over.

Billingsley consolidated his platoon around the overrun position. The wounded were brought forward from the previous position. Billingsley saw Fralich assisting two men in the open area. They were eventually brought into the treeline.

"This is Bravo Two," Billingsley called to English. "We've taken the position by assault and have secured this area. We've got some people who need medical care."

"I've got APCs on the way to your position. We will escort. Half a klick to the southeast."

"Roger, hurry," Billingsley requested.

Billingsley surveyed the destruction within the treeline. Enemy bodies, and pieces of bodies, covered the ground in a grotesque blanket of death. The artillery shelling had killed most of them. He noticed a strange odor as he stood looking at the bodies and the carnage. The smell of power lingered, as well as that of freshly dug earth. And even though the rain continued, he became convinced that the smell of blood was the odor that stood out above the others. He winced at the thought, and brought his attention back to the business at hand.

"Call the arty and tell 'em they did a number on a whole platoon of NVA," Billingsley said to Martindale. "Tell 'em Bravo Two sends his compliments and his thanks."

Thirty-seven dead NVA soldiers were counted. Parts of others would have brought the total even higher had Ambrosetti and his men bothered to count the pieces. Billingsley watched as the bodies of four of his Marines were brought into the position and covered with ponchos. He was surprised to see that the man with the hip and leg injuries had died. Strange, he thought. By all rights, that man should have made it. Some were horribly mangled, and lived. Others sometimes died from wounds which, at least outwardly, seemed far less serious. Most of the time, a combat veteran could tell with a glance whether a wounded man would survive or die. But not all of the time.

English arrived, accompanied by two personnel carriers, along with First and Third platoons. The wounded and the dead were loaded, and First Platoon escorted the APCs back to Con Thien.

English and Billingsley stood together underneath the trees after the casualties had been evacuated.

"We'll get dozers out here and fill in these trenches as soon as the weather breaks," English said. "And while we're at it, we'll get this area defoliated to keep 'em out of here."

"Sanchez," Billingsley called. "Come over here."

Sanchez carried his rifle by the handle as he approached the two officers. "Yessir?" he said dutifully.

"Captain English," Billingsley said, "this man's performance was outstanding. His conduct under fire kept us from having a much harder time of it than we did. I just wanted you to know that Sanchez was a great deal of help to us, sir."

English stared into the Marine's dirty face. The young squad leader's eyes reflected the fatigue felt by nearly all the others.

"That's good to hear, Lieutenant Billingsley. Good job, Marine."

"Thank you, sir," replied the self-conscious Sanchez.

"Write it up when you get back," English ordered when Sanchez had returned to his squad. "We'll see about getting him a decoration. Now let's get ready to shove off."

"What about these gooks?"

"The dozers can push 'em under when they get out here."

The remainder of the company trekked back to Con Thien under the dreary, overcast skies. The rain still came in hard, steady streams. The compound was reduced to a thick goo of red mud as the men sloshed their way to their bunkers. Billingsley entered his damp bunker to find a can of beer with a note of congratulations from Tom Compton on the day's action. Compton had left the area with the APCs.

Fralich peered into the bunker, calling Billingsley's name.

"Come on in, doc," Billingsley said.

"You wanted me to give you a report on the WIAs," reminded Fralich as he stepped into the hootch.

"Right. What's the scoop?"

"Clifford and Vandiver are the worst off. They're in surgery now. The others look like they're gonna be okay."

"What about Clifford and Vandiver? Will they make it?"

"Clifford, maybe. Vandiver, I don't know. He lost a lot of blood, and his vitals were getting weak. As soon as the ceiling rises, they'll be shipped on to the rear. You'll probably get some of the others back in a couple of weeks, or so."

"What the hell did Robinette die from?"

"The one with the leg and hip?"

"Yeah. I didn't think he was hit *that* bad. The next thing I saw after hearing him moaning in the treeline was somebody covering him with a poncho."

"I don't know, sir. I thought I had him stabilized okay. When I came back to him, he had stopped breathing and I couldn't get a pulse. I couldn't get him back after that."

"Weird, ain't it?" Billingsley asked as he passed the last of the beer to Fralich.

"Sure is, sir."

Fralich drained the beer in two gulps. The blood of Billingsley's Marines was still evident on Fralich's drenched utility shirt.

"Your people enjoyed what you did today, lieutenant."

"What's that?"

"The artillery. On the ride back in with the APC, Dantley was tellin' everybody that one minute he thought he was dead, and the next minute he knew he'd make it when word came that the platoon was goin' over into the attack. And he kept asking everybody if they'd seen the arty workin' out on the gooks," Fralich said, smiling.

"They probably enjoyed it more than I did. I was too puckered to enjoy it," Billingsley laughed.

"You weren't the only one with the tight ass, sir. It's some kinda trip when the stuff's that close."

"Yeah, Fralich. I know exactly what you mean. It's one *hell* of a trip."

Fralich squeezed the empty can and then changed the dressing on Billingsley's arm. The wound had nearly healed, with little consequence other than the itching.

Ivester came in later and assisted Billingsley with the wording of the draft recommendation for Sanchez's Bronze Star medal.

The rain cleared on the following day, allowing for the evacuation of the wounded and re-supply of the compound. English arranged for the bulldozers to fill in the trenches at the scene of the fighting, with Bravo Company as security. The NVA had removed their dead under the cover of night, leaving nothing but the scarred terrain to show that a violent battle had been fought there.

Throughout the remainder of April, the perimeter patrols and forays into the adjacent areas were conducted with relative impunity. There were few challenges from the enemy, and only sporadic shellings of the compound. What few enemy

units were encountered in the field were destroyed systemati-
cally. Those enemy units were generally small, however. The
weather became the greatest irritant to the Marines, not the
enemy. The unseasonable rains, alternating with periods of
intense heat, created more than enough discomfort. There was
always either too much water during the rains or too little
water during the debilitating heat. Rosser had finally returned,
full of stories about his tempestuous two weeks in Japan and
one week in the Da Nang hospital for treatment of
gonorrhea.

At the end of the first week in May, English gathered his
platoon leaders at the CP to advise them of Bravo Company's
impending move to Quang Nam Province where, along with
the remainder of First Battalion, they would set up shop in
the Da Nang complex. A three-day rest would be the first
order of business, however. That piece of news was well
received.

"I was just getting used to the mud," Ivester joked when he
later joined Billingsley atop their bunker where they took
advantage of the sunny weather to read their mail and dry
their wrinkled, blistered feet.

"There's plenty of mud in Nam, Art. You'll feel right at
home as soon as we get back in the bush around Da Nang,
and it rains on us."

"What's the deal down there?"

"Beats me. I don't get the impression that it's anything
major. I guess we'll find out when we get down there."

"It'll be nice to lounge around Da Nang for a while," Ivester
said as he reclined on the sandbags. "I think I'll buy me a nice
watch in the PX and send it home. I hear you can get a good
deal on one for fifty bucks. First-class watch, I mean."

"Hell, I coulda got you one for free the other day if I'd
known you were in the market."

"What kind?" Ivester said, sitting up.

"Seiko."

"Damn, I wish I'd known. That's the kind I want, too."

"Well, it was a pretty one."

"Yeah? What color?"

"Gold."

"No shit? Why didn't you let me know?"

"I didn't know you wanted a gold Seiko, Art. Goddamn, I

can't read your mind."

"Where was it?"

"On the arm of a dead gook," Billingsley said with a grin.

"What?"

"Yeah, man. Real pretty watch. Looked brand spanking new."

"What happened?"

"Well, Willingham's squad surprised the dude on a patrol to the northwest of here. The gook was takin' a shit in some brush when the point spotted him. Dude was all by himself. Anyway, the point and the others near the front blew the guy away before he could even get his trousers above his knees. Willingham walked over to the guy, and he was really shot all to hell, and lifted the dude's arm up with the Seiko on it and said, 'keeps right on ticking.' Cracked everybody up, man. I had to chew their asses to get them to shut up. Then, on the way back in, I started thinkin' about the gook tryin' to finish his shit before the shootin' started, and then Willingham's stunt, and damned if *I* didn't almost break up."

"Who ended up with the watch?"

"Hell if I know, Art. I didn't want it."

"Don't think I would have, either."

"I probably would've taken it off every time I took a shit, if I'd ended up with it."

Billingsley was still laughing as he opened a letter from Andrea. In it, she detailed the flight schedules from Washington, D.C., to Honolulu in preparation for their planned meeting in Hawaii in June. Andrea chastised Billingsley for lack of letters from his end, complaining that she was doing all the writing. She had sent several snapshots, including one that showed her in a snug, ice-blue bikini swimsuit. Obviously Andrea was taking exceptional care of herself, Billingsley judged, looking closely at the curves and contours only partially obscured by the bikini.

"Damn, I'm ruined for the rest of the day," he lamented as he stared at the photograph, with Ivester straining for a glimpse.

The withdrawal from Con Thien started. The battalion was flown by helicopter to Dong Ha where prop-driven transport planes waited to fly them to Da Nang. They arrived in Da Nang in the early afternoon. On the way from the airfield to the Quonset huts where they would be quartered, Billingsley watched the heavy air traffic of jet fighters and transports at the Da Nang airfield. Marines shouted "Freedom Bird" when a chartered DC-8 made its climb away from Da Nang in full view of the combat-laden troops. Stateside bound. Maybe someday, Billingsley thought as he walked along in the hot sun.

The cleansing ritual began for Second Platoon as soon as the men were quartered. For those not assigned to various working parties, weapons cleaning and clothes washing were the major activities. The large PX at Da Nang offered enough merchandise to satisfy the needs of those with the money to afford it. Billingsley and Ivester went to the O-Club their first night at Da Nang for an evening of revelry and relaxation.

They awakened the next morning to the inevitable price one must pay for such a night.

"How you feelin', Art?" Billingsley asked when he returned from morning chow to find Ivester comatose in his bed.

"Sick," was Ivester's feeble reply.

"It was the Vietnamese beer, Art. Could also be those women we were with."

"What women?" Ivester asked, sitting up, displaying eyes the color of tomatoes. "I don't remember us being with any women. Who were they? *What* were they?"

"We weren't. I just wanted to see if I could get any movement out of you."

"Fuck you, Billingsley. I'm dying, man. I think I'm gonna need a blood transfusion, or something. *Everything* hurts."

"I could have come in here screaming that we're moving out."

"Are we?"

"No."

"Well, fuck you, then."

"What if the skipper walks in here?"

Ivester remained on his back a moment longer, mumbling in a strained voice, "Fuck him, too," before rising from his bunk. He groaned and held his head after pulling his trousers and boots on. He hurried to the door of the Quonset hut and held fast to the sides of the entrance.

"You gonna puke, Art?"

Ivester could only manage to nod his throbbing head in the affirmative.

"Well, get away from the door, for Christ's sake! Get between the hootches, where I did on the way to chow."

Ivester made it a few paces away from the door and was violently sick.

The second night in Da Nang was considerably more moderate for Billingsley and Ivester.

The final day of the break found English going over the plans for a new operation. The company was to conduct a sweep in the mountainous jungle southwest of Da Nang in an area called, incongruously enough, Happy Valley. While the enemy was not suspected to be concentrating large numbers of its forces in the region, enough concern existed in the Da Nang command structure to warrant a search. The operations of previous months and years, conducted primarily by units of the Seventh Marines, had left clearings suitable for fire support bases and landing zones. English, who was familiar with the region from his previous tour in-country, smiled at his platoon leaders when he mentioned that the hills and jungles would represent "quite a challenge" to Bravo Company.

Early the following morning, Billingsley and his mates discovered what he meant. The entire battalion moved up the Charley Ridgeline-Hill 1235 complex after being deposited by helicopters at the base of the high ground. The lower valleys and the ridgelines were matted with tangled vines, scrub trees, and bushes. The jungle canopy was 100 feet high and three layers thick, with few breaks except where artillery and air strikes had cleared small portions. Huge teak, ironwood, and mahogany trees rose from the jungle floor and disappeared into the solid canopy. Heat was a problem for the Marines in the steamy, stuffy vegetation.

Billingsley led his platoon along the slopes of a ridge toward a previously cleared opening near a high point. The objective of the platoon was to ensure that the site was free of booby traps and adequate for delivery of supporting artillery. First and Third platoons trailed behind the exhausted men of Second Platoon. The point of the column was within 500 meters of the clearing when Billingsley radioed English that his troops needed a break.

"*Take five*," English answered.

"Think we may need more than five. We're close to taking heat casualties up here."

"*Take five*," English repeated.

Billingsley considered a caustic response but thought better of it. Four hours in the jungle had extracted a heavy price for the beers and sodas at Da Nang. He watched his men slump to the ground with blank expressions on their faces. Some were able to fall asleep almost instantly while bracing their pack against a tree and sitting upright.

They were up and moving again in five minutes.

At the cleared area atop the ridge, the sweat-drenched men had to first search for booby traps. Finding none, they began chopping away patches of growth and removing logs which had been left by the previous American inhabitants. Two hours of work were needed before the position was secure and ready for the guns. The troops were allowed to rest at last.

The first of the fire support to arrive were the mortars—81mm and 4.2-inch tubes. Bravo Company dug itself into the slopes of the ridge while the mortarmen emplaced their weapons and aiming stakes. The choppers ferried ammunition loads which hung by sixty-foot nylon straps. The location was also suitable for touch-down landings of the helicopters. Fletcher and his headquarters staff came into the position to set up their CP once the mortars had become operational.

Meanwhile, companies A and C patrolled the regions adjacent to the support area. Fletcher's plan called for one rifle company to remain in the position as security while the other two patrolled for periods of three or four days. Thus, Bravo began the operation as the "in" company while the others were "out." To the south, another Marine battalion set up on a hilltop in similar fashion.

Billingsley saw to it that his troops were adequately dug-in around the perimeter's portion assigned to him. The mortars began their registration with their deep, thunking pops. The lush green valleys beneath the position, in their scenic, simple beauty, belied from a distance the heat and the vines and the uncertainty which each man had come to associate with the jungle. Though it looked peaceful and serene, each of the men knew all too well the sweat and toil which the jungle withheld from sight. Not to mention the enemy.

Tom Compton was touring the company positions, and

with him, Gunny Kennerley was sketching the fields of fire on a piece of cardboard. They came near Billingsley, who stood sketching his own fire plan.

"Lovely day, huh gunny?" Billingsley said with a wink toward Compton.

"Yessir, beautiful," Kennerley said gruffly without looking up from his drawing.

"You might consider some pastels for your sketch, gunny. The accent might give it a little more depth. Know what I mean?"

Kennerley shot a quick look at Billingsley before turning and walking away. Compton was irritated.

"Dammit, Mike. Why don't you leave the old fucker alone? He's scared shitless of you, and he didn't want to come over here to begin with."

"Fine with me 'cause I don't want him over here. He ain't worth a shit and you know it, Tom."

"Look, I just want you to leave him alone. I try to get him to get off his dead ass and contribute, and you intimidate the hell out of him. I know how you like to screw with his head."

"He'd contribute a great deal to this unit by throwin' himself on a frag grenade."

"Mike, leave his ass alone, dammit. You copy?"

"I copy, XO. Tell him I still love and respect him."

"Just stay out of his shit."

"Okay, Tom, I said I would. How about you staying out of mine?"

"I'm not in yours. And I didn't come over here for a pissin' contest, either. I came over here to tell you that the 05s will be in here in the morning, and that we go out day after tomorrow. Alpha's already had some contact."

"Bad?"

"Nah. They chased a gook squad for awhile, but lost 'em in the bush. They wasted two of the bastards."

"Good. We're off and running."

"And there's one other thing, Mike," Compton allowed with a repressed smile.

"Yeah?"

"A journalist will be coming out here in the morning to gather some material for a story on the 'real war.' Fletcher gave the dude the okay to go out with Bravo Company, and Captain English has given his okay for the guy to go with—"

"Oh, no," Billingsley protested. "Don't hand me that bullshit about the dude going out with me."

"It's true, pal. You got the short straw," Compton giggled.

"Come on, Tom. You're shittin' me, aren't you?"

"Nope. The guy's supposed to go out on a few patrols and take some pictures and generally stay out of the way. The skipper's gonna talk to him about the ground rules before he gets to you."

Billingsley stared disgustedly at Compton, satisfied that his friend was telling the truth. "Would it help if I bitched to English?" he asked, hoping but not really expecting to extricate himself from the arrangement.

"No, it wouldn't. Captain English isn't going to put the guy with Kupton, and Ivester's not as seasoned as you are. So, there you have it, hoss. He's all yours."

"Tom, how do you think I'm gonna feel if the joker goes out with me and gets his ass blown away? Or if he trips a wire and kills one of my people? That's the kind of shit that can happen in 'real war', dammit!"

"It's my understanding that the guy's been in the bush before."

"Swell. That's all I need. Why don't you put him with Kennerley? He'd be safe that way. Besides, if something unusual happened and they both got zapped, it really wouldn't make a shit."

"No way." Compton turned to leave. "You've got him, Mike. And I don't want to hear anymore about it. That's the end of it."

Billingsley sighed, realizing the futility of his objections. Compton's expression was firmly cast, the expression which Billingsley had come to know as being non-negotiable. He was stuck with the journalist.

"Compton, you communist fucking faggot."

Compton laughed and turned to see his disconsolate friend wadding the paper on which his fire plan had been sketched and tossing it angrily to the ground.

"Son of a *bitch*!"

Shortly after dawn, three Marine A-6 Intruders took turns

dropping napalm in a valley to the west where Company C had discovered a lightly defended NVA bunker complex hidden in the thick jungle. Dense black smoke rose from the valley as the pilots released the silver canisters of deadly napalm. The mortars took up the slack after the aircraft departed and fired dozens of rounds into the NVA position. The muffled concussions from the explosions followed several seconds after the flashes from the detonations. Billingsley sat outside his hole eating his C-rations while watching the show in the valley below, visualizing what he thought to be taking place on the ground. The NVA position was eventually overtaken by the Marines with little difficulty.

The howitzer battery was lifted by helicopters onto the hill after the mortar fire had lifted. English called his platoon leaders to the CP for a briefing. In attendance was a short, stocky, red-haired visitor whose round face and thick, bushy moustache created a distinct resemblance to a walrus. He wore jungle utilities, clean and pressed, and carried his bush hat in his back pocket. Nearby on the floor of the bunker was a Nikon 35mm camera in its case, along with extra lenses and tubes of film. Though his hair had thinned appreciably on top, the visitor's curls on the back of his head were a sharp contrast to the crewcuts around him. His brown eyes and ruddy complexion gave him a weathered look. And in the presence of lean, fit Marines, his sizable belly seemed to flop over his belt in impious disregard of physical conditioning.

English introduced the man to his officers and staff as David Kemp, a freelance writer/photographer making his fifth trip to Vietnam. Mr. Kemp's purpose, English explained, was to gather material for an updated report on the war's activities. He was on assignment for a national magazine. This prompted Billingsley to hope that his own picture might appear on the glossy pages which might be scrutinized in a certain Reston, Virginia, residence.

Kemp greeted each of the platoon leaders with a firm handshake and an affable, engaging grin. His voice boomed, and his words were flavored with just a trace of a British accent, no doubt the result of his parents having moved to New York from their native London shortly after World War II. Kemp's father was a broadcast journalist; his son had favored the print media after earning his degree at Yale. Kemp's manner seemed wholly pleasant, his demeanor relaxed. He thrust his hand and smiled widely when introduced to Billingsley.

"So you're the chap with whom I'll be going on safari?" Kemp said with a laugh.

"That's what I'm told, sir," Billingsley replied with a hard glance at Compton. "That is the plan, isn't it, Lieutenant Compton?"

"That's the plan," answered Compton. "Captain English had an opportunity to speak with Mister Kemp on the procedures we'll insist upon as far as his being in the field with us. He understands that this is a military organization and that he's going out on a military mission."

"That's right, Mike," English added. "This won't be his first time out with Marines. He was at Hue City last year."

"I've heard the proverbial 'shot fired in anger' once or twice, Mister Billingsley," Kemp said.

"I should say so," Billingsley agreed.

"If you have no objections, I'd like to join you for dinner tonight," Kemp suggested as he looked at Billingsley.

"That would be fine. You can find me in the Second Platoon sector," Billingsley advised.

"Good. I'll see you this evening."

Billingsley and his men spent the day improving their position. Fighting holes were dug deeper, barbed wire was strung, sandbags were filled, claymores were emplaced, and fields of fire were coordinated with adjacent platoons.

As planned, Kemp found Billingsley that evening in the Second Platoon area.

"Might we get a table for two?" Kemp asked facetiously as he approached wearing his bush hat and carrying a box of C-rations.

"Probably," Billingsley said. "I have a little influence on this side of the ridge."

"That's what I admire—a man with influence. What do you suppose is going on over there?" Kemp pointed at a CH-46 hovering over a distant stretch of jungle.

"Looks like he's got a sling in the trees, so it may be a medevac. Could be re-supply, though. There aren't many breaks in the canopy where a chopper can set down."

They chose a spot on the ground near the edge of the perimeter and placed their meals on a wide tree stump. The heat had diminished somewhat, although it was still warm enough to keep them sweating. Their elevated position showed a sweeping panorama of green hills and valleys which seemed to stretch eternally beyond the distant horizon. Each opened his box of Cs and the packets which contained spoon, salt, sugar, and other enrichments.

"Got a John Wayne?" Kemp asked.

"You *have* been in the field before," Billingsley laughed at Kemp's reference to the small can opener which, inexplicably, carried the name of the popular movie actor.

They warmed their food with heat tablets and discussed their respective backgrounds. Kemp, in his mid-thirties, wanted to know Billingsley's impressions of Vietnam, the country, as well as his thoughts on the current conduct of the war. His questions were pointed and direct, causing Billingsley to feel that candid answers could hardly benefit him in the eyes of his superiors.

"Mister Kemp, I'm just concerned with doing my job as best I can, and beyond that I'd really prefer to keep my personal opinions to myself. You can understand that, can't you?"

"But surely you must often think about the meaning of all this chaos."

"Why the hell should I?" Billingsley countered testily. "My opinions don't make any difference right now, outside of purely military matters. And on a small scale, at that. If I do my job, keep my people squared away, then maybe we can see this thing through. You see, Mister Kemp, life in the field isn't all that complicated. You just try to survive, that's all. But that can be heavy enough without cluttering your head with a lot of philosophical bullshit that you can't resolve in the bush anyway."

Kemp wiped his mouth with a paper napkin from his goody packet. "Do you agree with the rather popular notion that stipulates this conflict is, by its very nature a civil rebellion and not an incursion by an invading force?" he asked.

"I neither agree nor disagree," Billingsley answered between bites of canned apricots. "I'm an unthinking, uncaring, jaded warmonger hell bent on pillaging and plundering the Orient."

"Nonsense! Your Captain English informs me that you're a gentleman of considerable intelligence and resourcefulness.

Let me try another angle, then," Kemp said with a thoughtful expression.

"Okay."

"Do you, Mister Billingsley, hold to the opinion that the war can be brought to a successful conclusion by continued military force?"

Billingsley glanced quickly at Kemp before settling his gaze upon the hills in the distance. He deliberated silently for a moment, lost in the abstractness of concepts and the experience of reality. He answered finally, "I don't know."

Kemp waited while Billingsley continued to look away for a moment longer with the distant expression of one who is absorbed in deep thought. He finally turned and stared at Kemp, the same expression still fixed on his face.

"I really don't know," he repeated.

"Perhaps you would prefer the succulence of your C-rations to my annoying chatter, Mike," Kemp said in an almost apologetic tone.

"No, I don't mind. You're not annoying me."

"Are you sure?"

"I'm sure."

"Well, then. Do you hear from home often?"

"Yeah, pretty regularly."

"Are you able to draw any inferences about the war from your correspondence?"

Billingsley laughed and said, "I don't need any inferences in my correspondence, Mister Kemp. If you'll notice, I'm ass-deep in the Goddamned war where I *am*."

"I'm aware of that, old man. But the news from home can be most revealing."

"How's that?"

"Are you aware of the level of opposition to the war back in the States?"

"I haven't paid much attention to anything back home since the Super Bowl. It's hard enough to know what's going on in the rest of I Corps, much less back in the States. People back home have no idea how isolated you feel after you've been over here for a while."

"There *is* significant opposition to the war."

"I know that. I haven't been over here all my life, it just seems that way."

"And it's growing by the day."

"Well, that's not surprising. But the people who are the most vocal, I would bet, don't know shit about this country and even less about war."

"An element of cowardice, would you say?"

"Probably. It's usually not too dangerous to bitch about something when you're comfortable and safe, and want to stay that way."

"Do you defend the war, Mister Billingsley?"

"No, Mister Kemp. Just this part of the ridge."

Kemp smiled faintly at the rejoinder with a look of admiration in his eyes. He sensed that Billingsley was opinionated; he also sensed the caution in the answers to his questions.

"What will you do when you're back, my friend?" Kemp asked.

"There's a young lady in Virginia . . ."

"Ah, yes. I'll bet you won't be quite as elusive with her as you are with me."

"I'm not elusive!" snapped Billingsley. "I'm a line infantry officer who takes orders and gives orders in a combat zone."

"I didn't mean to offend you."

"I'm not offended, Mister Kemp. I just don't care to sit on hills and walk through jungles debating the issues with a reporter. Okay?"

Kemp held two fingers aloft with one hand while his other supported the canteen from which he took a drink. "Peace, brother," he slurred with his mouth full of water.

"Yeah, right," laughed Billingsley. "Speaking of peace, we may run across some unpeaceful characters who mistakenly judge that this area belongs to them. In that event, I think you ought to have a helmet on your head and a flak jacket around that gut of yours when we leave here in the morning. Get rid of that bush hat, mister."

Kemp raised his eyebrows in mock insult. "Are you aware, young fellow, that none other than Lieutenant Colonel Fletcher himself has made the wearing of helmets and flak jackets an optional feature for jungle patrols?" he asked with an exaggerated smirk.

"Indeed, I am. And are you aware that Captain English has asked me to shoot on sight anyone not choosing the Bravo Company option where a helmet's on your head and a flak jacket's around your upper body?" Billingsley said with a straight face.

"Brutes," replied Kemp as he stood to leave. "I could be enjoying a whiskey about now in Saigon, but instead I must endure this wretched heat and whatever it was in those cans of Cs. Not to mention being threatened by a typically vulgar and coarse Marine."

Billingsley laughed out loud.

"I bid you good evening, Mister Billingsley," Kemp said as he extended his hand.

"Good night, Mister Kemp."

Billingsley had begun to enjoy Kemp's free spirit and wit. He had also enjoyed talking with an American whose recent experiences included something other than the noise of gunfire. And Billingsley envied the fact that Kemp would finish his assignment and climb aboard a plane for home in only a matter of days, as opposed to the long months ahead which he himself faced. How liberated Kemp must feel, he thought. Able to come and go as he generally saw fit. What a difference, Billingsley concluded.

The calm and quiet of the night enabled Billingsley to sleep for several uninterrupted hours in the deep hole. He felt rested when the new day dawned with bright, clear skies, and he joked with Martindale that combat could hardly be had on a more lovely day. The men ate their rations and then adorned themselves with full packs, stuffed with provisions for three days, and as many canteens as they could find. Most carried at least five.

Soon Bravo Company was filing out of the perimeter and heading into the jungle on its slow swing through the valleys and over the hills to the southwest. Ivester's platoon took the lead. Billingsley's group, with Kemp, brought up the rear. As usual, heat became an immediate concern as soon as the long column entered the canopy. Sweat soaked the uniform of every man. It burned their eyes and salted their tongues. English moderated the pace, rotated the point platoons often, and called for frequent rest breaks. The company assiduously avoided traveling along ridgelines, choosing instead to fan out along the slopes, no matter how steep. English's aim was unpredictability and difficulty in being fixed as an easy target. Although a rifle company was hardly inconspicuous, English refused to make it even more so by walking along ridges, which would certainly alert the enemy to its presence.

Scout dogs accompanied the Marines to warn of potential trouble spots along the way. The two German shepherds signaled an alert on three separate occasions during the first six hours of the patrol. Each time the company halted while artillery pulverized the area under suspicion.

During the late afternoon, gunfire erupted to the front of the column when Kupton's platoon came upon five VC soldiers who were resting near the cool waters of a stream bed. Two of the VC eluded the rifle fire; the remaining three met their deaths in the stream. The shallow waters diverted around their bodies, carrying blood downstream. Billingsley noticed Kemp photographing the corpses, which had been dragged out of the stream by the time Second Platoon was upon the scene. Kemp appeared exhausted, his face red and his expression blank as he aimed his camera and clicked.

"You okay, Mister Kemp?" Billingsley asked when he passed beside the journalist.

"Yes, especially if you consider the fate of these unfortunate gents," Kemp responded.

The company moved on, numb from their exhaustion and depleted body fluids. The difficulty of the route also made them irritable. Vines, rocks, slopes, and the inevitable command to "tighten it up" provided each man with his own minor hell, a hell which included aching feet and soreness virtually everywhere else. Skin irritations, particularly in the area of the crotch, added to the discomfort of the entire ordeal.

The company swept through a valley floor and climbed the crest of an adjacent hill. English halted the advance and ordered the company into a defensive perimeter. Word finally came that the hill would become the company's night position. "Dig in," the command echoed along the top of the hill.

"This has got to be the worst fuckin' day of my whole fuckin' life," Martindale sighed as he and Kemp started their digging. "The absolute fuckin' worst, man."

Billingsley and the other platoon leaders met with English to discuss the security of the position and the locations of the listening posts. English warned the group of the relative insecurity of their location, adding that indifference to proper security could turn out to be extremely harmful.

"Wouldn't surprise me in the least if Charles attempts a probe before the sun rises in the morning," English explained.

Billingsley and Tyler designated the listening post occupants and ensured that the platoon positions were adequately manned and dispersed. Billingsley returned to the three-man hole and settled back with Kemp and Martindale for dinner. Less than an hour of daylight remained.

"These things are abominable when they're cold," Kemp said with a grimace as he stared at a rude spoonful of his C-ration spaghetti and meatballs.

"They ain't all that great hot," Martindale said.

"Better than nothin'," Billingsley commented.

"I think the lieutenant here is the ultimate pragmatist," Kemp said. "Wouldn't you agree, Martindale?"

"Careful, Kemp," Billingsley warned. "You can knock the chow, but you start putting words into the mouths of my men and you'll risk being ejected from this hole."

"There he goes again, being brutish. He's also the ultimate brute. Don't you think so, Martindale?"

"That's it, Kemp," Billingsley said, stifling a grin. "Get the hell out of this hole. You're on your own now."

"But where, may I ask, do you expect me to go?" Kemp asked, rising to glance around the perimeter.

"Burma, if you like."

Martindale burst out laughing at the exchange. He knew that Billingsley was enjoying the banter with Kemp.

"You have my apology and my sincerest plea to remain where I am, no matter the food and the verbal abuse. I shall say nothing further, gagging as I am from the body odor," Kemp joked.

"You should talk," countered Billingsley. "You sweat like a mule at the slightest movement. Another fifteen or twenty years at this pace and you'd be rid of that obscene beer gut."

"That's not a beer gut, my good man. It's a condition derived from the enjoyment and appreciation of fine cuisine," Kemp explained. "Do you think, Mister Billingsley, that we'll see any action tonight?"

"I don't know. That'll be up to Charles, for the most part."

"Me and the lieutenant have been in some holes in the

ground when all kinda shit was goin' on around us. Right, sir?" Martindale said.

"Sure have. We've been in our share when nothing happened, too."

"If we start havin' to bust some caps, Mister Kemp, you just keep your head down and watch Lieutenant Billingsley zap 'em with his pistola," said the grinning radioman.

"To be frightfully honest with the both of you, I would be most grateful to Charles if he would permit me a needed night's rest."

"Get any leeches on you today, Mister Kemp?" Martindale asked.

"Christ, yes! After a bit I became so tired that I just let the bloody savages have their fill."

Martindale giggled as Kemp continued with his stories of the day's activities. They eventually became quiet as exhaustion overtook them. Billingsley remained awake for some time, wary of an enemy probe.

The night passed slowly but uneventfully, gradually giving rise to a steamy, overcast dawn. Billingsley awakened first.

"Let's go, people. We'll be pulling out in a half-hour. Up and at 'em," Billingsley spoke as the groggy faces and eyes of Kemp and Martindale came to life.

"Oh dear God," sighed Kemp, propped sideways against the earthen interior wall. "What a shame to leave my fantasies of ecstasy for another day of agony."

"Get him on his feet, Martindale. I'll be at the CP."

The men ate their rations and the company moved off the hill. Billingsley's platoon was situated in the middle of the column, with English and the CP, as the patrol headed north.

Movement was difficult as on the previous day. The route chosen by English kept the company off the ridges and trails and in the very teeth of the jungle and hillside slopes. Billingsley noticed fresh feces in several places along the path cut through the jungle by Ivester's troops. He sent word by messenger to English, calling the CO's attention to the droppings. Before long the column halted near a small opening in the canopy created by previous aerial strikes. The company waited while a medevac chopper arrived and lifted the two dogs, along with their handlers, through a break in the jungle by extending a nylon sling to the ground to which an aluminum fold-out seat was attached.

"One dog's got the shits and the other's showing signs of heat problems," English commented, disappointed at losing the effective warnings of the teams.

Billingsley's platoon rotated to the point after the helicopter had departed. An hour's travel along high ground led to a downward slope and a thick, narrow, overgrown valley. Sanchez moved the point men of the platoon perhaps twenty meters into the valley before he called for a halt.

"*You'd better take a look at this,*" Sanchez radioed to Billingsley.

Billingsley and Martindale walked to the front of the column and found Sanchez quietly studying the terrain in front of him. Ahead lay a partial clearing, a sort of channel through the brush, ten meters wide, with less vegetation. The opening appeared to extend for at least 100 meters. Though covered overhead by the intertwined branches of trees, the spacing between the limbs provided glimpses of the light of the sky.

"Got anything?" Billingsley whispered.

"No, sir. But I don't like the looks of it," Sanchez replied.

"Could be booby trapped."

"Sure as hell could. There's plenty of cover, and pretty decent light to set up an ambush spot. It'd be easy to just slide away into the bush once the ambush was sprung."

"What do you think, Sanchez? Think we ought to skirt it?"

The perspiration rolled down the sides of Sanchez's face and dripped steadily from his chin. His eyes remained fixed up ahead, searching, inspecting, considering. "I think so, sir. I'd a helluva lot rather break brush on the high side as I had to walk through there," he said, finally.

"Let's take a look," Billingsley said as he unfolded his map.

"It'll take an offset of half a klick, sir. But I'll bet there's something in there. It just looks too natural to suit me."

Billingsley and Sanchez studied the map spread on the ground. Martindale touched Billingsley on the arm with the handset of the radio.

"Skipper's on the hook, sir."

"This is Bravo Two, over," Billingsley spoke over the radio.

"*This is Six. What's the delay?*"

"We've got a pretty shaky looking spot up here. There's a

218/BENT, BUT NOT BROKEN

lane through the valley, and it might be best for us to slide around it."

"*Should I take a look?*"

"I'm working out an offset that'll take us back to the high ground before we cross the valley on north of here."

"*Roger. Standby and I'll be up there soon.*"

"Roger that."

Billingsley gave the handset back to Martindale. Just then, several AK-47 rifle shots echoed loudly along the valley floor about fifty meters away. One of the bullets found its mark, striking Martindale squarely in the forehead and slightly below the rim of his helmet. Billingsley saw Martindale's expression turn blank from the shock of the bullet passing through his head. His hand jerked toward Billingsley as he reeled backward and fell. The other Marines along the point dove for cover and began returning the fire of the enemy. Billingsley lunged at Martindale as bullets whooshed over his own head. Martindale had fallen over onto his back, on top of his pack and radio, with his helmetless head dangling above the ground. The exit wound on the back of Martindale's head was warm on Billingsley's hand when he attempted to support his young radioman's head and neck. His hand was covered in blood and pieces of brain, and Martindale was completely limp.

"Oh Jesus Christ . . . corpsman . . . CORPSMAN . . . Oh God, Martindale, hang on . . . CORPSMAN, GET UP HERE . . . c'mon baby, stay with me . . . GET UP HERE CORPS-MAN . . . Martindale, c'mon dammit . . . hang on, please . . . FRALICH, GODDAMMIT HURRY."

The Marines' firing intensified. Billingsley remained on the ground, cradling Martindale's head. Sanchez started maneuvering a fire team against the ambushers who kept up their own firing.

"I'll have you out of here soon, Martindale . . . c'mon, just hang on a little while longer, babe . . . FRALICH . . . c'mon, man . . . FRALICH . . . breathe, Martindale . . . breathe, dammit!"

Billingsley heard English's calls coming through the handset on the ground beside him.

"This is Bravo Two," he radioed. "We've been ambushed on the point. Request a priority medevac. Urgent, over."

He ignored English's repeated calls for additional information. Fralich arrived in a crouch and attempted to detect a pulse in Martindale's arm. There was none. Billingsley crawled forward, trying to locate his forces up ahead. The VC fired an RPG which exploded directly over Billingsley's head, twenty feet above him and within the canopy of the trees. His leg and hip burned. He clutched the ground and awaited another burst. Only the gunfire at the point continued.

"Stay down, lieutenant. You've been hit," Fralich said.

"Just see after Martindale. I'll be fine."

"Ain't nothin' I can do for Martindale. Now stay on the ground."

Through the ringing in his ears, Billingsley could vaguely hear the sounds of his pursuing Marines as they fired rifles and grenade launchers at the fleeing VC. More of his men ran by him to join in the chase with Sanchez and his squad. Tyler arrived and radioed a report to English while Ambrosetti set the remainder of the platoon into a defensive perimeter.

Billingsley winced as Fralich applied dressings to his leg and hip. Another call for Fralich sounded from the brush nearby for the benefit of two other injured Marines. Billingsley felt his blood-soaked leg, satisfied that at least it was still attached. The corpsman gave him a morphine injection and dressed the wounds before he ran to answer the call from nearby. Billingsley rolled onto his side and tried to stand up. He was stopped by a firm hand on his shoulder.

"Stay down, Mike. There's still some firing," Tom Compton said as he knelt beside Billingsley.

Billingsley felt groggy and rolled back onto his stomach. He overheard Compton order a nearby Marine to cover Martindale's body with a poncho. He heard English as the CO stood nearby and transmitted a situation report to Fletcher's headquarters.

"Three WIAs and one KIA at this point," Billingsley heard English say.

The grogginess intensified.

"Hey, Tom," Billingsley called weakly.

"Yeah. What is it?"

"Am I goin' into shock?"

"Nah. You'll be fine, hotrod."

Compton left to move up ahead. English leaned over and

gave his wounded platoon leader a lit cigarette. "How 'bout it, ace?" he said.

"I'm okay, sir."

"You've got another hole back there, Mike. Might come in handy when you get back out here and start eating Cs again."

"I was happy with the one I had, sir."

"We should have you out in a few more minutes. Just take 'er easy for now."

Billingsley recognized the sound of an approaching helicopter. Soon, a CH-46 was hovering overhead and extending the nylon sling into a partial clearing in the valley. The two other wounded men were able to walk to the sling, with the aluminum seat attached, and seat themselves beside one another. They were then raised into the body of the chopper.

"Off you go, sir," Tyler said while assisting Billingsley to his feet.

"Look after 'em until I get back," Billingsley shouted as he limped toward the sling.

"No sweat. Take care," Tyler shouted in return.

Fralich and Tyler helped Billingsley into the seat, leaning him on his side to keep his weight off the painful hip wound. Tyler nodded and slapped Billingsley on the boot as Fralich signaled for the sling to be raised. Billingsley noticed the odor of the engine exhaust and the high-pitched whirring through his grogginess, as he was pulled into the hovering chopper. He was placed on a litter on the deck while the other Marines sat with their arms and hands bandaged. Martindale's body was then pulled aboard and placed upon a stretcher near the back, his boots protruding from underneath the poncho. Billingsley felt the chopper pitch forward, then bank and head toward Da Nang.

"God bless you, Martindale," Billingsley said softly as he rested on the cool deck of the helicopter.

When he awakened, Billingsley found himself in bed, in clean sheets and air-conditioned comfort, at the hospital in Da Nang. He remembered only bits and pieces of his arrival by helicopter and his removal to the operating ward, and nothing beyond his having been prepped for surgery. The fragments from his leg and hip had been removed and he had later been wheeled into a partitioned room of the Quonset hut and left to sleep away the fog and haze. Sleep had come easily, with the drugs separating him from the horrors and sights which only hours before had been so real, so close. He rested on his stomach, unsure for a moment after awakening exactly where it was he had found himself. The stiffness in the back of his leg reminded him of where, and of the reason why. He looked back to see a physician, not much older than himself, standing at the foot of the bed and studying the papers attached to a clipboard.

"Good morning," spoke the doctor.

"Good morning," he answered groggily.

"Were you able to rest?"

"Yes, sir. Out like a light."

"Three fragmentation wounds, two in the leg and one in the hip. Not too bad."

"How bad is 'not too bad?' Will I be in here very long?"

"If there's no infection, something on the order of ten days or so should be sufficient," said the doctor.

"Is all the metal out?"

"As nearly as we can tell. There may be some slivers, but the big pieces are out."

The doctor unwrapped the dressings and viewed the area of the wounds. The clean, laundered sheets smelled fresh and felt good as Billingsley buried his face in his pillow. The doctor's probing caused little pain. Billingsley tried to feel the wounds but was reprimanded by the physician.

"Hands off, lieutenant. Like I said, you'll be out of here much sooner if there's no infection."

"How does it look?"

"You're healing normally. A corpsman will be along in a minute to apply clean dressings."

A corpsman arrived with sterile bandages. "You'll need to start thinking about what you're going to tell her, lieutenant," he observed as he dressed the wounds.

"Tell who?"

"The first girl who'll feel the two-inch scar on your butt."

Billingsley did not respond to the chuckling corpsman. He was trying to suppress jumbled thoughts of the previous day in the jungle valley. The good memories of Martindale, the impish grin and boyishness, seemed overshadowed by his appalling death. Billingsley had become attached to

Martindale, more so than to anyone else under his command. He felt Martindale's loss almost as much as he would the loss of his own brother.

"That's it, lieutenant," the corpsman said, finished with the dressings. "Decide what you're going to tell her?"

"Get the fuck out of here, doc. I'm not in a joking mood."

After two days of recuperation, Billingsley could walk around the ward with only a moderate tightness remaining in his leg and hip. He visited the other Marines from Bravo Company, two of whom were from his platoon, and found them in good spirits. His own attitude was aided by the brief talks with the other men. Observing several critically injured Marines, fighting for their lives during each moment, made Billingsley realize just how fortunate he had been.

The next day Billingsley was reading an old issue of *Sports Illustrated*, savoring a glimpse into that carefree world so far removed from his life, and so vaguely remembered. David Kemp walked into the room.

"Is this the gallant Mike Billingsley, reduced to a bed from an ass full of Soviet metal?" the affable Kemp bellowed.

"And this must be the terror from Happy Valley," Billingsley said, smiling as he received the warm greeting and handshake from Kemp.

"How are you, my tattered friend?" Kemp asked softly and sympathetically.

"I'm fine. And what about you?"

"I'm also doing fine. Your Bravo Company will be back tomorrow when the operation concludes. Or so they told me. Impossible for me to stay long, as I've a plane to catch to Saigon in an hour. Here, I brought you some reading," Kemp said, handing Billingsley a paper bag filled with news and sports magazines.

"Hey, thanks a lot. I can use them to pass the time."

"You're quite welcome. By the way, the others send their regards."

"Did you get what you needed to do your story?"

"Yes, I certainly did. I've also discovered that jungles are no place for civilized creatures. I was terribly distressed at what happened to you and the young Martindale. Will you recover without complications?"

"Sure. I'll be out of here in a few more days."

"It was a dreadful sight, the ambush."

"Where were you when the stuff hit the fan?"

"You didn't see me?"

"No, I don't remember seeing you."

"I came up with Sergeant Tyler, just after the explosion. My heart sank when I saw the two of you on the ground, and all the blood. I poured water on the back of your neck and handed you the canteen for a drink. You don't remember?"

"No, I don't," said Billingsley, puzzled at the void in his memory.

"I stayed with you for a while until Lieutenant Compton told me to 'scram' when he came up with the CO."

"Is everybody okay?"

"I think so. Your man Ambrosetti said he would bring some 'ladies' by to cheer you up when the company got back to Da Nang," Kemp said, raising his bushy eyebrows and smiling.

"I don't doubt that Ambro could find 'em."

"It's good to see you, old man. It wasn't quite the same afterwards."

Billingsley thought of Martindale's laughter as the three of them joked in the cramped confines of a faraway hole in the ground.

"It never is," Billingsley said.

"I would enjoy sitting down with you at some future time and buying you drinks until you fall out of your chair. Perhaps we can arrange that when you're back in the States."

"I'd like that, too."

"I must warn you, though. I do tend to dominate conversations with my ramblings about the comparisons of the world's women. Especially when I'm drunk and inclined toward taking liberties with the truth."

"I would enjoy listening to your ramblings."

"Then we shall arrange such a session. You must do everything to ensure a complete recovery so there can be no excuses at your not being able to keep up with me once the first round is served."

"I'll be healthy and happy when our time comes, I can assure you."

"I must catch that flight, my friend." Kemp glanced at his watch. "I'll be passing through D.C. early next week. Can I pass along any messages to your young lady in Virginia?"

"Yeah, if you don't mind."

"Of course not. The company of pretty women is far preferable to jungles and bloody Marines."

Billingsley wrote Andrea's name and address, both home and school, on a piece of stationery and gave it to Kemp.

"Tell her that I'm fine, and that I'll see her soon," Billingsley instructed.

"I will, Mike. I'll send your best." Kemp folded the slip of paper and placed it in his wallet. "Anything else I can do for you before I have to shove off?"

"No, Mister Kemp. I do appreciate your visit. I wish you luck."

"And I wish ample portions of the same. My best to you and all the men of Bravo Company," Kemp said, extending his hand.

They grasped one another's hand in a long, sincere handshake.

Billingsley read the magazines from cover to cover, especially the portions dealing with Vietnam. The Vietnamization issue was featured in one of the articles. There was a photograph of ARVN troops, waiting in an LZ for the choppers which would ferry them "into combat against the stubborn enemy." Quotations from high-ranking American officers, in and outside Vietnam, indicated their apparent satisfaction with the program. "It's working," they all agreed. There were statistics— ARVN troop levels, hamlets under control of the South Vietnamese government, and equipment expenditures by the U.S. government on behalf of the South Vietnamese. Big numbers. Big aspirations.

Billingsley's mind flashed back to several previous encounters with ARVN troops. He remembered their tight, pegged, camouflaged uniforms. He remembered the contempt which his troops held for the ARVN. He remembered Tom Compton's observation that the NVA and the ARVN were "basically the same breed of gook. So why is it that one fights like a tiger and the other runs like a deer? Sure as hell ain't *bio*logical; it may be *socio*logical; whatever it is, it's damned sure *il*logical." It's working? Billingsley wondered. Really working? Do the generals really believe that? Do the reporters? Do the American people? And if the American people do, would they *still* if they knew clearly how many American troops were in the field? Or in the hospital? Or in the stinkin' friggin' morgue?

Billingsley came back to the photo of the ARVN soldiers. He felt a sudden rush of anger, as if there was no credit due his role—America's role—in handling the lion's share of the fighting and bleeding. "My ass," he muttered, tossing the magazine aside.

The next day brought visits from Compton, Ivester, Tyler, Ambrosetti, and several others. The battalion had returned to Da Nang with only meager results to show from the grueling jungle operation. Compton and Ivester talked of the heat and rashes and infections which had afflicted nearly all of the men in the company. Ivester himself sported a swollen, reddened upper arm.

"It was a bummer, Mike," explained Compton. "Not a whole lot to show for it, either. You were better off in here, to tell you the friggin' truth."

"A guy from Kupton's platoon even got bit by a Goddamned *snake!*" Ivester said. "It didn't kill him, but it made him sick as hell. Just up and bit the piss out of him."

Compton brought a letter from Andrea, scented with perfume, along with a letter from Bill Blanton.

"How long will you guys be in Da Nang?" Billingsley asked.

"Couple or three days," replied Compton. "Enough time to get rid of this jungle rot, I hope. When will you be ready to get out of here?"

"Hell, I'm ready now, Tom. But they tell me it'll be a few more days before they turn me loose."

Compton and Ivester kept Billingsley laughing with stories of the struggle in the jungle, not so much from the events as from the deliberate and ridiculous exaggeration. So Billingsley laughed obediently at their efforts, and they left fifteen minutes later, feeling satisfied with the results of their visit.

Billingsley opened his letter from Andrea. He held it near his nose and breathed its perfume, reminded of the softness of her. She wrote about their scheduled reunion.

> My parents are still cool toward the Hawaii thing, though they don't come right out and say it. As for me, I'm anything but cool over the thought of spending ten whole days with you. And nine whole nights,

I might add. I'm having trouble deciding upon the clothes I'll need to bring, and I'm sure you'd be of little help in offering some suggestions. You'd probably grin and tell me that I won't need any clothes. And you know what? You'd probably be right. You usually are, anyway. As soon as your leave is approved, be sure and let me know the exact dates. Until then, baby, please be careful. Please!

I Love You,
A.

News from Blanton was encouraging. He had begun an exercise program at his home in California. Blanton joked about the pitch of his voice having risen since his injury. If Blanton could joke about it, Billingsley thought, then his recovery must be nearly complete.

He had completed one paragraph of a letter to Andrea when Captain English walked into his room.

"Hello, Mike. Feeling better?"

"Much better, sir," Billingsley replied, pleased at seeing English.

"That's good. Can you get around now?"

"Yes, sir. There's still some pain, but a few more days and I'll be ready."

"That's outstanding. I can sure use your help."

"Tom and Art came around to tell me about the operation. Sounds as if I didn't miss too much."

"I would consider it a success, but we sure as hell didn't set the woods on fire. I think the higher-ups were generally pleased, though."

"Any word on what's next?"

"Not yet. I'd like to be able to give the men a few days off before we go back out there. Almost all of 'em have jungle rot and a few got sick from drinking water out of a stream."

"Sounds like Bravo Company's had enough for a while."

"Yeah, I think so. Well, now you've got *two* Purple Hearts," English said with a laugh. "Stupid medals, that's what those things are."

"That fits me, sir," Billingsley grinned.

"Got something I'd like to bounce off you," English said, turning serious.

"What's that, skipper?"

"I'm going to transfer Gunny Kennerley to a support section here at Da Nang. Colonel Fletcher's helped me work it out."

"I don't blame you, sir. I think it's a good move."

"Will you think it's a good move if I take Sergeant Tyler from you and put him in Gunny Kennerley's place?"

"I think Sergeant Tyler would do well in that job," Billingsley said after a moment's hesitation.

"Can you get along without him?"

"Ambrosetti would be an adequate replacement, sir."

"So you agree with the move?" English asked with a slight smile.

"You're the CO, sir," Billingsley said, also smiling.

"Listen, Mike, I'm not taking advantage of your being away. It wouldn't happen for a couple of weeks, anyway. But we have a mission as a rifle company that requires us to put people in positions where they will do the most good, with seniority as the guide. We're going to lose a certain number to wounds, R&R, sickness, you name it. So when we get to the bush, we've got to have good people in the key leadership billets. Sergeant Tyler can help us a lot more as Gunny Tyler. That is, if you have a replacement you're confident can do the job."

"And I do have a competent replacement, sir. You have no arguments with me over the move, I'll assure you. Tyler's a perfect platoon sergeant, but Ambrosetti's not far behind. I'll support the move wholeheartedly."

"Good. I want you to understand that our mission is foremost. Everything else is secondary."

"I think I understand that, skipper."

"I think you do, too," agreed English. "I just wanted to reinforce it."

"Any particular reason, sir?"

"No, other than the fact that we've still got a mission and we've still got a war."

"I noticed the war the other day, sir. And I'm reminded of it every time I turn over."

"Very well," said English.

Billingsley suddenly felt uncomfortable with English. What had started out as an easy and light conversation had somehow become almost an adversarial confrontation.

"You know, of course, that the round that killed your

radioman was likely intended for you," English said as he glanced through a *Pacific Stars and Stripes* newspaper which he had picked up from the stand beside Billingsley's bed.

"I've thought about that, yes. But I think they recognized that Sanchez and I weren't too happy with walking through the area where they had the ambush set up, and so they decided to spring it early."

"That was the only time we were ambushed."

"What the hell does that mean?" Billingsley asked sharply.

English folded the paper and placed it at the foot of the bed on which Billingsley reclined. "It means that it was the only time we were ambushed," he said calmly.

"Sir, if I screwed up," Billingsley protested, "it wasn't because I blindly walked the platoon into the ambush. We pulled up short before they had a chance to do a *real* number on us."

"I didn't mean to imply that you had screwed up. And I don't think that you did, as a matter of fact."

"Well, I'm beginning to feel as if I'm on the stand. Like I need to defend myself."

English stared at Billingsley for several seconds. "I think you're a little sensitive in more places than one. Just hurry up and get yourself well and back with us," he said.

Billingsley stared back at English. "I will, sir. I'll be ready soon," he replied after a pause.

"Good. Anything I can do for you? Anything you need?"

"Everything's fine, skipper. Thanks for the offer, though."

"Okay, then. Take care and I'll see you soon," English said as he left the room.

Billingsley was perplexed by the conversation and bewildered by his own seeming inability to communicate with English. He felt uncomfortable in not knowing where he stood with his CO, suspecting that English either distrusted him or doubted his abilities as a combat officer. Billingsley began to feel a creeping doubt about himself, doubt over his own worth and proficiency. And those were new feelings for him, strange feelings. He was discouraged, a feeling brought on by the events of the previous five months as well as the conversation of the previous five minutes.

The hospitalization, though comfortable and removed from

the threat of imminent danger, dragged by. His thoughts were full of the faces and voices of those whom he had known and those who had met death on the battlefield. Stacey, Page, Maroney, Billy the Kid, Martindale, and others whose names he had forgotten but whose faces he remembered with clarity. Always the faces. Frozen faces. Frozen in the irrefutable and unalterable mask of death. So final, and so sudden. Especially the kid Martindale. He just couldn't shake Martindale. The boyish face, the gap-toothed grin, the loyal and willing follower. No matter how hard he tried, there was the voice and the face of Martindale.

He spent hours listening to the radio Sergeant Ambrosetti— now promoted—had loaned him. And he could sometimes push away the thoughts of loss and death by indulging in long, delightful daydreams of Honolulu excursions with Andrea. Restaurants, showers, ocean breezes. Suntan oil, cold beer, white sandy beaches. Television, room service, sleeping late. Daylight sleeping and nighttime lovemaking. Daylight love-making and nighttime sleeping. He could imagine it all with such intensity that he could close his eyes and know the sight or smell or taste or feel of just about any object or activity. And he could clearly visualize Andrea. Her skin, her touch, her long hair, her lovely smile. The Smile. It was the next best thing to being there.

"Dear God," he whispered as he stared at the curved ceiling over his head, "please keep me out of one of those body bags until I can have all of that again. Even if it's only one more time. That's all I ask, God. And I realize that it's a selfish request, but you understand how much it would mean to me. Please, just a little while longer."

On the afternoon of his eighth day in the hospital, the doctor said Billingsley's release for duty would occur on the following morning. He was also told that he was free to enjoy a night of liberty, if he so chose.

Bravo Company had left the day before to provide security for a village south of Da Nang. Before they left, Tyler had brought Billingsley a clean uniform and his gear, ready for his return to the platoon. Billingsley decided to change into the uniform and venture into town.

The streets along Da Nang's gaudy bar strip were crowded with servicemen, some wobbling from the effects of excessive alcohol. Loud music and foul odors assaulted Billingsley as he walked along the street. He eventually selected a reasonably uncrowded bar and took a seat at a table that faced one of two unsmiling, scantily clad Vietnamese dancers. The go-go girls danced suggestively to juke box records of American rock music. The music, Billingsley noticed, was at least two years old, and some of the records were badly scratched. Shapely girls undulated atop elevated wooden platforms directly opposite the wide bar.

He ordered a beer and sat alone on the bench seat of the corner table, watching the dancers and the crowd of American servicemen who shouted occasional lewd invitations to them. Not long after his beer was served, an attractive Vietnamese girl, dressed in dark slacks and light blouse, walked to his table and motioned with her hand for permission to join him. When he nodded his approval, the girl slid along the seat alongside him. She had been extravagant with her cheap perfume.

"You buy me drink?" she asked, leaning toward Billingsley and placing her hand lightly on his thigh.

"Yeah, why not," he acquiesced.

"Scotchy-watah," she ordered when the waitress appeared.

"Another beer, too," Billingsley added.

"You are Marine, yes?" she asked softly when the music had stopped and the dancers had stepped down from the platforms.

"Yeah."

"You not come in bar before, yes?"

"Right. I haven't been in here before."

"You offy-cer, yes?" she asked, carefully gauging Billingsley's response.

"Right. How did you know?"

"You act like offy-cer," she replied with a smile.

"All I've done is sit and drink beer. What's so unusual about that?"

"Many Marine come in bar," the girl giggled. "Many talk loud, call for girl. You quiet, like gentle-man. I think maybe you offy-cer."

"Gentleman and officer," Billingsley laughed. "You're pretty smooth, sweetheart. I'll give you credit for that."

They sat in the corner table and talked. Each time he ordered another drink, she ordered another drink. He knew the prices for hers were inflated, but he cared little. He was enjoying the company. She had long, flowing hair and an oval, attractive face. She smiled often and prettily. She became more appealing to him in a direct relationship to the number of beers he consumed.

They talked for more than two hours, through a half-dozen shifts of the go-go dancers. The stiffness in his hip and leg from the sitting was numbed by the eight beers.

"I've gotta get back," he finally announced. "I'll be too messed up if I stay here much longer."

"You stay one more drink. Okay?"

"No deal. I've got to get back."

"You very nice. I like you very much. Stay one more drink. Okay?"

The girl leaned toward Billingsley and kissed him softly on the mouth. He felt her tongue flicker inside his mouth and felt her hand touch him discreetly between the legs. Her lipstick tasted good, her touch even better.

"Ah, what the hell," he conceded. "One more drink."

The girl smiled and ordered another round for each. The dancers began anew, pushing and grinding their hips while their small breasts bounced from the motion. Billingsley felt lightheaded, from the taste of the lipstick as much as from the beer.

"Girl have nice body, yes?" she asked, pointing at the nearest dancer.

"Real nice," he replied as if in a trance.

"My body good, too. Numbah one. You see, you like."

Billingsley turned and faced his companion. "Well, get up there and dance and I'll let you know."

She leaned close to his ear, pulling at his neck with her hand. "I dance for you in bed, *s'il vous plait*. I have room behind bar."

"*A la bonne heure?*" said Billingsley with a bit of a slur.

"Yes," laughed the girl. "*A bras ouverts.*"

Billingsley stared at his enticing companion, surprised at how quickly his noble intentions of a quiet evening alone had vaporized. His judgement was cloudy, he knew, but little else mattered except the delicate features of the girl.

"What's you name?"

"My name Donna."

"Donna, right," he laughed.

"You go? We have good time?"

"Yeah, let's go," he said, summoning the bill. "I could use a little good time."

They left the bar from a rear door after Billingsley had paid for the drinks. They walked to a spindly, two-story dwelling down a darkened alley past other shanties of wood and sheet metal. The air was foul behind the bar, worse than on the street to the front. They walked up creaky wooden stairs and into a small apartment.

"Come, please," she said as she escorted Billingsley through the small den and into the single bedroom. Light came from a lone lamp on a small wooden table beside the bed. A bamboo-woven chair and a dresser with mirror were the only other pieces of furniture. Financial details were negotiated before the girl undressed to her black bikini underwear. She wrapped her arms around Billingsley's neck and kissed him fervently. Once in bed, he discovered that her body was as good as advertised—soft, active, pleasing. He quickly tired and allowed her to do most of the work. She was equally effective in that capacity.

"You like, yes?"

"Yeah. Keep going."

She moved herself over him, pushing, swiveling, rolling. She moaned, though Billingsley wondered about its authenticity. He moaned, and made her wonder. The first was quick, the second thereafter.

Afterwards, Billingsley lay on his back and smoked a cigarette. He laughed out loud when he thought of the girl as a rental object, one for which a fee was paid for the use thereof. So absurd, he thought. A real person, with feelings and a mother and a place in this world. A place as a whore, he thought as he laughed. He had never paid for sex before, and the whole concept suddenly seemed so ludicrous.

"Whattsa mattah you?" the girl asked.

"Nothing," he said.

"Why you so funny?"

"It's nothing, really."

"You wounded, yes."

"Yeah, I was wounded."

"Do hurt you?"

"Not much."

"You have girlfriend in States?"

"Sure," he answered as the girl rubbed his chest and shoulders.

"You marry when you go back States?"

"I hope so, if she'll have me."

"She have you. You nice."

"I *dinky dao*. She may no have me," he said in an Oriental tone.

The girl laughed. He reached for her again and pulled her close to him. Return on his investment, he thought as he laughed softly again.

When Billingsley woke later, daylight filtered through the thin drapes over the window. The girl's thin arm rested on his waist, her body still close to his. She awakened when he climbed from the bed to begin dressing.

"You leave now?" she asked sleepily.

"Yeah. Don't get up."

"You come back. Okay?" she said as she sat up and pushed her long hair behind her head. "Come back to bar."

"If I get the chance," he muttered as he laced his boots.

Billingsley winced at the stench of the alley as he stepped out into the already hot morning air. He hitched a ride with a Marine driving by in a jeep and returned to the hospital.

He went to his room and was gathering his belongings when a corpsman entered the partitioned area. "We thought you might have gone UA, lieutenant," the corpsman said.

"Nope. Anybody miss me?"

"Doc Baldwin wanted to know where you were. I told him you went to see a buddy in another ward. He told me to let him know when you got back so he could send you back to your unit."

"I appreciate that. Tell him I'm ready to go."

"Okay, sir. Take care if I don't see you again."

The physician appeared and advised that treatment should be continued until Billingsley's wounds were fully healed. He started to leave, but turned and smiled.

"At least you'll smell good when you get back out there."

"Sir?"

"You smell like a French whore, lieutenant. Cheap perfume, but rather fragrant, still."

"I've had nothing to do with any French whores," Billingsley said innocently.

"So I was only partly correct, then. Good luck to you," said the physician with a wave.

Billingsley left the hospital and walked in the hot sun to First Battalion Headquarters to arrange transportation to Bravo Company's position. When he entered the Quonset hut serving as the CP, he saw Lieutenant Colonel Fletcher standing in front of a color-coded map, chatting and pointing. A major stood alongside, quietly.

Fletcher turned and noticed Billingsley. "Hello there, sport," he called.

"Morning, sir. Think I might could get to where Bravo is?"

"Sure thing. We've got some vehicles about ready to shove off for that area."

Fletcher told a clerk to make the necessary arrangements.

"Feelin' okay, lieutenant?" Fletcher asked.

"Fine, sir. I'm anxious to get back."

"Attaboy," smiled Fletcher. "Good hunting when you get down to Hoi An."

"Thank you, sir."

"This way, sir," said the clerk. "I'll take you to Motor T."

PART THREE:
For Conspicuous Gallantry

7

The greetings from the men of Second Platoon were enthusi-astic and raucous when Billingsley returned to duty. There was ample kidding about his having been "in the rear with a hole in his rear." He enjoyed the joking for what it was—a comfortable way for his troops to welcome him back to the fold. Everything was back to normal.

Tyler, Ambrosetti, Sanchez, and Willingham were gathered with Billingsley under the shade of coconut palms within the village of Hoi An. The talk centered on the current security operation underway. Bravo Company had been assigned to protect the village from VC interference. During the previous week, before the Marines arrived, VC teams had entered the village requesting food and enlistees and had spoken of the American abandonment of the village for the comfort and security of Da Nang. The word of the meeting had soon spread throughout the district, resulting in the deployment of the Marines as a commitment to the safety of the village and the hamlet. Fletcher had finally relented, sending Bravo Company after having argued fruitlessly for sending an ARVN company who, instead, operated in the mountains to the northwest. In addition to security and patrolling, the Marines had been assisting with civic action programs, distributing foodstuffs and medical care.

"Beats the hell out of the bush," commented Willingham as three shapely Vietnamese schoolgirls walked nearby, giggling and talking rapidly in their high-pitched tones.

"I don't know about that," countered Ambrosetti. "The VC are probably all over the place, the sorry pricks."

"Any signs of 'em so far?" Billingsley asked.

"No, sir. But you know how they are. They'd rather set out

booby traps or shoot you in the back than come at you like a Goddamned man," Ambrosetti answered spitefully.

"They ain't *even* like the NVA, man. I'm with Ambro. I'd rather be up north bustin' caps than messin' around with these slimy motherfuckers," Sanchez added.

"Well you ain't up north, girls," Tyler snapped. "You can piss and moan all you want, but you know good and damned well what it is we've got to do. Got anything else, sir?"

"No," Billingsley replied. "I think I've got a pretty clear idea of the situation."

"Okay. Sanchez, you get your people ready for the night ambush. Willingham, you'll take your squad out first thing in the morning," Tyler ordered.

"And Ambro can fuck off, right Sergeant Tyler?" laughed Ambrosetti.

"If you can fuck off with my K-bar tickling your nuts," Tyler said, "then have at it."

The squads went about their patrolling of the areas surrounding Hoi An, finding little tangible evidence of VC operations. English staggered the patrol times and locations, and ambushes were moved to keep the VC guessing. The villagers went about their work in the long rice fields which quilted the deltas and alluvial planes in a velvet-green blanket. They exchanged glances with the passing Marine patrols who searched for the elusive guerrillas. The hot sun and brutal heat were constant companions. The patrols were short and the terrain was flat, significantly reducing the misery of "humping." When not patrolling, the men sought relief from the heat underneath the shade of lean-tos made of their outstretched ponchos supported by sticks or limbs. They listened to radios, played card games, or merely lounged on the ground.

The first contact with the VC occurred when a patrol from Ivester's platoon detonated a booby trap and came under light sniper fire in an area south of the village. One Marine was dead and two had been wounded when the half-hour skirmish ended. A sixteen-year-old boy, captured during the action, was brought to Hoi An for questioning. He gave information that caused English to deploy Billingsley's platoon 2,000 meters southwest of the village. English suspected a larger VC presence in that vicinity.

Billingsley and his squads arrived at their assigned location and dispersed within an island of trees surrounded by open terrain. Billingsley positioned himself in the center of the formation, with Willingham's squad. Ambrosetti, on the left, and Sanchez, on the right, protected the flanks. They dug their holes and waited for darkness, maintaining radio contact with each of the squads as well as with English, who remained in the village. Each squad had brought a light-intensifying scope to the field for night visibility. Dusk brought a perceptible cooling from the intense heat of the afternoon as the men settled into their holes to break out their rations.

Billingsley's new radio operator was PFC Philip Tetrick, a short, wiry, dark-haired nineteen-year-old from Detroit. His Adam's apple protruded from his thin neck, and his glasses rested on a prominent, pointed nose. A product of a broken home, he had viewed the Marine Corps as an alternative to the mean streets of the city and a welfare existence. He looked older than nineteen. He had been in Vietnam only five weeks.

"Is it true what they say about the night belonging to the VC, sir?" Tetrick asked after Billingsley had completed a radio report.

"Nope," Billingsley replied, glancing up from the schematic of the fire plan.

"But they *are* more active at night, aren't they?"

"Sure they are. And if they *didi* in here, we'll be pretty active ourselves."

"Think they know we're here?"

"Yep, most likely."

Billingsley noticed Tetrick's concern and heard insecurity in the young radioman's voice.

"Think they'll show up?"

"Possibly. But if I were them, I'd want a lot of help."

Billingsley reached for his cigarettes inside the pocket of his flak jacket and discovered an unopened letter from Andrea. He had forgotten it since receiving the word from English to mobilize the platoon. He was pleased with his unexpected find and delighted to be able to start the long night with fresh word from Andrea.

Billingsley's expression turned from joy to shock as he read the two-page letter on the yellow stationery. He came to the end and then looked away silently and blankly for a moment. He read it again.

Dear Mike:

This is the most difficult letter I've ever had to write. This is also the most difficult period of my entire life. Late yesterday afternoon, after a court appearance with a client, Daddy was stricken with a massive and fatal heart attack. The news has stunned Mother and me beyond belief, as I am sure you can understand. Daddy's health had never been a problem, so the suddenness of his death has left us crushed and bewildered.

Mike, with less than two weeks remaining before we are to meet in Hawaii, this tragedy forces me to cancel the trip which I so desperately wanted. I cannot leave Mother so soon after this terrible loss. I just cannot do it. Please try to understand, my darling.

I have not stopped crying since yesterday, and I cry now as I write this letter. My world has suddenly turned upside down, and I find it impossible to express to you all the emotions I feel as I sit here in my room. I wish that you were here to be with me. I've never needed you more, Mike. Or wanted you more.

I want you to know that my love for you has never been greater, and our being together again remains the central focus of my life, particularly now. I know that you, too, will be hurt that our plans are changed.

David Kemp called and notified me of your having been hurt, which also upset me greatly. Mike, why didn't you tell me? I was terribly frightened until David assured me that he had seen you, and that you were recovering. And then this terrible thing with Daddy. Oh Mike, I just don't know what to say. I feel so alone, and so lost. And I'm afraid.

I will have to write more later when I can sort out all the things that I want to tell you. I must now greet the friends and relatives as they come to pay their respects.

Please, please be careful, Michael. I could sure use
a letter from you.

I Love You,
A.

Billingsley folded the letter gently and placed it in the pocket
of his flak jacket. He felt a tremendous sympathy for Andrea
as she, too, experienced the profound sense of helplessness
that inevitably followed in the wake of such a loss. He thought
of the trip to Hawaii, deeply disappointed that he would miss
the chance to be with Andrea. But mostly he felt sympathetic
toward the girl whom he so dearly loved. He knew the pain
of a sudden loss.

The thought and sight of death had always been so remote
to him before the military. Death had always seemed a concept,
a condition reserved for others, a function of advanced age.
Life had always been a constant, a guarantee. He had known
little of death and thought little of dying. In Vietnam, however,
everything had changed. Death was as natural a sight in
Vietnam as a baseball box-score in a sports section. There
were no irregularities in either, no incongruity with the surroundings. There were bodies of the dead in Nam and
Killebrew and Kaline in the box-scores. But now death had
reached out beyond Vietnam, touching his life in a different
manner apart from the abstract cause-and-effect relationship
of battle and death.

"Bad news, sir?" asked Tetrick, breaking the silence.

"What?"

"Did you get some bad news, sir?"

"Yeah, pretty bad. Just one more downer," Billingsley
replied.

Tetrick sensed that his platoon leader preferred to leave the
subject unaddressed, so he was silent. Several more minutes
elapsed before Billingsley began to recover. Some comfort
came to him in knowing that, at the least, Andrea was safe
and secure.

Nightfall blackened the fields and paddies around Second
Platoon as the squads scanned their sectors with the three
Starlight scopes attached to M-16 rifles. By the time midnight
had come and gone, Billingsley was dozing in his position. All
was quiet except the buzzing of the mosquitos. Billingsley

would awaken on occasion to check with his squads by radio on the perimeter's security.

Then a muffled but perceptible shouting was heard in the distance, somewhere in front of the platoon. Nothing was seen, but the shouting became louder over the next few minutes. All else was still in the black of the dark night.

"Marine. Hey, Marine," came the high-pitched shrill.

Billingsley radioed Willingham to his front and asked if he could see anything in the scope. Willingham's response was negative.

"Hey ... Marine ... Marine."

"Jesus Christ! How many do you think are out there?" asked Tetrick, who was getting increasingly more jittery as the cries continued.

"I don't know," Billingsley answered calmly. "At least one, but maybe a zillion. I don't know."

"Marine ... hey, Marine. Fuck you, Marine."

Billingsley reported the incident to English's CP and was told to provide reports on all developments. "No shit," he muttered to himself. Moments later, Tyler called from his position to the right and suggested that Billingsley blast the area with artillery.

"Not yet," he radioed. "Let's see what he's got in mind."

Another shouter to the left-front began alternating with the first taunter.

"Marine ... fuck you, Marine."

"Hey, Marine."

Ambrosetti reported that nothing had been sighted in the field of view of his scope.

"Hey, Marine."

"Fuck you, Marine."

The platoon was awake and edgy as the shouting continued. Dawn was yet several hours away and the darkness was to the advantage of the enemy. Billingsley had considered the possibility of an impending mortar or rocket attack, but thought it odd that the enemy would prematurely announce its presence. The VC, he knew, were routinely unconventional, though he had never known them to initiate an attack with verbal taunts.

"Marine ... you die, Marine."

"Hey, Marine."

Billingsley radioed an artillery battery near Da Nang for a check on the clarity of communications. The voices on the other end were clear and crisp. The squad leaders continued straining to see the outline of a human form through the lenses of the scopes.

"You die, Marine."

"Marine . . . fuck you."

Again the squad leaders reported seeing no one. Billingsley advised each to maintain noise and fire discipline until clear targets existed. He kept a flare nearby and was sorely tempted to illuminate the area for a sweep from the automatic weapons and machine guns. Maybe he's bluffing, he thought. Maybe he just wants to screw with us, or get us to give our positions away so he can shell the piss out of us. No dice, he concluded. It was eerie and unnerving.

The longer the wait continued, the less frequent the taunting became. English was kept informed of the situation, since he held a reserve force at Hoi An. The Marines' anxiety changed to frustration as the loss of sleep and the lack of action heightened their aggressiveness. They wanted a shooting match, not a shouting contest. And they particularly wanted a clean shot at the chest cavities of the two taunters. Only an hour before the first light from the rising sun came into view did the shouting suddenly cease.

Dawn appeared in an orange cascade as Billingsley gathered his tired squad leaders for a meeting. They reviewed the events of the preceding hours, deciding that the enemy had intended only to harass them.

"Sergeant Ambrosetti, how far was it from your position to where the gook was shouting, in your estimation?" Billingsley questioned.

"Two hundred meters, max. Probably less."

"What about you, Willingham? What's your estimate of the distance from you to the other gook?"

"About the same, sir."

"Sergeant Tyler, those distances should be within the range of the scopes, shouldn't they?"

"Should be, sir."

"Okay," said Billingsley. "So they obviously weren't standing up and moving around while they were shouting at us. They were low, maybe even prone. Agreed?"

The men nodded their concurrence.

"So it might make sense that there's a tunnel out there, at a distance of less than two hundred meters. And they just conveniently slipped underneath when they thought we'd come after them at dawn," surmised Billingsley.

Tyler's raised eyebrows indicated that the logic of the suggestion was sound, and that he thought the likelihood of the existence of a tunnel was strong. "Makes sense to me," he agreed.

"The ground's not wet out there to the front. The tall grass would make it easy. I've seen tunnels in terrain like that before," offered Ambrosetti, turning to look to the front.

The squad leaders tensed with anticipation. They wanted a hunt.

"We'll move out on a line, go out two hundred meters and, if we haven't found anything, turn around and come back. We'll leave the M-60s here in the trees to watch the back door. Stay on your toes and watch the ground closely, especially for booby traps. Anybody got any questions?" Billingsley said.

There were no questions, but there were several wicked grins.

"Well, let's go wake up Charley and blow his shit away," suggested Ambrosetti.

Billingsley radioed his plan to English, who agreed immediately. They left the treeline and spread out with all three squads abreast. The men moved along cautiously in the high grass, examining the ground at their feet and snatching quick glances to their sides. Billingsley knew that his men were exposed, though he hoped the size of his force would discourage any attempts by a smaller enemy force at initiating contact.

The Marines reached the predetermined distance without finding any evidence of tunnels, then turned and started back toward the treeline. After moving about twenty meters, one of Ambrosetti's observant fire team leaders pulled up a clump of high grass, thatched together to resemble the natural condition of the ground, and discovered a small, circular opening to a tunnel.

Tyler ordered a quick perimeter as members of Ambrosetti's squad began dropping frag grenades into the hole. "Fire in the hole" was shouted a half-dozen times before Billingsley called for the men to cease. Rosser, Ambrosetti's most senior and experienced subordinate, stripped to the waist, exposing the rippling muscles that plated his chest and stomach. Rosser was small enough to fit into the tight opening, too small for larger men to enter. Armed with a flashlight and a .45, Rosser unhesitatingly lowered himself into the hole, feet first. Ambrosetti and Billingsley crouched near the opening.

The time passed slowly after Rosser disappeared.

"Hey, Ambro," came the muffled shout of Rosser, finally.

"Yeah. What have you got, man?" answered Ambrosetti as he knelt beside the opening and gazed downward.

"There's another level."

"You want another frag?"

"Naw, man. It's too damned close. I'm going down to take a look," called Rosser.

Billingsley was apprehensive about Rosser's searching the lower level. His preference had been to gas the tunnel with CS, but none of the gas had been brought to the field. Dammit, he thought. Might have known we'd need it when we don't have it.

Five minutes elapsed before Rosser emerged from the hole. His black skin and hair were powdered with tan soil. He wiped his face with his utility shirt before dressing himself.

"Anything down there?" asked Billingsley.

"Ain't no gooks. Motherfuckers done booked. Ain't nothin' down there but some mess gear and a five-gallon water can. I left everything just like it was, 'cept I took a piss in their water," grinned Rosser.

"Any other exits?" Billingsley questioned.

"Naw," shrugged Rosser. "This is the only one."

"Damn. I thought we had 'em by the short hairs," commented Billingsley while reaching for Tetrick's radio to advise English of the results.

"This is just for storage, probably. Ain't got but one tube for ventilation, and only one way in and out," pointed out Ambrosetti as he pulled on a short, hollow pipe hidden a few feet away in the grass.

"Get 'em ready to leave, Sergeant Tyler," Billingsley ordered.

English ordered Billingsley to return to the village. As the platoon was leaving the area a Marine to the rear of the column shouted in a high-pitched shrill toward the front of the group, "Hey, Marine . . . fuck you."

"Pass the word back to knock off the bullshit," ordered

Billingsley, managing a straight face amid the laughter.

Back at Hoi An, they were met with the word that Second Platoon would remain in the village for the rest of the day. The troops were pleased to hear they could get some "crash time." Many took the opportunity to spread out under their shelters and sleep to the sounds of the rock music emanating from the many transistor radios.

Billingsley was summoned by English to the CP, after which he walked somberly back to the platoon area. He saw Ambrosetti ambling toward the village hut where a medical team was treating Vietnamese patients.

"Where the hell are you going?" shouted Billingsley.

"To that hootch, sir," Ambrosetti said, pointing toward the location of the medical team.

"Are you sick?"

"No, sir. Those gook nurses who were in here last week looked pretty good. Thought I'd check 'em out and see if it's the same crew."

"Negative. You go back and turn your squad over to Rosser. Then you get him, Sanchez, and Willingham, and meet me at my hootch in zero-five," ordered Billingsley.

"What the fuck, over?"

"You are now the platoon sergeant," Billingsley replied. "Don't stand there staring at me like a bumbling idiot. Get to it."

The men gathered at Billingsley's lean-to and heard the announcement of the changes in the command structure. Sergeant Tyler was now Gunny Tyler, though in billet only. Gunny Kennerley was being transferred to a meaningless job in Da Nang, though Billingsley downplayed the delight he felt over the transfer. He spoke of his confidence in both Ambrosetti and Rosser as each stepped up a notch in responsibility. "Nothing changes, as far as I'm concerned," he said. "You know how we go about our business. You've all been in the bush together. You know my procedures. Do your jobs and everything's cool. Any questions?"

"Yes, sir," Ambrosetti said. "Who the hell's the platoon leader when you go on R&R?"

"Why *you* will be, 'Lieutenant' Ambrosetti."

"One good deal after another, sir," allowed Ambrosetti,

shaking his head in mock disgust. "Those nurses will be pissed when they hear I'm not gonna have time for 'em."

"They'll understand," grinned Billingsley. "You're making a sacrifice for your country. They can make one for theirs."

After the meeting Billingsley put in a request that his R&R address be changed from Hawaii to Japan. Captain English, upon hearing the news of Andrea's letter, had suggested that Japan would be an entertaining and enjoyable vacation. English had visited Japan with his wife and had found it to his liking. Top Day entered the request for the change through the normal administrative procedures, promising Billingsley that he was confident he could "swing it."

Word began circulating that President Nixon had authorized the withdrawal of a large number of combat troops from Vietnam. Rumors placed the number of men to be withdrawn from 10,000 to three entire divisions. Only the relative new-comers, those with less than three months in-country, placed any store in the rumors. The salty veterans smiled faintly at the rumors, paying little attention to anything other than their mail and their weapons cleaning. They knew better, the veterans.

Billingsley wrote to Andrea, expressing his sympathy and concern over the death of her father. He understood her need to be with her mother, he wrote, and considered the trip cancellation to be a responsible decision on her part. He wrote of his recovery and return to duty, and of his plans to visit Japan. He encouraged her not to worry about him, that the dangers were minimal and the duty was easy. When he completed the letter, Billingsley went looking for Fralich to obtain something for the throbbing headache which plagued him.

Gunny Kennerley departed for his new duties in Da Nang in the early afternoon. Tyler gathered his belongings and assumed his new duties at the CP. It was unanimously agreed throughout the entire company that Tyler's presence in his new capacity would benefit the unit.

The ambush teams left during the late evening and the security and listening posts settled into their places as the village became quiet. A gentle breeze carried the aroma of Vietnamese cooking into the Second Platoon sector on the fringes of the settlement. In the distance to the west, rumbling indicated that unseen B-52s were unleashing tons of explosives upon targets many thousands of feet below them. There was an odd contrast in the togetherness of village families so near the impersonal, destructive airstrikes which thundered on the western horizon in rapid orange flashes.

After an uneventful night, squads left the next morning for their short patrols into the adjacent fields and paddies. The routine of the day was altered twice, each time as squads called for medevacs to rush to their field locations to retrieve the victims of booby traps. On two separate patrols, two men from First Platoon and a man from Sanchez's squad were critically injured by explosions from booby traps. Not a single shot was fired by the Marines; they encountered the enemy only in the explosive devices he had rigged and left behind.

"This is total bullshit, sir!" protested Billingsley while he and English monitored radio reports from Sanchez at the CP. "If we stay here long enough, we'll lose everybody we've got without a single contact."

"If we don't patrol, we don't provide adequate security," countered English, staring straight ahead. "And our mission is to provide security for this village."

"Can't we provide adequate security without having to patrol so much, sir? Damn, they're bleeding us to death."

"It's not the frequency, lieutenant," snapped English. "If a Marine steps on a booby trap, whether it's one patrol or a dozen, it's gonna cause casualties. Our people are careless. *That's* our problem."

Billingsley disagreed but decided against pressing the issue. He knew that further argument would only irritate them both. If it was patrols English wanted, Billingsley decided, then patrols English would get. Fine, he thought. We'll patrol until we're blue in the face, if that's the way it's got to be. Or dead.

And patrol they did. The next five days produced a grand total of two VC dead, both caught in a night ambush near the southeast corner of the village. Three more explosions from booby traps took the lives of two more Marines and sent three others to Da Nang with serious injuries. Tyler even intimated to Billingsley that he suspected that some of the squads were "sandbagging" their patrols, resting under whatever shade they could find, out of sight of the village, and calling in fictitious situation reports. Billingsley was informed, however, that Second Platoon squads were not among those under suspicion.

"Skipper don't know about this, lieutenant. I'm just telling you so you can keep your eyes open," Tyler said.

"I appreciate that, gunny," Billingsley said. "Will you tell the CO?"

"If I find out for sure, I'll have to. But first I'm going to bust a few platoon sergeant's asses. Lieutenant Compton's gonna talk to you platoon leaders."

The word went out to the troops. A gentle reminder it wasn't.

A day later, on a routine patrol southwest of the village, a squad from Ivester's platoon ran into trouble with a numerically superior Viet Cong force. The squad, accompanied by Ivester, had been caught in the open and was unable to maneuver. They were in danger of being overwhelmed by the VC. The fighting had drawn to close quarters when Ivester shouted into the radio, fixing his location and requesting immediate help. English suggested artillery, but Ivester declined because of the closeness of the contact. Ivester sounded desperate.

"We're in high grass and we're pinned down by automatic weapons from a treeline to the southeast," radioed Ivester. *"We can't get loose, and the bastards are movin' on us! They're movin' on us right now! I can see 'em! We gotta have some help, over."*

"Roger. Be advised that Bravo Two is on the way to your pos," replied English. "Hang tough until we can get 'em to you."

Billingsley's platoon left the village in a trot and moved quickly toward the steady popping of the gunfire. English kept a small force within the village and recalled the other patrols in the event that more help was needed.

When Billingsley's point was 200 meters from the firing, VC in a treeline to the left-front of the approaching Marines turned their automatic weapons upon the reinforcements. The remainder of the area was mostly open terrain covered in waist-high grass. Bullets swooshed over his head as Billingsley struggled in the grass to spot Ivester's position. Sanchez and Willingham had their men fire into the narrow stand of trees from which the VC sprayed the entire area. Marine grenadiers fired M-79 rounds at the enemy before ducking under the return fire. Billingsley saw that Ivester's position was to his right-front, creating a triangle from their positions to the treeline. He raised Ivester on the radio.

"Can you move toward us?" asked Billingsley.

"Negative. They're between us, and I swear to God they're throwing more men into it!"

"Roger. I'll come to you, then. But first I've got to get the treeline off my back."

Billingsley turned to the Forward Air Controller, a Marine lieutenant, whom English had sent with the patrol. The FAC, himself a pilot, was responsible for the coordination of airstrikes. The artillery FO had been out with another patrol when the platoon had mobilized.

"I want some napalm on that fuckin' treeline," Billingsley shouted to the crouching FAC.

"Can do," the FAC replied as he unfolded his map.

Billingsley contacted his squad leaders and told them to halt until the airstrike had neutralized the treeline. He then intended to shift the line of the platoon toward Ivester and assault through the VC forces in the grass.

"You gonna mark the pos with smoke?" asked the FAC.

"Negative. We've got enough distance from the target. Tell him he can have all he can take in those trees. But tell him to keep it in the damn trees."

The VC, meanwhile, had concentrated the fire from the trees exclusively upon Second Platoon, pinning down Sanchez's squad at the front. Fralich dashed around in the high grass responding to calls for his assistance.

Ten minutes passed while the gunfire popped.

"Where's the air?" Billingsley called to the FAC over the noise of the battle.

"On the way."

Ivester radioed to Billingsley that his situation was nearly untenable. His casualties were heavy, he reported, and the VC were close to overrunning his remaining troops. *"They're in our position! They're popping up all over the place!"* he radioed, seemingly near panic.

"We'll be over there as soon as we bust up the treeline, babe. I can't reach you over this open ground until we do that. Just hang on."

Billingsley's relief force held it's ground and returned the fire of the VC to the front and left-front. He saw a grenadier rise to fire a blooper round at the treeline, only to fall from a burst of AK-47 gunfire from the man's direct front.

"WHERE'S THE AIR, GODDAMMIT?"

"Above us now. First run's ready to commence."

A pair of A-6 Intruders, of the Marine Corps variety, were overhead. The VC gunners turned their weapons toward the sky. The pilot of the first aircraft made his pass along the length of the treeline, and roughly parallel to the axis of the platoon's advance. The pilot banked the aircraft sharply away from the battle area as soon as the napalm had been released. The black and orange explosion ignited in a trail of fire and left a thick cloud of black smoke. Seconds later, the second jet sped toward the treeline and unleashed its napalm, again splashing the target with fire.

"Good! Beautiful! Tell 'em thanks and then get me a gunship over the position," Billingsley called to the FAC when he noticed the silence from the smoking treeline.

He strained to see Ivester's group. "Okay, we're gonna be movin' up on your left," he radioed to Ivester. "Try to maneuver around so that your backs are toward us when we get over there. We'll take care of the Victor Charlies who get between us."

"Roger, hurry. I'll mark the center of my pos with smoke."

"Negative on the smoke. They may have mortars."

"Roger that. Hurry, babe."

Second Platoon moved toward Ivester's unit in the face of small-arms fire from the VC to their front. Two VC soldiers from the blackened treeline attempted to dash to safety away from the area. Their clothes had been burned from their bodies. Sanchez's men dropped the two men after only a few paces, kicking up dirt around the fallen enemy soldiers.

Still on the move, Billingsley radioed for heavy artillery to pound the area to the rear of the attacking VC. He gradually moved the shelling around in an attempt to discourage any more VC from joining the fracas. The artillery shells exploded on and around all convenient avenues of approach from behind the 600 meters of open space in which the fighting continued. Billingsley constantly referred to his map and talked to the artillery battery which supported the rescue operation. He had never encountered such a large VC force before, and in broad daylight, to boot.

And just as Billingsley had feared, mortar fire from a VC

team began impacting near his forward troops. It was close enough to be of concern, though the explosions seemed to indicate shells of about 60mm. Thank goodness it isn't any bigger, he thought.

"Where's it comin' from?" called Ivester.

"Southeast, as best I can tell," Billingsley answered as he checked his map for a likely emplacement site.

Billingsley shifted the artillery onto the reverse slope of a small knoll which, at a distance of half a klick, appeared from his map to be a potentially good location for a mortar position. The artillery reached out to the knoll, but the mortars kept exploding around the Marines. He shifted the artillery to another location, also without silencing the mortars. A nearby Marine fell after being showered with fragments from a burst.

Billingsley was in constant motion as he directed the counterattack in the open terrain. He shouted a steady stream of orders, coordinating infantry and artillery strikes. He could occasionally see a helmet cover from one of Ivester's men as he would rise and fire a quick burst at the VC. Billingsley felt in control, though he feared that Marines might fire on Marines in the chaos and closeness of the fighting. He was satisfied, though, that the VC's will to press their attack was diminishing, and he was exhilarated from controlling such a powerful and destructive array of weapons. All seemed to work as it should, except the continued harassment from the mortars. In that regard, the closeness of the fighting worked to his advantage.

Word finally came that Willingham's squad was tied into the flank of Ivester, unifying the front. Billingsley stood in the high grass, holding two radios to his ears, too absorbed to flinch from the gunfire around him. He halted the artillery fire when the helicopter gunship arrived.

"This is Delta Dragon," called the gunship pilot. "Anything left for me?"

"Roger, plenty. Steer clear from the area to the south of your pattern. We've got mortars coming from the southeast. Can you identify my position without smoke?" asked Billingsley as he turned and saw the approaching Huey Cobra gunship.

"Roger, I have you fixed. Coming from the southeast, you say?"

"Affirmative, southeast. Get 'em off us."

"We'll have a look see."

The entire Marine force was advancing, trying to clear the field of the remaining enemy troops. Ambrosetti was busy keeping the squads on line, occasionally halting one squad or the other when the advance became disjointed. Rifle fire continued from isolated pockets of VC. The enemy mortars exploded mostly to the rear and sides of the Marines.

It was not long before the mortars were silenced.

"This is Delta Dragon. You still getting mortar fire?"

"Negative, " confirmed Billingsley. "Did you get 'em?"

"One tube and three gooks. Got anything else?"

"Roger, I do. I'll halt the advance and you take whatever you can get to the south, which will be to our front."

"Ready when you are," called the pilot.

Billingsley halted the advance with shouts and radio contacts. The chopper behind the crouching Marines circled overhead searching for enemy targets. When Billingsley ordered the attack, the Cobra's mini-guns popped a loud and steady stream of fire. Sporadic bursts from AK-47 rifles were directed at the helicopter, bringing immediate reprisal fire from the Marines on the ground. The gunship's help in clearing the battlefield was considerable, in actual and in psychological terms.

"We're gonna need medevacs. I don't have a number, but I suspect it's gonna be pretty heavy. We can start to bring the birds in to the rear," Billingsley radioed to English.

"Get 'em ready and I'll get you the birds," English called.

Two squads from Kupton's platoon moved into the area behind Billingsley. Kupton had been dispatched to help, though it mattered little by then. Billingsley ordered one of Kupton's squads to set up and secure an LZ and directed the others to join in on the left flank of the sweep. Meanwhile, the single gunship moved its darting passes farther out from friendly troops in its search for VC stragglers.

The firing gradually ceased except for an occasional volley from the Marines. Billingsley stood helmetless, just to the rear of his men, and ordered the squad leaders to spread their people out and collect as many enemy weapons as could be found. He also ordered that the friendly wounded and dead be moved to the rear where the LZ had been established. Ambrosetti took a group to aid Ivester with his five dead and six injured Marines. Two of his wounded were critical.

"How many Victor Charlies are on the ground?" called Billingsley to the chopper pilot.

"'Bout fifty, I'd say. I don't see any left. Are you still getting any ground fire?"

"Negative, not at the moment. We've got medevacs on the way in. Can you cover us a while longer?"

"Affirmative, Bravo Two. It's your party."

The Marines recovered as many weapons from the dead VC as they could sling around themselves. Billingsley avoided extending his lines too far, keeping the searches close to the main area where the fighting had taken place. He was concerned about sniper fire from any surviving or arriving VC, and he notified the gunship pilot accordingly. The chopper circled at a higher altitude while the pilot observed the entire vicinity. The two medevac helicopters came into view to the rear of the position and eventually settled into the high grass of the LZ. Ivester's men were boarded, along with the eight wounded from Billingsley's platoon. The second chopper was loaded with the dead Marines and the weapons collected from the VC. Billingsley noticed that Ivester was bloody from a fragmentation wound to his forehead and suggested that he climb aboard and have his injury seen about in Da Nang. Ivester refused with a shrug and a wave of his hand. The last medevac nosed forward and flew away.

Billingsley's new radioman, Tetrick, had watched as his platoon leader sifted through the confusion of the battle to coordinate movement on the ground as well as the artillery fire and air support. Billingsley had seemed fearless; now, although Tetrick was unaware of it, exhaustion was overtaking him.

"Get 'em ready to *didi*, Sergeant Ambro. I don't want to stay out here any longer than we have to," ordered Billingsley.

Art Ivester walked near Billingsley as the column moved toward Hoi An. "Man, was I glad to see you," he said. Dried blood was caked on his unbandaged forehead.

"Kinda hairy for a while, Arthur," Billingsley responded with a grin.

The column passed Billingsley as he waited to join the middle of the group. The faces of his men were the faces of

combat infantrymen, transformed from the youthful, exuber-
ant faces of only a few months ago. There was a certain look
in their eyes, that glazed expression common to combat
veterans. It was a look that told of the inconceivable emotional
strain they had experienced and had somehow managed to
reconcile themselves to. It was a look which seemed to say,
"I've been there, I've seen it, and I've made it through one
more time." There was fatigue on those faces, assuredly. But
no emotion. No self-pity. No sorrow. And little indication of
the fear which resided in the bellies of them all.

The gunship remained above until the returning Marines
were within sight of the village.

"Delta Dragon, you're free to find yourself a Happy Hour
somewhere. Thanks much, babe," Billingsley radioed.

"Roger, Bravo Two. Glad we could lend a hand."

The pilot made a low pass over the column and motioned
a thumbs-up to his fellow Marines on the ground. The chopper
then disappeared over the horizon.

They entered the positions around the village as if nothing
had happened. Billingsley unloaded his gear at his hootch and
removed his utility shirt to dry. He noticed his trembling hands
when he began unlacing his boots to get at his aching feet.
While concerned about his wounded, he was generally pleased
that the intense action hadn't created many times the number
of casualties that it had. He sympathized with Ivester, knowing
how he felt about the high percentage of dead from his platoon.
That was always the worst part, by far.

"They got hot chow, sir. Just came in. Want me to bring
you some?" Ambrosetti said as he passed by Billingsley's
hootch.

"That's okay. I've got to see the skipper, so I'll eat when I
get up there."

"Hey, sir," said Ambrosetti, "not too shabby a job out there,"

"Thanks. I'm glad to be the hell away from there."

Ambrosetti grinned and moved closer, almost directly in
front of Billingsley's face. "You know something, lieutenant?"
he asked in a whisper.

"What's that?"

"I'm glad to be known as the one who taught Lieutenant
Billingsley everything he knows about being a field Marine. I

consider it an honor and a privilege to carry that distinction."

"You've got to be the most arrogant prick in the history of the world," replied Billingsley with a smile.

The men were served their hot food at the edge of the village, away from the villagers and in the shade of the trees. English and his platoon leaders, along with the FAC, sat on the ground and ate their hamburgers and beans in picnic style. Ivester sported a bandage on his head from the creasing wound. Tom Compton had yet to return from Da Nang where he had been sent for treatment of several painful and impacted wisdom teeth. Day and Tyler also ate with the group, their paper plates piled high with food.

After the meal, English invited Billingsley to join him at the CP. The two were alone in the tent. English leaned back in his field chair and offered Billingsley a cigar from among several which remained in the brown Tampa Nugget box. Billingsley removed the wrapper and lit the cigar. It was stale, but he said nothing.

"Art gave me a pretty good account of what went on today. That, and the monitoring of the nets has given me most of the picture," English said as he propped his feet on a stack of ammo boxes.

"I'll add anything I can, skipper."

"Okay, fine. Do you know what happened today?" English asked from under a thick cloud of smoke.

"Well, sir . . . I, uh . . . well . . . of course. I was in the middle of the whole damned thing."

"I recognize that, Mike. But tell me what went on."

"You want it from the top?"

"Start from the very top."

Billingsley drew a deep breath and arranged the sequence of events in his mind. "Well, I got the word from you to saddle up and move to the area where Art's patrol—"

"Stop right there," interrupted English. "What was that last word you said?"

"Uh, patrol."

"Hmmmm."

Billingsley looked at English's raised eyebrows and immediately grasped the ploy. "Okay, sir. Chew my ass about the way I bitched about the patrols the other day," he said.

"I'm not gonna chew your ass, Mike. No, as a matter of fact I'm gonna see to it that you're decorated for the way you handled the situation out there," said English with a grin.

"I didn't do anything spectacular, sir."

"Maybe not spectacular, although that could be debated. What you did was relieve a small force, coordinate supporting arms, and kick the hell out of what was probably a larger enemy force than that of your own. Not many young officers are able to do all of that with such flair."

"Flair, sir?" said Billingsley, feeling sheepish.

"Sure. I suppose you realize by now that the VC force you just jumped would surely have been in this village at some point, be it tonight or some other time, if you hadn't stopped them."

"Yessir."

"And you know how you were able to stop 'em?"

"Yessir, because they were discovered by a patrol."

English smiled with the cigar still protruding from his teeth. "That's exactly right," he said. "I much prefer that my officers understand the reasons I do what I do. If my officers understand, then the troops will likely understand. We may disagree, like we did on the subject of the patrolling, but I give orders based upon my estimate of the situation and what I judge to be the most effective way to carry out my mission. You and the others who implement those orders do a better job if you have a clear understanding of just what it is that we're trying to do."

"I would agree with that, sir."

"Mike, you have the potential to become an exceptional officer. I'd be pleased to see Tom and yourself both decide to stay in the Marine Corps. You both have a lot to offer, and I think the Corps could offer the both of you a great deal. But that's another matter we'll take up later."

"Fine with me, skipper. My future plans aren't fixed at this point. I really didn't have any intentions of staying in the Corps when I came in, though."

"Neither did I, not for a minute," said English. "Anyway, you're second in command of the company until Tom gets back from Da Nang."

"Aye-aye, sir."

"Your leave for Japan was approved, by the way. Top Day told me it came through today."

"Great," Billingsley grinned.

He left English's tent, still smoking the cigar, and returned to his hootch for some rest. He slept soundly that night.

The patrols were back out the next day. Billingsley accompanied Rosser's squad as they moved to a forested area to the west of Hoi An. The growth of trees and brush was thick, though not nearly as dense and enveloping as the jungle canopy. Once inside the forest, the men moved carefully and avoided all trails and clearings. Since none of the night ambushes emplaced in the same area had produced any results, a squad had been deemed sufficient to handle the daytime patrol. Many of the men were wary, however, thinking of encountering an enemy force of the size of the one from the previous day. Nobody, especially Billingsley, wanted another fight like that.

The heat and humidity were only slightly improved once the perspiring men reached the shade of the forest. The pace was moderate, but still their eyes burned from the sweat and their mouths became dry from the exertion and the tension. They moved 200 meters into the trees to the west, then turned sharply to the south for another 500 meters. Billingsley finally halted the column for a break.

Billingsley and Rosser sat on the ground together, twenty meters behind the point men. Billingsley unfolded his map and made a quick check of the terrain characteristics ahead. Rosser, glancing to the sides and rear of the spot where he and Billingsley sat, suddenly straightened and glared intently at something in the nearby foliage. He rose quietly into a crouch and began ordering his squad to spread out with waves and hand signals. Men resting on the ground were nudged into alertness. Rosser's eyes were wide as he continued to stare at the object of his interest.

"What the hell is it?" Billingsley asked in a whisper, having neither seen nor heard anything to arouse his own suspicions.

"There's a bush over there, with the wide leaves. See it?" said Rosser, pointing with the barrel of his M-16.

"Yeah."

"It's dripping."

"Damn sure is."

"Nobody here pissed on it."

"Think they're on to us?"

"I doubt it," Rosser answered quietly with a shake of his head. "Not unless the dude had to piss some kinda bad."

"Let's get 'em on the move. Get the word to Lippman that it looks like we're not alone. Tell him to keep on the course."

"Right."

Rosser moved softly to PFC Lippman, his point man. Soon, the movement had begun again. Each of the men was newly sensitive to the sights and sounds around him. It was one thing to be in the bush with an enemy who was thought to be in the same area, but another thing altogether when the enemy was *known* to be close by. The squad traveled less than 100 meters before the point man turned to the east on a course designed to take them out of the forest and into the open terrain and to the village.

The column halted soon after the turn to the east. Tetrick handed the radio received to Billingsley and advised him in a hushed voice that Rosser had reported movement to the front.

"How many?" Billingsley radioed.

"Not sure. The point saw some bushes movin'," replied Rosser.

"Check it out."

Rosser took a fire team forward and searched the thicket under suspicion. *"Seems okay,"* he eventually radioed.

"Swing the point due north for a hundred meters, then turn back to the east," Billingsley ordered.

Billingsley was worried about booby traps, and so were the men. He felt confident that only a few VC were in the forest with them. Probably less than a squad, he thought. Hopefully just a few of 'em who are as interested in avoiding us as we are in avoiding them. Hopefully.

The course was modified as prescribed. There were no further breaks in the progress of the patrol until the point came to within fifty meters of the treeline's eastern fringes, near the open area. There was a muffled shout to the front, followed by a stirring in the brush. No shots were fired, but the middle and then the rear elements of the squad stiffened at the sound of the disturbance up ahead. There was a wait of several minutes, seemingly hours, before Billingsley's radio crackled.

"*We need a corpsman up here,*" radioed Rosser.

"What's the situation?" Billingsley inquired.

"*Point's been stung by a bunch of bees and it don't look good at all.*"

"Is it secure up there?"

"*Roger.*"

Billingsley motioned for the squad to move up with him and spread out. Fralich was summoned. They found Lippman kneeling on one knee and pouring water from his canteen over his already swollen face. Red lumps covered his face, neck, and arms from the multiple stings. One other man had also been stung but said nothing while Fralich began examining Lippman. Suddenly, Lippman fell over onto his back and began to breathe in short, strained gasps. His eyelids drooped heavily and his face took on a resemblance to that of a badly battered prizefighter.

"I'm dizzy, doc," Lippman said in a panicky voice.

Fralich looked at Billingsley with an expression of concern. "He's been stung at least a dozen times, and the swelling ain't normal. I think we'd better get him out," he said.

"Can he make it to the ville?" Billingsley asked.

"Better get him out quickly," Fralich suggested.

Billingsley radioed a report of his location and his predicament to English, requesting that a medevac be hurried to the scene. The men of the squad kept a close watch on the surrounding brush for any signs of movement. Their rifles were at the ready.

"*Bees?*" questioned the astonished commander.

"Affirmative, lots of 'em. He's in a real hurt locker."

A chopper took Lippman away ten minutes later.

"Fuckin' bees, man," Rosser said. "Gooks all over the damned place and Lips get zapped by a bunch of motherfuckin' bees."

The squad was unmolested as it made its way over the open country and returned to the village.

It was evening, and the fishy odor of *muoc mam*, the rank smelling additive for nearly every Vietnamese dish, made its regular passage through the village and its fringes. Few of the Americans considered the odor appetizing. They made ribald jokes about their heightened sexual desires when the evening breezes brought it in. "Reminds me of that bitch who worked at the all-night diner," Billingsley overheard from a nearby hootch. "Smelled like fish but tasted like candy."

Tom Compton returned to Hoi An, sans three wisdom teeth, and set out to find Billingsley for an account of the fire fight of the day before. He found Billingsley composing a letter to Andrea. Compton listened with great interest when Billingsley explained the events leading up to, and including the battle.

"You should've been there, Thomas. It's gonna rank right up there with Iwo, Tarawa, and all the biggies," said Billingsley with mock seriousness.

"No shit? That big, huh?"

"Yeah, man. I'll bet they make a movie out of it."

"Skipper told me that you were a real stud. Air, arty, all that good stuff."

"Actually, it was kinda neat. Everything worked just like it's supposed to. The gooks went apeshit when the zoomies dropped the napalm on 'em. I knew we had 'em after that."

Compton gave Billingsley one of the warm beers he had brought from Da Nang. "Should've cooled them with a blast from the CO_2 extinguisher on the vehicle," he said, opening his.

"Ain't bad warm. At least it's beer."

Compton told the details of his ordeal with the dentist. "Man, there was blood all over me *and* the damned doc. I could hear the teeth tearing loose from the roots when he was yankin' on em with those pliers," he explained.

"Hurt much?"

"Nah. They shot me full of something good," said Compton with a grin. "They hurt plenty while they were still in there. I'm happy as shit to have 'em out."

They talked on longer until Compton finally returned to the CP. When darkness had fallen, Billingsley detected what he thought to be the odor of burning marijuana. He summoned Ambrosetti quickly and the two of them inspected the Second Platoon positions. The troops gave the appearance of alertness as Billingsley and Ambrosetti moved about the sector. Billingsley was concerned that the VC might actually attempt a probe of the village defenses and accordingly lectured Ambrosetti.

"Goddammit, we get hit when the troops are all fucked up on dope, and we're screwed! We'll never live to talk about it," said Billingsley.

"Hope they don't mess with us, sir," Ambrosetti said.

"That's just it. We can't lay around and get high and hope that nothing happens. This shit's too serious to take like that."

"I agree, sir."

"Keep an eye on it."

"I will, sir."

Ambrosetti returned to his hootch and later finished his reefer. The night passed peacefully.

The day of Billingsley's R&R leave finally came. He stopped in to see English before departing.

"I'm not sure where we'll be when you get back," the commander said. "I don't think we'll be here much longer."

"I'll find you, sir," replied Billingsley.

"Make sure you do, Mike. Have a good trip and be sure to take that night tour of Tokyo that I told you about."

"Will do, sir."

Within a few hours, and after a brief stopover on Okinawa, Billingsley found himself at Yokota Air Force Base, Japan. He soon was walking through the Yokota terminal, carrying his seabag. He spotted two Marine aviators who were dressed in their flight suits and on their way out of the building. He hurried to catch them.

"Where you headed, sir?" he asked when he had caught up with the pair.

"Atsugi, but with a stop at Yokosuka," answered the pilot, identified by the patch on his suit as A.H. Webb, Captain, USMC. "Can I give you a lift, Marine?"

"Yessir, sure could. Yokosuka would be perfect. Name's Lieutenant Billingsley."

"You checked-in, and all that?"

"Right," answered Billingsley, uncertain of the check-in procedures and lying for the sake of expediency.

"Let's go, then," said the pilot.

Billingsley boarded the CH-53 helicopter and took a seat along the bulkhead. He was the lone passenger. The flight to Yokosuka, the large U.S. Navy complex, seemed strange, until Billingsley realized that ground fire and hot LZs were needless concerns. The sights and sounds were otherwise those which he associated with "down south."

At Yokosuka, Billingsley signaled his thanks to the crew and located a base taxi which took him to the BOQ. There, he procured a private room, complete with bath. He wasted little time in climbing into the cool shower for thirty minutes of relaxation and cleansing. He began to fee dirt-free for the first time in what seemed an eternity.

"This is fantastic!" he said aloud, stretched on his bed. "God, what a relief! Things like this still exist."

Billingsley bought clothes and film at the large PX on the base. He changed from his jungle utilities and glanced into the mirror in his room. Jesus, who are you? he thought as the lean, tanned figure in the mirror looked back at him. He had trouble remembering the last time he had seen himself full-length in a mirror. It was the leanness, he decided. But there was something about the expression, too. Something different.

The Officers Club was adjacent to the BOQ. He walked the short distance in the warm darkness, feeling a little uncomfortable in his civilian clothes. They were tighter than the loose, comfortable utilities he was accustomed to wearing. He entered the spacious dining facility and was struck by the sight of an extravagant hunk of roast beef which was being carved and served by an attendant at the end of a long, well-stocked buffet line. He stared incredulously at the roast. "Would you look at the size of that motherfucker!" he muttered aloud, drawing stares of reprehension from a senior Navy officer and his wife as they passed with full plates in their hands. He got in the line and took some of everything except a greenish souffle. Looked like the pus from a skin infection, he thought.

He found a table and ate alone. He couldn't finish all that he had heaped upon his plate. He relaxed with a cup of coffee. He felt stuffed and uncomfortable as he looked around at the carefree diners. He heard laughter and envied men in the company of their ladies. He was reminded of Andrea. He longed for Andrea to be there, to be with him. He still had to remind himself, almost convince himself, that he was not in Vietnam, not in a war zone where he had to worry about war. Something was weird, he thought. Either him or this place or just the idea of being away from Nam. But it was weird, he concluded. For damn sure!

Billingsley slept soundly through his first night, but he was wide awake at dawn. His excitement over the freedom from combat and the sightseeing and leisure to come made him restless. He decided to leave Yokosuka for the strong entice-ment of Tokyo.

At the train station, Billingsley exchanged pleasantries with a well-dressed American who was employed as an executive with a Japanese airline. The middle-aged man boarded the train with Billingsley and offered a host of suggestions on economical ways of seeing Japan.

As the train pulled away from the station, Billingsley noticed several Japanese Navy ships which were docked in port, their flags flapping in the ocean breeze. "Seems funny to see those flags with the red circles and rays," he remarked as he recollec-ted photographs of Japanese warships flying the same flag during the Pacific campaign of World War II.

"Brings back a lot of memories for me, too," added his American companion. "I was a carrier pilot during the war, and some of the memories aren't too fond."

"Do the people you work for know that?" Billingsley asked.

"Sure. One of the first things they asked me during the interview sessions was what I did during the war."

"What did you tell them?"

"That I tried to sink as many of their carriers and ships and destroy as many of their aircraft as I possibly could."

"What did they say to that?"

"They only smiled at one another. They said nothing to me."

They talked on, of the bygone war in the Pacific and the ongoing war in Vietnam. The businessman, who returned frequently to the States, spoke of the American public's denun-ciation of the recent battle at Ap Bia Mountain, or Hamburger Hill as it was being called. He spoke of the general malaise of the public's attitude toward the long conflict. They continued their conversation until the train pulled into Tokyo's Shinbashi Station, at which point Billingsley wished his friend well and departed.

A fast, darting taxi ride from the station took Billingsley to the old Sanno Hotel, an American-operated facility which served as a billeting establishment for military officers and government officials. The rates were cheap, food and drink were available, and it was near Tokyo's sightseeing districts. He checked into his room on the second floor before lunching on chili and beer in a small bar adjacent to a larger, more crowded lounge.

Armed with his camera, Billingsley took a taxi to the famous Ginza, the entertainment and shopping district of Tokyo. He walked along the crowded sidewalks, snapping pictures of the people and the buildings along the way. He spent nearly four hours shopping and photographing. Back at the Sanno, he mailed the gifts he had bought for his family and Andrea.

After dinner in the hotel's main dining area, Billingsley paid a visit to the steam bath and massage service, also within the hotel. The young Japanese attendants, all female, enjoyed a steady stream of business from the hotel's guests. The attendant who worked Billingsley's body was so skillful he nearly dozed off. Afterward, he returned to the lounge for a beer and met a Navy pilot who was waiting for his wife to arrive from the States. Billingsley and the pilot talked of their experiences in Vietnam, and of the contrasting nature of their duties. The pilot was assigned to the aircraft carrier *Ranger* and was familiar with many of the areas within which Billingsley had operated. Seated nearby were several American stewardesses and the flight crew from their chartered plane, which had stopped over in Japan. One of the women, a shapely red-haired beauty, kept glancing at Billingsley. The group at the nearby table partied with vigor, and Billingsley noticed her glances and smiles.

"She's interested," suggested the pilot as he watched the proceedings at the other table.

"You think so?"

"Yeah. There's three guys and four girls. Can't you Marines count?"

"I can count," Billingsley answered.

"You can move in on that. If my wife wasn't showing up in the morning, I'd damn sure go after it."

"She's all yours, pal," said Billingsley as he got up to leave. "I'm going to make a call to the States. Good meeting you."

Billingsley nodded at his Navy acquaintance and glanced at the redhead as he left for his room. When he placed an overseas call to Reston, Virginia, the operator advised him to hang up and await the connection, which she would signify by ringing his room. One minute later his telephone rang.

"Go ahead, preeze," spoke the Japanese operator.

"Andrea?"

"Mike, is that you?"

"Yeah, it's me. How are you, counselor?"

"Oh God, it's so good to hear your voice. Are you in Japan?"

"Right. I got up here yesterday. How are you and your mother getting along?"

"Much better. We try staying busy. Mike, are you still hurt?"

"No, no. I'm fine. I'm sleeping like a log and eating everything but my shirtsleeves."

"Are you sure you're okay?"

"I'm sure. I miss you, Andrea. I'd give anything if you could be here with me. That would make it perfect."

"Oh Mike, you don't know how I wish the same thing. I love you more than ever. Do you hate me for canceling our plans?"

"Only when I go to bed."

He heard her laughter, and he could envision The Smile.

"You do understand, don't you?"

"Yeah, I understand completely. And I love you, too, Andrea."

They talked for twenty minutes, gaining a somewhat remote but nonetheless real sense of comfort from the sound of one another's voice. The loveliness of her face was clear in Billingsley's mind as she talked over the slightly echoing connection. He could visualize her as she stood at the phone, motioning with her hand while explaining her life's activities. Late in the conversation, Billingsley detected her sniffling, and she paused as she began to cry.

"Will you promise me you'll be careful, Mike?"

"I will. And you do the same. It won't be all that much longer, kiddo. A few more months and I'll be home again."

They ended their conversation with the usual vows of love. As elated as he had been at the initial sound of Andrea's voice, Billingsley suddenly was filled with depression as he sat alone in his room. He didn't feel like sleeping, yet he cared nothing for another venture to the bar. Instead, he remained in his room and fought the depression which seemed to descend on him like a sudden fever. He called his parents in Atlanta, but was cheered very little. He was alone with his thoughts of the past, and his questions about the future. He stayed awake through much of the night.

Billingsley returned to the Ginza on the following day to see the things he had missed before. He also visited the

Emperor's Palace, photographing the guardhouse and the old bridge from outside the grounds. Later he enjoyed the night tour of Tokyo which Captain English had so highly recommended. Included on the tour was dinner at a fashionable restaurant and visits to a theater, geisha house, and cabaret. It was late by the time he returned to the hotel, and he went to his room and slept. He awakened after a few hours of sleep with his heart pounding and his body perspiring. He sat upright, realizing he had only dreamed of being surrounded alone by dozens of shouting, advancing VC soldiers. He was eventually able to compose himself from the frightening effects of the nightmare which had seemed so real and believable. Once calm, Billingsley sat and stared out of window of the hotel room, thankful that his danger was only imagined.

On his third day in Tokyo, Billingsley walked to the Tokyo Tower where he enjoyed the breathtaking and panoramic view of the city and the bay. The air was clear and he could easily distinguish on the horizon the spectacular symmetry of Mt. Fuji. He spent several hours in the Tower's lower level which housed demonstrations of various electronic equipment, including stereos and televisions. He decided then that he wanted a complete stereo tape system before he left the Far East. It was evening by the time he returned on foot to the hotel.

After his shower, Billingsley wanted a beer. The Saturday night crowd in the Sanno made it difficult to find an empty table in the lounge, so he took his beer and threw a handful of nickels into the nearby rows of slot machines. He won nothing, but in the meantime a small table in the corner of the lounge became vacant. He sat alone at the table, sipping his beer and noticing the volume of noise created from the multiple conversations in the crowded bar.

Billingsley also noticed an attractive, early-thirtyish woman playing the slot machines. He watched her as she, too, surveyed the floor for an empty table when her luck, and her change, had run out at the slot machines. She noticed that Billingsley was alone and decided to approach the table.

"May I sit here?" she asked.

"Please do," he replied with a motion toward the chair.

"Thanks. It's a little more crowded than usual, don't you think?" she asked as she wriggled into a chair in the cramped corner, facing Billingsley.

"It's busy, for sure. I'm not aware of what the usual crowds are like."

"What brings you to the Sanno?"

"R&R."

"You're up here from Vietnam?"

"Right. I've only been up here a few days."

"Great," she smiled. "I hope you enjoy yourself. My name's Sherry."

"Hello, Sherry. I'm Mike," he offered, gently shaking her extended hand. "What brings you to this part of the world?"

"I'm an elementary-school teacher at Tachikawa Air Base. I usually try to get away for the weekends, and I come up here as often as I can manage. What branch are you serving with, Mike?"

"Marine Corps."

"My goodness!" she grimaced. "You probably need some time off, don't you?"

"Yeah," Billingsley laughed. "Vietnam's an exciting place."

"Is it as bad in Vietnam as everybody says?"

"What does 'everybody' say, Sherry?"

"That it's bad."

"Then they're right," said Billingsley, gazing around the bar.

"Do you think it will end soon?"

"I don't know. It was still going on earlier in the week when I left from down there."

"What do you do, Mike?"

"I'm an infantry platoon leader. Try to be, anyway," he said with a grin.

The waitress, a short, smiling Japanese girl, took their order for drinks—a Mai-Tai for Sherry and another Kirin beer for Billingsley.

"So where's your home in the States, Sherry?" he asked when the waitress had left.

"Upstate New York, just outside Buffalo. What about you?"

"South America."

"Yeah?" She looked confused. "Whereabout?"

"Atlanta, Georgia."

"That's not South America," Sherry said, giggling.

"It's the American South, ain't it? Same, same."

Sherry laughed and touched him lightly on the arm. The

drinks came and they talked for the next half-hour on the customary topics of hometowns, educational backgrounds, and their experiences in the Orient. Sherry was more aggressive than the majority of females he had encountered in school and elsewhere. Billingsley admired her independent and adventuresome spirit, but he was uncomfortable. She had come to Tokyo in search of companionship and a good time, he reasoned. And she had chosen him for openers, he also reasoned. She was attractive and available.

He was flattered, though he tried not to show it, but still he felt ill at ease.

"I'm going to have dinner before it gets too late," said Sherry with a glance toward the dining area. "I'd really like it if you would join me, Mike."

"I don't think so. I'm not really very hungry."

"Well, come with me and have a cup of coffee or a drink, or something. You can do that, can't you?"

"I think maybe I'll just sit right here and get blind drunk. Thanks anyway," he said with a grin.

"Oh, c'mon, Mike."

"Some of those people are wearing coats and ties. I don't have anything to wear if that's a requirement. You go ahead and I'll be here when you get back."

Sherry stood and gathered her purse. "Come with me, Mike. Don't worry about a coat and tie. C'mon, I'd really like for you to sit and talk with me."

Billingsley finally relented and followed her into the dining room. She immediately commanded the table of her choice. Billingsley stood awkwardly behind her. Though she was attractive and feminine, Sherry was most assuredly no meek, retiring belle.

They were seated at a table with a view of the outdoor courtyard and the exotic plants around it.

"I'll bet you're something in the classroom, Sherry," Billingsley said casually.

"Why do you say that?"

"You're possessive as hell!"

Sherry closed the menu and stared at Billingsley. "You're blunt as hell!" she countered sharply.

"Did I offend you?" he asked, noticing her expression.

"Were you trying?"

"No, not really. I was just trying to establish myself before you ordered me to fetch you an ashtray or a napkin."

"Oh, I see," she said with a knowing look. "The Marine Corps lieutenant's used to being in complete charge. Right?"

"Somethin' like that," he answered with a self-conscious smile.

"Would you rather go back to bar, Mike?"

"No," he laughed. "I'd rather stay here with you. That is, if you'll let me. Please let me stay, Sherry. Please."

Sherry's face broke into a wide grin at that. He sensed she had grasped his point. Andrea's a pistol, but Sherry, she's *really* a hard charger, he thought.

"I promise I won't order you to fetch me anything," she said with a coy smile. "But I've made my choice for dinner and I'm ready to order."

"Miss!" Billingsley issued a crisp summons to their waitress. "The lady is ready to order."

Sherry was laughing when the waitress hurried over. They continued their conversation. Sherry laughed repeatedly, and she clearly enjoyed his company. And he began to feel much more at ease with her. She was pushy, but she was likable.

"I think I like you," she giggled.

"Yeah, I noticed," he answered which caused her to feint a slap at his arm.

Sherry picked at her food and listened while Billingsley explained his travel plans for the remainder of his R&R. She nodded her approval at his intention to visit Hiroshima and the shrines and temples of the old imperial city, Kyoto. Sherry made suggestions with respect to hotels and transportation, and it was clear she knew her way around Japan.

They decided to return to the lounge after Sherry had refused Billingsley's offer to pick up the tab. She had even declined to accept his payment for his own cake and coffee.

A table in the middle of the lounge became available almost immediately upon their entrance. They sat down and ordered drinks amid the din of laughter and conversation within the lounge. She was lovely, he thought. Better than at first glance. Not as pretty as Andrea, but . . . who is? He fixed her age at thirty-two or thirty-three. Older and more experienced, he contemplated. Probably not as good as Andrea. But . . . who is? Nice body. But not as nice as Andrea's. He looked at Sherry, he gave the appearance of listening to Sherry as she talked, but he thought of Andrea.

"Why are you grinning, Mike?" asked Sherry, breaking off her description of travel aboard the Bullet Train.

"Oh, sorry. I was thinking of something else."

"Some*thing*, or some*one*?"

"I was just daydreaming. Sorry about that," he said with a sudden flush of embarrassment.

"Are you married, Mike?" Sherry asked with a careful and observing gaze.

"Nope," he grinned.

"Engaged?"

"Nope. Are you either?"

"Neither. Is there a 'girl you left behind'?"

"Yep."

Sherry glanced at her empty glass and then removed two dollar bills from her purse. "I think I'll have one last drink at the Gaslight Lounge before I go back to Tachikawa. Care to come with me?" she asked.

"To the Gaslight Lounge, or to Tachikawa?"

"To the lounge."

He looked into her eyes for some signal, some indication of her interest. He could read nothing in her expression. "I don't think so, Sherry," he said, finally.

"What are you going to do, then?"

He searched for the signal again. Nothing still. Her eyes revealed no clues. "I'm going up to my room and go to bed," he said.

They said nothing for a moment while Sherry stared at him.

"You're welcome to join me," Billingsley said softly.

Sherry leaned back and toyed with the plastic straw from her drink. Her hesitation, he concluded, was a result of her serious consideration of his pointed overture.

"You really don't expect me to walk out of here and go to bed with you after just meeting you two hours ago, do you?" she asked after a long pause.

"I'd like for you to."

"But you don't expect it, do you?"

"No, Sherry. Not really. But the offer stands, just the same."

She smiled and stood, slinging her purse around her shoulder. "I'll be at the Gaslight Lounge if you change your mind about that drink. It's about a mile and half from here, near the Russian Embassy."

"I'm in Room 209 if you change *your* mind."

She smiled again and proceeded toward the door. He briefly considered following her but soon decided instead to retire early and attempt to get a full night's sleep. He left the lounge and told himself as he climbed the stairs to his room that Sherry would not return to be with him.

His prediction held. He fell asleep eventually and slept well.

The train trip to Kyoto on the following morning was pleasant and leisurely. A light rain and low clouds obscured the countryside but did little to dampen his spirits. The shrines and temples at Kyoto were a sightseer's delight. He walked among the crowds of Japanese adults and children, though a few American tourists could occasionally be seen and heard. He spent two days in Kyoto and left with a broader understanding of Japanese history and a fuller appreciation of Japanese food. Raw fish and squid were the notable exceptions, however.

The tour of Hiroshima was equally informative, but quite sobering, if not altogether frightening. Photographs of the horrible destruction to life and property were dramatically displayed in the city's museum. He had only remotely considered the incomprehensible effects of nuclear war until he stood alone in Peace Park and imagined the suffering which had been heaped upon so many of Hiroshima's citizens. Sure, it was war, he thought. And these were the enemy. But they bled and suffered and died on an unimaginable scale by the single flash of an atomic bomb. They were, after all, real people. Billingsley was genuinely moved and genuinely disturbed at the prospect of even larger, more powerful weapons being unleashed upon other cities. And other people. American cities. American people. He cringed and later prayed silently that God would be so kind as to spare civilization from extinction under the heat and fury of nuclear warfare. He knew only too well the destructive capacity of conventional warfare. He was glad he went to Hiroshima, but he was uncertain why.

Billingsley spent his last few days in Japan relaxing. He stopped at a lakefront hotel near Mt. Fuji before returning to Tokyo for a final jaunt. He went to a steambath and got a massage. He went back the next day and got a "special" massage. He went back the same evening, for the same deal. He was alone most of the time, and he tired of a vacation alone. Though he dreaded another six months of combat duty, and although the sinking feeling returned to his stomach, he was anxious to return to Vietnam and get it over with. He was homesick in Japan, just like he got homesick in Nam. In Nam, though, he wasn't alone.

He soon caught the bus to Yokota at Tokyo Station. He took a seat in the rear, next to the window. A young Japanese, perhaps college age, sat next to him when the bus eventually filled with passengers. Once the bus was free of the Tokyo traffic, the ride was smooth and even. The Japanese boy beside him read magazines and noisily ate oblong crackers wrapped in what appeared to be seaweed. The smooth ride and constant groan of the engine soon lulled Billingsley into a doze.

Sleep once again produced a nightmarish dream. Alone in the jungle, he desperately attempted to locate the platoon from which he had become inexplicably separated. The enemy soldiers shouted at him and at one another, though they were nowhere to be seen. He crouched with his rifle, uncertain which direction to take. It was as if he was paralyzed from his uncertainty. The noise of the VC kept getting closer. The bushes, the shouts, the breathing. He wanted to cry in his dream, to jump up and fly away through the trees. He aimed his weapon. He squeezed the trigger.

The dream ended abruptly when an elderly Japanese woman, returning from the restroom in the rear of the bus, slammed the door loudly after experiencing difficulty with its closing. Billingsley jerked at the noise and felt as if his heart had thrust upward into his throat. He breathed heavily. The Japanese boy in the adjoining seat was amused, but decided against showing it when he noticed the grim expression on the face of the American. Billingsley slept no more.

The bus finally arrived at Yokota. He claimed his seabag and travel bag and caught a cab to the base. He paid the cabbie and went into the terminal to change into his utility uniform.

Here we go again, he thought.

8

A dreary, steady rain greeted Billingsley at Da Nang. It was hot and sultry, despite the rain. Billingsley learned at regimental headquarters that Bravo Company had left Hoi An and joined the remainder of First Battalion in the hilly country northwest of Da Nang. He also discovered that a convoy was going there in a few hours. Billingsley was soon aboard a truck and moving away from Da Nang.

First Battalion's position was among a series of hills and ridges in the rolling terrain ten miles from Da Nang. The eight-vehicle convoy stopped short of the position on an unimproved and soggy road while a platoon from Company C met the trucks. The supplies, mainly of ammunition and food, were unloaded and carried by the wet replacements. Billingsley talked with the platoon leader about the progress of the operation before walking up a ridge to find Bravo Company.

Captain English welcomed Billingsley with a handshake when he saw his returning platoon leader enter the tent which served as the CP. English asked about Billingsley's trip, and then explained the nature of the current mission. In the three days in which the company had operated from its present location, English related, contact with the enemy had been light. Billingsley was pleased to hear that Ambrosetti's tenure of command had been carried out satisfactorily and, for the most part, uneventfully.

"There was a bit of a problem back in Da Nang before we came up here," English said.

"What kind of problem, sir?"

"Several of your people were involved in a fight in the chow line. Some white Marines claimed that some black Marines

275

broke in the line, but the black Marines denied it. It got down to where a few punches and a bunch of slurs were thrown back and forth before your squad leaders and Ambrosetti broke it up."

"Anybody hurt?"

"Not much more than the usual cuts and bruises. Everybody was returned to duty. Tom Compton's been investigating the incident, so I want you to check with him."

"I will, sir."

"We can't have that, Mike. Not our own people at each other's throats. Hell, there've been riots in some units in-country. There are plenty of ways to lose control of the troops, and this racial stuff appears to be one of the easiest. Get back on top of things."

Billingsley walked in the rain to the Second Platoon sector. Ambrosetti greeted him with a wide grin when Billingsley jumped into the covered hootch of his platoon sergeant. Ambrosetti was eager to return the command of the platoon to its rightful bearer. The story of the racial incident disturbed Billingsley almost as much as the thought of a sizable encounter with the enemy. He had heard the reports of unrest on other occasions, particularly among Marines confined to brig areas. He had often seen black Marines raise their fists in the symbolic greeting and demonstration of unity. The potential for racial confrontation in his platoon had not escaped him, though on the whole his people had given him few reasons for concern. He listened carefully to Ambrosetti's assessment of the state of the platoon.

"I don't think it's one group or the other that wants to stir things up, lieutenant. It's a few people in both. Most of the guys don't need that bullshit. They just want to put in their time and get the hell out. But some of the brothers think it's cool to act different, and some of the whites don't help by talking about them the way they do. And we've had so many people come and go that there's bound to be a few shitbirds passing through, black and white. Scares the hell out of me, sometimes," explained Ambrosetti.

"So whaddya think?"

"There's some mean dudes in this platoon, sir. Crazy dudes. You'd shit all over yourself if you knew everything about these guys. And if you knew it and tried to hard-ass it, you'd probably get yourself fragged."

"So, should I go back to Japan, or hide out in Da Nang?" joked Billingsley.

"Most of the guys respect you, sir. And it's mostly because you don't fuck with 'em, especially when we're in the rear. You know, spitshined and that kind of horseshit. Nah, I don't think you need to hide. The war'd find you any damn way," grinned Ambrosetti.

"We're gonna control this platoon, Sergeant Ambrosetti," Billingsley said with a sudden seriousness. "I know a lot more than you may *think* I do about the kinds of people we've got. Some of the whites hate the blacks, and some of the blacks hate the whites, and some of each hate everybody. No different than anywhere else. Some of 'em are lazy, some of 'em are crazy, and some of 'em think only of themselves. We've got people who'd just as easily kill somebody as they would buy 'em a beer. We've got people who would be in jail somewhere if they weren't in the Marine Corps in Vietnam. We've got people who are holding down their first jobs, by going off to war and being told to kill other people. And some of 'em think it's neat. We've got people who'll screw anything, drink any-thing, and shoot anything. We've got people who like to smoke a little herb when we come back from the bush, yourself included. And we've got a majority who go about their jobs as best they possibly can, yourself again included. But we're gonna *control* this platoon, and we're gonna make *damn sure* that everybody gets a fair shake and a fair chance to survive this thing. You with me?"

"Yessir," said Ambrosetti in amazement.

"And when I say *we're* gonna control it, that means you and it means me. You still with me?"

"Yessir, I'm with you. Goddamn, you *do* know more than I thought you did."

"Gonna frag me?" Billingsley asked with a slight grin.

"No, sir. I don't want your damned job no more."

"Now tell me about these new replacements. Are they blending in with the others?"

"Yessir, pretty much."

"There were some more on the convoy I came up with. I'd

expect us to get some of them, too. Is the platoon still as tight as it used to be a few months ago?"

"It's not as tight as say, when we were at Quang Tri. Some of these new dudes just aren't worth a shit. That's all there is to it."

"Think being out in the bush will help?"

"I hope so, sir. Oh, before I forget, Sanchez rotates in ten more days."

"Ten days," Billingsley sighed enviously.

"Right, and Mayson will replace him 'cause he's the senior man."

"Okay, good. Let's start to ease Sanchez out of things."

"I was gonna suggest that, sir. You know how the little shit likes to be right in the middle when the shit hits the fan."

"Yeah, I don't want him to miss his flight home. Ten days . . . ain't that a sweet sound?" Billingsley mused.

"Hell, sir. I ain't got but forty-eight days and a wakeup," bragged Ambrosetti.

"Stick it in your ass."

"Sir?"

"You heard me."

"You'll get there, lieutenant. Five thousand more miles of humpin' and a hundred more pounds of C-rats, and you'll be there," said Ambrosetti with a laugh at Billingsley's dour expression.

"I suppose so. Who's got my mail?"

"Tetrick. Your hootch is over there to the left, just the other side of those big rocks. See 'em?"

"Yeah. Thanks, and I'll see you later."

"Lieutenant?" Ambrosetti called as Billingsley climbed from the hole.

"Yeah."

"Good to have you back."

Billingsley grinned and left, making his way through a large portion of the sector on his way to his own hootch. His men began to notice as he walked in the rain. Several shouts greeted Billingsley as the men nudged one another in their positions and pointed.

"Couldn't stay away, huh, sir?"

"Should've booked to Sweden, sir."

"At least the weather's nice for you, sir."

"What'd they do to you in Japan, sir? Cut your hair and send you to Vietnam?"

Billingsley nodded and waved to those he could see in the covered holes. He had every reason to feel dejected and miserable at being back in the "discomfort zone," but instead he felt as if he had come back to the next-best thing to actually being home. It felt good to back with the platoon again.

"Get any on you, lieutenant?" came a shout which Billingsley recognized as the voice of Willingham.

"I'd *still* have it on me, Willingham, if this damned rain hadn't washed it away," he lied, provoking laughter from Willingham and others within earshot.

"Welcome back, sir."

Two letters from Andrea and one from his family occupied his time after settling into the position with Tetrick. Afterward, he listened while Tetrick described the activities of the previous two weeks. No big battles, not many casualties, very few enemy contacts. Just the heat and the rain and the same old "ration of shit." Not much had changed except the passing of June and the beginning of July.

The wet weather continued throughout the next day. Bravo Company left the ridge shortly after dawn on a long patrol. They returned later the same day. Not a single shot had been fired on the grueling, exhausting patrol. Virtually every man had begun to have problems with damp, blistered feet. Later the same evening, Compton reviewed with Billingsley the results of his investigation into the racial incident. There was insufficient evidence in Compton's view to warrant the bringing of charges against anyone and the entire matter was closed. In the aftermath of Compton's remarks, Billingsley convened his squad leaders and Ambrosetti and demanded firm and fair treatment of all troops in the platoon. Any further altercations, he warned, would only serve to destroy the unit's integrity and would pose a consequent real and dangerous threat to every man. And there were enough real and dangerous threats, he added, without creating any more.

The quiet of the next few days was broken when the NVA shelled the ridge with mortars and rockets for twenty minutes one night. Most of the explosions were in and around the Bravo Company positions, injuring slightly two men from the fragmentation. One of those hits was Sanchez. The news disturbed Billingsley until he discovered that the wound to his squad leader was only superficial. Mortar fire from the battalion tubes was returned at the enemy, though no results were known.

Bravo Company was ordered off the ridge the morning after the shelling to conduct a long sweep of the hills to the west. That same morning, the Ninth Marines were preparing to pull out of Vietnam as part of President Nixon's withdrawal plan. One group left looking for a fight while the other made ready to disengage completely.

The men of Bravo Company quickly discovered that the enemy troops in the area were still active. They had covered less than 1,000 meters when the lead elements, from Ivester's platoon, tripped a booby trap which took the life of one Marine and the leg of another. One other man escaped with only minor wounds. The bad weather hampered the evacuation, and only the skill and courage of a low-flying chopper pilot who maneuvered his craft in the dense fog at great risk to himself and his crew got the wounded men out.

Movement began again once the medevac had left for Da Nang. Billingsley's platoon brought up the rear of the column as the company snaked its way through the increasingly thick jungle. English permitted frequent rest breaks during the long patrol, deviating from his previous routine of extended, tortuous intervals between stops. Though the rain helped compensate for the debilitating heat, the men were burdened by their heavy, soaked gear and their blistered and bleeding feet. They slumped wearily to the ground when the orders for the breaks came. Very few of the Marines bothered to shield themselves from the rain; they were drenched already. Some even fell asleep as they propped against trees with their weapons across their legs and their helmets tilted forward. Misery was once again their constant companion.

The order to move out after one of the numerous rest breaks was sounded. Ambrosetti walked among the men and woke the tired and sluggish troops. "Get on your feet, I said. We're movin' again," he said to a reclining newcomer to the platoon.

"How much longer's this bullshit gonna go on?" asked the young replacement as he struggled to stand under the weight of his pack.

"It'll never end, sweetheart. Now take your place and get

your ass in gear," snapped Ambrosetti. "You'll be here for the rest of your life."

Billingsley's platoon moved up to the middle of the column while Kupton's group rotated to the point. The steepness of much of the terrain made the footing especially treacherous in the mud. Each step became an effort to avoid a stumble, uphill as well as downhill. Boots were caked with the slick mud, hampering traction and adding weight. Marines could be heard cursing vehemently after slipping and taking a hard fall. But they continued on, moving and resting, over the hills and through the valleys. By early afternoon, Billingsley's feet, legs, and shoulders ached steadily. By late afternoon, a numbness had gradually supplanted the aching. His fatigue made it impossible for him to think clearly as he plodded forward in a test of willpower. He wondered why it was that his straining seemed so monumental, and he became concerned that his conditioning had been lost during his R&R. A look at the faces of his men, however, told him that misery like his own was intimately familiar to the rest. Tetrick walked alongside, pale and open mouthed, too exhausted to remain alert and too numbed to care about it.

English made his decision for the company's night position and directed his men up the slopes of a prominent piece of high ground. With two hours of daylight remaining, the men dug their holes as quickly as their tired muscles would permit. Billingsley helped Tetrick dig their hole in the damp ground. It mattered little that, in addition to being soaked, they became covered with dark, slimy mud. There were gradations of misery, they knew, but beyond a certain point additional increments made absolutely no difference.

Ambrosetti and Billingsley checked the Second Platoon positions as night fell over the hill. The men had virtually disappeared into the landscape underneath the cover of the ponchos and the foliage. Satisfied that his sector's defensive layout was adequate, Billingsley returned to his hootch to eat a meal and rest his weary body.

Darkness had enveloped the hill for nearly three hours when Billingsley was summoned to English's CP. He stumbled along in the dark and the rain until he was met in the open by English, Compton, and the other platoon leaders. Something's up, he knew.

"We're pulling out," English stated abruptly. "I want each of you to have your people ready to move in fifteen minutes."

"Sir?" asked Billingsley in disbelief.

"That's right. We've moving to a hill about half a klick to the west of here. The XO will lead the way, since he's familiar with where we're going."

"Keep 'em quiet," added Compton. "Like the skipper said, it's about half a klick to the west. We'll dig in when we get up there. We'll leave from Third Platoon's area. I want your people on the point with me, Lieutenant Billingsley. Lieutenant Ivester, you'll follow. Sergeant Kupton, you'll bring up the rear. Let's get 'em up and ready to shove off."

The platoon leaders started back to their areas. Billingsley pulled Compton aside, out of range of English's hearing.

"Have you two lost your fuckin' minds?" he whispered.

"No, we haven't. Get 'em on their horses, Mike. I don't want to have to wait on you," Compton replied firmly.

Unbelievable! Billingsley thought as he returned to the platoon.

Billingsley and Ambrosetti managed to have the platoon ready within the required time. The stunned men emerged from their holes in angry but silent compliance. Compton joined Rosser's squad at the head of the column and led the company down the slopes. Billingsley briefly considered the possibility that English had become delirious from his exhaustion. Billingsley wasn't sure of English, and he never had been. But Compton, too?

They moved slowly to the new position. Billingsley strained at the uphill climb which had begun after they crossed a shallow stream running along a thick, dense valley. The crest of the hill was finally reached and the men assumed the same defensive formation as before. Second Platoon faced to the southeast as the troops dug their holes and hoped for some unimpeded rest.

The company had been settled into its new position for nearly an hour before explosions started booming to the east. Billingsley looked out of his damp hole to see the orange flashes on and around the high ground from which they had recently departed. The explosions appeared to be from medium artillery, certainly heavier than mortars. Tetrick stood up alongside him as they watched the shelling across the valley.

"Get the CO on the horn," Billingsley said.

Tetrick gave the handset to Billingsley. Compton was on the other end.

"This is Bravo Two, over," Billingsley spoke.

"Bravo Five," replied Compton.

"Roger, Five. Is that ours or theirs?"

"It's ours. We'll see what shows when we get some light. Be advised there will be more to follow."

"Roger, out," replied Billingsley.

"They knew what they were doing all along," Billingsley said as he left the hole to get word to Ambrosetti that the firing was friendly.

Billingsley tried to snatch a few more hours of sleep. But he couldn't help but mull over English's strategy of moving his troops and shelling the previous location. Pretty nifty, Billingsley concluded. Respect for English came grudgingly from Billingsley, though he knew English to be a competent and able professional—one who had an excellent knowledge of his craft. Whatever he lacked in communicative skills, English nevertheless understood explicitly what it was he was doing in the bush. Maybe the damn guy *is* good, Billingsley thought. No, he concluded, there ain't no maybe. He *is* good. And Tom knows him better, and thinks he's good. Don't know, though, he thought. English may be good, but he's still a little strange.

Another volley of artillery rounds was fired onto the adjacent hill an hour before dawn. The sudden concussions from the explosions awakened Billingsley from his napping, startling him until he remembered the circumstances. He was groggy, the kind of stupor felt when exhaustion is only partly remedied with three hours of sleep. The rain appeared to have slackened, judging from the sound of the drops falling on the poncho. Billingsley shifted his feet and noticed that his boots were resting in water up to his ankles. He managed to get a few more minutes of sleep before the hazy, overcast dawn brought the first dull light of day.

The company came to life on the hill. While they ate their morning ration, the rain had slackened to a drizzle; the skies were grey and dreary. The troops were stiff, and many began stretching to loosen their aching joints. Nobody wanted another day like the previous one.

Bravo Company left its position and began moving toward

the adjacent hill to the east to inspect it for enemy bodies. Captain English placed Second Platoon on the point to start the patrol. Billingsley had recently begun to position himself near the front of his platoon instead of in his usual place in the center. He had also put two men on the point. He and Tetrick followed close behind. He reasoned that the revised formation would permit him to observe the situation more closely than before and, hopefully, to react more quickly. There were additional risks, he knew, but he chose to ignore them.

At the crest of the hill, only the evenly spaced holes and shell craters were there to greet them. The Marines moved carefully, wary of ambush. Fog enshrouded much of the hill, reducing visibility to perhaps thirty meters. It was quiet and eerie, and Billingsley had to fight the grogginess that still bothered him. The abandoned fighting holes were partly filled with murky water. An occasional crushed cigarette package or a soggy C-ration box were the only indications of previous habitation. Some of the trees that surrounded and covered the position had been felled from the shelling. It seemed desolate to those who searched the premises.

Rosser and his squad examined the far slopes of the hill. In the dense growth, they found evidence that the enemy had indeed made an appearance on the site.

"They were here," Rosser radioed after a search of ten minutes.

"You got bodies?" asked Billingsley.

"Negative on the bodies. But we got some pieces over here on the south side."

Much of the company was still climbing up the slopes when Billingsley radioed the preliminary findings to English. Ambrosetti maneuvered Sanchez's squad into a position to cover the squads of Willingham and Rosser as the searches continued. Billingsley walked across the hill to Ambrosetti, near the searching squads.

"Got a foot over here," called one of Willingham's men. "Looks about like a size seven."

"Piece of a uniform sleeve over here," called another.

"Jesus," shouted still another. "There's guts strewn all over the motherfuckin' ground over here."

By the time English arrived, enough proof had been accumulated to confirm that a number of enemy soldiers had died on the hill during the previous night. The patches of clothing were from the khaki uniforms of NVA regulars. The bodies had been dragged away down the hill to the south, leaving a trail of intestines and an occasional splotch of blood which had yet to be washed away by the rain.

"It worked, sir," Billingsley said as he and English surveyed a spot where blood-stained battle dressings lay scattered along the ground.

"Yeah, but it's hard to tell how many were up here. What's your guess?" English queried.

"Maybe a squad of sappers. Seems like they would have shelled it themselves before jumping off with a main force."

"Okay, sounds good. So how many did we get?"

"Well," Billingsley said with a slight chuckle, "judging from the pieces, I'd say we got most of 'em. Ten sounds like a good number."

English also smiled faintly. "I'll buy that. Too many split bellies for three or four. Let's get ready to go find the rest of 'em," he said as he turned to leave.

Compton met them as he came for a look. "Get any of 'em, sir?" he asked.

"Lieutenant Billingsley seems to think so," grinned English. "There were definitely some hurtin' gooks up here last night. Right, Mike?"

"Sure as hell were," agreed Billingsley.

"How many?" asked Compton.

"Ten pounds of guts. How does ten KIAs sound?" Billingsley asked.

"Outstanding," smiled Compton. "Just outstanding."

"Get 'em on their horses, gentlemen," said English as he walked briskly toward his radioman.

Word quickly spread among the troops that English's ploy had claimed a number of enemy victims. The troops realized, as Billingsley had the night before, that what had seemed so needless a move at the time had avoided an NVA assault. Furthermore, there was the good feeling among the troops that, for a change, the cunning enemy had walked into a trap in his own territory, at a time and place of his own choosing, and been methodically blown to pieces in the process. It was a real good feeling to know that the cunning Charles had been conned.

The weather remained overcast and drizzly as Bravo Company began its patrol to the south. Second Platoon remained on the point with the typical instructions to avoid trails, ridges, and any other likely ambush spots. The NVA were known to be in the area and, according to English, were probably underneath the canopy to the south. With Willingham's men on the point, Billingsley followed close behind. Soon the two point men were chopping and hacking their way through the undergrowth which unavoidably slowed the progress of the advance.

By the early afternoon, the company had advanced only several thousand meters through the jungle. The heat had become a factor again, and the light rain didn't help much. English continued to halt the company for frequent breaks and at one point kept the company stopped for nearly an hour. The men were able to fill their canteens and bathe their heads in a clear, shallow stream. During the breaks they found leeches on their arms and legs. The leeches, burned from the skin with cigarettes, would fall to the ground, swollen with the blood of their victims. Rashes broke out on many of the men's arms and hands, and blistered feet continued to irritate the majority. Another common affliction was raw, abraded skin in the crotch. Underwear and trousers never dried completely in the wet weather, causing irritations between the legs. Some of the men removed their undershorts and stuffed them into their packs.

The first contact came during the late afternoon of the patrol's second day when Kupton's men opened fire on a squad of NVA who were carrying weapons and supplies on a narrow jungle trail. The first two NVA had been cut down by gunfire and were sprawled on the trail. Kupton maneuvered his troops to cut off the remainder. Billingsley, whose platoon was located to the rear of the column, stayed near the ground in the thick foliage. The firing to his front intensified as more Marines were able to join in the fighting. The AK-47 rifles of the NVA were easily distinguishable from the American M-16s as Billingsley listened to the popping gunfire. Judging from the volume of their fire, Billingsley thought, the enemy had decided to stand and make a fight of it.

"Bravo Two, move up and set up on our left flank, to the east, and protect the far side of the trail while we finish with

the rest," came the radioed order of English. Billingsley moved his platoon forward and emplaced them along either side of the trail, fifty meters removed from the fire fight. Grenade explosions began booming from where the shooting continued. English was able to maneuver Ivester's platoon through the foliage to a position behind the enemy. Within ten minutes, the NVA had been outmaneuvered and silenced. Billingsley remained on the trail to the left of the main body as the firing ceased. He could hear orders being shouted for the preparation of blocking positions along the trail in the event other NVA appeared from the same direction. The valley in which the company was located was long and narrow, not an unlikely location for NVA supply columns.

Billingsley noticed that some of his troops appeared on the verge of falling asleep. He moved among his men, nudging several on the tops of their helmets with the stock of his weapon.

"Wake up, Marshall. Get those eyes open and keep 'em on the Goddamned trail. Anything wrong with you, Mironovich?"

"No, sir."

"Shut those eyes again and there damn sure will be."

He walked on further, his troops fully aware of his presence. "See anything, Ledbetter?" he asked.

"Nothing, sir."

"Looking for anything, Ledbetter?"

"Yessir, gooks."

"What about you, Pendley?"

"I'm okay, sir."

Billingsley glanced across the trail and saw Ambrosetti also endeavoring to maintain the alertness of the platoon's other half. He motioned to Ambrosetti by pointing to his eye and then making a circular motion with his finger to the front of his eye. Ambrosetti nodded his understanding and continued to move among the men.

English summoned Billingsley to a spot near the bodies of the first two NVA slain during the fight. Both were lying on the trail, on their backs, one with a leg bent awkwardly underneath. Their khaki shirts were drenched with blood. A rain-filled hole in the trail near one of the enemy dead was red with the swirling blood which had streamed into it. The

288/BENT, BUT NOT BROKEN

other dead NVA were being dragged onto the trail by Kupton's Marines.

"We've got one man with a graze. Won't need to evacuate him," Gunny Tyler said to English.

"Is that all?" Compton asked incredulously.

"That's it, sir. One man nicked on the arm."

"How many NVA?" asked English.

"Eight, sir. We got 'em all."

Billingsley and Compton were amazed that the violent and noisy battle had produced only one friendly casualty, and that a very minor one. Billingsley would have expected five or six Marines to be killed due to the closeness of their contact. The NVA were considered to be excellent marksmen. One minor casualty was a mystery.

The enemy bodies were buried off to the side of the trail and the weapons were taken by the Marines. English moved the company out of the narrow valley, across a ridge, and finally to an unusually steep, rocky hill. Movement up the hill was slow and cumbersome, but by early evening Bravo Company ringed the crest with its fighting holes. The rain continued in a mist, though lighter than at any time since the patrol had begun. Low clouds and fog obscured much of the surrounding terrain, casting a grey and white haze along the tops of the adjacent hills.

The position occupied by Bravo Company had been employed as a fire base in the recent past. Ample clearing of the trees at the top of the hill provided visibility from one end to the other on days without fog. Once the troops had dug new positions or improved old ones, they were encouraged to remove their boots and socks and air their blistered feet. The corpsmen attended to the worst cases of immersion foot.

Billingsley walked to a sandbagged gun pit where Art Ivester sat wiping his moist eyeglasses with a rag.

"I'll bet you never dreamed you could have so much fun and still get paid for it," Billingsley said as he took a seat on the sandbags.

"Son of a bitch if this is fun," replied Ivester, inspecting his lenses before sliding the glasses over his eyes.

"C'mon, Art. You could be bored stiff in some office building in Indianapolis, watching all those secretaries wiggling their asses on the way to the water fountain."

"You're right, Mike. This is where I belong, out here where the air's clean and the livin' is easy. How are your feet?"

"I'm afraid to look. Think they might be stuck to my socks. What about yours?"

"Not too bad. What bothers me is the rash I've got in my crotch. Burns like hell, man."

"Get some stuff from the corpsman. Some of my guys are using a salve that Fralich's got, and it seems to help. Tell the doc you need the stuff for 'athlete's ass'."

"I'm beginning to get bad vibes about this whole trip, Mike," Ivester said with a sigh of resignation. "It's like the war's gonna keep drawing down and drawing down, but the units in the field will have to play it out to the very end. It's spooky, man. Don't you think so?"

"Yeah, I do. I don't want to lose any people. I'm gonna do all I can to see that my people get a chance to leave here in one piece. I kinda feel responsible every time one of 'em gets messed up."

"Do you think Captain English feels the same way?"

"I didn't before, but I'm beginning to think so now. Tom seems to think the guy's coming around, or that maybe we're coming around to him. Whatever, I know he's not taking any stupid chances. And I respect the hell out of him for that."

"I don't know, man. I guess I'm still a little afraid of the dude."

"He's not the easiest guy in the world to understand, that's for sure. But best I can tell, he's got his shit in one bag. And that's what counts, anyway. If I've got to be out here, I don't feel too bad about being out here with English."

Captain English, unnoticed by either Billingsley or Ivester, walked up behind the pit.

"Are you two plotting for the overthrow of the government?" asked English jokingly.

"No, sir," Billingsley answered. "Just taking a load off."

"I want to have a look at your positions. I'll meet you at yours, Art, after I've had a look at Second Platoon."

Billingsley escorted English to the portion of the hill occupied by his Marines. Many of the men sat outside their holes, their weapons nearby, and aired their bare feet. English observed the positions and the occupants, nodding occasionally to a familiar Marine.

"What kind of shape is your platoon in?" English asked as they walked through the mud.

"A bunch of 'em have foot problems. A few others have jungle rot. Other than the usual crud, I think they're okay, skipper."

"Keep 'em on their toes. I don't expect us to keep getting a free ride while we're out here."

"Will do, sir," replied Billingsley as English turned to trudge through the mud toward Ivester's location.

The rain fell harder after dark, turning the hilltop into a sea of red mud. The sound of raindrops hitting the ponchos made other sounds nearly indistinguishable. The sucking sounds of footsteps were audible only from a close distance. Seepage of water into the holes was a continual problem for the dug-in Marines. Most stood in several inches of water, which severely aggravated the already bothersome condition of their feet.

Billingsley experienced an anxious interlude in the middle of the dark night when one of his squads reported possible movement to their front. No shots were fired, however, as the men waited for a clearer view of the possible targets. Only when Sanchez radioed that the sector was secure did Billingsley suspend his temptation to order a sweep of the area by fire. The remainder of the night passed without incident.

Although the skies remained overcast, dawn brought relief from the driving rain. The damp troops emerged from their holes and hoped for a clear day. After chow, the company left the hill and headed in the direction of the battalion position to the northeast. One more long day, one more night out, and the final leg of the triangular sweep would be complete. Perhaps then, the men quietly hoped, they could rest and attend to their feet and rashes.

Again the high temperatures and humidity joined with entangled terrain to slow the patrol. After two hours in the jungle heat, one of Billingsley's point men fainted and collapsed in a limp heap. The column halted for forty minutes while the man was revived and eventually judged able to continue.

"I just got real dizzy, sir," explained PFC McGannon, a rifleman whose face looked even younger than his age, eighteen. "It was just like when they gave us polio shots in grammar school. I got light-headed and before I knew it, I'd done hit the deck."

Billingsley looked at McGannon's eyes, which had eventually cleared with the long rest. The young Marine was able to stand without wavering.

"You know where you are, and what's going on, and all that shit?" asked Billingsley.

"Yessir, I'm fine now. Just got a little too hot. It's a bitch up there on the point, sir."

"I know it is. Stay off your feet until we're ready to saddle up again. And get that canteen to your mouth," ordered Billingsley.

"Yessir."

"I'll take the point," offered Sanchez.

"Negative. Get another man up there and you stay where you're supposed to be."

"But I can—"

"Sanchez, did you hear what I said, dammit? Get another man up there," snapped Billingsley.

"Ledbetter, get on the point," Sanchez said with a trace of irritation.

The order to resume the patrol soon came from English. Billingsley and his men took their places at the head of the column. Not long after they started, Billingsley felt his fatigue reach a new plateau. He labored under the weight of his pack. His feet hurt with every step. His muscles ached. His irritation grew at being so tired and so uncomfortable in the stifling, stinking jungle. A headache, carried over from the previous night, throbbed incessantly. He hated everything—the Marine Corps, Vietnam, English, the jungle, everything and everybody. He couldn't imagine a situation more miserable. His mood became dark and sullen and he fought a temptation to shout out a single profanity which would capture the essence of his attitude toward Vietnam and duty therein. He gritted his teeth and trudged on. Every step, every movement became a chore, a challenge to his will. Vines clutched at his arms and feet as if to prolong his agony by prohibiting his escape. His eyes burned from his sweat, the same sweat which darkened his uniform from his collar to his boots. His stomach churned, though he had no appetite. He kept moving, struggling, hating, aching.

Billingsley was startled from his deep fatigue by the sharp crack of a rifle to the column's immediate front. The single shot was instantly followed by bursts from M-16s.

"Sniper!" Sanchez warned from up ahead.

Billingsley listened to the Marines' gunfire and noticed that the enemy firing had ceased. He moved up the column in a low crouch, with Tetrick close behind, and overheard the faint cry of a wounded Marine from a thicket of vines and tangled undergrowth.

"Somebody (cough) help me . . . I'm hit (cough) . . . somebody (cough)."

"Corpsman up," Billingsley shouted over the shouts and shots to the front of the column. Tetrick spotted Ledbetter, gravely wounded and slumped on his back, partially supported by the undergrowth. Ledbetter's open flak jacket, along with the front of his utility shirt, was covered in dark blood. He had been shot near the center of the chest, slightly above the breast. The color had already begun to leave his face and his eyes were glazed. He coughed up his own blood in mouthfuls.

"Pull the flak jacket off him," ordered Billingsley when Tetrick had freed the limp Ledbetter from the vines.

Fralich arrived and quickly began his attempt at saving the fading Marine. The bullet's exit wound had left a gaping hole in Ledbetter's upper back. Billingsley turned his attention to the men ahead, where he could hear shouts and see Sanchez moving. He notified English of the sniping and the single casualty. When English inquired as to the condition of the wounded man, Billingsley turned to see Fralich attempting to detect a pulse from the wrist and chest of Ledbetter. Fralich looked at Billingsley and shook his head solemnly, his hands covered with the blood of the dead Marine.

"As you were on the friendly WIA," radioed Billingsley. "It's a KIA now."

Billingsley moved ahead cautiously and found Sanchez still probing for the sniper. Sanchez strained for a noise or a glimpse of the enemy sniper. He and Billingsley knelt alongside one another, with Tetrick just behind them, searching the tangled jungle.

"I ain't believin' there ain't a blood trail in here somewhere," declared Sanchez. "I know I hit the motherfucker. Garland, you see any blood, man?"

"No, not yet."

"I know I hit the motherfucker, sir. I *know* it! How about you, Ledbetter? You got anything, man?" called Sanchez.

"Ledbetter's bought it," advised Billingsley.

"You're shittin' me," said Sanchez, stunned.

"No. He took the round from the sniper, right through the chest."

"He was just next to me in the bush, before the gook fired. I thought the sniper had missed us."

"He was shot clean through," Tetrick added.

"I got a blood trail," shouted one of Sanchez's men who was several meters forward.

"Good." Sanchez sounded grim. "I want that dude . . . bad."

Billingsley radioed that the chase was on for the sniper. English's advice was to proceed cautiously.

The six Marines, including Billingsley and Tetrick, followed the dark splotches of blood on the ground and in the foliage. Sanchez led the way, alert to every sight and sound in the jungle. The trail of blood became more pronounced in the thick vegetation as the hunt continued slowly through the first twenty meters. Billingsley's heart pounded as he awaited the sound of another shot from the wounded enemy soldier who was in danger of bleeding to death. They searched through the next twenty meters. The blood became thicker. They slowed, knowing they were close. Still more blood. Another ten meters. Slowly. Another five. More blood. He's here, Billingsley thought. He's here and we're here, and somebody's gonna fucking die! Another ten meters. Couldn't be much farther, Billingsley guessed.

Suddenly, the anticipated shot rang out from a thicket of brush fifty feet to their front. Sanchez opened on full automatic while Billingsley shouted for the others to spread out into a line, facing the thicket. The Marines fired dozens of bullets into the target, partially defoliating the limbs and vines of the hiding place. Billingsley stood and watched, not firing his weapon, while the others continued with a change of magazines. The sniper's bullet had passed harmlessly over the head of Sanchez. The Marines kept pumping rounds into the thicket.

"Hold your fire. Cease firing," shouted Billingsley, finally gaining control of the men. "Move forward on a line. Keep your weapons trained on the target. C'mon, stay on line. Hold your fire. Who's going in after him?"

"Pull his ass out of there, Garland," Sanchez ordered to the man closest to the thicket.

They tightened the noose around the brush while Garland probed the thicket with his rifle barrel. He then separated the vines and pulled with one hand the riddled body of the NVA soldier. Another man stepped forward to assist Garland in freeing the body while Sanchez leaned in and recovered the AK. The body was dragged away from the brush and dumped in front of the gathered Marines. The multiple gunshot wounds had so ripped and shattered the man's body that identification from even his own next of kin would have been difficult. The dead man's left arm was the only portion of the body that remained at least somewhat intact. All else seemed a mass of blood, bones, entrails, and cartilage.

They all hovered over the body for a look.

Sanchez impassively aimed his camera at the corpse and took several snapshots. "Anybody want pictures?" he asked as he completed his photographing and stored the camera in his trouser pocket.

"We got what we came for. Let's get back to the position," interceded Billingsley, finally able to look away from the body.

Sanchez leaned over the man's body and grasped the undamaged hand. He placed the arm of the body across the chest and curled the fingers of the hand into the universally recognized gesture of defiance. The others laughed at the grotesque sight. Except Billingsley.

"I said we got what we came for. Now get moving," Billingsley said forcefully.

Sanchez focused his camera once again. "Let me get a shot of this," he said.

"Negative. We're moving out. Put the fuckin' camera away," said Billingsley sternly while staring at Sanchez.

Sanchez also stared at Billingsley. Each had a menacing expression on his face. Neither moved a muscle, nor did any of the others.

"Now, Sanchez!"

Sanchez complied, though clearly upset with his platoon leader's sharp tone and lack of humor. Billingsley, it seemed to Sanchez, had been especially uptight since his return from R&R in Japan. They left the body and made their way back to the company.

A helicopter passed them overhead on the way back.

"Comin' after Ledbetter, huh, sir?" asked Tetrick.

"Yeah, Goddammit." Billingsley spoke through clenched teeth.

The chopper lifted Ledbetter's body through the opening in the trees and departed. Bravo Company continued onward with Billingsley's platoon occupying the middle of the column. The heat intensified and by late afternoon the men were drenched with sweat. About 3,000 meters from the battalion position, English ordered the company to halt.

A ridgeline, with a knob at either extreme, was chosen for Bravo's encampment site. A platoon was emplaced on each of the knobs while the remaining platoon was extended across the compact ridge. Second Platoon was situated on the northernmost hill, overlooking a long valley to its right-front. A shallow stream wound along the valley floor in a glimmering line, fading into the northwest. The terrain, in general, was not as thickly overgrown as was the green jungle to the nearby west. The ridge occupied by the battalion headquarters staff, along with Company A, could be seen from the heights of the Bravo position. In the opposite direction, Company C's position atop a prominent rise could also be seen.

Colonel Fletcher was flown by helicopter into the Bravo Company perimeter about two hours before dark. He and English toured the positions and discussed tactical considerations. Billingsley watched as Fletcher pointed toward the west, toward the hills and jungles which appeared so tranquil from a distance. The aide with Fletcher brought mail for the men of the company—a small favor, but a meaningful and appreciated one. Fletcher left after the twenty-minute visit and flew south to the Company C location.

The morale of the tired troops improved dramatically when the letters were distributed. Billingsley received a letter from Andrea but chose not to open it immediately. Instead, he observed his troops as they waited for their names to be called by the company clerk who held the stack of letters. He was relieved to see that nearly all of his men received at least one piece of mail. He knew that Willingham's parents had been injured in an automobile accident on a recent Oklahoma day. He watched as Willingham read the two-page letter, after which the young squad leader drew a deep breath and folded the pages into the envelope.

"Willingham," called Billingsley. "Come over here."

Willingham walked over. His eyes were tired and puffy as he looked inquiringly at his platoon leader. "Yessir?" he asked.

"Any word on your folks?"

"Yessir, a letter from my sister, Janet."

"Everything okay?"

"They've both improved a lot, sir. It's mostly cuts and bruises. You know, shit like that. Mom hit the windshield and got a slight concussion and Dad broke a coupla ribs. But Janet says everything's a whole lots better, sir."

"That's good, Willingham. I'm sure it's a relief."

"Sure is, sir. Kinda been on my mind for a while."

Billingsley went to his fresh hole to read the news from Virginia. As usual, the letter was invitingly scented, a delight to the grimy man holding it in a muddy hole. Andrea's letter contained her typically optimistic views on the winding down of the war. She also wrote of her progress in law school.

> I'm now a third-year law student. Can you believe it? In five months you will return, and in eleven months I will graduate. Fantastic, huh? Mike, I've been thinking a lot about my life, especially since Daddy's passing. There's still a lot of questions in my head, but I've got a good idea about what I want to do and who I want to spend my life with. I don't mean to pressure you or put words in your mouth, but don't you think we'd make a great team? Why, we could take on the whole world. With your looks and brains (and my money), who's going to stop us? Interesting, isn't it? I think about it a lot. Hope you do, too. Please be careful, my love, and hurry home. I'm waiting for you.
>
> I Love You,
> A.

Billingsley could sense from the tone of her letter that Andrea was regaining her spirits. He could hardly contain himself as he thought of the day when he would once again be with her. He held the envelope close and breathed the sweet odor which reminded him of so many pleasant and joyous times. The scent and the memories stirred him.

"One of *those*, sir?" said the grinning Ambrosetti as he walked toward Billingsley's hole.

"Damn right. Want a whiff?"

"No way, sir. Too distracting for a serious Marine like myself. I've got business to look after."

"Bullshit. How many letters did you get?"

"I got three, sir."

"From how many different women?"

"Three."

"And how many of the letters were perfumed?"

"Three."

"How many of the women wrote erotic things in their letters?"

"Hell, all three, sir."

"And you can stand there and tell me that you're not the least bit distracted?"

"Sir, there ain't nothin' they can tell me about myself that I don't already know," said Ambrosetti with a grin. "When you got it, lieutenant, there just ain't no hidin' it."

"Well," sighed Billingsley, "what causes you to come over here and disrupt my quiet moment of reflection and contemplation?"

"In other words, what the fuck am I doing here?"

"Precisely."

"Okay, sir. The way I see it, if the gooks hit us they'll probably come right up the middle, 'cause the climb's easier. So that means Third Platoon gets jumped first. With me?"

"I'm with you."

"If they try to flank us, they're gonna come our way 'cause this hill's easier to climb than the one First Platoon's on. Okay?"

"Okay."

"Us and Third need most of the claymores out in front of *us*. But I was just over there lookin', and First Platoon's got most of 'em out in front of *them*. That's a crock of shit, sir. We oughta get us some more before it gets dark."

"You certainly weren't distracted, were you?" Billingsley asked admiringly.

"Business before pleasure, sir."

Billingsley later saw Tom Compton and explained Ambro setti's logical contention on the distribution of the claymores. Compton readily agreed and, upon English's approval, several additional claymores were installed to the front of Second Platoon as darkness enshrouded the hill.

"Satisfied, killer?" asked Compton as he, Billingsley, and Tetrick looked out over the position from Billingsley's hootch.

"Yeah, Tom," Billingsley replied. "It's impenetrable now. A whole horde of 'em couldn't move us off this hill."

"I don't care to see no hordes tonight," Compton said softly as he cupped his cigarette. "Six more weeks and I'll be back in the saddle again, in Baltimore, USA."

"Do I detect a note of softness in my hard-bitten XO?"

"No," smiled Compton. "The closer it gets, the harder I get."

"More ways than one, probably," Billingsley chuckled.

"There it is. Not much more of this shit left for me. If they come up this hill tonight, they're really gonna piss me off."

"If they come up this hill tonight and I happen to hear somebody shouting 'chieu hoi', I'll know it's you."

"Ah," shrugged Compton, "needless concerns. The famous Lieutenant Billingsley is here to uphold the prestige and glory of the Corps. All I'd have to do is watch."

"I hope to sleep like a baby tonight, Tom. You and the CO have run my ass off out here."

"Speaking of the CO," Compton said as he extinguished his smoke in the bottom of the hole, "I've got to hoof it back to the CP and go over the artillery plots with him."

"Send him my love." Billingsley helped Compton out of the hole with a solid push at his friend's backside.

"I will, Mike. I'll tell him that you've got a big, wet kiss that you're just dying to put on him."

Tetrick snickered.

"He's probably tired of your nose up his ass, anyway. It'd be a welcomed change," Billingsley whispered loudly at the departing Compton.

Compton stopped and returned to the hole. He leaned down and looked at Billingsley in the subdued light. "One more word of disrespect out of you, mister, and I'll have your ass shipped out of this unit posthaste," he said softly.

"Where to, sir?" asked Billingsley, stifling a grin.

"Back in the rear, to some place like Reston, Virginia."

"You'll have no more problems with me, XO. I just want to stay out here and do my duty and serve my country. Please don't send me away, sir."

Tetrick continued his snickering.

"I'll take it under advisement. Just remember, you're being observed closely," Compton said as he turned and left.

"I ain't believin' you two, sir," Tetrick said afterwards. "I didn't know officers shot the shit like that."

Billingsley smiled and stared into the darkened horizon.

A full moon provided enough light for Billingsley to see most of his sector indistinctly. The lack of rain had prompted the men to construct their positions without any overhead cover. Buzzing mosquitos annoyed them as much as the previous rains. Billingsley slapped a mosquito on his forearm and felt sticky blood between his fingers. Several more encounters with the pests prompted him to bathe the exposed parts of his body with the "bug juice" he carried in his first-aid packet.

Billingsley settled back into the hole and exchanged small talk with Tetrick. He looked forward to the forthcoming and well-earned rest period at Da Nang. He even considered paying a return visit to the girl in Da Nang whom he had discovered during the foray from the hospital. She had not infected him on the first encounter, he thought, so maybe his luck would hold for a repeat. The more he considered it, the more appealing the idea became. The thoughts of her soothing powers had been flickering intermittently in his head for days.

"Man, am I gonna jump her ass," he muttered softly.

"Do what, sir?" asked Tetrick.

"Nothing. I just don't seem to be able to get with the program tonight."

His distraction continued for another two hours before he was able to nod off to sleep. Andrea paraded from his subconscious. She was smiling in the dream, doting over her returned hero, embracing and cuddling him in a gush of affection. The pleasant, relaxing dream was cut off by NVA mortar and rocket rounds exploding on the ridgeline. Flashes and booms shattered the stillness of the night.

Bravo Company mortars began answering the enemy with

shells of their own once English's FO had identified a target area. To the south, English could see from his CP the intermittent flashes occurring within the Company C position as they, too, came under attack. Moments later, English watched as tracers began crisscrossing the sky, both from and into the Company C position. A ground assault was underway to the south.

"This is Six," English radioed to his platoon leaders. *"We've got a hot one starting to the south. Stand ready."*

The mortars and rockets bursting throughout the Bravo Company position were heavy enough to discourage anyone from all but a quick glance. An explosion several feet behind their hole showered Tetrick and Billingsley with falling debris. Billingsley's ears shrilled from the concussion. The heaviest concentration of the shelling seemed to be directed toward the center of the ridgeline, with the connected knolls only sporadically affected. Heavy explosions were scathing the ridge.

"Hold your fire until you've got something to shoot at," Billingsley advised his squad leaders by radio. "Don't give away your positions until you have to."

Only isolated shots were fired by the Marines at suspected probings by the NVA. Illumination rounds began to cast an eerie glow over the Company C area to the south where the steady popping of gunfire was muffled by the distance. Marine artillery soon opened up on the valley from which the NVA were emerging to join in the assault. Bravo's position continued to take fire, but it soon became clear that the enemy's initial efforts were being directed at Company C.

Billingsley heard a series of gunshots from several of the positions occupied by his men. The firing was light, however, and came from the portion of the sector manned by Willingham's squad. The mortars had lessened, and shouts for medical assistance came from Billingsley's left, near the ridge. He became convinced that a ground assault was imminent.

"They're just pickin' their spots right now. They gotta be comin'," radioed Ambrosetti.

"Have you still got live claymores?" asked Billingsley.

"Affirmative."

The situation with Bravo remained unchanged for the next half-hour. Friendly artillery from batteries to the south and northeast pounded the suspected enemy assemblages. Company C still resisted determined enemy thrusts. The artillery later shifted its fire into the valley to the front of Bravo when a prop-driven airplane arrived and circled over Company C's position. The aircraft unleased "Puff" at the enemy ground forces in a spectacular stream of tracers. Once the plane had completed the mission and cleared the vicinity, the Marine artillery once again began firing at the enemy near the Company C site.

Meanwhile, English notified his platoon leaders that preparations were being made to reinforce Company C's position to the south. Billingsley's heart felt as if it had jumped into his throat when he heard English mention over the radio that Bravo might soon leave its location to join the action elsewhere. Soon Tom Compton jumped into Billingsley's hole and began explaining the rudiments of a plan for moving Bravo to the Company C area.

My God! Billingsley thought as he listened to Compton. This ought to be interesting. This is some all-out stuff, he concluded. He could see his friend's tenseness. Though English had put it together quickly, it was a good plan—uncomplicated and logical. Bravo would slip out of its current location, move along the stream to the rear of the position, and break toward the Company C position to the west to reinforce them from the rear. What resistance would they meet? Billingsley wondered. What about an NVA blocking force to prevent the reinforcement from any direction? How many gooks are down there? What if they shell us when we're along the stream? What if they overrun Charlie Company before we get there, and then *they* have the high ground? Jesus! he thought. We'll know soon.

"Shit, Tom. I hope they can hang on," Billingsley said after Compton's review of the plan.

"God, so do I. But we can't leave 'em down there if they can't," said Compton.

"I know. How much longer before we'll have to pull out?"

"Not long, if it's gonna happen. Skipper's in touch with battalion, and he's also monitoring the C Company net."

Compton raised his head and glanced around the position, though the Company C position to the south was obscured by the gentle rise of the ridgeline. He returned to the bottom of the hole where Billingsley and Tetrick sat unmoving. Occasional bursts from rockets and mortars continued to shake the ground occupied by the Bravo Company troops.

"What do you think, Tom?" asked Billingsley.

"I think I'd like to leave the party early and drive home."

"No joke, sir," interjected the nervous radioman.

"Got any questions about the plan?" Compton asked.

"Nope," answered Billingsley. "Have you talked to Art and Kupton?"

"Art, yeah. Not Kupton. I'd better get over there."

Heavy small-arms fire erupted on the far side of the Bravo perimeter. Mortars and rockets once again exploded rapidly within the position after a period of relative calm. Light gunfire could also be heard from the middle of the ridge.

"If we have to pull out, we'll go out just like I explained," Compton said, still kneeling in the hole. "I gotta get back up there. Sounds like we may have problems of our own."

"Better stay here," suggested Billingsley. "Let 'em waste their fuckin' ordnance before you stick that empty head of yours up."

"Still disrespectful, aren't you, asshole?" Compton pulled himself onto the rim of the hole. "Stay in touch, ace."

"Keep your damned head down," Billingsley shouted as Compton sprinted toward the ridge.

The gunfire intensified to the left of Billingsley's position. Incoming explosions pounded at the ridgeline. The signs still favored an assault by the NVA. Billingsley radioed English to inquire if the attack was underway on the far side of Bravo's perimeter, the area which Ambrosetti had argued would be the least likely avenue of the enemy's approach.

"Negative," replied English. *"It's a rear-guard force to keep us up here. If it's gonna come, it'll be somewhere else."*

"How can he figure all that shit out, sir?" Tetrick asked.

"Beats me," Billingsley answered as he piled hand grenades within easy reach.

The situation remained unchanged for another long hour. To the south, Company C continued to hold its own. The shelling and small-arms fire rang out through the Bravo position, though no assault came. Several NVA soldiers, attempting to probe the Second Platoon sector, were discovered and killed only a few feet from the closest hole. One of the dead NVA was carrying a satchel charge. English radioed Billingsley with a terse message that Bravo Five, Tom Compton, was WIA and that he, Billingsley, was now second in command of the company. English said nothing about Compton's condition. The news stunned Billingsley.

"Dammit, I told him to keep his head down," Billingsley said in disgust.

"Who is it, sir?" asked Tetrick.

"The XO's been hit."

"Bad?"

"I don't know. Jesus, I hope not."

Another mortar round exploded near Billingsley's hole only seconds after he had risen to inspect his sector and dropped back in the hole. He kept waiting for the enemy to try to overrun the hill, feeling certain that large numbers of NVA troops would soon be upon the slopes of the ridge. He felt a detached, sinking sensation, but no feelings of panic. It was as if the NVA commander was calling all the shots, leaving the Marines to wait and guess. And Billingsley was unsure just how the picture was developing. He wondered who might be winning.

The time passed in dreadfully slow chunks.

"They're coming up, they're coming up!" Sanchez radioed excitedly as gunfire erupted from the platoon positions. In the center of the company's defenses, Third Platoon also began firing into the advancing NVA troops who moved up the ridge. Concussions from exploding claymores reverberated through the air when Ambrosetti activated the devices in the Second Platoon area. The firing was so intense that stacks of enemy bodies piled up only twenty feet from the positions of the defenders. The Marines flung grenades at swarming NVA soldiers and fired M-79 rounds into the attackers at virtually point-blank range. Billingsley could judge from his radio reports and his visual scans that the enemy was failing in its attempt to breach the perimeter. English's FO moved supporting artillery fire to within 200 meters of the slopes of the ridge. The attack lasted forty minutes, though it seemed an eternity to those closest to the darting figures in the khaki uniforms and the pith helmets.

"Think that was it?" Billingsley radioed to English.

"Roger, I do. The main event's to the south. Are you still engaged?"

"A few snipers, nothing big. What's it like to the south?"

"It's cooling a good bit. I think it may be breaking up," English said in a calm, even tone. *"Keep 'em alert and don't go to sleep at the wheel."*

"Roger, not much chance of that. Any word on the X-ray Oscar?"

English paused before replying, *"Not good."* The conversation concluded when English requested a casualty report as soon as the number could be determined.

Billingsley was uncertain of the meaning of English's reply on the condition of Tom Compton. He had not asked for clarifying information in the strange hope that by not knowing for sure, Compton could be assumed to be alive and well. He wanted to believe that, anyway. But really he knew that his friend's life was in the balance, at the very least. And in the inexplicable, natural buffering function of the human brain, Billingsley was somehow prepared for the worst.

His mind came back to the situation of the platoon wounded. He crawled to Ambrosetti's hole, and soon both moved off in opposite directions to inspect each of the platoon's fighting positions. Billingsley found five seriously injured men, all of whom had been treated by Fralich, and Ambrosetti reported one dead and four wounded. Billingsley crawled back to Ambrosetti's location, to the left of the sector, and radioed his report to English.

"Who's the KIA?" asked Billingsley after having transmitted the count.

"Fernandez, in Rosser's squad," answered Ambrosetti.

"The grenadier?"

"Yeah, that's him. Caught a round in the fuckin' gourd."

"Damn."

"I'll bet we skated by a lot better than Charlie Company did, sir. Could've been a shitload worse if they woulda come at us like that."

"Yeah, sure could have. Get 'em ready to go out. Skipper says we'll try to get 'em all out, but get the worst cases on the first bird in case the ground fire's too hot."

Dawn was still nearly two hours away. Billingsley knew that at least two of his wounded men would likely not survive an extended delay in being evacuated. With Fralich's help, the injured and the dead were carried up the ridge to an LZ in

the center of the company position. Billingsley noticed that
the medevac point was crowded with injured Marines.

The choppers made their approach from the southwest and
were guided toward the Bravo location by Marines with flashlights. The first chopper to reach the position drew light
small-arms fire from isolated enemy stragglers from the nearby
valley. Still, the pilot was able to touch the ground while the
wounded were literally tossed aboard the CH-46. Once the
severest of the casualties had been loaded, the chopper rose
and banked sharply toward the east. A second helicopter
approached the ridge and attracted crisscrossing small-arms
and automatic-weapons fire from many directions. English
advised the pilot by radio that the serious cases had already
been taken on the first load and suggested that Company C
might need another bird. Eleven wounded Marines, and the
bodies of nine others, remained in the position while the
chopper swung to the south amid a string of tracers.

Billingsley returned to his hole and lit a cigarette. He was
drained from the tension and fatigue. He prayed silently, asking
that the enemy be made to go away and leave them alone for
the rest of the night. As always after a major action, a feeling
of gratitude at being alive and well came to him. He wondered
how much more action he could see before his luck ran out.
Luck had run out for quite a few people on and around the
hill who, only a few hours before, had undoubtedly hoped to
enjoy a quiet, peaceful night. He cupped his cigarette with one
hand while with the other he wiped his dirty, sweaty face.
Another long night in an endless, hellish vortex of long nights,
he thought.

Tears were streaming down Tetrick's face as he slumped
into the hole. "Sir, the XO's dead."

"How do you know that, Tetrick?" Billingsley asked calmly.

"I heard two dudes from First Platoon when we were up
there with the chopper. They hollered and asked Gunny Tyler
if he wanted them to put Lieutenant Compton's body on the
first bird, but he told them to hold off until the next one. That
was before the skipper sent the next one away. I asked Gunny
Tyler what had happened and he ..." Tetrick wiped at the
mucous at his nose, then sniffed, "he said the lieutenant was
killed from a rocket burst that landed only a few feet from

him when he was comin' back from Sergeant Kupton's position."

"Son of a bitch," Billingsley said softly. All the air seemed to have left his lungs. "I was afraid of that."

"I'm sorry to have to tell you that, sir," Tetrick said, wiping his face. "I knew you and Lieutenant Compton were tight, so I thought you oughta know."

"Thanks, Tetrick. I'm glad you told me," Billingsley said after a long pause.

Tetrick coughed and wiped his nose with his sleeve. The tears still streamed from his eyes. "I feel sick to my stomach, sir. I thought we were all going to buy it. I just knew I was gonna die. I didn't even know if I could do my job," he said.

"You did fine, Tetrick. You did your job as well as any Marine in the platoon."

"Does it ever get any easier, sir? I mean, do you ever get used to it?"

"You learn to deal with it, yeah. You'll feel a lot better with a little sleep. Why don't you try to get some rest before we pull outta here in a few hours," Billingsley said with a faint slap on Tetrick's shoulder.

"I'm still shakin', sir."

"If it makes you feel any better, so am I. And so is every other man on this ridge. Ain't nothin' strange about that."

Billingsley stood and leaned against the top of the hole. And he *was* still shaking, as he had claimed. Twenty minutes later, he heard deep breathing, which indicated that Tetrick had succumbed to his fatigue. Billingsley climbed quietly from his hole and walked the fifty meters to the CP where he found Gunny Tyler still awake in his small hole.

"What's up?" Tyler whispered.

"Where's the XO?"

"Over there with the others," Tyler said, pointing. "He's the last one on the right."

Billingsley found the body of Compton among the other dead Marines. His left arm protruded from underneath the poncho which covered his body, displaying a watch and wedding band that Billingsley recognized easily. That was proof enough. He knelt in the dim light alongside the remains of his closest friend. He arranged Compton's arm so that it, too, was completely covered.

"I'm gonna miss you, hotshot," Billingsley said softly.

He thought back to his first encounter with Tom Compton, the already salty veteran with a mixture of swagger and compassion. He thought of Compton's infant daughter who would never lay eyes upon her father. But mostly he thought of the mere six weeks left on Compton's tour, six weeks which stood between this end and Compton's return to his Baltimore home for the long-awaited reunion. Only six weeks. Compton had endured the heat and the slime long enough to feel as if the completion of his tour was at hand. The light at the end of the tunnel; the pot of gold at the end of the rainbow; the beginning of the end. Only six weeks. And now had come the most cruel and dreaded of scenarios. So close and so unfair, Billingsley thought. But not especially surprising. Not over here. Not really. Not anymore.

Billingsley had difficulty accepting that the still corpse underneath the poncho was all that remained of the man whose friendship had come to mean so much to him. He could hear Compton's voice, see Compton's face, enjoy Compton's wide smile beneath the dark moustache. It almost seemed a joke to Billingsley, as if at any moment Compton would hurl back the poncho and fling an obscenity at him, laughing heartily in the process. But Billingsley could only wish, could only hope. For Tom Compton would live no more. *Six weeks!* Billingsley lamented. Why, in God's name? Why, dammit? Why?

Billingsley slapped gently at Compton's boot. "Take care, babe. I'll keep an eye on Chris and the baby for you. You have my word on that," he said firmly.

The walk back to the hole was filled with memories of Compton.

The remaining hour of darkness passed quickly for Billingsley, who sat in his hole, numb. When the sun appeared behind him at dawn, he woke Tetrick and then went about rousing his tired platoon. As he gazed down the western slopes of the hill, he could see piles of stiffened NVA dead. English soon joined him for a walking tour of the carnage. They estimated that at least sixty enemy soldiers had been stopped short of the perimeter.

"Reports over the net seemed to indicate that Charlie Company lost over half its people last night," remarked English, his eyes puffy and bloodshot.

"God almighty, they *were* in a hornet's nest," exclaimed Billingsley.

English explained the facts of the battle which he had pieced together from radio reports. Companies A and B had been harassed to block any attempts to reinforce Company C, the major object of the enemy's attentions. The NVA planned to isolate and destroy Company C with its main force while committing only enough troops toward the other companies to keep them occupied. "It almost worked. Came within a gnat's ass," English concluded.

English's radioman came running toward the two officers, extending the handset to the CO. "It's Colonel Fletcher, sir," he advised.

Billingsley listened as English reported on the estimate of enemy casualties in the Bravo Company area. After English returned the handset to the radioman, he took a deep breath. He placed his hands on his hips and gazed about the position, a slight smile on his face.

"What's the scoop, sir?" Billingsley asked.

"A change in plans. We'll get everybody together at the CP and go over it. Get your people fed and I'll see you in ten minutes."

Billingsley and English went their separate ways—English to the CP and Billingsley to find Ambrosetti.

"Get 'em ready to go out as soon as they've had chow," ordered Billingsley.

"What's comin' down, sir?"

"I'm not sure. Just have 'em ready."

Billingsley joined the others at the CP, taking a seat on the damp ground next to Tyler. A few feet away was Compton's body, his pack, helmet, and weapon stacked alongside. Billingsley quickly looked away. English appeared and, after a glance at his watch, took a seat on the ground. All eyes focused upon the CO.

"Okay, people. We've had a change in plans," English said, speaking slowly. "Choppers will arrive in less than an hour to take out the rest of the dead and wounded. The good news is that the choppers will also take us and Charlie Company out, too. Alpha's already on the way to Da Nang in trucks. So, instead of humping over to the battalion position, we'll get a ride to Da Nang and a few days off before we go back out. That shouldn't be too hard to take, huh?"

The platoon leaders indicated their unanimous approval with smiles and laughter. Billingsley smiled with relief and winked at Tyler, who looked impassive as always.

"You're not pissed, are you?" Billingsley asked out of the corner of his mouth.

"I go where the Corps needs me, sir," Tyler cracked, unable to suppress the slight smile which crept across his face.

"That's probably Colonel Fletcher there," said English as he pointed toward an approaching helicopter. "He'll likely stop here, so get back there to your platoons and be ready to shove off in forty minutes."

Fletcher did stop at the Bravo position, but only after he had first visited the Company C area. He was accompanied by Chaplain Sherwin, a large, middle-aged Protestant minister whose popularity with the troops was immense. Chaplain Sherwin had a reputation of fearlessness in the face of gunfire. He had been decorated for administering to the needs of wounded Marines within embattled areas. He also had an alleged appreciation for an occasional cocktail, for which no decoration had been forthcoming except the unabashed admiration of the Marines of First Battalion.

Fletcher walked with English toward the perimeter's edge to view the dead while Sherwin moved freely among the positions of the troops. Fletcher's face was stern as he gazed at the clusters of NVA bodies. Several Bravo Company Marines walked among the dead enemy, collecting weapons and searching for documents. Fletcher completed his tour and thereafter left with his small party in his Huey command chopper.

Billingsley glanced around his platoon area as he stood smoking a cigarette alongside his hole. He noticed that his men were gathering in groups, laughing and joking, comparing stories of the previous night's action, while they waited for the choppers. Many had taken off their helmets and flak jackets. They were alive, and they were about to get a rest, and they had chosen to concern themselves with little else.

"Sergeant Ambrosetti," called Billingsley.

Ambrosetti walked over from where he had been inspecting

the stacks of NVA weapons. Ambrosetti was already perspiring in the warm, morning sun.

"Yessir?" he said as he faced Billingsley.

"If Charles decides to send a few mortar rounds as a going-away present, he'll have some nice targets," Billingsley said with a nod toward the clustered troops.

Ambrosetti walked slowly toward several of the men. "You people having a good fucking time? I hate to be the one to break up the party, ladies, but four or five rounds and some of you cocksuckers will be leaving this hill in a fuckin' *spoon*! Get your Goddamned gear on, people, and get back to your positions. You'll get the word on when you can come out. You squad leaders start paying the fuck attention to what's comin' down. Rosser, I want some of your men to carry these AK's out when they go," he shouted.

The troops did as they were told; they usually did when under orders from Ambrosetti. Billingsley considered Ambrosetti to be a very able replacement for Tyler. Though he lacked Tyler's experience and maturity, his intelligence, resourcefulness, and toughness were recognized by everyone. He didn't often shout, and rarely needed to. He knew the nature of the men in the platoon, he knew what had to be done, and he knew how to get it done without a lot of fanfare. The troops respected Ambrosetti, and they knew he wouldn't tolerate any foolishness once the platoon was in the bush. Ambrosetti knew what it took to stay alive once the shooting started. Everybody admired that quality, especially in those with leadership positions.

The first of the helicopters, the long CH-46s, landed amid the swirling red smoke which marked the LZ in the Bravo position. Two gunships roamed the skies above, ready to pounce upon any ill-advised resistance. First Platoon was the first to board. Sergeant Kupton and two others carefully lifted the body of Tom Compton so that their former platoon leader could make his final journey with them. The men of the platoon had requested such an arrangement, and English had quickly agreed. There were no tears, though lumps were in the throats of many of the young men who had followed Compton over countless hills, through countless valleys, across countless streams. They were bringing him back now, as one of their own, for the last time.

The remainder of the bodies were taken with Second Platoon. Billingsley glanced over the deserted ridge as the last of his men ran aboard the chopper. A few empty cardboard boxes, several C-ration cans, lots of spent cartridges, a lot of holes in the ground surface. And a lot of dead enemy soldiers on the slopes. Billingsley stepped up the ramp of the helicopter and motioned a thumbs-up to the helmeted crew chief. He took a seat in the rear, near the ramp. The chopper edged forward and began gaining altitude while Billingsley watched the hill become only a green blur in the exhaust. At his side sat Willingham, who opened a small can filled with a brownish substance. Willingham held the can toward Billingsley.

"A little snuff, sir?" shouted Willingham over the engine noise.

"No thanks. You wouldn't happen to have a beer on you, would you?" Billingsley shouted in return.

"No, sir. But I will have soon, and you can have one on me."

Billingsley grinned and nodded his head approvingly. He fully intended to have more than one.

9

The stuffy afternoon air in the Quonset hut was moved about only slightly by the two pedestal fans procured by Ivester. Billingsley had fallen asleep on his bunk and lay propped by his full pack. He had involuntarily succumbed to the effect of a hot meal after thirty continuous hours of no sleep. On his lap was an unfinished letter to Chris Compton, Tom's wife. The few words which were already written had come with great difficulty as he tried to express the sorrow and sympathy he felt over the death of his best friend. He had known what he felt, what he wanted to say, but the words had not been there.

Billingsley was awakened from his nap by three sharp raps on the door of the hootch. He called out for the person to enter and saw Ambrosetti open the door and step inside.

"Sorry, sir. I didn't know you were crashing or else I would've left you alone," said Ambrosetti.

"No problem. What's up?"

Ambrosetti held a sandbag toward Billingsley. Inside the bag was a single can of beer, still cool and moist. "Willingham told me to be sure you get this," he explained.

"Send my thanks to Willingham, but you drink it. I'm groggy enough as it is."

"Any word on how long we'll be here?"

"Two days, the last I heard."

"What I came to tell you," Ambrosetti said, stopping to savor a sip of the beer, "is that I got all the squad leaders together and jumped in their shit about keeping a close eye on this racial stuff. I told them that if any more shit starts like last time, somebody's gonna go to the brig. And that'll be one less pack they'll have when they get back out in the bush. I hope they listened."

313

"Maybe everybody's too tired to get into anything like that. I know I am," said Billingsley with a yawn.

"That's all I had, sir. I just wanted you to know that I got 'em together, like you said."

"Good. Sit down and finish the brew."

"Troopies ain't supposed to be in officer's country, sir. Especially drinkin' beer," grinned Ambrosetti.

"What are you worried about? Afraid somebody's gonna cut your hair and send you to Vietnam?"

"Month and a half, sir, and this dago's bookin' from this scumbag. Man, am I gonna do a job on some of those hogs in the neighborhood. It's gonna be 'groan city' when I get my hands inside their skivvies."

"You keep braggin' to me about how short you are and I'm gonna tell the CO that you want a six-month extension."

"I'll write my Congressman, sir. He's Italian, too. Got a bunch of dudes on his staff with names like Bruno and Bugsy."

"In that case, you'll have no further problems from me," Billingsley said, and they both laughed.

Ambrosetti left after finishing the beer. Billingsley returned to the letter to Compton's wife, completing it with a minimum of words but with a great deal of compassion and sympathy. Art Ivester soon appeared in the hootch carrying beer and snacks, along with several magazines and paperback novels. Ivester and Billingsley had the Quonset hut to themselves.

"Caught up on your correspondence?" asked Ivester.

"Yeah, pretty much."

"Good. You can help me devour these goodies. We can be shitfaced by evening chow if we get after it right now. How 'bout a beer?"

"Why not?" Billingsley said as he put away his pen and paper. "I'll probably fall asleep again whether I drink or not, so I may as well cut some drunken z's."

They had barely downed the contents of the first of Ivester's beers when Captain English opened the door to the Quonset hut and stepped inside. He was followed by a man of medium build with short, dark hair and dark eyes. The man carried his gear into the hootch and tossed it upon an empty bed.

"I see you gentleman have acclimated yourselves," English said with a slight smile.

"Help yourself, skipper," offered Ivester.

"No, not now. I want you to meet the new XO of Bravo Company." English turned toward the newcomer. "This is Bob Saliba. Bob, meet Mike Billingsley and Art Ivester."

Saliba accepted their greetings indifferently, neither smiling at nor thanking them. He barely even looked at Billingsley and Ivester when he shook hands; instead he gazed about the hootch's interior. His eyes finally settled upon the cans of beer which were stacked at the foot of Ivester's bunk.

"Bob's new in-country," English added. "He's just getting over here from Twentynine Palms. He's all checked-in and filled-in on the unit, and so forth, so why don't you fellas get him a rack and make him feel at home."

"Will do, sir," Billingsley said.

"I'll see you a little later, Bob. Welcome aboard. You'll be in good company with these two officers," English said as he walked to the door.

"Okay, sir. Thanks," Saliba responded. He immediately reached for a beer, opened it, and turned his attention toward his unpacking.

Saliba said nothing as he arranged his clothing and gear for the next five minutes, stopping only for an occasional gulp of beer. Ivester, who stood in front of his own bunk, glanced over at Billingsley. Several moments of uncomfortable silence ensued.

"Have a beer, Bob," Billingsley said sarcastically.

Saliba turned and looked briefly at Billingsley before drinking the remaining contents from the can. He then crushed the can with his hand and leaned over to take another from the stack. "Thanks, I believe I will," he said.

All the warmth and charm of a car repossessor, Billingsley thought. And all the courtesy of prostate cancer.

"Where you from, Bob?" Ivester asked in a friendly gesture.

"Colorado."

"Married?"

"Yeah."

"Any kids?"

"Nah."

"Where'd you go to school?"

"Colorado State."

"What'd you major in?"

"Liberal arts."

"Got any tattoos?" asked Billingsley.

Saliba shot a quick glance toward Billingsley and made no effort to answer the question.

"Think you're gonna like Bravo Company?" Ivester quickly asked.

Saliba sat upon his bed and sighed deeply, as if inconvenienced by the questioning. He rubbed the cool can across his forehead, then sipped from it. "It'll be fine, I guess. I'm not real impressed so far with Gunny . . . what's his name. He'll need some work. Other than that, it seems like it may be a pretty decent outfit," he said.

"His name's Gunny Tyler," Billingsley said sharply.

"Yeah, right. Gunny Tyler. Where'd you people get those fans? This heat is something else."

"Use this fan," said Ivester as he slid the fan near his own bed in Saliba's direction, again receiving no acknowledgment of appreciation.

Art, you stupid shit! Billingsley thought to himself. Let the idiot suffer. Let him *really* suffer. Maybe he'll melt and liquefy and flow into the pores of the concrete deck.

The spotty conversation between Saliba and Ivester continued for another half-hour. Saliba seemed bored with Ivester's conversation and much more interested in his beer. Saliba spoke only when spoken to, and then with a "yeah" or a "right" or a "we'll see about that." Not once did he initiate a topic of conversation after reclining on his bunk and enjoying the breeze from Ivester's fan. He sipped the beer, belching occasionally, and wiped his face repeatedly with a handkerchief. He perspired heavily from the unaccustomed humidity of Indochina. Saliba finally left the hootch to meet further with English.

"Well," said Ivester after Saliba's departure, "what's your opinion of your new XO?"

"I think you know what I think of him, Art. And I hope to God nothing happens to English," replied Billingsley.

Little else was mentioned about the new officer.

Billingsley walked to his platoon area during the late afternoon and found Fralich treating blisters and rashes which had plagued many of his men. Tetrick received the platoon mail at the CP and returned to distribute the letters to the outstretched hands of the troops. Billingsley was generally satisfied with the condition of his platoon, both in body and in spirit, and he left the men to their mail.

After evening chow, Billingsley and Ivester returned to their hootch to find Saliba stretched out with both fans directed toward his bed. Saliba nodded at the two as they entered, glancing upward from a magazine. Billingsley resisted a terrific urge to retrieve his fan, as well as the inclination to advise Saliba of his dislike of him. Instead, he said nothing. He started a letter to Andrea.

"You people gonna go to the club tonight?" Saliba asked when he had finished with the magazine.

"I'm not, Bob. I need some rest," answered Ivester.

"What about you, Billingsley?"

"Nope."

"Both of you must be out of shape, huh? A little brew and bullshit session might improve both your attitudes."

Billingsley felt a rush of indignation and fought to control his temper, for he wanted badly to snatch Saliba from his bunk and pound him unmercifully. But he controlled the urge with a deep breath and a warm can of beer. He wadded the letter and started over.

Saliba suggested once more that Billingsley and Ivester join him for the trip to the Officers' Club, and was again refused. After he left, Billingsley and Ivester went next door to join some friends from Alpha Company for several rounds of drinks and a few hands of poker. They later returned to their Quonset hut and arranged the two fans to their own liking. They turned off the single bulb and settled into their beds for a needed rest.

Saliba returned shortly before midnight, finding Ivester and Billingsley asleep. He closed the door sharply and turned on the light, jolting Ivester awake. Saliba undressed slowly and clumsily, and he stumbled as he struggled to remove his boots. Once undressed down to his undershorts, he belched loudly and fell into his bed. He opened and began to read a magazine in the illuminated hut.

"How 'bout turning the light out, Bob," asked Ivester, shielding his eyes with his arm as he lay in the bed next to Saliba.

"I will in a few minutes."

Saliba belched again when he rose to leave the hootch to urinate on the ground nearby. When he returned, he continued with the magazine, rattling the pages as he turned them. He breathed deeply and loudly.

"C'mon, man. Cut the light out," Ivester said in a louder voice.

"Yeah, okay. A few more minutes."

Billingsley, across the aisle from Ivester and Saliba, was now awake and lay on his back shielding his eyes from the light.

Ten minutes passed and Saliba continued his reading. He ate peanuts from a can which he had spotted near Ivester's bunk.

"I can't sleep with that light on, man!" Ivester said, clearly becoming irritated.

"I'll turn it off in just a second."

The same scene continued for the next fifteen minutes—the rattling of the pages, the belching, the crunching of the peanuts. Saliba made another trip outside, near the door. Billingsley and Ivester listened to his urine splashing onto the ground. Saliba slammed the door and fell into his rack with the magazine and the peanut can. All the while, the light remained bright.

Billingsley turned onto his side. He slowly reached beside his bunk for his cartridge belt and pulled it quietly toward him. He felt for the black leather holster, opened the flap, and withdrew his loaded .45 caliber pistol. With his other hand he silently reached over and slowly pulled the chamber back to seat a round. He then bolted upright, aimed upward, and fired a single, deafening shot. The overhead bulb exploded into thousands of pieces and the bullet tore through the roof of the Quonset hut, on out into the dark of the Da Nang night. Pieces of glass showered Saliba's bunk as he lay stunned and unmoving in the dark hootch.

"Think hard before you light any matches, cowboy. I've got six rounds left," Billingsley said calmly.

"And don't fuck with the fans," Ivester added as he rolled over.

Saliba needed no further warnings. He remained motionless for the rest of the night. He was in the same position, with the magazine still in his grasp, when the first light of dawn appeared.

The first to dress and leave the hootch was Saliba, but only after he had picked the particles of glass from his bed. As soon as he had closed the door behind him, Ivester quickly sat up and began cackling and pointing to the hole in the roof.

"Welcome to Bravo Company, Lieutenant Saliba," said Ivester and a laughing spell overtook him.

"I'll probably go to jail for that," grinned Billingsley as he, too, sat up. "We're gonna need us a broom, Art. There's glass everywhere."

"I can't believe you *did* that, Mike," said Ivester, tearful from his laughter. "He came off that rack about two feet. Made this real low, guttural sound . . . like you'd just blown his fuckin' face off, or something. And the surprise was total. Absolutely total! Man, I ain't *even* believin' you shot the light out."

"I would have looked like a jackass if I'd missed, wouldn't I?" said Billingsley, also laughing hard. "Sitting there in the fuckin' light with a gun in my hand."

"But you didn't. I could've kissed you when you did it. I woke up early and the son of a bitch was still sitting there with his eyes open. I had to turn over away from him to keep from breaking up. He was still breathing heavy."

They laughed about the incident as they rose and dressed. After breakfast, they cleaned up the broken glass on the concrete floor of the Quonset hut. When their housekeeping was completed, they made plans for their day: trips to the barber shop, the PX, the hospital to visit their wounded, and finally, a night at the club. Saliba had yet to return to the hootch.

Gunny Tyler dropped by later in the morning to inform Billingsley that Captain English expected him at the CP in five minutes. Gunny Tyler had a serious look on his face.

"What the hell for, gunny?" Billingsley asked innocently.

"I don't know, sir. Him and the new XO have been talkin' for a good while already. He just told me to come by and give you the word that he wanted to see you."

"Okay, gunny. Tell him I'm on my way," Billingsley said, resigned.

Tyler left to return to the CP.

"There it is, Art. Saliba's spilled his lousy guts to English. They've got me by the balls, now," Billingsley said as he reached for his cap.

"Maybe not. Maybe it's about something else."

"Like what? He'd want both of us if it was about an operation."

"Don't worry about it, Mike. The worst you'll get is an ass chewing."

"If I don't get back," said Billingsley as he walked to the door, "will you bring me my things at the brig?"

"Hell, no. I don't affiliate with known criminals. You *dinky dao*, boy."

"Thanks, Art. It's been good knowing you."

English greeted Billingsley curtly when he reported to the hut which served as the CP. Saliba stood beside English's desk, staring coldly. Neither spoke, but each nodded to the other as their only form of greeting. English glanced at his watch and then reached for his cap which hung from a nail in the wooden support at the back of the Quonset hut.

"Colonel Fletcher wants to meet briefly with you, Mike. Bob and I are going along, too," said English.

Billingsley was confused. Why would English pack him off to see The Man without even hearing his side of the story? Though he knew what he had done was out of the ordinary, he at least wanted an opportunity to explain himself to his CO. As the group entered the headquarters of Fletcher, Billingsley's mood changed from one of helplessness to one of defiance and anger. He fully intended to have a go at Saliba as soon as the proceedings with Fletcher had ended.

Billingsley waited outside the entrance to Fletcher's office while English and Saliba stepped inside. A few minutes later English looked around the corner at Billingsley and nodded for him to enter. He stood between English and Saliba, facing the seated Fletcher who held a typewritten document in his hand. He suddenly felt his mood change back to helplessness. He felt outnumbered, outranked, and outcast. "Lieutenant Billingsley reporting as ordered, sir," he said.

"Stand at ease, Lieutenant Billingsley," said the unsmiling colonel. "Do you know why I've asked that you be brought here?"

Billingsley paused and drew a deep breath. He finally decided to answer, safely, "I'm not sure, sir."

"Well, the reason you're here," Fletcher said as he put on his reading glasses, "is because of what's written here. Let me read it to you."

Billingsley waited to hear Fletcher speak of "charges" and "specifications" and "willful violation," but instead something astonishing began to unfold. Fletcher read from a citation which described Billingsley's part in the rescue of Ivester's imperiled patrol near Hoi An. He was stunned. Instead of admonishment, he was going to get a *decoration!* He listened as Fletcher read.

"... For conspicuous gallantry in the face of a numerically superior enemy force in or about the vicinity of Hoi An, Quang Nam Province, Republic of Vietnam ..."

Billingsley's expression was one of bewilderment. He glanced quickly to his side and saw a proud smile on English's face.

"... commanding a reaction force sent to the relief of an endangered friendly force, succeeded in repulsing the attack of an estimated enemy company. Coordinating the use of supporting arms with extraordinary skill, Lieutenant Billingsley led an aggressive and determined ..."

He had difficulty grasping it. It all seemed so unreal and, only minutes before, so unlikely. He wondered if the whole thing could be a practical joke by Fletcher and English.

"... actions were timely and forceful and he employed his smaller force with tactical resourcefulness. He accomplished his mission with a minimum loss to his own forces ..."

Billingsley felt an urge to laugh, not at Fletcher's words, but at the strange twist of fate. He knew, though, that laughter would be anything but appropriate.

"... courage and professionalism were an inspiration to those who were witness to his exemplary leadership, and was in keeping with the highest tradition of the Naval Service."

Fletcher removed his glasses and stood up. He produced a flat cardboard box which he opened with a series of shakes. He walked around the desk to stand facing Billingsley, who felt the back of his legs shaking.

"Lieutenant Billingsley, I commend you on this award of the Silver Star," Fletcher said. "I'm proud to be able to make this presentation, and I know Captain English also shares in that pride. First Battalion, Third Marines is the outstanding unit it is because of the leadership from men such as yourself. And I want to tell you straight up that I'm damned glad to have you in my command. Congratulations, Marine."

Fletcher pinned the red, white, and blue medal, with the dangling star, upon Billingsley's jungle utilities. A handshake from Fletcher was followed by the same from English and Saliba.

"I'd like to have a hundred more just like him, Captain English," Fletcher said with a slap at Billingsley's shoulder.

"That would be outstanding, sir," agreed English.

"Lieutenant Billingsley," Fletcher added, "you've done yourself proud, and you've done the Marine Corps proud. I sleep a hell of a lot easier at night knowing I've got men like the three of you under my command."

The *two* of us is what you mean, Billingsley thought. Saliba's harmless. He nodded his head and said, "Thank you, sir," before cutting a quick glance in Saliba's direction.

"Keep up the fine work, son," said Fletcher in closing the short ceremony.

Back in English's office, the CO handed out cigars. Billingsley removed the medal from his uniform and put it back in the box.

"You gotta be shittin' me, sir! The Silver Star?" questioned the self-conscious but appreciative Billingsley.

"You earned it, Mike. Tom had already written the draft and all I had to do was touch it up before sending it up the chain of command. It went through a good bit faster than I thought it would. I had intended to have a ceremony in front of the entire company, and I suppose we could still do that," pondered English.

"I'd really rather let it go at this, sir, if you don't mind."

English looked away in silence for a moment. "Okay, then. Congratulations, Mike. You can get on with whatever it was you were doing," he concluded.

Billingsley thanked English and turned to leave, but stopped when he heard the voice of Saliba. "Were you surprised, Mike?" Saliba asked with a cunning smile.

"Yeah," he replied. "Damn sure was."

Billingsley walked past Tyler, who was standing in the front of the CP. Tyler was drinking a cup of coffee, a ritual practiced with a complete disregard for the soaring temperature. He grinned when he saw Billingsley.

"Congratulations, Mister Billingsley. Another one of my products has made good," he said.

"Gunny, you don't know how true that is," replied Billingsley as he shook Tyler's outstretched hand.

"You're gonna look funny wearing that medal in the brig."

"Why? What have you heard?" Billingsley asked.

"That you're a real dinger with a .45," Tyler said with a wink.

Billingsley returned Tyler's wink and left.

Billingsley couldn't help but feel elated over his decoration as he returned to his hootch. He hoped, though, that the pistol incident would eventually just blow over. Ivester was still lounging in the Quonset hut when Billingsley entered.

"Get your ass chewed?" Ivester looked serious.

"Nah. Got the Silver Star," replied Billingsley, tossing the box with the medal inside to Ivester.

Ivester opened the box and stared at the prestigious decoration. "Jesus Horatio Christ!"

Bravo Company waited near open rice paddies in an LZ to the west of Da Nang. Two days of patrolling had resulted in no contact with the enemy, though three booby traps had killed as many Marines. Word had come in early morning that Bravo Company was to serve as a reserve force while a village to the south was searched by an ARVN unit. The ARVN were already positioned in an assembly area to the south, awaiting Bravo. Word also had it that a sizeable VC force was active in and around the village.

Billingsley sat alone, near his troops, and watched his men as they readied themselves for the choppers which would hurl them toward the objective and the possible cataclysm of combat. The men were anxious, though nothing certain was known of the resistance that might face them. They preferred not to show the tension. They checked their equipment. They chuckled at some nonsensical comment from the self-appointed jokesters. They were tired, but there was no time for sleep. They related their tension, to a large degree, to their boredom. They kept busy. They checked their equipment again. Weapons clean. Ammo clean and loaded into magazines. Plenty of water. First-aid kit. Extra bootlaces. C-rats. Socks. Rifle grease. All set. Let's get it on. Let's get it over with!

They waited.

There was time for a quick smoke. "Gimme a light, sweetpea," Billingsley overheard. He thought of home, of what was happening at this exact moment in time. His own C-ration Marlboro had the taste of chewing gum from the Chicklets which were part of the goody package. What the hell, he thought. They're free. Someone cracked another joke— inevitably sexual and just as likely facial. The laughter helped. Ten thousand miles would have helped, too. What a crock. What a *deal!*

They waited.

English and Tyler went over a few final details. Billingsley had another flash of life at home. He hoped for mail later in the day. God, how good it would be to sleep, he thought. How better it would be to get laid. Or would it? If the dream was good enough, sleep could cover 'em both. Yeah, sleep. Definitely sleep would be the choice. Man, what's it like to have choices? he wondered.

They waited.

Radios were checked. The time neared. Red smoke began to spread around and spiral above the breezeless fringes of the LZ. Last time was red smoke, Billingsley remembered. And nothing much happened. Hope the luck holds.

There were some new dudes; there were always new faces. And they're always new-guy dumb. Don't know diddly shit. Hope they can get snapped-in in a hurry. Like the old salts. Combat vets of what . . . nineteen? Maybe twenty? Amazing what a few months in this place does. Speaking of old salts, it sure seems odd to be in the bush without Sanchez. Billingsley laughed softly. Little shit's back in Texas now. Probably drunk and disorderly, too. A damn good squad leader. A damn good Marine.

"Two minutes, people," Tyler shouted.

Billingsley took one last drag of his cigarette while Ambrosetti jostled the troops to their feet. He flicked one last clump of dried, reddish mud absently from his boot's underside. One last sip of water. His mouth was as dry as a Mohave landscape. Then there was the weight of the pack; the heat of the afternoon; the stale odor of the helmet liner; the first sound of the choppers, though still unseen.

"Standby, people," Ambrosetti called.

The pensive moods changed. The CH-46s, with their Cobra escorts, approached close to the ground. Billingsley noticed the tightened jaws of his troops, betraying their nonchalant facades. The company area was alive with anticipation, and equal parts of knowing dread. The heightened feelings in the LZ always reminded Billingsley of his former days as an athlete, when the remembered games of what seemed ages ago were near their start—the exit from the locker room; the frenzied crowd; the excitement of the kickoff. This time he was struck by the crucial, stunning, inescapable difference between a game and a combat operation—the stakes—and he dismissed the similarity as an inane and cruel product of his imagination's devilment. Winners and losers, victory and defeat. The scoreboard told one story; the bodies the other.

They were soon running up the ramps in the rear of the choppers. They crowded together on the bench seats along the bulkhead, their weapons pointed toward the deck.

"Lock and load," shouted Ambrosetti once they were airborne.

The helicopters were taking Bravo to an assembly point north of the village, in the paddies. The ARVN would be several hundred meters to the east and northwest of Bravo before they moved into the village. The ARVN platoon to the northwest was scheduled to remain in place unless otherwise needed.

Billingsley glanced out the window of the chopper when the approach into the LZ began. Preparatory artillery fire into the LZ had been decided against in order to achieve surprise, a point which was lost upon Billingsley since the choppers themselves were hardly quiet. English had agreed with him, but orders were orders. Maybe we'll be lucky Billingsley hoped.

A sudden burst of fire from the door gunner's M-60 machine gun confirmed that which was always feared and dreaded—a hot LZ. From a treeline to the west, a VC force directed sporadic fire upon the helicopters and the disembarking Marines. The feeling of helplessness inside the chopper, with bullets slamming into and through its thin skin with sounds like sledgehammer blows, was allayed only when the opportunity came to set foot on firm ground and dash for cover. The regular fears of battle then took over.

Billingsley crouched behind the cover of a dike while bullets whizzed over his head from the distant treeline. Gunfire popped steadily throughout the area, making verbal communications difficult. The choppers continued their sorties until the balance of the company had been successfully landed.

Billingsley established radio contact with his squad leaders and immediately ordered fire from the grenade and rocked launchers into the treeline. The rounds burst with loud crunches, but the VC still held to their positions. Billingsley judged that casualties among his troops were light, since he had heard few shouts of "corpsman" since disembarking.

In order to get a better vantage point, Billingsley, followed by Tetrick, quickly sloshed forward in a crouch to the next dike and dove for cover. He was near the front of his platoon's advance, and in the center. A lone figure lay behind the dike, a few feet away. Billingsley thought the Marine was dead or wounded until the man raised his head and turned toward him. It was Saliba.

"You okay?" Billingsley shouted over the gunfire.

"Yeah. I got separated. How many do you think are up there?"

"Couple of squads, I'd say."

"Can you tell what's going on?" Saliba asked in a shout.

"Yeah, Bob. I'd say we're in a Goddamned firefight," shouted Billingsley in return. "And I'd also say we're pinned down."

"What'll happen now?"

"I'd imagine the skipper'll try to flank 'em with the friendly gook unit."

Billingsley talked with his squad leaders by radio and advised them to hold their positions and return the fire. "Stay low and stay put," he advised while waiting for instructions from English, who huddled behind a dike fifty meters behind Billingsley. Bullets splashed throughout the paddy, sending geysers of water several feet into the air.

"What do you think?" called Saliba.

"Stay down, Bob."

"Think we ought to rush 'em?"

"Stay down, Bob."

"We can't stay here. We'll get cut to pieces."

"Stay down and shut the fuck up."

Saliba adjusted his helmet and remained motionless behind the dike.

English called to report that the ARVN unit to the northwest was moving toward the VC's flank. A few minutes later the ARVN soldiers arrived to throw themselves into the fight. The VC recognized their tenuous position and decided to try an escape to the southwest. When several of the VC rose to leave, heavy gunfire and grenades from the M-79s were hurled at them from the Marines in the open paddy.

"Start moving up," Billingsley called as he stood and urged his men forward. "Let's go . . . quickly . . . get up there . . . move, dammit . . . MOVE."

The Marines moved swiftly in the assault and overtook the remaining VC. The ARVN swept behind the treeline and chased those VC attempting to flee. The bodies of six enemy soldiers were scattered over the position by the time the resistance ended. Another two VC were alive but severely wounded from the rocket and grenade explosions.

Saliba moved into the treeline with Billingsley.

"I got a live one over here," shouted Rosser from a nearby stand of trees.

Rosser stood over the bloody, semi-conscious enemy soldier. The dying man breathed laboriously. Blood soaked his entire chest and abdomen. His eyes blinked slowly and he coughed up blood from his lung and stomach injuries. In addition to the fragmentation wounds, a gunshot had penetrated the man's belly.

"He won't live to fight another day," Billingsley concluded nonchalantly after viewing the man.

Saliba stood with his eyes fixed on the VC clinging desperately to the last moments of life. The man's breathing finally ceased, his eyes partially open in the empty stare of death.

Bravo Company suffered seven casualties, only one of which was serious. Two of the injured Marines were from Billingsley's platoon. Lance Corporal Mayson, the squad leader who had replaced Sanchez, endured his groin wound with the help of a morphine injection from Fralich.

"Hang on, Mayson. You can do that, can't you?" Billingsley asked of the husky, black Pennsylvanian.

"I think so, sir," was Mayson's woozy reply.

"You'd better, hoss. The Phillies are gonna need your stick in the lineup," Billingsley said. Mayson had been selected in the pro baseball draft before the other draft had delayed his athletic career. "You'll be able to tell 'em that stopping a hot grounder will be a piece of cake now that you've stopped a round in the gut."

Mayson grinned weakly through the effects of the morphine.

The helicopter's rotors could be heard on its approach into the smoke-marked LZ.

Captain English entered the treeline and consulted by radio with the planners of the operation in Da Nang to determine if the village search was still a "go." English thought a continuation of the mission would likely be pointless, particularly from the standpoint of surprise. He argued for a cancellation of the mission, though not vehemently. He was told to remain prepared for execution of the plan while the new situation was assessed. Bravo and the ARVN units stayed on the outskirts of the village waiting for the decision from Da Nang.

"What's the word, sir?" asked Billingsley after returning from the scene of the medevac.

"None, yet," replied English. "Have you seen the XO?"

"Not in the last few minutes."

Saliba came out of the trees and walked over to English and Billingsley. His face was drawn and pale, his uniform soaked and muddy.

"Anything I can do to help?" Saliba asked, self-conscious over his lack of experience in the field.

"Hold on a second," English replied as his radio crackled. "This is Bravo Six, over." English listened to his instructions while Billingsley stepped away for a cigarette. Saliba hesitated for a moment and then joined Billingsley who sat against a tree. Saliba sat on the ground, studying the face of his calm, composed contemporary.

"Not a bad little fight, huh?" remarked Saliba.

"Not bad for putting down in a hot LZ," Billingsley answered without looking at Saliba.

"What happens now? Think we'll stay with the plan?"

"I don't know. I think the skipper's finding that out now. One thing you have to remember about a plan."

"What's that?"

"They usually don't work like they're supposed to. You always have to have a plan, always, but you've got to be ready for some changes once things get underway. Especially once the shooting starts."

"Let me ask you something, Billingsley," Saliba said after a short pause.

"Go ahead."

"You don't especially like me, do you?"

"That's affirmative," Billingsley said, staring straight at Saliba. "You haven't given me much reason to, so far."

"You've probably got the ass because I came in here as XO, when you thought you should've had the job. Right?"

"Affirmative, again."

"Look, that was the luck of the draw as far as me being ordered to Bravo Company. You can't hold that against me."

"I don't."

"So what's the deal?"

Billingsley drew deeply on his cigarette and then fixed Saliba in an icy stare. "You know what the damn deal is, Bob," he said sharply. "You don't have to ask me."

"Well, I *am* asking you."

"You come into this outfit with a chip on your shoulder and you act like a complete prick and you want me to tell you what the fuckin' *deal* is?"

"So it's been the way I've acted toward you and Ivester. Right?"

"You know the answer to that, too. You came in here acting like Julius Caesar, when the truth is you couldn't carry Tom Compton's dirty jock."

Saliba breathed deeply and looked away.

"Okay, then. You don't have to like me, but I'd sure appreciate it if you would offer any advice you think might be helpful to me. It's not easy for me to say this, but I can use all the help I can get."

"We all need help from time to time. There's plenty of experience in the company. If you want to know something, all you've got to do is ask. Cemeteries are full of stubborn, bull-headed people who wouldn't ask, and full of people who were led by stubborn, bull-headed people who wouldn't ask."

"I'd like to have you on my side," Saliba said with a look of sincerity.

"I *am* on your side."

"The plan's been scrapped and the operation's off," English said as he joined the two lieutenants. "Some other time, gang."

"Next time, skipper, we ought to go in at night," Billingsley said as he and Saliba stood. "Come in by trucks to about a klick away, then move in quietly."

"No shit," agreed English, who then explained that the ARVN were staying in the general vicinity to continue a sweep of the area. Bravo Company was to return to Da Nang. He ordered Saliba to see to it that the platoons were prepared to move to a dirt road to the east to meet the vehicles which had already been dispatched for them.

"Aye-aye, sir," Saliba said as he left to carry out his duty.

"You want the point in the convoy, Mike?" asked English.

"Absolutely, sir. First in, first drunk."

Billingsley began to feel good on the hot July day. The reprieve from the remainder of the operation, which meant another night of comfort in relatively secure Da Nang, was one of those small favors which buoyed the spirits of the infantryman. That the favor was unexpected made it all the better. To have an operation canceled and to be pulled out of the field was, indeed, a favor.

Word soon came from English to move out across the paddies to the road to the east. The company moved in a column, with Second Platoon in front, until they reached the dirt road after a march of fifteen minutes. The column halted while the road was inspected and secured.

"They ain't here yet," Rosser shouted from up ahead.

"Move across and spread out. They should be here most skosh," called Billingsley.

When the trucks came in sight ten minutes later, Rosser and two of his men stepped out into the road. The lead vehicle was a jeep whose driver wore a grimy, green undershirt and a soft utility cap.

"You guys Bravo Company?" the driver called as the jeep came to a stop.

"That's us," replied Rosser. "You gonna turn around, or what?"

"Naw, start loadin' now. There's a trail to the south of here that cuts over to Route One."

"He's ready to take us," Rosser shouted to Billingsley.

Billingsley motioned for Ambrosetti to begin loading the platoon onto the six-by trucks. Other trucks were still arriving when Second Platoon started to board the first of those in the line.

"That dude's got a real decent radio in the jeep, sir. Mind if I ride with him?" asked Tetrick.

"Go ahead," Billingsley said, and he climbed into the passenger side of the first truck.

The jeep and three trucks pulled away with Second Platoon while First Platoon continued to board the other vehicles. The truck in which Billingsley rode followed the jeep on the two-lane, dirt road. The driver of the truck was a young, red-haired private whose smile showed a missing front tooth. They bumped up and down in their seats while the truck moved along the uneven road.

"You an officer?" asked the driver.

"Yeah, I am. Do you know where you're going?"

"Not really, sir. First time I've been down here. Sergeant Pembroke does, though."

The convoy followed the jeep, turning to the left, toward the east, at the intersection of a single-lane road. Farther south lay the village that had been the object of the intended search.

"Sir, did you hear anything about them astronauts?" the driver asked.

"No. What about them?"

"They blasted off," exclaimed the driver with a look of amazement. "They gonna go to the damn moon! Ain't that some shit, sir?"

"No kidding? When will they get up there?"

"Land on Sunday, I think the guy on the radio said. Yessir, that's it. Sunday's the day."

"What's today?"

"Friday, sir."

"I knew they were going, I just didn't know when. It's amazing how isolated this place is."

"It's a bummer, ain't it, sir? I been over here goin' on four months and I ain't seen a thing that's good about it yet. Whoever the dude was who thought up this place for a war ought to have his butt kicked."

Billingsley smiled faintly at the young Marine's suggestion. He agreed entirely, though he remained silent. He reached for a smoke but remembered having given his last cigarette to Tetrick while they waited for the trucks.

"Got a cigarette?" he asked the driver.

"Yessir," the driver replied, tossing a crumpled pack of Pall Malls.

Billingsley took a cigarette from the pack and lit it. Hope they've got mail in Da Nang, he thought. He propped his right arm on the door of the truck where the window had been rolled down. The jeep up ahead created a steady haze of red dust as it bounced along the narrow, rutted road. The thick foliage alongside the road broke open occasionally to reveal the flat openness of the coastal terrain. Vietnam looked beautiful, such a contrast to the horrors she held within her boundaries. So green and lush, he thought. So slow and easy. Billingsley relaxed, thinking ahead to a cool beer in Da Nang and perhaps a letter from a certain young lady in Virginia.

The ambush struck with dreadful swiftness.

The vehicles were less than a mile from Route One, still on the single-lane road, when the jeep hit a powerful mine. Billingsley saw the mine explode, hurling the jeep several feet into the air and tossing the inhabitants onto the road. The jeep landed on its side and toppled upside down, pinning one of the occupants underneath. Debris from the blast shattered the truck's windshield and covered the hood. Oh God! Billingsley thought, disbelieving. No, God! No!

The driver of the truck had slammed on the brakes at the sight of the mine detonation. Gunfire erupted from the foliage on Billingsley's side of the road, only a few feet away. Billingsley and a dozen of his Marines in the back of the truck sat, helpless. Both the cab and rear of the vehicle were under small-arms fire. Before he could move, one bullet struck Billingsley in the right arm, slightly above the wrist. Another round ricocheted off the front of his flak vest after passing through the metal door. A third bullet passed through the door and penetrated his upper thigh. He could hear bullets slamming into other parts of the cab.

Billingsley pulled his arm inside and dived forward in as tight a crouch as was possible. Other rounds pounded the cab. He heard scrambling in the back of the truck, along with rifle fire from M-16s. He glanced at his arm to see bone protruding from the wound. Both wounds were gushing blood. He pressed on the arm injury with his other hand, but it did little to slow the bleeding. More bullets flew into the door and the cab.

"Get out the door," he yelled at the driver.

The driver made no move.

"Get the hell out. Stay low and get out."

Billingsley saw a thick pool of blood forming in the floorboard beneath the driver. The young private was leaning forward, motionless and propped against the steering column.

There was a gaping gunshot wound in his temple. Billingsley began to panic as his mind flashed before him the prospect of a rocket explosion and a burning vehicle. No, please no, he was screaming silently. No, God, don't let 'em do it!

The firing from the Marines intensified. Billingsley heard piercing screams and wailing from an injured man in the back of the vehicle. He waited, still crouched in the floor of the cab, for the VC to move close to the truck, to toss a grenade inside or spray the cab with a burst of gunfire from an opened door. He felt weak. His arm wound spurted blood into his face and his thigh injury dripped into a puddle underneath his trousers. Another round banged into the door. He thought he was hit again, that he might be mortally wounded, until he realized that the pressure he felt in his lower back came from his canteen which had wedged upward from his cartridge belt. Please, no, he thought again.

Billingsley's pistol remained in its holster, on his right hip. He had given his rifle to Tetrick to transport aboard the jeep up ahead. He tried to grab his pistol with his left hand, first across his front and then behind his back. He couldn't reach it without straightening up. Still more rounds slammed into the cab. "C'mon, dammit," he said grimly as he groped for his weapon, again without success. The driver's body shook as more bullets struck it. "God, c'mon!" he said as he moved his limp right hand toward his pistol. He couldn't grab it. He wanted desperately to defend himself, to greet the first VC who opened the door with a .45 round. Instead, he felt helpless.

Suddenly, the door on the driver's side of the cab was opened. He gasped, waiting for the gunfire. Instead, he saw Ambrosetti.

"Ambro," he called weakly.

Ambrosetti pulled the dead driver from the truck and dropped the body into the road. Billingsley leaned to his left, painfully extending himself across the seat, and felt Ambrosetti's hands beneath his armpits, pulling him roughly from the cab and dragging to safety.

"Jesus, you're bleedin' like a stuck pig! Corpsman. CORPSMAN," shouted Ambrosetti from a ditch on the side of the road opposite the fighting. "CORPSMAN, OVER HERE."

"Fralich's hit," shouted Willingham from nearby.

"Get down there and meet those other trucks and get us a

doc up here. We've got people up here who are pretty fucked up," Ambrosetti called.

Billingsley heard the booms of two grenade explosions from the other side of the road. He attempted to sit up but was shoved down forcefully by Ambrosetti.

"Stay down, dammit," Ambrosetti said.

"Get 'em off those trucks. They're gonna blow the trucks!"

"Those are our frags. We've got it under control now. The gooks ain't firing no more."

Ambrosetti tied Billingsley's arm with a tourniquet fashioned from a web belt and bandaged the thigh wound. He then rose to check on the rest of the platoon.

"Stay down, sir. I'll be back in a minute. And I *mean* stay the fuck down," Ambrosetti said firmly.

Billingsley remained on the ground, leaning back in the ditch. Events around him began to blur. He fought to clear his head, aware of his pain but not yet overcome by it. The dressing applied by Ambrosetti was soaked in blood. He could hear additional vehicles arriving on the scene. He could also hear and feel the footsteps of men running in his direction. The firing had ceased except for an occasional round fired by a Marine in the direction of the enemy's escape route. There were several shouts for medical assistance.

"Over there, in the ditch," he heard Ambrosetti call to a corpsman. "He's bleedin' like a motherfucker."

The corpsman, unrecognized by Billingsley, arrived at his side. "You ain't had morphine yet, have you?" he asked.

Billingsley shook his head.

The corpsman injected the morphine and started an IV in his left arm. Another man held aloft the plastic bag containing the clear liquid.

"How you feelin'," asked the corpsman.

"Okay," Billingsley said, woozy.

Captain English arrived and told Billingsley to remain still and to "hang tough." English then walked to his nearby radioman and began transmitting a message.

The morphine eased the pain in Billingsley's limbs. He stayed on his back, unaware of the passing time and only vaguely aware of the movement around him. His mouth was terribly dry and gummy. He noticed the odor that had always reminded him of hospitals. And he noticed the sound of the medevac chopper only when it had started its approach in a clearing off the side of the road.

"Gonna need some help over here," shouted the corpsman.

Ambrosetti grabbed Billingsley's legs and another man lifted him from behind. The corpsman held the plastic bag. They carried him across the road and into the dust and wind created by the chopper's rotors.

"You've been a royal pain in my ass today," shouted Ambrosetti as he leaned near Billingsley's face before lifting him aboard the helicopter. "I'll probably get a bulgin' hernia from having lugged you all over the fuckin' Nam. You must weigh a motherfuckin' ton."

Billingsley looked at Ambrosetti's sweaty face. He managed a weak smile for the man to whom he quite possibly owed his life.

"Make 'em keep their heads down, Ambro."

"Will do, sir. Now get the hell out of here and don't come back."

Billingsley never noticed that Bob Saliba was one of those who had helped carry and lift him aboard the chopper. Once inside, he rested on the cool metal floor of the aircraft and surrendered to the fog and the haze which seemed to encircle his brain. Neither did he notice as the lifeless bodies of Fralich, Rosser, Tetrick, and two of the drivers were pulled aboard with five other wounded Marines. His only awareness was that of the vibration of the deck on which he reclined.

The chopper pitched forward and began its climb away from the string of vehicles and men on the narrow road.

"Gimme some water," Billingsley requested when a corpsman aboard the medevac had leaned over him and asked of his condition.

The corpsman produced a canteen from his own belt and supported Billingsley's head for a short drink. He took another sip and then rested his head on an extra medical pouch. It was hard to focus his eyes and a slight nausea had crept into his stomach. The morphine gave him a limp, floating sensation.

He was out before the chopper landed in Da Nang.

PART FOUR:
The Return

10

Six weeks of treatment in hospitals in Vietnam and Okinawa had preceded Billingsley's return to his Georgia home. Three separate occurrences of being wounded, and three Purple Hearts to go along with his Silver Star and various Campaign and Service Medals, had enabled him to return early from his overseas tour. Three had been a charm.

Billingsley was back at home almost exactly nine months from the day on which he had departed for Vietnam. His wounds had adequately healed, though he still wore a soft cast on his right arm, below the elbow and over the wrist. The flesh wound in his thigh had caused minimal damage to the muscle, and none to the bone. Only a slight stiffness in his leg remained, along with the purplish scar. His arm had atrophied slightly from the wound and resultant lack of muscle stimulation. Squeezing exercises with a rubber ball were gradually returning the gripping ability to his right hand.

Billingsley's worried family had been waiting at the Atlanta airport to greet him when he had walked into the crowded concourse. And once he was back at his home, in many ways he felt as if he had never left. But in other ways he felt as if he were an alien, a stranger, in the secure and comfortable surroundings. It was a peculiar sensation. He was physically removed from Vietnam, of that he was certain. No orders, no jungles, no gunfire, no screams. His clothes were clean and his meals were substantive and unhurried. Emotionally, however, he was still in Vietnam, with Bravo Company. He still slept lightly, in snatches, and was aware of the silence of his room as he lay awake in his bed. He was happy in many ways, sad in a few others, but mostly just relieved.

He spent five days in Atlanta and then boarded an airplane

for Washington, D.C., and traveled by cab and bus to the naval medical facility at Bethesda, Maryland. There he spent the better part of a day waiting to be examined. Finally, he was seen by a physician who spent little time with him. He was advised to keep wearing the soft cast for an additional ten days. Otherwise, his condition was judged by the physician to be satisfactory. The hospital was crowded with grievously wounded Marines and servicemen from Vietnam. He left the hospital late in the day.

Another series of bus and cab rides eventually deposited him in Reston, Virginia, where he checked into a motel. After showering, he waited in the lobby for the cab which would take him to Andrea's home. He was ecstatic that the long-awaited reunion was near. He was also nervous. He had deliberately neglected to call and advise Andrea of his trip, preferring instead to surprise her. She knew that he was home, as they had spoken daily by telephone, but she did not know he was in Reston. His coup at having had Bethesda approved as his treatment facility came only after a long plea of his case to a sympathetic doctor on Okinawa. Otherwise, he would have been assigned to a facility closer to his home, perhaps Memphis or Jacksonville.

The taxi whisked Billingsley the short distance to Andrea's home. His apprehension mounted as the taxi stopped in front of the house. This is it, he thought. This is the moment that's been dreamed about for so long, and so often. He wished he didn't have to wear the silly cast, for it made him feel less than whole. He wanted it to be perfect, just right, just as he had imagined it during so many long days and nights in Vietnam. *This is it!* he thought. It's really here, and *I'm* really here! He paid the taxi driver and faced the house. A bulb illuminated the front porch and a light could be seen inside. Billingsley listened to his footsteps on the walk up the driveway to the porch. He stepped up onto the porch, his heart pounding, and rang the bell.

There was no immediate answer and no sound of movement inside. He rang the doorbell again.

"C'mon, Andrea. Be *home*, for Christ's sake!" he said out loud.

After a long pause, he heard footsteps. The knob of the door turned. It wasn't her.

"Hello, Mrs. Strickland. It's good to see you again."

"Mike?" Andrea's mother was startled. "My goodness, what a wonderful surprise! Please come in."

Mrs. Strickland warmly embraced Billingsley and noticed his bandaged arm. They talked in the foyer for a moment before she guided him to the family room with her arm wrapped around his waist. She smiled broadly.

"Mike, it's so good to see you again. You look fine. When did you come up from Atlanta?"

"This morning, early. I'm on leave, but I came up to get checked out at Bethesda. And, of course, to see Andrea."

"Please have a seat, Mike. Could I fix you a drink?" she asked after she had embraced him once again.

"No, ma'am. Well, wait . . . yes, ma'am. I could use something to settle me down. Is Andrea here?"

"She will be soon. What can I fix you to drink?"

"Beer's fine, Mrs. Strickland."

"Andrea would have a fit if she knew you were here. She's involved with planning a party for a group of third-year law students before they all return to school. She's making the arrangements with a downtown hotel, and she should be back in no more than an hour. Could I fix you something to eat? Surely you must be hungry," she said as she passed Billingsley a glass and a bottle of beer from the bar.

"No, please. Sit down and relax. I'm not disturbing anything, am I?"

"Of course not, Mike. Are you sure you're not hungry?"

"Yes, ma'am, I'm sure. Sit down and tell me about your daughter."

They talked cordially, of Andrea, of the changes since the death of the elder Strickland, of Billingsley's experiences overseas. He spoke little of combat and referred to Vietnam only in generalities. Over an hour elapsed while they sat in the family room and conversed. She showed him the photographs taken during the trip with Andrea to the Catskills, earlier in the summer, where they had relaxed and enjoyed a week-long vacation. She spoke of Andrea's oft-repeated concern for his safety, and of Andrea's near-hysteria over the news of his having been wounded again.

"She turned pale, Mike, when your mother called to give her the news. And afterwards she went to her room and cried.

Then she got mad and cranky and stayed that way for several days."

Billingsley smiled faintly at the picture in his mind of a furious, raging Andrea, throwing objects against the walls of her bedroom and screaming obscenities at anyone within earshot.

"Mad, was she?" laughed Billingsley.

"Oh, Lord! I'm afraid Andrea inherited the Strickland tendency toward hot-temperedness."

Billingsley laughed again but stopped when he noticed the reflection of headlights in the bay window. He heard a car pull into the driveway and stop. He heard a door close, then another.

"That should be her now," said Mrs. Strickland as she smiled and remained seated.

Then Billingsley heard Andrea laughing when she entered the foyer, followed by a male companion. Andrea continued to laugh and talk with her guest until she noticed her mother in the family room.

"Hi, Mom. You remember Robert Sloan, don't—"

Billingsley had risen from the sofa and come into her view. She stared in disbelief. Andrea was stunned and speechless.

"Long time, no see. Hello, Andrea. You look great," Billingsley said.

Andrea stared at him for a moment longer, as if to seek some sort of visual confirmation of his actual presence. She then rushed to him, embraced and kissed him, and locked her arms tightly around him. Mrs. Strickland and Sloan quietly left the room as the embrace continued.

"Oh, God! Is it really you? Is it really my wonderful Mike Billingsley?"

"Yeah," he said as he embraced her. "It's finally happened, baby. Finally."

"Please hold me, Mike."

He squeezed her, almost lifting her off the carpeted floor. They said nothing for several minutes as they swayed and rocked and kissed and clung tightly to one another. She felt wonderful, he thought. And smelled wonderful. And looked wonderful. And sounded wonderful. It's here, he thought. It's finally here.

Billingsley could feel the slight trembling in the back of his legs.

"How do you feel?" Andrea asked softly, her head resting upon his shoulder.

"I've never felt better."

They kissed again, with more passion. She pushed away a short distance to get a better look at him.

"Why didn't you let me know you were coming, Mike?"

"Thought I'd surprise you."

"You succeeded!"

"I thought so."

"How long have you been up here?"

"Since this morning."

"This *morning*?" said Andrea as she raised her eyebrows in surprise. "You could have called me, Michael. I almost called your home in Atlanta to see how you were doing this afternoon."

"I flew up this morning to get checked out at Bethesda, then I came directly out here to see you. My intentions were noble, counselor."

"What did they say?"

"Who?"

"The doctors at Bethesda."

"Told me not to get shot for a while," he said with a grin.

"C'mon, Mike. Tell me."

"I'm fine. Just got to keep this cast on for a little while longer. But I'm fine, really."

They embraced and kissed once more. Andrea clung tightly to him and sighed deeply.

"I've been worried sick about you. When your parents called to tell me that you'd been hurt again, I was physically ill."

"So was I," he added with a chuckle.

"Thank God you're finally safe."

"Thank God I'm finally next to you."

"I've never worried so much in my life."

"It wasn't that bad," Billingsley said, as his mind flashed back to the ambush scene, prompting him to add, "considering."

"Considering what?"

"Never mind. Who's your friend?"

"A classmate who's helping me make arrangements for a party. His name's Robert Sloan. Where are you staying?"

"At a motel, not far from here."

"You can check out and stay right here. And you can go with me to the party tomorrow night. Come with me and we'll get you an upstairs room fixed up. It won't take long," Andrea said excitedly.

"Wait a second, Andrea. I'll stay at the motel. I'm not gonna come barging in here on you and your mother. And I really think you should go to your party without me hanging around. I'm not gonna be up here long, anyway."

"What's wrong, Mike?" she asked, taking his hand.

"Nothing's wrong. I want to go over to Baltimore tomorrow and visit the family of a friend, and I want you to go to your party and have a good time with your friends."

"Will you please stay here with us?"

"No, I'll stay where I am."

"I'll drive you to Baltimore tomorrow and you can go to the party with me later. That way, we'll be together all day."

"Andrea, I—"

"Oh please, Mike," she pleaded. "My gosh, we've been apart for nine months!"

He stood looking into those incredible blue eyes. "Okay," he relented, reaching to embrace her.

"Oh, Mike. You feel so good to me. I can't believe you're finally here. I've waited so long for this."

"So have I, baby. You wouldn't believe how many times I've thought about this."

"I knew you'd be back. I just *knew* it!"

"Almost seems unreal, doesn't it?"

"Unh uh. You seem awfully real to me, lieutenant."

"I'm shakin' like a damned leaf."

"Do you feel okay?" she asked, concerned.

"I feel fine."

Several more kisses were exchanged before Andrea asked her mother and friend back into the family room. Robert Sloan politely excused himself after a short while and returned to his home in McLean. The other three talked for another hour, and Mrs. Strickland later prepared sandwiches for all.

After the snack, Billingsley accepted Andrea's offer to drive him to his motel but continued to refuse politely the pleas for him to stay. They left after Billingsley had embraced and thanked Mrs. Strickland for her company and her hospitality.

Andrea drove to the motel in her sporty new car. She parked near his room's ground-level entrance. She left the engine idling as Billingsley reached across with his left hand to open his door. He noticed Andrea making no effort to open her door and follow him into the room.

"What's the matter?" he asked.

"Nothing."

"Are you gonna come in with me?"

"Do you want me to?"

"What ?" he asked with a small laugh.

"I mean, you're not feeling too bad or anything like that, are you?"

"Andrea, are you kidding?"

"I just want to be sure," she said.

The keys remained in the ignition, the motor still running. Andrea's hands remained on the steering wheel and her eyes looked straight ahead.

"What's the matter, baby?" he asked softly.

"Nothing, Mike. I just don't want to impose on you."

"Are you uncomfortable, Andrea?"

"A little, yeah."

"Do you want to go home?"

She looked over at him, staring into his eyes. "Of course not," she said convincingly.

"Then what's the matter?"

"I'm nervous."

"At what?"

"I don't know," she said looking at the floorboard of the car. "Maybe at this whole thing happening so suddenly. I'm sorry, Mike. I feel like such a fool. I'm just nervous, that's all."

"Been a long time, hasn't it?" Billingsley said with a tender smile.

"Sure has."

"I love you, Miss Strickland."

"And I love you, Mister Billingsley."

"Tell you what," Billingsley said as he reclosed his car door. "I think I might know what's bothering you. I think I might know *exactly* what's bothering you."

Andrea said nothing. He reached for her hand. The engine idled.

"You've been waiting a long time for this," he spoke. "And

so have I. You've wondered what it was going to be like when we were together again. So have I. You've thought of all the neat things that you were gonna say when we met again. So have I. You've hoped and expected and anticipated that everything would be exactly the same with us as it was before we parted, but you really weren't absolutely sure. Neither was I. And when we met, finally, it seemed as if it would be as good as ever, but you wondered what it would be like when we were all alone. So did I. And then you may have felt that, after all the waiting, after all the many times of thinking about it, there may be a chance that you'd disappoint me when we were ready to make love. You may have wondered about what my reaction would be, if you were satisfying me, and all that. And you know what, Andrea?"

She looked squarely at him in the dim light of the car.

"I feel the same way," he said. "You can't possibly be any more nervous than I am."

She smiled faintly and leaned her head onto his shoulder. He kissed her softly on the top of her head. He reached his arm around her and pulled her close.

"You're really something, Billingsley," she said quietly.

He kissed her on the forehead and squeezed her tightly.

"I don't believe the part about you being as nervous as I am," Andrea said, grinning at him.

"I am, really."

"I know how to find out," she said, still with the mischievous grin on her face.

"So do I."

The ignition switch was turned off and the keys were removed.

Andrea returned for Billingsley late the next morning. He got into the passenger side while she drove to the interstate and, eventually, to a suburb of Baltimore. Billingsley had explained the trip's purpose to Andrea on the previous evening. They found the brick, modern apartment complex which corresponded to the address which Billingsley had written on a scrap of paper. They parked the car in front of the door to unit number 777.

Billingsley knocked lightly. The knock was answered by an attractive, blonde-haired woman in her early twenties. She was dressed in dark slacks and wore a bright orange sweater. They could hear a baby crying inside.

"Chris? Chris Compton?" asked Billingsley.

"Yes," the woman answered, partially obscured by the door.

"This is Andrea Strickland, and my name's Mike Billingsley."

The woman smiled warmly and fully opened the door. "Please come in," she motioned. "Your name's very familiar to me, Mike."

Tom Compton's widow led them into an attractive living room. A picture of Compton in his Marine Corps dress blues was prominently displayed on a coffee table to the front of a long sofa. The baby, crying in a playpen in the center of the room, quieted as her mother returned to the room.

"I would have called first, Chris, but I couldn't find a number in the book," Billingsley explained.

"It's unlisted. I'm glad you came, though. Please have a seat," she said as she led them to the sofa.

Chris raised the infant, Karen, from the playpen and proudly displayed her daughter to her guests. The child resumed her crying until Andrea asked to hold her. Andrea coddled the baby and quieted her.

"You have a nice way with babies," Chris remarked to Andrea. "She's been irritable the whole morning."

"Thank you," smiled Andrea, glancing quickly at Billingsley.

"Would you like some coffee? I made some earlier and haven't taken the time for a cup, myself," asked Chris.

"Sure," said Billingsley. "Can I help you with it?"

"No, no. It's no trouble."

Chris stepped away into the adjacent kitchen.

"Karen was born right about the time I got hit the first time," Billingsley remarked softly to Andrea while Chris was still in the kitchen. "Tom was proud as hell. I'll never forget the look on his face."

Chris returned with cups of steaming coffee on a silver tray and lowered it onto the table in front of the couch. After another trip she returned with cream, sugar, and spoons.

"Andrea, my mother's reading in the back bedroom and she'll be glad to watch after Karen while we talk," said Chris.

She accepted the child from the gentle grasp of Andrea and disappeared into the back.

Andrea and Billingsley took their coffee and remained on the sofa. Chris returned and after maneuvering the playpen out of the way, took a seat in the chair across from them. They made small talk for a half-hour, avoiding any references to Tom and Vietnam and speaking mostly of Karen and her daily development. Chris was tiny, smaller even than Andrea. Her skin was fair, her hair nearly white in its blondness. She giggled often, and nervously. She glanced repeatedly at Billingsley, but not with the conspicuousness of a stare. Billingsley recognized the strain in Chris' words, on her face, and even in himself. The identity with Tom was close in each of them, and each brought remembrances of him to the other. But they enjoyed their chance to talk.

Finally, Billingsley felt the conversation begin to drag.

"I'm glad we got the chance to come by and see you and Karen, Chris," Billingsley said.

"I'm certainly glad both of you took the time to come by," responded Chris.

"One other reason I came, Chris, was to tell you how much I admired Tom. He could have been my own brother. He meant a great deal to all of us, and he had the complete respect of every man in the unit. And because he and I were so close, I want you to know that you can call on me for anything. I don't want you to feel that you don't have anyone to help you, and I mean it when I say that I'll do anything I can to assist you."

Billingsley reached into his shirt pocket and produced a piece of paper which he handed to Chris.

"Here, you can call this number in Atlanta if you need to contact me. I've requested duty at Quantico, and if I get it I'll call you and give you my new address."

"Thank you so much, Mike," said Chris. "Tom wrote often of you, and I could tell he thought a great deal of you, too. He even wrote of you, Andrea, and told me about how Mike talked about you all the time."

Andrea smiled. Chris was speaking with difficulty, and her eyes began to fill with tears.

"Anything at all, Chris," emphasized Billingsley. "I mean it. I always knew I could count on Tom, and I want you to feel the same way about me."

"You're both very kind," said Chris as she bit her lip and wiped at the tears which began to stream down her face.

Andrea passed a tissue to Chris, who then apologized for her inability to stem her crying. She was overcome by Billingsley's sincerity and his identification with her dead husband. Finally she sighed, smiled faintly, and drew a shuddering breath.

"May I ask you something, Mike?" she said softly.

"Certainly."

"Were you with Tommy the night he died?"

"Yes, I was."

"The people who came to tell me about it said Tommy died instantly. Is that true?"

"That's correct, Chris. There was no suffering. Tom died as soon as he was hit, doing his job during a very tough time."

"For some reason, I just wanted to be sure that he didn't suffer."

"I can understand, Chris. And the people who came to tell you, told you the truth."

Chris regained her composure by staring out the window for several moments. Her eyes had reddened appreciably as she sat upright and clutched at the crumpled tissue.

"Will you be okay?" Andrea asked sympathetically.

"Yes, thank you. I'm learning to deal with it a little better each day. I have Karen, too."

"Can we do anything for you before we leave?" asked Billingsley. "Fix your car? Clean the shower? Wash diapers?"

"No," said Chris, laughing at the suggestions.

They rose from their seats. Billingsley led Andrea to the door. Chris smiled and followed them, still wiping her eyes.

"I can't tell you how much your visit meant to me. I hope you'll both come back again. I really—" her voice broke as the tears returned again.

Billingsley watched as she attempted to compose herself. She buried her face in her hands when she failed. He reached his bandaged arm around her shoulder and pulled her to him. As he did, she sobbed deeply. He turned to see Andrea, her face wet with tears and her hands clasped over her mouth. He reached and pulled Andrea close. They stood together, the three of them, holding one another and crying. Except Billingsley. He wanted to cry, tried to cry, but he couldn't. He could only hold them close to him.

Andrea and Billingsley left only after Chris was able to smile again. Billingsley humored her, remarking how difficult it was to manage two weeping females. "One's bad enough," he had said. "But *two*?"

They left Baltimore, with Billingsley behind the wheel of Andrea's car, and headed on the interstate toward Washington, D.C. Not much was said until they were moving along smoothly on an open stretch of freeway.

"She's so pretty," remarked Andrea, gazing absently out the window.

"Yeah, she is. She's prettier than the pictures Tom had shown me."

"God, I feel so sorry for her."

"It's been on my mind ever since the night Tom was killed. I just thought that somehow, Tom would always be there, always ready to listen when I wanted to talk. I wish he was here now. I miss him a lot."

A long silence ensued as Andrea tried to imagine her own reaction had she been similarly notified of Billingsley's death.

"I'm so glad you're back, Michael," she said softly. "Thank you so much for coming back."

"I always thought the chances were pretty good that I'd make it out okay. But I thought the same thing about Tom, too. I never really felt at any one time that I was gonna die, except that once."

"When was that?"

"When I got hit that last time. I was caught inside a truck during a close ambush. On my side of the damned door, too."

"Were you driving?"

"Nope."

"Were you conscious through the whole thing?"

"Yep."

"Where was the driver?"

"Blocking the door."

"Why?"

"Because he'd been shot in the head."

"Oh my God, Mike!" Andrea said with a grimace. "How did you get out?"

"A kid named Ambrosetti finally pulled me out. Until he

did, I just knew I was at the end of the line. I almost gave up, I was so sure they were going to blow me away. I don't mean surrendering, I mean just losing all hope that I'd get out."

"Were you afraid?"

"Terribly. You'd have to feel it to believe it. All sorts of things went through my head."

Andrea frowned and shook her head. "Do you think now that it was worth it, Mike?"

"I don't know," he replied with a shrug.

"Why?"

"Because I don't know, that's why. How the hell am I supposed to answer that?"

"Say what you feel."

"I don't *know* how I feel about it."

"Are you glad you went?"

"Andrea," he said, growing impatient, "if I say that I'm happy as hell that I went, then what does that make me look like? Somebody asks me what the country's got to show for it, what *I've* got to show for it other than the medals and the scars. And what if I say I'm hating myself for having gone? What does that do? What does that do to the fact that I tried my best, that we *all* tried our best, under circumstances that you wouldn't believe?"

Andrea did not respond.

"And after having been through nine months of it, do you know what some dude said to me when I was in L.A. waiting on a plane to Atlanta?"

"No. What?"

"I was in uniform, with my arm in this thing, and this guy walked up to me in the coffee shop and told me that I represent everything that's wrong with America. Tells *me* that."

"That's terrible, Mike."

"The dude had hair to his ass and he smelled like a water buffalo. I didn't say anything, just looked at him thought about how cool it would be to kick him in the groin. But the funny thing is, I think he really meant it. He was just as repulsed by me as I was by him. So if I say I really regret having gone to Nam, then does that make me like him?"

"Certainly not."

"But if I say I'm glad I went, then I'm not sure I'd be telling the truth. Do you think I was ecstatic about being in Vietnam when I saw Chris Compton's husband underneath a poncho, with only his Goddamned boots sticking out?"

"Of course not, Mike," said Andrea as she reached for Billingsley's hand.

"I don't think I could ever explain the way I feel about the whole thing, Andrea. And I don't think I even want to try," he said, almost in a whisper.

Andrea could feel the moistness of Billingsley's hand. They said little else until they stopped for a late lunch at a fast-food outlet near Reston.

After lunch, Billingsley drove the car to the motel where he was staying. He wheeled into a space in front of his room.

"Want to come in?" he asked.

"Mike, will you go with me to the party tonight?" she asked tentatively and quietly.

"Will you have to break a date with somebody else?"

"Absolutely not!" Andrea answered with indignation.

"I don't have any clothes, other than these street clothes. I can't show up there looking like I just got off work down at the supermarket. And besides, I can't hide this silly cast."

"Mike, you'll look fine. It would mean so much to me to have you there."

"C'mon, Andrea, cut me some slack. I'd be out of place."

"You would not, either. You said you'd go. Remember?"

"I remember."

"Then will you go?" she asked pleadingly.

"I said I'd go. Remember?"

"Then I'll pick you up at seven. Okay?"

"Shit," sighed Billingsley, yielding to several moments of silent pressure from Andrea. "I'll be ready."

"Good," she said with a broad smile. "Listen, I've got tons of things to do, so I'll need to leave you for a while. Will you be okay here?"

"No. You'd better send one of those English-soundin' butlers over to look after me," he said sarcastically as he opened the door of the car and climbed out.

Andrea opened her door, got out, and walked around the front of the car to the driver's side. Billingsley fumbled with his door key while standing outside his room.

"Are you upset?" she called before starting the engine.

"See you at seven."

Billingsley entered his room and closed the door. He turned on the television and attempted to adjust the fuzzy color, and lay down on the bed. He later showered and changed into another shirt and slacks. His civilian wardrobe felt baggy from the weight he had left somewhere in the Far East. The cool of the room and the comfort of the bed lulled him to sleep.

He was awakened at seven by Andrea's knocking. She was carrying four jackets and a half-dozen neckties from her father's wardrobe. A dark blue jacket and red-striped tie matched the blue shirt and grey slacks he wore. The fit of the coat was acceptable, and he left feeling considerably relieved over his appearance.

Andrea drove to the downtown Washington hotel where a ballroom of modest size had been reserved for the nearly seventy students, friends, and alumni of the law school. Once inside, Andrea mingled freely with the group and introduced Billingsley by maneuvering him from one gathering to the next. Billingsley shook hands with his left hand, wearing the borrowed jacket with only his left arm through the sleeve. He noticed Robert Sloan, whom he had met the previous night, standing unaccompanied off to the side and sipping a cocktail. He also noticed that Sloan's eyes followed Andrea around the room.

Dinner portions were ample—chicken, roast beef, vegetables, bread, salads, and a choice of three desserts. Andrea and Billingsley joined two of her classmates, along with their wives, at a table in the center of the ballroom. They ate heartily, the law students laughing, joking, and kidding one another over their common experiences. Billingsley smiled politely through it all. He was restless and uncomfortable, but he tolerated it obligingly.

After the meal, the bar re-opened and the band began playing.

Couples began wriggling to the lively music provided by the band. The floor became crowded with dancers as Andrea led Billingsley to the tables of several of the older alumni in attendance. One elder alumnus, an attorney in Andrea's father's firm, discussed the rigors of combat with Billingsley while Andrea left to dance with Robert Sloan. The older man was interesting and had an appreciation for the pressures and difficulties of commanding troops. Billingsley chatted sociably while Andrea returned to the table to enter into a continuous stream of chatter with the ladies.

They moved on, to other tables and other conversations. Andrea left to dance with Sloan again. And again. *Unchained Melody. Yesterday. Dock of the Bay. My Girl.* He smiled and returned Andrea's wave when she would acknowledge him from the dance floor. Inside, however, he began to seethe.

"No, my arm's fine, really," he would say to each group.

"It's nothing, really. This cast makes it appear worse."

"No, it doesn't hurt anymore."

"Yeah, it was interesting over there."

"No, I never burned any villages."

"Right, I'm in the Marine Corps."

"Yeah, a little homesick."

"Yes, ma'am. She was real good about writing."

"I hope not. Maybe it'll end by that time."

The chatter and the laughter and the dancing continued. Billingsley chattered, though he laughed only occasionally and danced but twice. He didn't enjoy wearing a tie any more than he relished the idea of deliberately remaining sober. He felt out of place, as he had feared, as Andrea talked and danced and delighted in the company of her friends. He finally went to the bar in the back of the room, ordered a beer, and stood off to the side. He emptied the can with three large, burning gulps and then ordered another.

Billingsley took a seat at a table in the rear of the room, near the bar. Andrea was engaged in a rambling conversation with a group of wives at the table of the older alumni. He removed his jacket and loosened his tie as he sat alone and sipped his beer. Some fun, he thought. He saw Andrea look around the room for him before being asked to dance by the older, friendly gentleman from her father's firm. It was a slow dance.

"May I sit down?"

Billingsley looked over his shoulder to see Robert Sloan pointing to the empty chair at his side.

"Please do," he said with a nod.

Sloan slipped into the chair and loosened the brown tie that matched his tweed jacket with the patches on the elbows. Sloan's hair dangled over his forehead and was matted with perspiration. He looked drunk, or close to it, Billingsley thought.

"Well," Sloan said ceremoniously. "How does it feel to be a Marine war hero?"

"You'll have to ask one," Billingsley snapped.

"I thought I just did."

"No, you didn't."

"I heard you were hell-on-wheels, man."

"Yeah?"

"Yeah, hero. A real bad-ass."

"Who'd you hear that from?"

"Why, Andrea. She's made it a point to tell everyone that her guy won the Medal of Honor, or something, and that he was a genuine, authentic hero."

"I'm no hero," Billingsley said self-consciously.

"Not according to Andrea. She made it sound as if you'd won the Battle of the Bulge," Sloan said with a laugh.

Wrong war, asshole! Billingsley thought. But that's okay. What's twenty-five years and several thousand miles?

"The Battle of the Bulge, huh?" Billingsley said with a grin.

"Yeah, man. You must've been something, hero."

"I was no different than any of the others. Just tried to survive, that's all."

"Well, they'll never get me over there."

"They'll get by," Billingsley said, looking away and returning Andrea's wave as she went back to the table of the alumni.

"That Andrea's a great chick," said Sloan, also waving. "She's got it all except one thing."

Billingsley turned slowly and glared at Sloan. "What might that be?" he asked.

"Me," said Sloan with a grin and a point at himself.

"She'll get by, too."

"I'm of the opinion that I could have taken her from you if I had really tried."

"Oh? Well, I suppose I owe you a debt of gratitude, then."

"Nah, not really. I didn't try very hard."

"Lucky for me, huh?"

"If I had tried, hero, she'd be here with me instead of you."

Not much further, Sloan, Billingsley said to himself. Not much further, and you're moving at the speed of sound.

"How 'bout another drink, hero?" Sloan asked as he stood.

"No, I don't think so."

Sloan soon returned to the table with a fresh Scotch. Andrea stopped by the table and chatted briefly, then excused herself to go the rest room after declining Sloan's invitation to dance.

Thank God, Billingsley thought. That would have done it, for sure.

"Yeah, hero, I just might start trying harder," said Sloan, watching Andrea as she walked away.

"Lean over here, hotshot," Billingsley said with a motion toward himself.

Sloan shifted his chair and leaned in Billingsley's direction. His expression was one of amusement. His eyes were slightly droopy and his movement a little uncoordinated.

"Don't call me 'hero' again," Billingsley said calmly.

"What should I call you, then?"

"Anything else you want, pal. Okay?"

"Okay, pal."

Sloan attempted to slide his chair back closer to the table but was stopped by Billingsley's hand gesture.

"One other thing, pal," Billingsley said.

"What's that, pal?"

"This is a nice party. Wouldn't you agree?"

"Sure, great party. Why?"

"Because I don't want to spoil it."

"How?"

"Listen, cocksucker," Billingsley said as he moved close to Sloan's face. "I really think you're gonna do something or say something very soon that's gonna cause me to become angry. And I don't want to become angry with you, Sloan. You know why?"

Sloan's smile left his face. "No. Tell me."

Billingsley reached over with his left hand and grasped Sloan's tie, pulling him even closer. "Because I'll tear your spleen out and stuff it in your fuckin' ear! And let me promise you, tiger, that if I get on you it's gonna take a putty knife to get me off."

He turned loose of Sloan's tie, though he still looked wicked.

"Billingsley, let me tell—"

"Careful, Goddammit! I'm just about ready to jump."

Sloan straightened his jacket and leaned away. He then got

up from the chair, placed his drink on the table, and hurried out the door of the ballroom. Billingsley remained at the table for another five minutes before Andrea appeared and took a seat beside him.

She glared at him icily.

"Hello, counselor," he smiled.

"Mike, will you please tell me why it was necessary for you to be so crude toward Robert? I passed him in the hallway, and he's leaving the party."

"That's too bad."

"He said he wasn't very comfortable with you."

"That all he said?"

"Yeah, for the most part."

"He'd *better* be uncomfortable around me."

"You're beginning to make *me* uncomfortable," said Andrea as she looked at Billingsley's stern expression.

"Andrea, that guy sat here and called me 'hero' and told me how he was going to take you from me. I didn't start anything with him. I only warned the drunken asshole that he'd better be careful what he said to me," said Billingsley, suddenly feeling defensive.

"Does everybody, including me, have to be careful what they say to you, Mike?"

"Okay," Billingsley said as he rose abruptly from his chair. "That's enough for one night. I'll take a cab to the motel so I won't screw up anything else. I'll return the coat and tie before I go to the airport in the morning."

Billingsley grabbed the jacket from the chair and started toward the door. Andrea watched for a moment and then quickly followed him out the door of the ballroom.

"Wait, Mike," she called to him. "You can't leave yet. Mike, come back here and stay. Mike *wait*, dammit!"

Billingsley stopped and turned to face her from ten feet away. The jacket was slung over his shoulder. His face was sullen and red.

"For God's sake, Billingsley! We've never had a cross word before, and now we're fighting. *What* in the name of *God* is *going on?*"

"I don't *know* what's going on, Andrea. I get a jerk out of my friggin' face and I offend you in the process. You tell *me* what's going on."

Andrea walked toward him. "Are you really going back to the motel?" she asked, standing directly in front of him.

"I'm really going back to my motel."

"Why?"

"So I won't offend you or chase anybody else away who might want to call me 'hero' and tell me how they're gonna snake my girl away from me."

"You're uptight, Mike. You're so uptight it's *unreal!*"

"I'm sorry. I didn't want this to happen any more than you did. But it did, didn't it?"

Andrea's lips were pressed together and her face reflected her concern and bewilderment. She had never known Billingsley to become so stubborn and gloomy. And she noticed his tenseness.

"Is this it, Mike?" she asked. "Is this the way the whole thing ends?"

Inside the ballroom, the music and laughter continued.

"I hope not, Andrea. I really hope not. I had every intention of asking you to marry me tonight when I could manage to get you alone for a while. Maybe I'm a little too optimistic, I don't know. But I do know that I love you more than anything else in the world. I'm gonna leave, though, and spare us any more angry words because I don't think I could take it. Not now. Not tonight."

He turned and left Andrea standing in the hallway. He hailed a taxi from the driveway in front of the hotel. It had begun to rain, which only served to further darken his mood. By the time he arrived at the motel in Reston, he was hopelessly discouraged. He paid the driver and went straight to his room. A throbbing headache added to his misery and discomfort.

He undressed and went to bed. He remained awake, pondering the unexpected changes which had occurred in the relationship which had sustained and buoyed him for so long. He was remorseful and disgusted with himself, with everything. He was fearful of what might happen to this love affair which had provided order and stability to his life. He was confused. He didn't know exactly what had gone wrong, or exactly what would be necessary to mend it. He was torn from coming from a world of danger and discomfort and strife to one which which seemed now to exclude only the danger. He wanted Andrea for himself, exclusively. No strings; no challengers; no irritations; and particularly no strife. He wanted to feel sorry for himself because everything was not perfect. But he knew better. Things were perfect only in his imagination.

It was after midnight before he fell off to sleep.

Billingsley had been asleep for over an hour when he jerked awake. He sensed he had heard something but when he sat upright, all was quiet in the darkened room. He had fallen back onto his pillow and closed his eyes when he heard the second knock on his door. He jumped out of bed and pulled on his trousers before glancing out the curtain to see Andrea's shadowy form. He opened the door and saw her, her face wet with tears, as she stood in the doorway. She was damp from the rain and still dressed in her evening gown.

"Okay if I come inside?"

He extended his hand and led her into the room. She dropped her purse in a chair while Billingsley turned on the light above the dresser. Andrea's eyes were red and puffy, and she appeared exhausted. Her shoulders slumped as she continued to sniffle and cry. Her hair and clothes were damp from the rain.

"Are you all right, Andrea?"

"I feel horrible. Will you hold me, Mike?"

Billingsley moved to her and pulled her close. He held her tightly while she continued to cry, though silently.

"I woke you, didn't I?"

"That's okay."

"Swell night, huh?" she asked with a forced laugh.

"It's my fault, baby."

"No it's not. It's mine."

"No it's not."

"Yes it is, Mike. I'm the one who needs to apologize. I ignored you for a lot of the evening, and I had no reason to speak to you the way I did. I've been very selfish, and I feel rotten about it," she confessed.

"It's not all your fault, counselor. I get my share of the blame, too. I'm sorry for being so antagonistic."

"It's mostly my fault, Mike. We could have had a quiet evening together if I hadn't pushed you into going. I wanted to badly to show you off to my friends, though. I should've thought more of you, Mike. A party like that was probably the *last* thing you needed."

Andrea breathed in sobs and held tightly to Billingsley. He pulled himself away and produced a towel from the bathroom. He dried her hair and arms.

"I look like a wreck," she said when she glanced at herself in the mirror on the dresser."

"I happen to think not," said Billingsley, sitting down on the bed and lighting a cigarette.

"I had reserved a room at the hotel for us, for after the party," she said as she sat in a chair alongside the table near the door.

"Yeah?"

"Yeah. I even went up there after the party broke up and went to bed."

"What made you decide to come out here?"

"I knew I wouldn't be able to sleep," she said, looking down. "And I couldn't stand the idea of your being here and my being there. Not after what happened, especially."

"What about your mother?"

"I told her not to expect me, that I didn't want to drive back out here after the party."

"But you did, anyway," Billingsley said with a smile.

"Yeah, I did."

"I'm glad, Andrea. I was afraid that maybe I'd lost you."

"Oh, Mike," she said as she came over to sit on the bed next to him. "You've gotten the wrong impression about my being with Robert Sloan. He's just a friend, that's all. That's all he'll ever be. I don't want anyone other than you. I've waited a long time for you to come back, and I love you with all my heart."

He lowered his head and ran his hand over his short hair. "It's not you, Andrea. It's me," he said without looking at her.

"What's you?"

"I feel the same way about you, baby, but I don't seem to feel the same about too much else. Since before Nam, I mean. I can't get it out of my head. It's like I'm still there, in a lot of ways. And so much reminds me of it—the rain, the taste of beer, the trees—hell, everything! Maybe I'll shake it later. I hope so."

"You will, Mike," Andrea said comfortingly.

"Yeah, no sweat. But you'll probably run me off, meanwhile."

She walked to the dresser where she turned out the light.

"I'll do no such thing," she said as she began unzipping her gown. She stepped out of her shoes, draped her gown on the chair, and climbed into the bed dressed only in her underclothes. She pulled the covers to her chin. He still sat on the side of the bed, his cigarette glowing in the dark.

"This is so much better than being at that hotel," she said suggestively. "Are you gonna sit over there and smoke all night long?"

"No."

"Good."

"I've got an eleven o'clock flight in the morning."

"It's a long time until eleven o'clock, if you won't waste any of it getting lung cancer."

"I can't believe you came back here."

"If you thought that I'd let you go on back to Georgia, without so much as a 'good-bye, see you later,' you need your head examined, Billingsley."

"I may need that anyway," he said softly.

She sat up and crawled close to him. She propped herself on her knees as she reached around him from behind and held onto him. He could feel her smooth skin on his bare back, her warm breath on his shoulder. Her arms were wrapped around his neck and her hands stroked his chest. He could smell her perfume, that sweet, incredible, intoxicating scent so familiar to him.

"What's the matter, Mike?" she whispered in the dark room.

"Nothing, now that you're here," he said as he ran his hands over her arms.

"Yes, there is something wrong, too. Want to talk about it?"

"I've just got a lot on my mind, that's all."

"Anything I can do to help?"

"Yeah."

"What?"

"Take off the rest of your clothes."

Billingsley lit another cigarette while Andrea removed the remainder of her clothes. She tossed her underclothes toward the chair on which her gown was draped.

"Why are you smoking again?" she asked, pressing her bare chest against his back and enveloping him with her arms.

"Guess what, babe?" he asked.

"What?"

"Colonel Fletcher and Captain English recommended me for augmentation into the regular Marine Corps."

"What does that mean?"

"It means I'd have an option of staying in, if I wanted to. The whole process has to be approved by Headquarters, Marine Corps. There's no certainty that I'll be selected."

She sighed and sat away from him, on her side of the bed.

"What's the matter?" he asked.

"You know good and well that they'll accept you."

"No, I don't."

"Oh, c'mon, Mike. With your record in Vietnam, with all those medals? You've got the Silver Star and all of those others like the Purple Hearts. And their recommendation, too. No way they'd turn you down."

"I'll at least have an option. That's important to me, Andrea."

"God!" she sighed as she fell back onto the bed. "You're impossible to figure out. I hoped that by the time I was ready to graduate, you'd be ready to get out of the service. Now you're talking about staying in forever. They'll send you back to Vietnam, or some *other* place in a few more years. Haven't you been hurt enough?"

"I didn't say I was going to stay in forever."

"Look what happened to Tom Compton. The same thing could happen to you, Mike, when they send you to Vietnam or wherever the next war'll be."

"What if there *ain't* a next war?"

"Yeah, right. What if frogs had wings?"

"Are we gonna fight again, Andrea?" he asked, more amused than serious.

"I'm not dressed for it, if you haven't noticed."

"I don't want to fight anymore."

"Then telling me you want the option to stay in the Marines doesn't fit with the 'don't want to fight anymore' business."

"I don't want to fight with *you*, counselor."

"You were ready to fight with Robert, though."

"Goddamn right, the swine."

Andrea snickered and drew a deep breath. "You're impossible, Billingsley. Just go away to Vietnam and leave me alone, dammit. I can't figure you out, no matter how hard I try. Sometimes you're brilliant and sometimes you're a complete jerk. And sometimes you're both at the same time. Just go away and leave me to my room," she said.

"It's *my* room. Remember?" He crushed his cigarette into the ashtray on the nightstand.

"This is my town, so this is my room. I don't want to hear any more about it. It's my room."

"You spoiled little missy," he said, removing his trousers.

"You unappreciative idiot."

"You rich little hussy," he said, sliding next to her in the bed.

"You fascist pig."

He leaned over her, his head against hers. He kissed her lightly on the forehead. "Sometimes you can be a real hassle, Strickland," he said in a whisper.

"Sometimes you can be a Goddamned bully, Billingsley."

"I've never heard language from such an upper-crust like yourself that so reeked of the proletariat."

"It must be the company I've been keeping today."

He kissed her again, feeling her lips part. Her soft breasts pressed gently against his chest.

"I don't know why I would become aroused over a dishrag like you, but it seems that I have," he said between kisses.

"You probably get aroused just *thinking* of me."

"I wouldn't know. I've never thought of you."

"Bull."

"What's your name again, sweetheart?"

"Suzy Wong."

"Yeah, right. The long black hair, the narrow eyes, the slight accent. Yeah, I remember now. It's all coming back to me. Sorry about that slip of memory."

"What else do you remember?"

"Why?"

"Because your hand is acting like it's very familiar with certain parts of my person."

"My memory's getting better."

"So is your sense of direction."

Their kissing continued. Their passion for one another began to mount. They were relaxed, free from the tensions which had affected them earlier. They embraced, trying to absorb one another in one common web of affection. His brain began to fog with the same passion which burned his body throughout. She was so soft, so close, so responsive, so fragrant, so warm, so perfect.

They rolled about underneath the covers, he pulling her to him, atop him, rolling, holding, tightly, passionately. The world seemed to halt, to stand still until they could fill themselves with their enjoyment of one another. The passion built to a fury and erupted with a forceful, simultaneous conclusion, leaving both spent and satisfied.

Afterward, Billingsley lay on his back while Andrea propped herself on her side and ran her hand over his damp chest.

"Whew," he said as he exhaled. "Think I'm out of shape."

"I don't think so," Andrea said soothingly. "I like your shape just fine, except for that scar on your behind."

"It's evidence that I've been there, babe. If anybody were to doubt that I'd served my country honorably, I could just drop my pants and show 'em my scar."

"That'd be smooth," she said with a laugh. "I can just see you doing that when we're at a classy cocktail party or something. Everybody gets real quiet and there's Mike on the other side of the room with his pants down, pointing to his scar."

"Right. 'See there, Frank and Eloise. I was really there. They got me right in the tail when I was tryin' to elude the entire North Vietnamese Army. The nerve of 'em, shootin' *me*!' "

"Poor baby."

He pulled her close to him, hugging her and burying his face in her hair. "Thanks, counselor," he said softly.

"For what?"

"For coming here."

"I'm glad I did."

"I don't want to lose you, Andrea. I want you forever."

"I want that, too. More than anything else in the world. It was well worth the wait, Mike."

He smiled and held onto her.

Andrea awakened first, shortly before noon. By the time Billingsley opened his eyes, she was emerging from the shower, draped in towels.

"Good morning, Lieutenant Billingsley, sir," she said cheerfully.

"Morning. What's the time?"

"Almost twelve."

"That's just dandy," he sighed as he reached for a cigarette on the nightstand. "My flight should be somewhere over North Carolina by now."

Andrea smiled as she stepped into the bathroom after gathering her clothes from the chair. "How can you do that so early?"

"Do what so early?"

"Smoke."

"Ain't early. It's almost noon. Remember?"

"So soon after waking up, is what I meant. I wish you'd stop. You smoke way too much."

"Yeah, I know," he mumbled, leaning against the bed's headboard.

"Did you have trouble sleeping?"

"No . . . well, no more than usual. Why?"

"You tossed a lot."

"Did I keep you up?"

"Not until you sat up and said something."

"Really?" he asked curiously, recollecting nothing involving dreaming or talking during the night.

"Yeah. You sat up and said, 'Get 'em off the trucks, God-dammit!' You don't remember?"

"No, I don't. Sorry about that."

"It was no problem. I pulled you back down and you mumbled something and then went back to sleep."

Andrea glanced at herself in the mirror near the bathroom before taking a seat on the bed next to Billingsley. "C'mon, Mike, let's get going. You can check out of here and come home with me," she suggested.

"Nah, I've got to check the airline schedule."

"You can do that at my house. Hurry up, let's go."

"Don't pressure me, Gunny Strickland," he said as he grabbed at her playfully.

"Hurry up, Mike."

They drove to her house after he had checked out of the motel and tossed his belongings into the car. The weather had cleared and the sun was bright and warm. When they arrived, there was a note from Andrea's mother detailing her plans for lunch and shopping with a neighbor. The empty house belonged to the couple.

He opened a can of soda and stretched out on the sofa in

the large family room. When she joined him, she had changed into tight, well-fitting slacks and the Marine Corps sweatshirt which he recognized from the photograph sent to him on the previous Christmas. She took a seat beside him.

"Want some lunch?" inquired Andrea.

"I need to check on the flights to Atlanta for tonight. Got a telephone book handy?" he asked, rising from his seat.

Andrea reached up and grabbed his arm. She pulled him back onto the couch. "Stay here, at least for a few more days," she said.

"Aw, I'd better not," he said with little conviction.

"Please, Mike. You know you'd be welcome. We could go back to Georgetown and visit—"

"I'd better not."

"Why *not*? You could use the guest bedroom. You don't have to be in Atlanta tonight and besides, we'd both be miserable with you down there and me up here. Now *stay here*, dammit!"

"How can I refuse you?" he smiled.

"You can't. Everything will be okay," she said suggestively, adding a smile of her own.

"Everything?" he asked, leaning to kiss her.

"Trust me . . . everything," she whispered. "This is a big house."

He kissed her and held her long enough to feel a rekindled surge of want. He pulled her to him. They extended themselves over the length of the sofa, with Andrea atop him.

"Will you stay?"

"I'm under your spell."

"You're under everything about me. Wouldn't it make for a lovely scene if my mother suddenly came into the house?"

"Yeah, it would. 'Well, hello there, Mrs. Strickland. It's me, Mike, under here with my hands on your daughter's posterior.'"

"Let's get up," she said, unable to elude his grasp.

"Nope. I'm taking you here and now."

"No, you're not," she giggled as she lightly bit his lower lip. "I'll make you some lunch and take care of your other appetite."

"Take care of this one first."

"I'm gonna have to put you in a cold shower," Andrea laughed.

"Will you get in there with me? I might have forgotten how to take a shower since gettin' back from Nam."

"You haven't forgotten *anything*, Billingsley."

Andrea freed herself from his pulls and grabs. "I'll make lunch. If you want to change your reservations or call home or whatever, feel free to use the phone. The book's in the desk drawer. Don't plan to leave too soon, though."

"What's today?"

"Saturday."

"I'll leave Monday."

"No, Wednesday."

"What?"

"Yeah, no earlier than Wednesday."

"Okay, then. Wednesday night you can come with me to Atlanta and stay through the weekend. Air travel and shit like that ain't no problem for a rich girl."

Andrea laughed and left the room. Billingsley changed his flight and made reservations for the two of them for late Wednesday evening. He also called his home and informed his mother of the change in plans, and of Andrea's intended visit. His mother mentioned that Bill Blanton had called from California with an important message. He took Blanton's phone number from his mother.

Andrea summoned Billingsley soon after he had completed the call to his home. He waited to return Blanton's call.

"Lunch is served, dearest," said Andrea.

"That was fast. What specialty of the house have you prepared for us?" he asked as he followed her into the kitchen.

"About the only thing I can—peanut butter and jelly sandwiches," she replied meekly.

"What's this? Do you mean that Andrea Strickland, the girl wonder, the girl who can do almost anything, is *lost* in the *kitchen*?"

"I can't even fry a blankety-blank egg," she confessed, looking embarrassed.

"Why didn't you tell me you couldn't cook?" he asked with a frown.

"Can you repair a broken dishwasher?"

"Of course not."

"Why didn't you tell me you weren't very handy around the house?"

Billingsley laughed and embraced her. She wrapped her arms around his neck and kissed him on the cheek.

"Know what I'm thinking?" he whispered.

"What?" she whispered in return.

"I'm thinking about overlooking the fact that my wife can't cook."

"Oh?" Andrea said aloud, leaning back away from him. "Why didn't you marry someone who could. And why didn't you invite me to the wedding?"

"Because it hasn't happened yet. And I certainly *intend* to invite you to the wedding."

"Swell. Hope she's nice. Where's it gonna be? Atlanta? Air travel and shit like that ain't no problem for us rich girls, so tell where so I can be sure and come," she giggled.

"Quiet."

"What?"

"Be quiet."

Andrea saw that he had turned serious. She held his hands, facing him. She heard him draw a deep breath.

"I want you to become my wife, Andrea," he said slowly and deliberately. "I know there's a lot left to work out about what we'll do and where we'll be, but I want you with me. I love you and I want to be with you for the rest of my life. We can set the date and choose the place later, work out all the little details later, send out all the little invitations later. It won't need to happen until you're finished with school. But right now I want you to know that I very much want you as my wife."

She looked shocked as his words and their meaning registered. Though she had expected a proposal of marriage from Billingsley, the fact that it had actually happened, that she had been told of his desire for her as his wife, stunned her with its gravity.

"Will you marry me, Andrea Strickland?"

Tears welled in her eyes. She looked at him, his hands in hers. She swallowed and took a deep breath, exhaling with a sigh and a grin.

"I'll marry you, Michael Billingsley."

She leaned forward and rested her forehead on his chin. They stood in the kitchen and embraced, both relieved and both happy.

"I had always wondered what this would be like," said Andrea, still in his embrace.

"Disappointed?"

"Not in the least. A little jittery, maybe. And happy. And excited. And proud. And in love. But certainly not disappointed. I've got the peanut butter and jelly sandwiches as my witnesses."

"Think maybe that you could schedule an elective before you graduate?"

"On what?"

"Cooking."

"You've already asked me now, buster," she grinned as she straightened up and looked at him. "You can't start adding special conditions to the basic agreement. Unh uh, too late for that."

"I suppose we'll have to live near a restaurant, then."

"And a dishwasher repair shop, too."

They laughed and embraced, swaying gently from side to side.

"Are you sure, baby?" he asked.

"Yes, I'm very sure," she replied, holding on to him.

They ate their lunch and decided when to break the news to their families. They decided to advise Andrea's mother on the same evening, as soon as she returned. Billingsley's family, they concluded, would be told during the coming week when Andrea would visit Atlanta.

With their plans for the announcement made, Billingsley went into the family room and placed a call to Bill Blanton in California. Andrea came into the room with a bottle of white wine to celebrate the occasion. Billingsley sipped the wine while he talked, telling Blanton the news of Andrea's acceptance of his proposal. Andrea then spoke briefly with Blanton and accepted his congratulations and best wishes. She gave the phone back to Billingsley and shortly thereafter watched as his expression became blank after an exclamation of, "Oh, no!" His face grew pale as he listened silently to Blanton for the next several moments. The conversation finally concluded with Billingsley promising Blanton that he would "stay in touch." Billingsley hung up the telephone and stared at the carpeted floor.

"Mike, what's the matter?" Andrea asked.

"Bill heard from a Basic School classmate of ours who told him that Dan Redwine lost both his legs in Nam a couple of weeks ago."

"Oh, dear God, Mike," said Andrea, placing her wine glass on a table and moving to embrace Billingsley.

"He's on Guam. Man, what news. Guess I need to get a letter off to him. I'll call his mother in Illinois and find out the address. Damn, Danny. They sure shot the old gang up, didn't they? Shot me and Bill all to hell and blew Dan's legs off. All the good times, all the laughs, all the long talks. None of us had any idea it would end up like this. No way."

"Mike, that's so sad. At least Dan's alive, though," Andrea said softly. "We've gone from one extreme to the other today."

"Sure have. Seems like it's been that way for me for the last nine months. It almost numbs you after a while. Kinda like burning your fingers so often and so bad they *quit* hurting, or at least you can't feel it anymore. Man, what lousy news."

They moved over onto the couch where they sat and made small talk for the better part of the next hour. Andrea was able to humor and sooth him, extricating him from the depths of the familiar depression which had darkened his mood. She made him laugh, fed him wine and cheese, proposed toasts to their future bonding as husband and wife, and generally raised his spirits.

Andrea's mother returned home in the early evening. She was invited into the family room where she heard the news of her daughter's engagement. Mrs. Strickland remained composed throughout, though her eyes were moist when she embraced each of them after hearing Andrea's pronouncement. She expressed her satisfaction with the decision to delay the marriage until Andrea's graduation and her pleasure in having Billingsley as a son-in-law. He grinned and embraced her again.

Later, all three of them dined on seafood at a nearby restaurant. They returned to the house and listened as Mrs. Strickland began notifying by telephone a few close relatives and friends of the family. Andrea would glance at Billingsley and wink each time her mother would remember yet another friend or relative in what seemed an endless stream of telephone conversations. He sat patiently, occasionally pinching Andrea in some private part of her body when Mrs. Strickland would look away to dial the telephone. Andrea would fix him in an ominous start after each of the light pinches.

It was late when Billingsley excused himself from their talking and planning. He took his belongings upstairs to the guest bedroom. He showered in the adjoining bathroom and then read *The Washington Post* in bed. An editorial attracted his attention, condemning the war in Vietnam, citing the loss of life, and alleging the failure of the South Vietnamese government to adequately rise to the occasion, either politically or militarily. Billingsley was impressed with the logic and the research of the columnist though he, himself, knew little of the political background of the events which had shaped, and were continuing to shape the character of the country and the war. As he read, he kept thinking of Vietnam—its geography, its people, its uncertain destiny. And he thought of Dan Redwine, his damaged but alive buddy recovering from his wounds in a Guam hospital. Hang on, Danny, he thought, almost as if Redwine could intercept the thought waves and receive the encouragement of his friend and fellow officer.

He finally dimmed the light in the guest bedroom and closed his eyes.

Billingsley had been asleep for nearly two hours when the door to his room was quietly opened and just as quietly closed again. He awakened with a recoil when he felt the movement of the bed and realized that he was not alone in the room. He sat upright, straining to focus his eyes in the dark.

"Shhh," whispered Andrea while placing her index finger across his lips. She pushed him back down in the bed and slid in beside him. She was dressed in her nightgown, he in his undershorts.

"What time is it?" he asked softly.

"Three o'clock. Missed me?"

"Yeah."

"You don't sound very enthused."

"I didn't know where I was, for a second. You just surprised the greatest jungle fighter in the world."

"I didn't come in here to fight. Can you dig it?" she giggled.

"Yeah, I can dig it," he said, feeling her bare arms.

"Reach over there and set the alarm."

"Do what?"

"The alarm. We may not need it, but set it for six so I can

be out of here in plenty of time."

Billingsley leaned toward the table, on his side of the bed, and picked up the small, electric clock. He studied it for a moment, in its own illumination, before feeling the dials behind it. He reached behind the face of the clock and turned one of the protruding dials. The alarm suddenly began a loud, sharp buzzing.

"Son of a bitch!" he whispered loudly, startled by the noise. Billingsley dropped the clock, then grabbed it up, madly fumbling with all the dials on the back. Andrea buried her face in a pillow and laughed uncontrollably as Billingsley struggled to quiet the alarm. Finally, in desperation, he stuffed the clock underneath his pillow, jumped out of the bed, and unplugged it. He listened for a moment in the hallway but heard only the muffled and near-convulsive laughter of Andrea. He climbed back into the bed, fully awake.

"You clumsy ape," said Andrea through her laughing spell. "The world's greatest jungle fighter, huh?"

"Your mom's gonna open that door any minute now."

Andrea rested her head upon his chest and covered her mouth with her hand to suppress the noise of her laughter. Her entire body shook from the effects.

"Andrea, be quiet, dammit," he said, wrapping his arms around her and gently shaking her.

She sat up, took a deep breath, and resumed her laughing. It took another effort from Billingsley to calm her, finally. She dared not to say anything for a moment, until the spell subsided. Her eyes were moist from tears of laughter.

"I think I've split my sides," she sighed, under control.

"Handled that well, didn't I?"

She started laughing again.

"Dammit, shut up before your mother comes in here," said Billingsley, more amused than agitated.

She giggled for another minute. She had him pass her a tissue from the nightstand with which to wipe her eyes. She then fell back onto the bed and exhaled loudly.

"I'm exhausted," she allowed.

"How exhausted?" he asked as he began to kiss her on her cheek and neck.

"I think I may want to sleep," she said coyly.

He moved his hands over her nightgown, rubbing, fondling,

caressing. She began to respond to the touches and kisses with touches and kisses of her own.

"Still want to sleep?" he asked.

The fondling continued. The only sound from Andrea was her breathing.

"Do you?" he repeated.

Still she did not answer.

"Do you?"

"Not usually, but I will with you," she giggled.

Billingsley was still sleepy when he joined Andrea and Mrs. Strickland in the kitchen's breakfast area.

"Well, good morning, Mike," greeted Mrs. Strickland when he entered and took a seat across from Andrea at the circular wooden table.

"Good morning, ladies," he said with a smile.

"I trust you slept well," said Mrs. Strickland, who stood at the electric range.

"I slept fine, ma'am. I did have a little trouble with the alarm, though, and it went off a bit early. I hope it didn't bother anyone."

"It didn't bother me, Mike. Are scrambled eggs okay?" Mrs. Strickland asked.

"They're fine, ma'am. Did it bother you, Andrea?"

"No," Andrea replied, squinting and looking away.

Mrs. Strickland started bringing the food to the table. First the bacon, then the eggs. When her mother had turned away for another trip to the range, Andrea firmly kicked him on the leg. She followed the kick by making a face at him and sticking out her tongue.

"Something wrong with your leg, Mike?" asked Mrs. Strickland when she returned to the table and noticed Billingsley examining his shin.

"No, ma'am. I was just making sure that my socks matched."

Andrea grinned smugly throughout breakfast.

The remainder of Billingsley's stay in Virginia was spent in leisurely walks, drives, picnics, and discussions with Andrea. They drove to Georgetown, to the restaurant where they had met. They had a drink in the lounge where they had gone afterwards, also during that first meeting. They picnicked at Manassas, Virginia, where Billingsley explored the grounds of the famous Bull Run battles of the Civil War. They slept late in the mornings and stayed up late during the nights, with little regard for time.

They left Virginia on Wednesday evening.

In Atlanta, the Billingsleys were gathered in the living room of their home when they heard the news of the marriage plans. Andrea sat on the couch alongside Mrs. Billingsley. The reaction of the family was emotional and enthusiastic. Andrea was received well by the family members, accepting the hugs from Billingsley's father and brother and the long, teary embrace from his mother. Even the usually unflappable Kevin was excited by the news, for he had been charmed by his brother's fiancee.

They spent the remainder of the week relaxing and enjoying themselves in the warm days and the cool, comfortable evenings of the beautiful Atlanta fall. They kept to themselves much of the time, still feeling the need to catch up after the long and difficult separation.

The day before Andrea's scheduled return to her home, Billingsley received his orders in the mail. He opened the letter quickly, as Andrea looked on, and smiled as he read the contents. " 'You are directed to proceed and report by 12 October 1969 to the Commanding General, Marine Corps Development and Education Command, Marine Corps Base, Quantico, Virginia, for duty. These orders constitute permanent change of station.' "

Andrea was smiling too when he glanced at her after reading the remainder of the orders. He kissed the papers and grabbed Andrea in a tight embrace.

"Thank goodness," Andrea said with feeling.

"This calls for a celebration," Billingsley said. "C'mon, let's go."

"Where to?" Andrea asked as she followed him out the door of the house.

"C'mon, I'll show you."

They drove for fifteen minutes, through an area of majestic, Williamsburg-style homes. They came to a light commercial district and parked on the side of the street. They walked for a block to a lounge with neon signs in the windows advertising popular beers. It was dim and musty inside. A half-dozen patrons sat at the bar and drank their beer from icy mugs.

Several more customers occupied tables at the far end of the room where a pinball machine was ringing. The bartender, a thin, balding man, called and waved to Billingsley as he and Andrea took a seat at one of the three tables directly in front of the bar. The bartender's wife, a plump, round-faced woman, moved toward the table from the far end of the bar where she had been enjoying a plate of fried potatoes.

"How you doin', Mike?" she smiled.

"Fine, Hazel. What about you?"

"Okay, I guess. What can I get for ya'll?" she asked as she placed two cardboard holders and a basket of pretzels upon the table.

"Hazel, this is the girl I was telling you and Jack about early last week. Her name's Andrea, and she's gonna become my wife," said Billingsley proudly.

Hazel smiled, displaying the product of neglected dental care, and raised her eyebrows in approval.

"Lord sakes, Mike! She sure is a pretty 'un. I knew you must've been hooked, the way you carried on about her the last time you was in."

"I am hooked."

Andrea grinned self-consciously, her chin resting upon her clasped hands.

"Yessir, Mike. She's as pretty as can be. Tell you the truth, hon, he's been in here before with some real lulu's, but none as pretty as you," Hazel said with a grin and a wink at Andrea.

"Aw, Hazel. Don't get into all that. Just bring Andrea a gin and tonic and me a beer."

"I'm gonna bring ya'll one on Jack and me, seein' as ya'll are gonna be married, and all," Hazel said as she left to fetch the drinks.

"You're a regular at this dump?" Andrea asked quietly.

"Used to be," Billingsley answered with a laugh. "I used to come in here a good bit, before I went into the Marine Corps. Thought I'd bring you in here and watch your expression when you see somebody eating peanuts and throwing the hulls on the floor."

"Classy joint, huh?"

"Here ya'll go," said Hazel, returning with the drinks. "Ya'll gonna make a fine couple, I just know it. Hon, don't let him go back over yonder to that Viet-nam again. We don't need no more of our boys goin' over there and gettin' hurt no more. You keep him home, hon. Okay?"

"Okay," agreed Andrea.

"She won't have to worry about that anymore, Hazel. I'm not going back," said Billingsley.

"Well, I hope not, son. It's a shame, that's what it is. The whole dad-blamed thing's a shame. There oughta be a law against it."

Hazel left and took a seat at the near end of the bar. Jack the bartender called out his congratulations from behind the bar. Andrea and Billingsley sipped their drinks.

"They seem like nice people," Andrea remarked.

"They are. They're really decent folks. Hazel doesn't talk much about it, but their only son came back from Nam in early '67 hooked on dope. They've done about all they could do, but I understand the guy's still pretty screwed up."

"That's terrible."

"They told me last week that he's still being treated by the VA."

"Is it working?"

"They don't seem to think so."

"What kind of drugs did he use?"

"Heroin, the big H. That's what he was stealing money out of their cash register to buy, when he first came back."

"Ever get the feeling that everything's coming apart?" Andrea asked as she shook her head in disbelief.

"Sometimes, I sure do. That's why you mean so much to me, counselor."

"Why?"

"Because you help me to keep things in perspective. You give me a sense of direction, a sense of purpose."

"You do the same for me."

"Do I, really?"

"Certainly."

"Well, I'll be damned. We ought to get married," he suggested with a wink.

"Not a bad idea. But there is one thing, Mike."

"What's that?"

"I'm pregnant."

"WHAT?" Billingsley asked loudly, his eyes bulging.

"I'm only kidding," Andrea grinned. "I just wanted to get

even for that stunt you pulled on me the other morning at breakfast. You know, asking me in front of my mother if I had been bothered by the alarm."

Billingsley slumped back into his chair in relief. He stared at Andrea for a moment before breaking into a wide grin. He reached across the table and grasped both her hands.

"Are we even now, counselor?"

"We're even now."

Hazel sat at the end of the bar, watching her customers as she sipped a cup of coffee. She motioned for Jack to come over. "Poor little thing's pregnant, Jack," she whispered with a nod at Andrea and Billingsley.

11

For those who had only recently returned from the tropical heat of Southeast Asia, the coolness of November at Quantico seemed pronounced. The trees had dropped their leaves, and the landscape had taken on a brownish hue under the clear skies of Virginia.

Billingsley had adjusted to his routine as an instructor at the Basic School. He enjoyed lecturing to the attentive students on squad tactics and the tenets of warfare, since he was only a year removed from being in their place. He had begun to feel comfortable and at ease in his assignment, especially when practical applications took the class and the instructors to the field. He wore a sufficient number of decorations on his uniform to provide him with instant credibility as a combat officer. The Silver Star and three Purple Hearts bore witness to his close exposure to battle. He was one of the young lions—decorated, confident, witty, and intelligent. He enjoyed the respect of the young officers at the Basic School.

He rented a two-bedroom apartment in nearby Triangle, Virginia. It was affordable and preferable to the BOQ, particularly on the occasional weekends when Andrea would drive over from Charlottesville to join him. He cooked infrequently, usually eating frozen dinners unless he chose to have dinner on the base. His refrigerator was stocked mainly with beer, milk, and orange juice. An aging, shorthaired cat had taken up with him almost immediately upon his arrival, strutting fearlessly into the apartment as Billingsley moved his things from the car and rented trailer. The old cat had quickly realized, however, that feedings would be left predominantly to its own initiative since its adopted master departed early and returned late. The friendly old cat was always waiting, though.

379

The routine for the past month had satisfied Billingsley's need to resume an active life. He studied and worked hard at his new job, reviewing the manuals and splicing his lectures with practical advice to the students on applications particular to Vietnam. Billingsley was patient in the classroom but far less tolerant when he observed a careless student in the field exercises. He often warned his students of the dangers involved with carelessness in the face of the enemy in Vietnam.

"Are you married, Nicola?" he had shouted at a student who had made a mockery of his failure to adequately move a group of others away from an area which had been designated as mined.

"Yessir, I am," the smiling student had answered.

"You just led your men into a mine field, and you and most of the others are dead. If you think it's funny, then ask your wife to join you in a big laugh tonight when you get home. And ask her if she's gonna think it's funny when she gets a visit from somebody in a few months who'll tell her that you did the same thing in Nam and blew yourself apart at the waist. They'll ship you home in a cigar box, Nicola, if you pull that kind of crap in Vietnam. And if you think it's funny, tiger, then go ahead and have yourself a good laugh. But if you think it's gonna be funny when you screw up and get other Marines killed, then step over here and let's you and me have us a little chat."

"I'm sorry, sir," the embarrassed officer had said. "I really don't think it's so funny anymore."

Billingsley recalled the encounter as he sat in front of the living-room window and gazed outside, comfortable in the bamboo papa-san chair he had bought and shipped home while he was recuperating in Okinawa. The chair was one of the few things he owned in the fully furnished apartment. It was Saturday, early afternoon, and he was watching eagerly for Andrea's car to enter the parking lot. She had remained in Charlottesville during the previous evening to recuperate from a difficult week of classes and quizzes. Billingsley stared outside while his stereo played rock 'n' roll music from a cassette tape. He sipped a beer and stroked the head of his cat, which rested contentedly in his lap. He had named the cat Bud after he learned that the elderly feline fancied an occasional bowl of beer.

His thoughts turned to his visit the previous night to the home of Chris Compton. He had enjoyed her dinner and companionship until the early morning hours. Chris had talked freely about her long days since Tom's death and of their bygone days together. She had spoken of her emptiness and loneliness, and had said that she felt a certain kinship in spirit with him which allowed her to open up and speak easily. And he had found in Chris an equally good listener. He had told funny stories about Compton and himself. There had been plenty of laughter during the visit—the joking with Chris and her mother, the stories, the fun with little Karen. As he had started to leave, he had been stunned by an affectionate kiss from Chris. Could've just been a friendly kiss, he thought. He hoped that was all it had been—just a spontaneous and appreciative gesture on Chris' part for his effectiveness in cheering her. The thought that Chris might be attracted to him bothered him deeply.

"If I can come back as something different, Bud," he said as he stroked the head of the purring cat, "then I want to come back and be just like you. No hassles, no problems, no worries. And if you're sitting there thinking the same thing, then request to stay with what you've got. You've got it made, man."

The cat opened its eyes, raised its head, and yawned widely. Soon it was asleep again with its head on its paws.

"Don't listen to me, then. But don't bitch if you come back as a person and get a set of orders to Nam. I won't listen to you, you old drunk."

The vigil continued. Billingsley held his arm aloft and checked its size. The strength had gradually returned in his grip, and exercise had improved its appearance. Deep scars, slightly above the wrist, on both sides, marked the entry and exit paths of the bullet. How in God's name did I get out of there alive? he wondered. Twice in the arm, twice in the leg, once in the butt. Countless encounters, countless bullets and fragments passing only inches away. How could they have missed me as often as they did? What would it have been like to have been gravely injured, in those final few moments in the passage from consciousness to eternity. Would there be shock? Pain? Slow motion? Resignation? Comprehension? Bright colors? He wondered, as he had often done, what Martindale had felt and thought, if anything, in those final moments. He grimaced and attempted to rid himself of the unpleasant thoughts by shaking them from his head. But, as usual, the images returned as if attracted by a magnet inside his mind. They weren't easily shaken.

Andrea's red sports car appeared at the entrance to the parking lot. She found a space, parked, and emerged carrying a single grocery sack filled to the top. She walked toward the door, not noticing Billingsley in the window until she neared the walkway. She smiled when she saw him and motioned for his assistance with the heavy bag.

"Hi, babe," Billingsley said as he greeted her at the steps of the ground-floor apartment.

"Take this thing before it breaks my back," Andrea said, pushing the sack in his direction and leaning to accept his light kiss.

Billingsley took the bag into the apartment and placed it on the kitchen table. Andrea closed the door behind them and removed her light jacket. She wore faded jeans and a bright yellow sweater over her white blouse. Billingsley embraced her tightly.

"I've missed you the last two weeks," Andrea said softly.

"Missed you, too. You feel so good, baby. You feelin' okay?"

"Why?"

"You look tired."

"I'm exhausted. Too much mental strain, dear."

"Can you stand a little physical strain?"

"Like what?"

He slapped at her rounded behind. "Like anything you want," he replied after kissing her.

"Have you gotten rid of that cat yet?"

"I can't do that, Andrea."

"Why not?"

"Bud and me have us a deal."

"What kind of deal might that be?"

"I pay the rent, I pay the bills, I provide most of the chow and all of the beer, I clean up after us, and he stays here and keeps me company."

"That's a lovely arrangement, Mike. Would you be kind enough to fix my lunch while I stay here and keep you company?"

"Sure."

"A hamburger would be fantastic. There's ground beef in the sack," said Andrea as she went into the living room and slumped in the papa-san chair. "I tried to call you last night."

"Yeah? When?" he called from the kitchen.

"Nine, ten, and eleven."

"I had dinner in Baltimore with Chris Compton."

"Oh," she said softly.

Billingsley cooked the hamburgers, spread the food onto the table, and summoned her to lunch. She picked at her food and broke the potato chips on her paper plate into small pieces.

"Why so quiet?" Billingsley asked.

"My head's splitting."

"Taken anything for it?"

"Yeah."

"You sure did clam up when I mentioned that I'd been with Chris. Anything else the matter?"

"I think I want to go back to the bedroom and rest a while. This headache is making me feel sick. Would you mind?"

"No, of course not. But you didn't answer me when I asked if anything else is the matter."

"I don't *want* to answer you," she said, standing and folding her napkin over the remains of her lunch.

Andrea went to the master bedroom in the back of the apartment. Billingsley cleaned the kitchen and then took a fresh beer into the living room. There he sat in the quiet, thinking and drinking his beer. She was here, he thought. Yet she wasn't.

Andrea was fast asleep on the top of the covers when he checked on her a half-hour later. He covered her with a light blanket. He left the bedroom, closing the door quietly and returning to the living room. He turned on his stereo and sat in his chair, the cat as his only company.

By the time Andrea awakened in the early evening, she felt refreshed. Her headache had gone. She glanced at the clock near the bed and discovered that she had slept for nearly three hours. She got up and walked into the living room to find Billingsley still occupying his chair. Next to him was a pyramid of empty beer cans, along with remnants of a bag of chips. He greeted the sight of her with a raised beer.

"Feelin' better, babe?" he asked.

"Yeah, much better. You look as if you feel pretty good

yourself," she said with a giggle as she took a seat on the sofa, facing him.

"Take a look at Bud," Billingsley said, pointing at the cat which had slumped on its side near one of the stereo speakers.

"What's the matter with him?"

"He's drunk as a skunk. He's had almost two bowls," he laughed.

"Mike, it might *kill* him," Andrea said reprimandingly.

"Nah. Want me to wake him up and get him to walk around? It's a riot."

"No, please. Just leave him alone for now."

She went into the kitchen and returned with a glass of Coke. She took her seat on the sofa and noticed the full ashtray at Billingsley's feet.

"Have you been sitting in here the whole time?" she asked.

"That's affirmative. Roger, dodger, over and out."

Billingsley smiled and pointed to the stacked beer cans next to his chair, knocking them over in the process. "Well, hell. Probably stain the carpet enough to where they'll keep my deposit now, sure as shit," he complained while stacking them again.

Andrea sipped her drink slowly as Billingsley lit another cigarette. The stereo volume was tuned low to a fast, snappy rock tune.

"So tell me what you've been thinking about while you've been sitting here for the past three hours," Andrea said with a faint smile as she circled her finger over the top of the glass.

"You," he replied with a point.

"Me? What about me?"

"I ain't gonna tell you," he said with a grin.

"Why not?"

"Later, it'll have to be later."

Billingsley rose and left the living room, walking straight and steadily. He soon returned from the bathroom in the hallway and took his seat in the chair.

"Know what, babe?" he asked.

"What?"

"I live a pretty boring life now."

"It's boring *already*?"

"Yeah."

"Why, Mike? You're really only just getting started again."

"I get up early . . . drive to the base . . . I eat breakfast at Basic School, if I eat at all . . . I teach tactics . . . I leave after work and meet some buddies at the club for a few beers . . . then I may eat . . . but sometimes I don't . . . then I come here and study for a while . . . then I may watch the tube and drink some more beer . . . then I go to bed and wake up feeling like a daisy cutter went off inside my head."

"What's a daisy cutter?"

"A bomb. A heckuva boom."

"Aren't there other things to do?"

"I could go to D.C. with some of the guys, but all they do is end up chasing whatever women they can find. I'm not as interested in that as I used to be," he grinned.

"I'm glad about that. Do you enjoy teaching?"

"Yeah, in most ways."

"What about the other ways?"

"I don't like knowing some of the things the students don't know."

"That's why you're the teacher and they're the students, isn't it?"

"I suppose so."

"Then you have to tell 'em what they don't know. Right?"

"Do you think I should tell 'em that some of 'em in the class are gonna be dead sons of bitches in a few more months?"

"Mike, please try to watch your language," Andrea said softly.

"Sorry."

"I didn't think that too many were getting orders to Vietnam now, not since the start of the withdrawal."

"It's not like it was a year ago, but enough of 'em are gonna go, still. And those that do are gonna have their chance. They don't have much of an idea of what it's gonna be like," he said with a sigh.

"Isn't it your job to tell 'em what it's like?"

"I can tell 'em what to look for, yeah. But I can't show 'em or tell 'em what it's like to see another human being's guts strewn all over the grass."

"Oh, Mike! Please," Andrea said with a grimace.

"See what I mean? How can you tell somebody what the smell of burning flesh is like? How can I tell 'em what they're gonna feel like when they hear an explosion and then see the leg of one of their troops on the other side of the trail? Or how can—"

"God, *stop!*" said Andrea as she lowered her head and placed her hand to her forehead. "Please, let's talk about something else."

Billingsley rose from his chair and went into the kitchen for another beer. He returned, asking, "What do you want to do tonight, counselor?"

"The quieter the better."

"We can stay here or go out. Which do you prefer?"

"I'd just as soon stay here, Mike."

"That's fine with me."

The telephone rang and he answered it in the kitchen. Andrea heard him say "Hello, Chris," as she sat waiting on the couch. The ensuing conversation lasted little more than five minutes before Billingsley returned to the living room. Andrea sat and stared at her glass, impassive and silent.

"That was Chris Compton," Billingsley said tentatively.

"How nice."

"She called to thank me for keeping her company last night. She just wanted to say that she had a really nice time."

"That's great, Mike."

"I thought so."

"Did she invite you to dinner tonight?"

"Of course not, Andrea. You're uptight again."

"I'm not uptight."

"You certainly are uptight. Look, her husband was my best friend. We both miss Tom a lot, a hell of a lot. Do you think I'd encourage anything other than a few laughs and some companionship?"

"No, Mike. I don't."

"Then what's the matter with you, then?"

"Did you ever consider that she might encourage you?" Andrea said, looking out the window.

"Yeah, I've considered that. But I don't think it's gonna happen because I'm not going to be around her very often and, besides, she's very well aware of my plans to marry you."

"You can talk to her about some things a lot easier than you can with me."

"Like what?"

"She's the widow of your best friend. You have Tom in

common. You both enjoy talking about him, and Vietnam, and all that Marine Corps stuff. She's like one of the guys, in some ways. Except that she's terribly attractive."

"You're terribly attractive, too."

"You don't talk much about Vietnam with me, though."

"Because I don't think you really care to hear about it."

"I don't know, Mike," she sighed. "I understand you're only trying to be a friend to Chris, and I don't mean anything derogatory about her. I guess I just wish you felt as easy talking to me about what's on your mind as you do with her. I don't know what's said when you're with her, but I sense that you can talk with her more openly than you can with me. And that bothers me."

"It shouldn't. I look at Chris as the widow of my best friend. I look at you as the woman I want very much to be my wife."

"How can you want me for your wife when you don't find it easy to talk to me, Mike?"

"I'm talking with you now."

"You know what I mean."

"I'm not sure I do," he said, suddenly becoming agitated. "Andrea, I'm as open with you as I can be, and I always have been. We've talked about a lot, about Vietnam, about the people I was with over there, and God knows you've been a good listener. And there are some things that I've not talked about with anybody, and probably never will. But that's no reflection on you."

"Yes, it is."

"No, it's not!" he snapped. "You've had a chip on your shoulder all afternoon, and you won't come right out and tell me what's bothering you. Yet you seem to be upset with *me* because you claim that I can't talk with you about some things."

"You're getting mad, Michael."

"Yeah, I'm gettin' mad because you've clammed up and acted kinda strange every time Chris Compton's name has come up. Do you really distrust me that much, Andrea?"

"I don't distrust you, Mike."

"I don't distrust you, either. There, we've settled that. We both trust each other. We're both talking to each other. And I'll talk about anything you want, anything at all," he said loudly.

Andrea started to walk into the kitchen.

"No, no. Don't run out of the room on me again," he said.

She turned and stared at him, making no further attempt at leaving. "You're uptight again, Mike. Your fuse is a lot shorter than it used to be."

"It doesn't help when you light matches around me."

"I've done nothing of the sort."

"I think *I'll* go back and take a nap," he said, rising from his chair. "It's beginning to get a little thick in here."

"Please stay," Andrea said comfortingly.

Billingsley returned to his seat in the chair. Andrea sat on the couch, noticing the tenseness in him. She said nothing, hopeful that his moodiness would pass. Billingsley leaned back, with his arms dangling over the sides of the chair. He stared at the ceiling for a moment, then looked at Andrea and smiled faintly.

"Let's talk some more," he said softly.

"Okay."

"Tell me what you want to talk about, counselor."

"Tell me what it was you thought about while I was sleeping."

"Bravo Company, mostly."

"Then tell me about Bravo Company."

"God, we were good," he said, perking up. "We were *damn* good. You should have seen those Bravo Company troops in action, babe. It was a spectacle. I'd have taken those guys to the Kremlin and raised the Stars and Stripes in Red Square, if they had told us to. Makes me feel good all over when I think about the way those guys performed."

"How can you look back on all of that so fondly? I know how much some of it bothers you."

"Some of it does. Hell, *most* of it does. But to command those guys was special, those guys in Second Platoon. I was involved with trying to keep those guys alive, but at the same time trying to kill other people. It's a wild thing to command troops, Andrea. Especially in that crazy war in Nam. But it's a good feeling to know that I was able to do it, and do it reasonably well."

"I'm sure it is."

"Let me tell you something about command. When I was in Atlanta before I reported up here, a buddy set up an interview with the bank he works for. You know, to see if they might be interested in hiring me when I got out. Well, I dressed up and went to meet the personnel dude, thinking that he was gonna interview just me. But there were a bunch of college kids there and they were running 'em through like cattle. Fill out an application, have a short interview, take a short test, and that was it. So I put up with it, just for the experience of interviewing. I had my interview with some guy about my age, and he told me that they were only interested in 'aggressive, motivated, results-oriented individuals.' Told me they wanted people who could 'make things happen.' Ain't that neat?"

"And?"

"Well, I thought of that skinny asshole leading a bunch of combat troops, and I almost laughed. But he seemed to know what it took to make it in the world, or he seemed to *think* he knew it. Anyway, I was thrown in there with the rest of the group, like I'd just finished up with Finance 301 and I'm ready to go out and grab the world by the stackin' swivel. And here I've run a platoon of infantrymen for the past nine months."

"They didn't know you, Mike."

"It doesn't matter. It'll probably be like that for a bunch of us. Some worm sits at his desk, sees that you went to Vietnam, and thinks you're a jerk for even having gone into the service in the first place. I looked at that dude I talked to, and finally realized that Killing Gooks 301 carried no water at all, as far as he was concerned. He wouldn't have been *less* impressed if I'd told him that I've been in a coma since leaving school, and that I'd just come out of it. Didn't make two shits to him."

"That's just one experience, Mike. You know better than to make sweeping judgements like that."

"I know. But it wouldn't surprise me to find out that it's gonna be the same every place else."

"You can do anything you want to do, and do well at it. I believe that with all my heart."

"Well, what I was gonna say is that I've commanded troops, under very difficult circumstances, and I don't care if nobody else appreciates it because not that many people can do it. That dude at the bank would have vomited all over his wingtips at the sound of the first round. It's hard to describe it, Andrea, but I'm glad I had a chance to command troops. But what bothers me is that when I get out, it'll count for nothing. And

I may even be made to feel guilty about it. That bothers the hell out me. See what I'm trying to say?"

"Yes, I think so."

"See why the idea of staying in the Corps isn't all that repugnant to me?"

"I see that, too. But I'm not sure that I agree."

"You want me out, don't you?"

Andrea hesitated before answering. "Yes, Mike, I do."

"Well, I'll have more to say on that later."

"Would you ever want to do it all again?" asked Andrea, studying Billingsley's reaction carefully.

"Command, yeah. But not in Nam."

"If they told you on Monday that you're going back again, what would you do?"

"I'd go."

"But how would it make you feel?"

"Bad, until I got over there and hopefully got another command and got busy again."

"Then what?"

"It'd be the same old crap . . . tryin' to stay in one piece."

"Did you ever get upset when you saw the people your troops killed?"

"Why do you ask me that?" he asked curiously.

"Did you?"

"Of course not. Not after a while, anyway. The first few, maybe. And then once, after an ambush. One of the dead NVA had a photo of his family on him, with some other papers. That one bothered me for an hour or two."

"And then it didn't bother you anymore?"

Billingsley's expression changed and Andrea immediately regretted having asked the question.

"Andrea, what the hell are you trying to make me out to be? A Goddamn murderer, or something?" he asked loudly. "That guy might have killed *me!* Jesus, what would've happened if he would have blown *my* chest open and looked at *my* heart, along with *your* picture? He wouldn't have needed any more than an hour or two to get over it, if *that* long. What kind of sick creep are you trying to make of me because I didn't whimper and cry every time I saw a dead gook, who just a minute before could've been aiming for *me?*"

"Please calm down, Michael."

"See what I mean, about talking about some things? I don't *want* to talk about it if you're gonna make me feel like I'm a friggin' murderer. I didn't like it, but I did it. I *had* to. We *all* did. If you're not supposed to kill anybody in a Goddamned war, then we sure as hell need to quit havin' wars. And that'd be fine with most of us who'd have to fight the friggin' things, anyway. But the rules were, if we found 'em, then we blew 'em away. And vice versa. And I ain't gonna sit here and let you make me feel like a creep about it."

Billingsley suddenly rose from his chair and stepped quickly into the kitchen. He leaned against the refrigerator, his arms folded tightly against his chest. Andrea waited for several moments to pass before she, too, walked into the kitchen. She stood beside him, facing in the same direction. Billingsley's face was drawn and taut as he stood silently. Andrea dropped her hand by his side and opened her fingers. He reached for her hand.

"You know I didn't mean that you're a murderer," she spoke in a hushed tone.

"I know, baby."

"Can I tell you something?"

"Yeah, sure."

"Do you remember Mister Worthington, the older fella who worked with Daddy at the firm?"

"The guy at the party?"

"Right."

"I remember him."

"Well, after you left the party that night, he talked to me for quite a while. He told me that when he had come home from Europe after World War Two, it had taken quite some time to get adjusted. He told me he wouldn't be surprised if it took you six months or more, especially since you didn't come home to happy VE celebrations like he did. He had been in charge of a lot of men, too. He said he knew kinda what you'd be going through, and that I'd just have to—"

"Put up with my bullshit?"

"No, he said that I'd have to be patient and to help you see it through."

"Same, same."

"No, it's not. You're showing the signs of the strain, and I'm not helping you much by irritating you like I've just done."

"Think I'm a basket case, counselor?"

"No, but I don't believe you've adjusted to being out of the war, or out of Vietnam. And I don't think you'll get over it in the next few days, either. It's still with you, and you're still with it."

Billingsley reached for Andrea and pulled her close. She wrapped her arms about his waist and clung tightly to him. She rested her head upon his shoulder.

"Mister Worthington's so sweet. He called me at school this week to ask about you, Mike."

"What did you tell him?"

"I told him you were fine. I told him *we* were fine."

"Do you still believe that?"

"Yes."

"Do you trust me with Chris?"

"Yes."

"Are you sure?"

"I'm sure. I know what you're trying to do. And I know you well enough to know you wouldn't create problems for yourself, like that *could* be."

"I shouldn't be around Chris without you. I'll make sure of that from now on."

"Whatever. Like I said, I know what you're trying to do. I know how much those people you were with in Vietnam meant to you. I know that even more, now."

"What would I do without you?" he asked, kissing her on the top of her head.

"You'd probably mope a lot more."

"Probably so. And drink a lot more, too."

"You've done enough of *that* today. There're eight cans next to your chair," she said with a chuckle.

"It relaxes me."

"It depresses you, that's what it does."

"Everything you say makes sense. How did you get so smart?"

"Good genes, I suppose."

"Know what I'm going to do now?"

"Probably go to the bathroom."

"Right. But after that?"

"I give up. What?"

"I'm going to take you out to dinner."

"What if I'd rather stay here?"

"Why?"

"I'm still tired."

"You got mono, counselor?"

"No, I'm just tired. And I'd rather stay here and cook for you."

"Cook what?"

"What do you have?"

"Two frozen pizzas."

"I'll cook 'em," Andrea laughed. "Show me how to work the oven."

The old cat sauntered into the kitchen from the living room. With a weary glance at Billingsley, the cat clumsily plopped into the floor and then yawned widely. Andrea and Billingsley broke out laughing.

"Poor thing," Andrea said as she lifted the cat and began cuddling it. "You're going to have the SPCA picketing your apartment if they find out you're giving beer to this cat."

"He's got a taste for it. Probably eases the pain in his joints, the old trooper."

The cat ate some leftovers from the refrigerator while Billingsley and Andrea dined on the pizza. They became engrossed in a movie after dinner, arguing over the eventual outcome during the commercial breaks. Near the movie's end, Andrea noticed that Billingsley had fallen asleep on the floor, his head supported by a cushion from the sofa. She watched the conclusion of the show without disturbing him.

"Wake up, sleeping beauty," she said softly as she shook him.

Billingsley opened his eyes and raised his head quickly. "What happened?" he asked, slightly dazed.

"You fell off to sleep. The movie's over."

"How did it end up?"

"I'm not gonna tell you. If you can't stay up and watch with me, you'll just have to guess. I'm gonna take a shower now."

"C'mon, tell me how it ended."

"Nope," she said as she left for the bathroom.

They took turns using the single bathroom in the apartment. When he emerged from the shower, shirtless and wearing faded utility trousers, he found Andrea sitting in the center of his bed. She sat with her legs crossed, wearing a crimson nightgown and looking through a scrapbook of photographs from his

Vietnam tour. Her long hair was pushed behind her ears and fell onto her back and shoulders. She studied the pictures intently.

Billingsley walked straight to the closet in the bedroom. He checked to make sure that her gaze had not followed him before reaching for a small box on the closet's shelf. He slid the box into his trouser pocket and then sat on the bed, beside her.

"These are interesting, Mike," she observed. "Some of the countryside looks so pretty."

"Some of it is."

"Where is this?" she asked, pointing to a photograph of green, shadowy mountains.

"Southwest of Da Nang, near Happy Valley."

"Was it a happy valley?"

"Only if you're happy when your life is constantly endangered. See that guy in the top picture on the right, talking on the radio?"

"Him?" she said, pointing.

"Yeah, the one with the radio. That's Tom Compton."

Andrea gazed at the mustachioed figure with the handset to his ear. "He was nice looking. Looks just like he does in that picture Chris has. How long after that did he . . ."

"Couple of months, I guess. I made an extra print of that one and gave it to Chris. She really appreciated it."

"It's such a shame," she signed.

"I agree."

"Is there a picture of that sergeant who helped you from the truck . . . what was his name?"

"Ambrosetti," said Billingsley, flipping the pages of the book. "There he is, the one who needs a shave. He's got the green rag around his neck."

"Why did he wear a rag around his neck?"

"Kept the snakes away."

"What?"

"I'm just kidding," he laughed. "He used it to wipe his face."

"What about Tyler? Where is he?"

"That's Tyler, standing next to him. The big one."

"He looks so rough."

"He was," grinned Billingsley. "They all were when they had to be."

"Who's the one who looks so young, next to Tyler?"

"That's Martindale."

"Wasn't he the radio guy you wrote me about?"

"Yeah, that's him."

Andrea stared at the picture of the group, studying the faces of those whom she had read and heard so much about. She finally sighed deeply and turned the page. "Thank you so much, Mister Ambrosetti," she said.

"Wherever you are," added Billingsley.

He began to rub his hands over Andrea's smooth, bare arms. She continued to look at the pictures, stopping occasionally to sweep her hair behind her ear.

"Oh, there's me in the Marine sweatshirt, standing next to our Christmas tree," she said with a smile of fondness. "The picture's so crumpled, Mike."

"I carried it inside my helmet the whole time. When I got hit that last time, Ambro found it and stuffed it inside my front pocket before the chopper came. He looked at the picture and told me to arrange to have it sent to him if I died, the crazy jackass. Smiled and told me he'd take good care of you. Anyway, I ended up with it back at the hospital. It got me through some long days, baby."

She leaned and kissed his hand.

"Do you look at these pictures often, Mike?"

"No."

"Is that you standing there, without your pants, in that hole full of water?"

"Yep, that's my beautiful backside."

"What were you doing?"

"Bathing," he laughed. "That was up at Con Thien. I kept my helmet and flak jacket on, just in case.'

"In case of what?"

"In case some irate gook gunner decided to try to blow my beautiful backside off."

"Your backside wasn't protected."

"I *know* that, counselor. I thought it'd be better to get hit in the butt than to get a sucking chest wound if they started sockin' it to us. That's why I wore the flak jacket. Any further questions?"

"Who took the picture?"

"Sanchez, one of my squad leaders. He was standing in the

next hole. He gave me that picture when he got 'em back."

"Bathing?" Andrea repeated, incredulously.

"Yeah, bathing," he replied, pulling her away from the book.

"I wasn't finished," she protested between his kisses.

"I've got something for you," he whispered.

"No kidding. I'm surprised you didn't jump me earlier, when you were loaded up on beer."

"No, it's something else. Everything has its place."

"Okay, then. What is it?" she asked, attempting to sit up.

"No, no. Don't get up. You smell so good and feel so good, I just want to hold you here for a minute longer."

"Well, you can whisper it to me, then. What is it?"

He continued kissing her on the neck and lips as he slipped his hand into his pocket and produced the small box. He then shifted Andrea to where she lay at his side, with her head supported by his shoulder. He kissed her once more before raising the box into her full view.

"Just stay where you are," he instructed, reaching around her with his other hand and opening the box.

Andrea gasped when he showed her the diamond engagement ring inside the box. He removed the ring and tossed the box toward the foot of the bed. Andrea's left hand rested upon his chest.

"Okay, kid. We'll make it official now. Here, let me have that ring finger," he demanded.

He slid the ring onto her outstretched finger. The fit was perfect and the stone reflected brilliantly. Andrea smiled widely and extended her hand to admire the beauty of the single diamond in its white-gold setting. She embraced Billingsley and lay back for another admiring look at the ring.

"It's lovely, Mike," she said after a while, resting her head upon his chest.

"Do you really like it?"

"It's the most beautiful ring I've ever seen."

"You're the most beautiful woman I've ever seen."

Andrea sat up in the bed, taken with looking at her hand and absorbed in the emotion which filled her. Her eyes became moist as she stared at the ring, reflecting upon its beauty and significance. She sniffed and wiped her eyes with her hand.

"Wow, this is really impressive," she said, her voice husky. "You've gone and done it again, Billingsley."

"It looks fabulous on you," he said, wrapping his arms around her and holding her left hand in view as he looked over her shoulder. "Just like the guy who sold it to me said it would."

"Where'd you get it?"

"From a pimp at Phu Bai."

"You did *not!*" she said, playfully slapping at his arm.

"I got it from a jeweler in D.C.," he laughed. "Your mom gave me your ring size and I picked it up Wednesday night."

"I'm very proud of it," she said, holding his arms which reached around her waist. "And I'm very proud of you, too. I want very much to be your wife."

"I want that, too. Now we've got something to show everybody that it's gonna happen."

"I wish the time would hurry up and get here," she said as she leaned back and braced herself against him.

"Me, too."

He kissed Andrea on the cheek and began massaging her neck and shoulders. He turned her around so that she rested on the bed as he continued with the massage. She closed her eyes and relaxed, occasionally stealing a quick glimpse of the ring. She smiled faintly at each glance. His touch soothed her into a relaxed and comfortable submissiveness.

"That's a beautiful gown, Andrea. Soft and smooth and sexy, just like you. Where'd you get it?"

"From a hooker in Annandale."

Billingsley laughed out loud as he continued massaging her shoulders. He was rarely able to best her in their ongoing game of matching wits, with breakeven being about the best he could hope for in their contests. Andrea was quick, even when relaxed. She shared his fondness for humor, and she delighted in his capacity for witticism. She, though, could usually match him when it came to adapting a clever remark for a particular situation.

He moved his fingers from her shoulders to her middle and lower back. He noticed that her eyes were closed.

"Don't fall asleep on me, kid. Not after I've sobered up and given you an expensive ring," he said with a pat on her behind.

"I'm not asleep. Keep it up. You're doing a terrific job."

"You have a great body," he mentioned casually.

Andrea turned and grinned sheepishly at him.

"Really, you do. Pretty face and pretty body. Especially this lovely little tail," he said with another pat.

"My bust is too small. That's why you notice the other parts so well."

"Not so. That's just not so. It's in perfect proportion with the rest of you."

"Thank you, sweetheart. Will you move back up to my shoulders again? Where did you learn to do that so well? It's absolutely wonderful."

"From a bar girl in Da Nang," he said, biting his tongue to keep from laughing at the thought of his encounter with the Vietnamese girl during his first hospital stay.

"Now *that's* probably the truth," Andrea said, and she raised her head to look at him.

"Get back down there and stop making such wild accusations."

"Well, it probably *is*. I was over here being lonely and you were over there chasing all those Oriental dollies."

"I was a combat officer, madam. I had no time for such nonsense."

"Yeah, right."

Billingsley still wanted to laugh but fought the strong urge to do so. He ran his hands over Andrea's smooth shoulders and attempted to ignore the thoughts of the girl, the dancers, and the stench from the alleyway behind the bar. The whole episode seemed hilarious to him now. But he knew Andrea would likely feel otherwise.

"Was she soothing, too?" Andrea asked softly.

"Who?"

"The bar girl in Da Nang."

"Yeah, very. But she gave my syphilis and I went blind. I've been meaning to tell you of my condition, but I just couldn't quite—"

"See fit. Right, I knew that one was coming."

"What about you, my dear?"

"What about me?"

"I show up in your house, fresh from being wounded in battle far away from home, and after nine months of not seeing you, and *you* walk in with that *dipshit* Sloan. Laughing and giggling and having a nifty ole time. What about that, huh?"

"He's not a dipshit."

"He *is* a dipshit! He's a slimy, crawling, cowardly dipshit. Of the first order. Probably a draft dodger, too. A complete worm of a man. What about him, toots?"

"It was nothing."

"Hah. Did he ever try to make a move on you? Huh, did he?" he asked, tickling her sides.

"Of course," she replied, squirming from his gouges.

"Just as I thought. Did you reject him?"

"Of course not. I had an abortion just before you came home. It was his, Mike. I must confess," she laughed, still squirming from his tickling.

"You hussy."

He grabbed her and they began wrestling playfully. Andrea soon tired and begged for a truce after promising him she had indeed been kidding about her affair with Sloan. He knew that, anyway. She reclined on the bed and breathed deeply, still laughing sporadically. She held her ring in front of her and admired it once more. Billingsley leaned over her and kissed her lightly at first, then forcefully. Their passion grew as they pressed closer to one another. They faced each other, on their sides, as they kissed and fondled.

"What about the Vietnamese bar girl?" Andrea whispered.

"What about her?"

"Did she really teach you about massages?"

"Yeah."

"Is that all she taught you?"

"Yep, that's it."

"No diseases?"

"Are you kidding? What do you think I am, crazy?"

"I certainly do."

"Gimme the ring back."

"No way."

"But don't you worry about being married to a crazy man?"

"Not this crazy man."

"I'm really not crazy, you know. I just act that way sometimes."

"Everybody does, sometimes."

"Even you?"

"Even me."

They continued their kissing. Billingsley reached his arm

around Andrea and pressed her to him. The momentum built, the fire became warmer. Suddenly, the old cat jumped onto the bed at their feet. The cat walked up the bed and raised itself on its hind legs to put its front paws on Billingsley's shoulder. The cat meowed loudly as it looked down into their faces. Andrea opened her eyes to see the cat staring at her intently, its eyes wide and its ears raised.

"We have company," she said.

"I know. He's purring in my ear."

"What should we do?"

"Ignore him. He'll go away."

"I can't ignore him. He's looking right through me."

"He'll go away."

"I'm afraid he's going to scratch me, Mike. I know he doesn't like me. He's jealous of me."

"He won't bother you," Billingsley said, kissing Andrea on the forehead.

"Mike, take him out."

Billingsley turned to where he could see the cat. The old cat meowed loudly again.

"Bud, get the hell out. Turn off the light on your way out."

Another loud meow.

"Mike, please take him out."

"Bud, don't stand there when I've given you a direct order."

"Come on, Mike. Take him out of here."

Billingsley got up and tossed the cat gently into the hallway. He closed the door to the bedroom and dimmed the light before returning to Andrea.

"That better?"

"Much. Thank you."

He pulled her close and kissed her again.

"Why don't we just go out and get married tonight?" he suggested.

"We can't."

"Why not?"

"We just *can't*, that's why."

"What if they send me back to Nam tomorrow?"

"They won't do that."

"They did it once, didn't they?"

"You volunteered. Remember?"

"A minor detail."

"It's *not* minor, either. You asked them to send you over there, and they did. If you'd not asked, you might have ended up with a job in D.C., or somewhere else."

"Nah. I would have gone no matter what."

"Baloney."

"Gimme my ring back."

"Nope."

"Then will you marry me tonight?"

"No. It'll be June, in the church, in front of millions of people."

"I can't wait that long."

"Why not?"

"There may be another war somewhere by then."

"And you'll volunteer. Right?"

"Of course."

"You hopeless jerk," she said, pinching him on the arm.

He turned and pulled Andrea on top of him, holding her tightly.

"Do you think it'll always be this good? After we're married, and all?" he whispered.

"Why not?"

"You don't think it'll wear off after a while?"

"I don't know. I've never been married before. Do you think it will?"

"I doubt it. I can't see myself ever getting tired of you."

"You'd better not or I'll take you to court. Remember?"

"Gosh, that's right."

"So you'd better behave yourself, and do as I say."

"I won't be intimidated by a girlie lawyer with a small bust."

"My body has nothing to do with it."

"Oh yeah?"

"Yeah."

He wrapped her in his arms and kissed her. "It won't wear off," he said.

Andrea got up early and found him already up, sitting at the kitchen table scanning the morning newspaper. He was squeezing a small rubber ball and sipping steaming instant coffee. Andrea entered the chilly kitchen dressed in jeans and sweater with Billingsley's camouflaged poncho liner draped over her shoulders. Much of the poncho liner dragged the floor behind her.

"Good morning," she offered as she leaned to kiss him on the cheek.

"Hello, kiddo. Your nose is cold."

"My nose isn't all that's cold. Can't you make this place warmer?"

"It's warming up. Shouldn't be much longer. Want some coffee?"

"Please."

Andrea took a seat at the table, still huddled in the poncho liner. Billingsley chuckled at her mummy-like appearance as he heated the water for her coffee. A transistor radio on the kitchen counter was tuned low to a rock music station. The curtains in the living room were open, casting light into the apartment from the clear blue sky outside. It was a slow, easy Sunday morning.

"The Third Marines have pulled out of Nam," Billingsley commented when he handed the ceramic cup to Andrea.

"Really?"

"Yeah, according to the paper."

"Where to?"

"Okinawa."

"What's Okinawa like?"

"A big island with Okinawans on it."

"Right. How long will they stay there?"

"I guess the unit will be there from now on. The troops will probably rotate when their tours are up, just like always."

Andrea held onto the cup with both hands, sipping lightly. Billingsley took his seat and lit a cigarette.

"I'll bet those guys are happy with that," he said as he resumed his reading.

"You would be if you were there, wouldn't you?"

"Darn right."

"What will they do on Okinawa?"

"Be rowdy, I would imagine."

"Is that what you did when you were there?"

Billingsley glanced up from the paper with a slight smile on his face. "Yeah, for one night," he answered.

"What did you do?"

"I went to the famous BC Street a few days before I left for the States."

"What's on BC Street?"

"Bars, bars, and more bars," he replied in the manner of W.C. Fields.

"So tell me what you did on the famous BC Street."

"No," he said casually, returning his gaze to the paper.

"Why not?"

"You probably wouldn't believe me."

"Were you rowdy?" she asked with a sly grin.

"Kinda."

"Did you go to one of those steambaths?"

"Naw, not with my arm and leg the way they were. Might've gotten infected, or something."

"Meet any Okinawan girls?"

"A few, yeah."

"So?" she asked with a forced expression of sternness.

"So what?"

"So, what happened?"

"I went with a wounded Marine captain from the hospital. All we did was drink beer and talk loud. And we sang along with the band."

"What did you sing?"

" 'Nah-nah-nah-nah, nah-nah-nah-nah, hey-hey-hey, good-bye', " he demonstrated.

"I don't believe you."

"Well, gimme my ring back, then," he said, reaching for her hand as she giggled to free it from his grasp.

"Stop, you'll make me spill my coffee."

"C'mon," he said as he stood. "We're gonna drive to Q-town and get some breakfast."

"Good, I'm starving. And freezing, too. Can I take this with me?" she asked, pointing to the poncho liner.

"Absolutely not. Put your jacket on."

They rode in his car for the short drive to the town of Quantico. They passed the old train depot and parked in front of a small restaurant in one of the old buildings along the tiny town's main street. A stiff wind blew at them from the direction of the nearby Potomac River.

They entered the restaurant and were seated in an adjoining room which served as the lounge during the evening. A stale odor hung in the air from the smoking and drinking of the previous night. A scattering of Marines, dressed in their civilian clothes but easily identified by their short haircuts, glanced admiringly at Andrea as she read the plastic-laminated menu. Billingsley noticed the stir she was causing among three young Marines at a nearby table as each turned to catch a glimpse of the attractive new customer.

"I think you've brightened up their day," he said softly.

"Think I'm safe in here?"

"Yeah, I think so," he laughed.

Each had a full breakfast of eggs, bacon, hash browns, toast, juice, and coffee. They ate slowly and relaxed afterward with a final cup of coffee.

"I've got an idea," Billingsley said as he sipped his coffee.

"What's your idea?"

"Let's take a drive to the river, over near the Air Station."

"Fine with me," Andrea shrugged.

"Let's go."

He drove to the base, just over the railroad tracks, and cruised slowly along its main street. Marines walked along the sidewalks, individually and in small groups, in and out of uniform, on leisurely strolls to and from the mess halls and snack bars in the area. Barracks and administrative buildings lined the street. The wind swayed the trees and blew leaves into the path of Billingsley's car. They drove to a fork in the road, turned toward the Air Station, and parked in a small lot. Andrea zipped her jacket as they strolled to the banks of the river.

The Potomac's greyish waters rippled from the wind. Across the water were the wooded shores of Maryland. Billingsley couldn't resist skipping a stone across the water, though he failed in three attempts to achieve multiple skips. He finally reached for Andrea and pulled her close.

"Wanna jump in and go for a swim?"

"Think I'll pass."

"We should've brought wine and cheese."

"In this cold? And after such a big breakfast?"

"Maybe you're right. What about marshmallows?"

"Need a fire for that," she said as she snuggled close to him.

"Yeah, that's right. I don't think the base people would be too hip on that."

Andrea held her hand before her and admired the ring on her finger. She smiled and embraced Billingsley.

"Are you gonna take it off when you go back to school?" he asked jokingly.

"Of course not. Why?"

"Will you see Robert Sloan anytime soon?"

"Yes, he's in some of my classes."

"Will you do me a favor?"

"What?"

"Stick the ring in his face and tell him that Mike Billingsley sends his warmest personal regards."

"I'll do no such thing. I'll wear it with dignity."

"That's fine," he laughed. "But around him, I'd like you to wear it with arrogance."

"I will not."

"You will, too."

"I will *not*!"

"Then gimme it back."

"I will not."

"I'll throw you in the river."

"You will not."

"Oh, yeah?" he said as he playfully grabbed her and began pulling her toward the water.

"Let me go or I'll scream for help."

"In you go, Strickland," he said, still pulling.

"No I'm not, Billingsley," she replied, giggling and resisting. "You'd better let me go or I'll call for help."

"Go ahead."

"HEY SOMEBODY, THIS JERK'S TRYING TO RAPE ME," she screamed at the top of her lungs.

Billingsley froze and glanced self-consciously toward the Air Station to make certain that nobody was sprinting to Andrea's rescue. Andrea laughed boisterously at his look of surprise and embarrassment.

"Andrea, you *idiot*!"

She doubled over in laughter. The thought of him, so ruffled and flustered, was too much for her. Her body shook from the loud laughing. His face was still crimson as he stood grinning sheepishly, with his hands on his hips. Andrea eventually regained control of herself after placing her hands on her knees and staring at the ground for several moments.

"You looked so pitiful, Mike," she said in a strained voice, still bent over.

He also started to laugh.

"Really, you looked so funny," she said as she straightened and wiped her eyes.

"Sometimes I just don't know about you," he said with a shrug.

Andrea walked to where he stood and draped her arms around his neck. She then kissed him on the cheek. "Promise not to throw me in the river?" she asked.

"Yeah, and I don't think I'm gonna rape you, either."

"I don't think you'll ever need to," she said, kissing him on the ear. "Just don't throw me in the water."

"It's a deal."

She placed her head on his shoulder, still unable to avoid an occasional giggle. He slapped at her behind and held her away from him. He held both her hands as she turned her head slightly to use the wind to blow the hair from her eyes.

"I've got something to tell you," he said.

"Okay, tell me."

"I've been accepted into the regular Marine Corps. My augmentation was approved."

Andrea stared into his eyes, her expression unchanged—no surprise, no disappointment, no consternation. She accepted the news gracefully, though not without a conscious effort to do so. She drew a deep breath and offered a faint smile.

Billingsley knew her smile was forced.

"Congratulations, Mike. I knew they wouldn't turn you down."

"All it means, counselor, is that it's an option. I can still get out if I want. It's not like I'm obligating for another hundred years."

"Why didn't you tell me yesterday?"

"Because I didn't think yesterday was the right time."

"Okay," she said, poised and pleasant.

"And besides, there's more."

"What's the rest?"

"It's something that I've been thinking about for a long time."

"Well . . ."

"And I really wasn't sure that I was ready to talk to you about it until I got up this morning. Then I decided what the heck, I'd tell you before you went back to school today."

Andrea drew a deep breath and exhaled slowly. She continued looking directly at him.

"Well . . ."

"And it's something that has a great deal of significance, especially with our plans for marriage."

"Well . . ."

"And I kinda think you'll like it. I know I'm really excited about it."

"Well . . ."

He produced an envelope, folded in half and partly crumpled, from the hip pocket of his trousers. Andrea looked at the envelope with great interest, though she could detect nothing of its contents. It remained folded in his hand.

"Do you know what this is?" he asked.

"I have no idea what that is."

"It's an acceptance of another kind."

"Oh?" she said as she raised her eyebrows. "And just what kind of acceptance might that be?"

He chuckled as he taunted her with the envelope. She strained for a revealing glimpse.

"Mike, *tell* me!"

He grinned, his eyes glimmering, until he cleared his throat and announced, "I've been accepted into law school at George Washington University."

Andrea was stunned into speechlessness. Her delight over his totally unexpected pronouncement gave her face the sort of wide-eyed joyous look typically reserved for small children in the early morning hours of Christmas. She bit her lip and pondered the news, and the possibilities associated therewith. Her mind raced swiftly through thoughts of a common legal practice; a husband-wife team; shared interests; shared potential; the excitement; the certainty of a clear objective. Nothing could be more perfect, she decided. No more separations, no more war, and no more dread over the prospects of either.

"How in heaven's name did you manage to do all of *that*?" Andrea asked with an astonished expression.

"I took the aptitude test when I was in Basic School. Then I went to George Washington University and talked to the dean of the law school, and I liked what I heard and saw. Then, when I found out in Vietnam that I'd made a pretty decent score on the test, I applied for the term beginning in the fall of '71. And they notified me the middle of last week that I'd been accepted."

Andrea reach for Billingsley and enveloped him with her arms. "You're unbelievable, Mike Billingsley. I love you, I love you, I love you," she repeated as she kissed him on the cheek with each declaration.

"You'll have to work and pay the bills, kiddo. It'll be three long years. Can you handle that part?" he asked.

"I can handle it, baby," she answered with a laugh of glee.

"Do you agree with my plan?"

"Do I *agree*?" she asked as she laughed and tugged at his neck. "He wants to know if I *agree*! I can't *believe* this *whole thing*! You're gonna get out of the service and not go off and leave me anymore and not get hurt anymore and go to school while I work in the Washington area and we're together and making great plans and making great lives for ourselves and having great fun and making great love, and you want to know if I *agree*? Of *course*, I agree. You *know* I agree. You really are a jerk sometimes, Billingsley."

"Then you do agree?"

She laughed loudly and bit at his ear. "Yes, yes, yes, a million times yes," she said joyfully.

He held her tightly and kissed her. He pulled away and noticed the tears of happiness which flowed from her eyes. He wiped at the tears with his fingers as they fell from her eyes.

"Andrea, I need you, baby. In a lot of ways," he said gently.

"You have me, Michael. Every day, every way."

He held her hands and faced her. Even with the tears, she was ever so beautiful.

"Can I keep my cat after we're married?" he asked.

"No way."

"Gimme my ring back, then."

"Nope," she said as she pulled away from him and walked several paces away, in the direction of the Air Station. She sniffed and wiped at her eyes, then drew a deep breath. She placed her hands to the sides of her mouth.

"Andrea, what the hell are you doing?"

"HEY SOMEBODY, I'M GONNA MARRY THIS JERK. SO DON'T WORRY."

She turned and ran at Billingsley, flinging herself at him in a tight embrace. He lifted her and swung her in a full circle.

"You can keep your stupid cat. Okay?" she said.

"Okay."

"And I'll learn to cook. Okay?"

"Okay."

"And I'll put you through law school. Okay?"

"Okay."

"And we'll go back to your apartment soon, to celebrate. Okay?"

"Okay."

"But you won't change your mind about all of this and stay in the Marines. Okay?"

"Okay."

"Are you gonna ask for your ring back now?"

"No way."

She looked at him with a mischievous grin. "I wouldn't give it back anyway . . . counselor," she said.

They held tightly to one another while the wind blew around them and the river flowed silently beside them. They were peaceful and happy. The world was a better place again. There was hope. And they had one another. So much had happened, so much had changed, so much was before them. Perhaps, they both silently thought, things were destined to work out, after all. Only time would be the true measure, the true test, as it always was . . . and always is . . . and always will be. Nothing was certain except the certainty of change itself—the inevitable, unalterable process of things being different tomorrow than they are today. But they could cling to each other and weather the changes, as they had before.

And, most important, they had hope.

THE END

GLOSSARY

AO: Aerial Observer. Usually an artillery officer who plotted and adjusted artillery or naval-gunfire missions from an observation aircraft.

APC: Armored Personnel Carrier.

Chieu Hoi: Vietnamese for Open Arms. In practice, an amnesty program that encouraged defection among NVA or VC.

CO: Commanding Officer.

DMZ: Demilitarized Zone.

FAC: Forward Air Controller. Typically an aviator who was assigned to an infantry unit to plot and adjust airstrikes.

FO: Forward Observer. Usually an officer, though sometimes an enlisted man, who was responsible for plotting and adjusting artillery missions.

Gunny: Marine Corps Gunnery Sergeant (E-7).

Klick: One kilometer.

Lifer: Military careerist.

LP: Listening Post.

LZ: Landing Zone.

411

MOS: Military Occupational Specialty. Job category.

NCO: Non-Commissioned Officer. An enlisted rank of Corporal (E-4) or higher.

NVA: North Vietnamese Army, or an individual North Vietnamese soldier.

OCS: Officers Candidate School.

05s: 105mm howitzers.

PFC: Private First Class (E-2).

Pogue: Office worker. Non-combatant.

R&R: Rest and Recreation.

RPG: Rocket Propelled Grenade.

Six-by: A 5-ton truck.

VC: Viet Cong.

Ville: Slang for village.

XO: Executive Officer.